THE KEYSTONE

ELEMENTS SERIES
BOOK 1

SEREN GOODE

The Keystone

Written and published by Seren Goode

Cover by We Got You Covered (Molly Phipps)

Grace's Image by RMGraphX (Rhiannon Gilmore)

Formatting by Goode Star

D2D Print ISBN 9798223515982

Print ISBN 978-1-7365387-0-8

Ebook ISBN 978-1-7365387-1-5

SerenGoode.com

DODGING 101

SAN FRANCISCO, *California*

I've found one of the best ways to avoid being picked up by the authorities is to just disappear. You sneak out, drop false trails, and double back, and when you are sure no one is following you, you swap out the plates on your vehicle. We always carried backups for Van Ekman, our ancient VW camper. Then, pull out a map, and with no rhyme or reason, pick a new town to call home.

Lather, rinse, repeat.

That's my life—sixteen years as a nomad.

I used to love it, just the three of us, a team, moving to the next adventure. Now, when my dad changes jobs like some people change underwear, it just gives me a stomachache.

Van Ekman lurched and, with a shudder, stalled two feet short of the parking space.

Click. Click. Click. Holding my breath, I reached for the stone on my necklace and closed my eyes as Dad turned the key in the ignition again. *Click.* There was no roar of sound. The engine was dead.

There had been no traffic when we left a pre-dawn Santa

Cruz, and we made good time heading south out of the beach city. Soon, we were looping and backtracking to our new destination. Hours later, struggling through congested San Francisco streets, my dad was white-knuckling the steering wheel as he looked for parking. I guess this was our new home. I had little say anymore. I don't know why he picked this city. It's so expensive, and driving was always a mess. Today was the worst. There was probably a big tech conference happening.

We had finally found a parking spot in a private garage. I hoped he didn't plan on staying long because this place was going to cost us a fortune. I mentally counted what I had left of our rent money, about eighty dollars, and I cringed. That wouldn't get us far.

"Okay, that's it." My dad slid out of the driver's seat and left the door open for me to follow. "Grace, let's go. We're late."

"Late?" I asked. He didn't respond. Something on his phone had already caught his attention. He was so easily distracted, and I was starting to wonder if he was depressed again and trying to hide it. We hid so much from each other now.

Turning, I flipped the long mess of my green-streaked hair out of my face and wiggled over the back of my seat and into the back of the van. Using my arms, which were strong from open water swimming, I snaked my tall frame over the neatly labeled and stacked boxes that represented all our earthly possessions. I grabbed the strap of my messenger bag and pulled. It was stuck, so I yanked on the corner of a box until the strap slipped free.

Knowing the passenger door tended to stick, I slid across the front seat and out the driver's door, pausing to push the gear into neutral, dragging the bag behind me.

"What are we late for?" I asked as we both braced against the frame of Van Ekman and pushed. As soon as the van started to roll, I jumped inside and stepped on the pedal, leaning my full weight into it. The brakes squealed in protest but finally relented, and the van stop neatly in the parking spot. Climbing out again, I checked the spacing. We were parked, or rather stalled, between an Audi and a BMW. The roof barely cleared the depressed ceiling of the parking garage. Van Ekman looked like a piece of bark wedged between two gleaming teeth.

Now what? I looked to my dad for direction. His brow was furrowed. His eyes were glued to his phone as he cycled through numbers to send a text, his fingers clumsy on the gadget's miniature keys.

Who was he texting? Neither of us had any friends. We moved around too much, and we were our only family left. He caught me leaning forward to look at the screen and shoved the phone into a frayed pocket in his khakis. We stared at each other.

Weren't we supposed to be in a hurry? The flutters in my stomach felt like guppies swimming around. I took a calming breath and kept my mouth shut as I settled my messenger bag over my shoulder and waited. Finally, Dad broke the silence.

"There are things about your mother's life you don't know... she was different; they all are—" He drew a long shuddering breath. Grief, longing, and fear all crossed his face then, but with a long blink, the emotions disappeared, like a door slamming shut.

Mom? What did she have to do with being in the city today? The churning in my belly grew as it always did when I thought about my mom.

"There's not enough time to explain. I'm so sorry—Grace, I've always meant to tell you, but I didn't know what to say, and now I've waited too long. Later, I promise, but now, we've got to go." He grabbed my arm and rushed us out of the garage, the pinch of his fingers on my skin an awkward connection I craved as I fumbled along behind him.

Leaving the parking garage, we walked briskly through

unfamiliar streets. The chilly, late-morning air held just a hint of salt. *Stars,* I missed the ocean. I paused at the top of a hill, breathing it in. The steep city was laid out around us, an urban quilt in shades of white, the occasional burst of green, and a border of blue that led up to the bridge. My dad trotted back and grabbed my hand, tugging me forward, a not so gentle reminder to keep up. He quickened his pace downhill into tightly packed residential neighborhoods, then up and down again and again, until my legs ached. We finally left the residential streets, the buildings changing to street-facing retail spaces, office buildings, and towering glass skyscrapers. The roads were packed with cars and the sidewalks with pedestrians late to work.

I had an impeccable sense of direction—and was completely lost. It must have been an hour before my dad stopped in front of a coffee shop and spun around. He glanced left, then right, searching for something. Then he looked me right in the eyes.

"Grace, if something happens to me, you need to run. Don't try to help, don't go back to the van, leave everything, and run. Promise me." He was earnest, and his out-of-breath plea ended in a whisper drowned out by the cadence of the city.

"What do you think is going to happen?" I struggled to understand.

"I don't know...something doesn't feel right. It's not like before. When your mom was here, she always seemed to know what was happening. She stayed connected to them. This time..." He trailed off.

When Mom was here, a lot of things were different.

The flow of people on the busy sidewalk cut around us like an ocean current, slamming us together then pulling us apart, testing the elasticity of our frayed connection. The last year held some winners for us in the most-craptastic moments category. I studied the gray in his dark hair and the lines spidering out from the corners of his brown eyes.

He had changed.

I had changed.

And somehow, we just didn't fit together anymore.

"Who are the 'them' you are talking about? Tell me what is going on." I grasped at his arms, snagging a handful of his red knit sweater. It stretched as he was pushed by people swarming past until there was a break in foot traffic, and he made his way back to me, the sweater sagging, not reforming.

"Grace." He made a strangled sound and pulled me into an awkward hug, whispering in my ear, "I can't. It's too dangerous. If you don't know, maybe they won't hurt you." I was drowning in questions, and all I could manage was to tighten my shoulders, which he must have taken for acceptance.

Sighing, he released me but kept a hand on my arm as he pushed me ahead of him into the coffee shop.

He headed toward an empty table by the front window. My feet dragged as I twisted backwards, listening to his whispered instructions.

"I'm going to meet some people, friends of your mother. You need to stay here where it's safe, well, safer." He made the correction like the rest of his statement wasn't completely insane.

"What?" I grabbed his hand. My mind shuttled from one fractured thought to the next. I needed order. *What do I know? Dad is here to meet family of my mother.* That was news to me. *And they are dangerous. How? How are they dangerous—physically? Why? Why meet with them? Why now?* I tried to sort through what I knew and analyze the situation, but I just didn't have enough information.

"Dad, what is going on? You and mom are orphans." The story ran like an omniscient narrator's voice in my head, recounting how they met and immediately connected when they recognized the loneliness in each other.

"Yes, I know. These are more than friends but not quite family. They're her foster siblings."

"What?" I stumbled and he pushed me into a chair.

The shop was packed. All the bistro tables were full, and a long bench table was loaded with a mix of lunchtime co-workers and laptop users. Our table was probably only free because the surface was littered with used coffee cups and sandwich wrappers and had a mix of mismatched chairs and stools.

Dad perched on the stool across from me, looming over my chair with his brow pinched up, deepening the lines around his eyes, and his breath puffing in my face. It smelled of the bitter coffee he drank when he was driving.

"Her foster family...um...they're different. Dangerous. That's why it's important you remember, Gracy, if something happens to me, *run* and don't go back to the van," he hesitated before adding, "and don't trust anyone."

I had so many questions. I opened my mouth to ask as Dad's phone beeped. A quick glance, and his eyes widened. He stood as he read the message. I rose to follow, but he pushed me gently back.

"No. It's safer for both of us if you stay." Concern for him was the only thing that kept me in my seat. "They are waiting. I have to go. Remember what I said." He backed away, his eyes soft as they studied my face. Then he left me there in a sea of questions.

I watched as he crossed the street, repeatedly looking left and right as he walked a half block and then entered a building as if he had known exactly where to go. The building was a wall of glass shooting up in the sky. With the first floor wrapped in advertisements about the advantages of living in the city, the structure extended so far up, even tilting my head, I couldn't see the top through the café's front window.

And so, I waited.

For the first hour, I stayed leaning forward, eyes glued to that door across the street, like a puppy waiting for its master to return. But as the adrenaline drained from my body, I slumped in the chair. I was so tired. Dad had woken me in the middle of the night and said we had an hour to pack up the apartment and leave.

This never would have happened with my mom. When it was the three of us, being nomadic was fun. We were the sailing three Musketeers, living on the boat with the world as my classroom. Mom turned everything into an adventure, and I got to help make the decision of where to go next. Once, I'd asked where the whales were going, and in a heartbeat, we had dropped everything and followed one of the migration routes for a week. I knew we didn't live like everyone else, but we had each other, and it was fun. I was too young to ask questions like, "What happened to Dad's job? How are we going to pay for food and dock slip rentals?"

For the last year, since Mom died, I've thought about nothing else.

When we lost her, we lost the captain of our ship who'd made our lives run smoothly.

Then we lost our home. When the boat was repossessed was when I first realized Dad wasn't paying any bills, and I had to take over.

When we lost Mom, we lost our joy.

No. Nope. No time to dwell on that. I had a problem to solve. For the next hour, I sat with my face scrunched, thinking of all the questions Dad would have to answer when he got back. *Why did Mom never tell me she had a foster family? Do they live here? Why haven't I met them? Why are they danger-*

ous? What happened that they don't care about her anymore? Because if they cared, surely, they would have turned up at her funeral last year. But they hadn't. It had just been Dad and me. I thought up more things to ask, but really, the answers to the first questions would dictate the next ones.

Maybe he wouldn't answer any of them.

That was a depressing thought. I don't know how long I sat hunched over, my sightline just barely over the rim of the windowsill, watching as the traffic that had eased after lunch started to pick up again for early rush hour.

My mind wandered as I fingered the stone in the necklace at my throat. It was my mother's, the only thing she had ever given me—well, the only thing of any value. The necklace was a strip of flattened bronze with a lumpy rock on the end. In the non-valuable category, I also got her freaky genetics that left me with green streaks in my hair, which made me look like I was being strangled by seaweed and got me a lot of strange stares, even in towns where half the high school student had brightly colored hair. That reminded me of the last school I'd attended, and I lost myself in bad memories.

The shrill ring of my phone startled me. Jumping, I knocked over one of the empty paper coffee cups on the table. Pulling my neon yellow and grey messenger bag into my lap, I quickly dug around, looking for my phone. It was when it sounded again that I was able to locate it and realized I had two text messages.

I read and then reread the text, hoping it would make more sense.

Dad: The Helios are here! Run! Find Waters.

Chills raced up my arm when I read the second message. It was a single word.

Dad: Run!

I looked across the street, and my breath caught. Something was very wrong. There was no traffic, and at some point, several white vans and cars had double parked in front of the apartment building Dad had disappeared into.

And then there were the suits. About twenty people in what even I could tell were ill-fitting jackets loitered across the street in front of the apartment building's entrance, and more were visible in the lobby through the glass. They looked so out of place. Since we had arrived I had rarely seen a tie, and it seemed suits were worn for ironic effect rather than corporate necessity.

A motion across the street caught my attention. The large glass doors of the apartment building opened, and a tall, blond man came out. He looked like a movie star with perfect features marred only by an angry scowl. His arms were at an awkward angle in front, and two men flanked him, holding onto his elbows until they pulled him into one of the white vans.

Who was that? Did this have something to do with why my dad telling me to run? My hands had been shaking since I'd read the text message. I kept thinking, *What if it was a mistake?* I quickly typed a message.

Me: Dad, what is going in?

I hit send before realizing it wasn't right. Hope swelled in my chest when, seconds later, my phone chimed.

Dad: All well, come home.

I read the message and blew out a sigh, and my skin began to buzz from the release of tension.

It was a minute before realization dawned, and I looked back at the message. It didn't make sense. Our home was stalled in an expensive parking garage.

Why would he say to come home? What was going on?

More action across the street drew my attention. My heart leaped into my throat as the glass doors opened again, and my dad was led out of the building. The stretched-out sleeves of his baggy sweater sagged down his arms, but I could see a white band tied around his wrists. Like an incoming text, a *ding* went off in my head as I watched a man force him into the van. He couldn't have typed the message. Looking down in horror at my phone, I had to resist the urge to drop it, like it was something dirty.

Some unknown person was sending me messages, and they wanted me to believe it was safe. I didn't know what was going on, but it was the furthest away from safe you could get.

I had to get out of here. I scanned the shop. Besides the front door, there was a side entrance.

Stars knew where that led.

Sliding out of the chair, I crouched down until I could barely see out the window and scanned both sides of the sidewalk in front of the shop. There was an overhang on my right and a marque for a mall entrance. Maybe that was where the side door led?

I looked back at the white van. There was a scuffle as a third group came out of the glass doors. The woman was striking. Her hair, dyed a bright red, was mussed, and a jacket hanging in front covered her hands. She looked furious. The disheveled man and woman on either side stood a head taller than her, and they roughly pushed her into the same van. As soon as the doors closed, the van took off, tires squealing.

A motion in my peripheral vision grabbed my attention. Two teens were fighting at the entrance of the mall. A boy about my age with curly hair and brown skin was restraining a younger boy who was trying to chase after the van. The curly-haired boy struggled to keep a hold without hurting the younger boy whose pale skin had flushed to match his red hair. I could see his face as he yelled the word "mom." Both boys were looking toward the disappearing van.

They were connected! Somehow, they knew the other people in the van with my dad. Maybe they knew what had happened, knew who those people in suits were. I bet they knew where they took my dad.

One of the men left behind at the apartment pointed toward the teens at the mall entrance. Then he turned and pointed directly at me. For a second, I froze in panic and then dropped low so I could just see over the window.

There was a burst of noise. The younger boy struggled free and, with a taunting glare at the people in suits, threw a skateboard on the ground and took off. Two men pursued.

I didn't have a second to spare. I had no idea why or where my dad was taken, but maybe the curly-haired boy knew. I had to get to him before the suits did.

I bolted for the side door and had no time for relief as it pushed out into a brightly lit space with shops. I looked left toward the mall entrance; Curly Hair was still staring down the street after the redhead. Lunging forward, I grabbed a handful of his shirt, and backing up, I pulled him with me through the door and into the mall. He turned, his eyes angry and chest heaving.

"Where did they take my dad?" I demanded.

I caught his anguished look as he stared after the redhead. It changed to panic as a man raced by, chasing the boy on the skateboard.

"Your mom was in the van with him. You know something." I commanded his attention, and his eyes crinkled in suspicion.

"Is your father, Noah?"

How did he know my dad's name? I was right. He did know something.

Curly Hair pulled away, dragging me with him as I held on to his shirt.

"Yes, Noah, that's my father's name. Tell me where they took him."

"No. If you want to get him back, follow me." The boy yanked free of my grip and backed away.

My heart was pounding, and my skin crawled with the urge to flee from all of this. I wanted to run after the van and pull my dad free, but I knew that couldn't happen, or whoever had grabbed him would have me too. I didn't know if I should follow Curly Hair, who was still walking backward toward the interior of the mall, his eyes as hard as yellow diamonds as they studied me.

"I'm getting out of here. You can come with me," he shrugged, "or don't. Your choice." He turned and raced up the escalator, taking the steps two at a time.

I made my decision in a blink, no thought, just instinct. Ignoring the shouts behind me, I followed the curly-haired boy up the escalator.

2

THE MALL

I ONCE READ that among the top ten of fears most people had, a fear of being left behind ranks near the top. I'd bet the fear of getting kidnapped ranks pretty high too.

The curly-haired boy was fast and hard to follow. I focused all my attention on not losing sight of him as he dodged through the mall like a veteran shopaholic on Black Friday. Whirling through the late afternoon crowd, he raced up another escalator, his sneakers stomping on the steel treads. At the top, he dodged into a bath shop, and I followed. We exited out of the connecting lingerie store, silk jammies and cotton panties fluttering as we passed.

We were in and out of three more smaller shops and made another floor change before we entered a large department store. I stayed with him as he zigzagged like a pro-quarterback. He scrambled around racks and down aisles until he came to a set of doors labeled "Employees Only" that swallowed him up. Racing up to the threshold, I hesitated, feeling the resistance that holds you back when you consciously bent a rule, even a small one. My heart pounding, I wiped sweat from my forehead.

A hand reached out and yanked me through the doors. I yelped.

Curly Hair shook his head at me, turned, and ran. We raced side-by-side down a fluorescent-lit corridor and a flight of stairs. The void of natural light ended as we burst through another set of swinging doors and back into the public section of the mall. Immediately, we were engulfed by jostling bargain shoppers and a cacophony of sounds.

I was distracted, a little panicked, and a lot out of breath, which is why I didn't see the stroller until it plowed into me.

In a sprawl, I hit the ground. Hard. My knee slammed into the concrete floor, and pain radiated through my leg. Frantic, I grabbed the side of the rocking stroller to steady it. The hipster, juggling a paper cup and typing on his phone while he pushed it, glared at me and, dropping the coffee in the cupholder, yanked the stroller back. With my knee stinging from the impact, I pulled myself up and backed away, looking around at the gathered crowd. I recognized no one.

I had lost him. Anxious, I spun in a circle and tried to think which way Curly Hair would have gone. We had zigzagged a lot, going up and down, trying to shake off the suits, but after we lost them, the general direction he had headed was down and away from where we had entered.

I staggered to an escalator, holding myself up by the railing. At the bottom, I get caught up in a large group of teens leaving a store, their multicolored hair shining in the mall's lights.

Wading through, I stopped and spun, searching the crowd. My heart was pounding when I finally caught a glimpse of curly hair disappearing into a store.

I had a moment of uncertainty as I remembered when I was seven and thought I was following my dad through the airport. It ended up being an older man with the same suitcase, which I didn't realize until we were in line to board a flight to San Jose,

Costa Rica instead of San Jose, California. I thought I had lost my dad forever and had cried for hours. I hoped this wasn't a repeat.

Crossing my fingers, I hobbled after him. It took a minute to adjust to the pain lancing my knee with every step. I kept moving, biting my lip as I put more weight on the knee and picked up speed. I paused in the fragrance section and sneezed. Out of the corner of my eye, I caught a flash of curly hair exiting a door. When I got there, the door was marked "Emergency Fire Exit Only." I chewed on my lip, breathing hard. Had I imagined it? I braced for the shrill of an alarm as I hit the bar opening the door and charged out into a brick alley.

I slammed hard into someone, our heads knocking together, causing my ears to ring.

"Ow." The curly haired boy rubbed his nose. I realized the impact was so hard because we were the same height. "What happened to you?"

Joy flooded me. *He had come back for me!* I almost threw my arms around him. The thought of being lost had me skipping past the splash zone and heading into the deep end of the panic pool.

Unsteady on my feet, I had a death grip on his shirt, wadding it up in a fist with one hand while I rubbed my aching head with the other. Add another bruise onto the count for the day. Gasping to catch my breath, I let go of his shirt and managed to get out, "Fell...hurt my knee."

The boy watched me limp and wobble alongside him for a minute before he put a tentative arm around my back to steady me. Tensing, I flushed and tried to ignore the tingles along where we touched. It felt awkward, different. The simple connection was alien, and I didn't know how I was supposed to respond.

When I didn't pull away, he pulled me close to his side and

grimaced. I couldn't tell if the look was pain or disgust at the idea of touching me. My first instinct was to push his arm away. I could walk without his help. But he held tight, and I realized I could go faster if I leaned on him. As he dragged me around the back of the building, he grumbled and made faces every time I rubbed against his hard body.

"This way." His voice was gruff and our bodies were stiff. Our muscles clenched where we knocked together in an awkward three-legged race. I was about to give up and start hobbling again on my own when, somehow, we latched onto a rhythm that worked, and his face relaxed a little. Locked in at shoulder and hip, he helped me down the alley. It surprised me how natural our rhythm was when we were working together.

I was still a little breathless from the running and the touching when I remembered to ask, "Who are you?"

Of all the questions I had, this was I blurted.

"Name's Shim." He glanced over but didn't stop. It was an odd name.

"I'm Grace."

"Yeah, that's what I thought. Noah is your dad, and your mom was one of them. Amy, right?"

I stiffened a little, wondering if this had been a mistake. "It's pronounced Amé—how do you know my mom's name? What do you mean 'one of them'?"

"One of the original five. She was the one that went missing, that started this whole mess."

"What are you talking about? My mom is dead. She died last year in a diving accident." I wasn't use to talking about my mom, and since Dad still wouldn't say her name, there wasn't much point in bringing her up.

Shim glanced over at me, his face puzzled.

"That's not what I heard. My mom said Amé was taken. That's why everyone's been on code red."

"What?" My stomach had always worked like my mood meter, doing a pretty good job of telling me what I was feeling, and right now, the guppies in my stomach were fighting. I was pretty sure I was going to throw up. Hope can be a terrible thing, and as it mixed with the sorrow I'd felt since her death, it turned to frustration. I stopped walking and almost fell on my face as my knee buckled under me. Gripping Shim's arm, I steadied myself. *Was it possible? Was she still alive?*

"Where is she?"

"I don't know anything else about it, but maybe the others do."

"Others?" I asked, reminded that my mother's death—disappearance—wasn't the most pressing concern at this moment.

"We are going to meet the twins and my brother."

I tucked that away to worry about later. "That was your mother, the woman in the van? Would she know who took my mom?" I thought of the short, Black woman with the bright-red hair and scowling face.

"Yeah, her name's Kindle. She doesn't know where your mom is, but she's one of the original five too. I bet you don't know about them, or her, do you?"

"Why would I know who your mother is? What's the original five?"

He had grimaced when I pulled on him for support, but otherwise, his face told me nothing. "Well, I know who your father is." He ignored the rest of my question.

"Yeah, how? How do you know my father's name?" I realized I couldn't do anything for my mother, but I might be able to help my dad.

"Kindle told me. She was meeting your dad at Arie's apartment. Arie is the twin's father. The Suits got all three of them." Shim shook his head, his lips pressed into an angry line.

"Who were those people in suits?"

"Don't know. That's what we have to figure out—fast. Come on, we are wasting time. The others are probably already at the meet-up."

I didn't know what he was talking about, but anywhere further away from people chasing us seemed like a good idea.

I wanted to ask him more questions, but he brushed off every attempt I made. I was still feeling a little wobbly and didn't want to tick off the person that was practically carrying me, and no matter what, I couldn't lose him. He had information I needed.

As we stumbled along, I looked over at him. His mop of curly hair fell past his ears, and up close, I could see it was in an amalgam of colors from dark browns to light golds, way too pretty for such a rough-looking guy. He had high checks, a broad nose, and full lips. His features were kind of crooked, but that made his face more compelling. He glanced over and glared when he caught me staring. I tried to keep my eyes forward, but they drifted back to him. He was intense, with compact muscle and bold stares, and I struggled not to shiver when it was his turn to look me over. I knew what he saw: a gangly girl with pale skin; long, weird-colored hair; and sad, gray eyes. I'd been cataloged before. I wasn't surprised when his nose wrinkled and one side of his mouth pulled up higher than the other. There was a tightness to his face. I felt a tinge of compassion and thought maybe he'd be more receptive to a question that wasn't about our parents.

"Who was the redhead?"

Seconds ticked by before he answered, "My brother, Jaxon."

"Why didn't he stick with you?"

Shim scowled. "Because he is a pain in my ass, but he's my responsibility."

Odd answer. But I didn't have any siblings, so what did I know?

Shim stopped and peered around the brick corner. "It's clear." He returned to help me, putting his arm around my shoulders again. "Lean into me so your limp doesn't draw attention." He snarled softly when I touched his side. I pulled back, but he jerked me to him again.

With his support, I left the alley, and we merged into the late rush hour foot traffic, looking like any other couple on the street.

I couldn't help wondering if I was heading the wrong direction.

3

THE WATERFALL

THE LATE AFTERNOON summer sun reflected off acres of glass. I briefly closed my eyes, blinded as we pushed through the doors to the outside, leaving the Metreon theater and the cacophony of music and voices behind us.

"Are we there yet?" I asked as Shim paused to get his bearings. I was stalling as I tested my knee out, eager to be independent of his awkward support.

"Almost. They said to meet behind a waterfall. Ah, there." Shim pointed with his chin.

Right. The mysterious twins. Maybe they would provide more answers than the taciturn Shim. I glanced around. I'd never been in this park. At the center was a large waterfall it must have been twenty feet tall. Water raced over the edges of the granite cliff, creating multiple waterfalls, glistening in the setting sun and dropping into a large rectangular basin. A relaxed atmosphere surrounded the fountain. People were sitting on benches talking while pedestrians wove along the path. Shoppers lay in the grass next to their bags. An idyllic scene in contrast with the desperation of my situation.

I hobbled stiffly beside Shim, along a path that led behind

the waterfall. The roar of the waterfall drowned out the noise of the city and across the pool a quote from Martin Luther King, Jr was etched in bronze into the wall. As I read it, stray droplets of water wet my clothes, and mist cooled the hot skin on my neck and face.

We rounded the corner to a covered walkway with etched glass panels on one side and the waterfall on the other. Two blond teens were sitting cross-legged on the floor directly behind the center of the waterfall. One gave Shim a chin lift in recognition, but his eyes narrowed on me tucked under Shim's arm. Before he could say anything, footsteps sounded behind us, and the red-headed boy with the skateboard appeared around the waterfall.

"Jaxon!" Shim lunged for his brother, pulling him into a hug. Jaxon grasped Shim close for a brief second, but the warm and fuzzy didn't last long, and he pushed Shim away with a swear.

"What the Stars is going on? Who were those creeps who took Mom?" It surprised me to hear one of my mother's favorite curse words coming out of Jaxon's mouth. It wasn't a common phrase. His face flushed, he glared at each of us, pausing briefly on me to spit out, "Who are you?" Then he moved on and fixed his gaze back on Shim. "Why did Mom go with them?" His voice rose to a shout.

"Quiet! Someone will hear." The twins made shushing motions, which increased Jaxon's glare.

"I don't know—I don't know what's going on," Shim stuttered as he paced the narrow space with angry steps. "Mom didn't go with them willingly—she was cuffed."

"They all had zip ties on their wrists," one of the twins said, both of their faces were crumpled in confusion, and I realized one twin was a boy and the other one, the one speaking so fast it was hard to follow, was a girl.

My knee wasn't going to hold me much longer, and as the twins seemed safer than the brothers, I slid down next to them, but not too close, and pushed my messenger bag under my sore knee. My jean-clad legs splayed out awkwardly, and I felt numb. I think I was in shock, and my body was carrying on instinctually with no real thought behind the actions. I so desperately wanted to demand answers, but I was learning more through listening.

"Dad told us something might happen to him, but I never expected this." The boy twin shook his head.

"What do you mean he thought something would happen?" I stopped fussing with my bag and stared.

"Who are you?" The twins asked at the same time, and everyone turned to me.

Shim stopped his pacing and squatted on my other side. "Guys, this is Grace, Noah's kid—and she knows less than we do."

"Hey!—no, well..." I started to protest, then stopped mid-sentence. I really didn't know what was going on. Resigned, I mumbled, "I guess that's true."

"The twins are Skylar and Breeze, or you can call her BZ. Arie is their dad, and everyone was meeting at his condo." Shim continued the introductions like I hadn't said anything. My eyes studied each of them. As if she was a bee, the girl twin positively vibrated at her name and the boy gave a toothy smile. If the models of Abercrombie & Fitch hooked up with the teens from the Gap ads, these would be their love children. The two had matching haircuts, blond bangs styled to the side over vivid blue eyes, and were dressed in identical short-sleeve button-up shirts in a shade of yellow probably called "lemon" or "sunshine," and expensive-looking jeans. I tugged the hem of my faded tee over my old jeans.

"And the redhead is Jaxon, my brother. I told you about him."

I compared the two brothers. They were both lean and muscular, but they didn't look like brothers. Jaxon had spiky ginger hair, skin almost as pale as mine, a smattering of freckles across his nose, and flushed cheeks. He had an earbud in one ear, narrowed green eyes, and the corners of his mouth turned down in a scowl.

"What is all that green shit in your hair?" Jaxon asked.

"It's my hair." I responded defensively. I put a hand to my head like I could cover up the streaks that had plagued me since birth. Breeze reached out toward my head. I pulled back. I wasn't sure I wanted any of them touching my head.

"You look like a freak."

I couldn't tell if Shim or Jaxon made that remark. They both stared at me like I was a freak.

"It's genetic, from my mom. She has it too—had it too," I automatically corrected and continued, "I get in trouble for it all the time. At one school, they thought it was dyed, and I had to get a doctor's note proving it wasn't." I was desperate to sound confident but failing miserably with my awkward verbal gushing. I ground my teeth. Why was I letting them intimidate me? My stomach did a flip.

"I've never heard of someone having green hair DNA before. I like it," Breeze said.

"Don't knock genetics. Jaxon and I are brothers." Shim held a dark fist up to Jaxon's pale freckled arm. "Weirdo." He gave his brother a friendly punch on the arm. Jaxon snorted and returned the punch.

"Can we focus?" I glared at them. "What happened to my dad, and what do you know about my mom?"

"And where did you get those bags?" Shim hijacked the question.

The twins ignored me and responded to Shim.

"Well—Dad is always learning survival tips," Skylar explained, wide-eyed, "Has been for years. He pretended it was all normal."

"Last year, he got really crazed. Started hoarding supplies and stashing stuff all over the city for us." Breeze looked pointedly at the backpacks. "He wouldn't tell us why, but now—"

"—now it makes sense. I think it was about the time that your mom went missing, Grace." Skylar finished Breeze's thought, and they both looked at me.

Everyone here thought my mom was still alive. Everyone—even me. I had always thought her disappearance was suspicious. But my dad had been so convinced she was gone, even when they hadn't found her body after the diving accident, he had insisted on burying an empty casket. I didn't know what to think anymore, and alarm bells were going off in my head. I couldn't figure out how all these events were connected.

"Why would someone take them? First your mom, now our parents—why is someone kidnapping our people?" Breeze whined.

"I didn't even know my mom was missing," I admitted. My declaration was met with shocked looks from the others. While Shim explained what we had talked about at the mall, I tried to organize what I knew so I could figure out what to do next.

"So Breeze and Skylar, your dad, Arie, was kidnapped with my dad, but none of you know why or by who?" The others nodded their heads, so I continued, "And Kindle, Arie, and my mom grew up together, like siblings, or something similar." I was mystified by the strange names but tried to stay on track.

"Kindle called them foster siblings. Said we all were cousins or some crap when she introduced us and dumped us off this morning with the twins," Jaxon said, his voice deadpan.

"I was so exhausted from driving all night, I didn't think to ask her more," Shim said, adding another thing we had in common. Later, I'd have to remember to ask where they were from.

"And you had never met before?" I had a strange feeling about all of this. There were too many coincidences in our stories.

"No. We were hanging out in the mall, waiting for the all clear, when I got a call from Kindle telling us to run. The twins must have grabbed the bags on the way here." The blonds bobbed their heads at Shim's summary.

I was incredulous that, collectively, they had barely more information than me.

"Ah man, this is so weird," Skylar said. Shim pointed to the pack in his hands.

"Maybe there is something inside that tells us what is going on."

There were three backpacks, and the twins each dug into one. Jaxon grabbed at the third bag, and Shim tried to pull it from him. They sank to the floor, struggling over it.

"Jaxon, leave it…" Shim shoved his brother back.

"I'll do it." I leaned forward and snatched the bag from the distracted pair.

We unzipped the backpacks and started rummaging through. There were a couple of smaller sacks inside mine, one with the usual survival gear. We had a bag like that on the boat. Then, the contents got strange. There was a sack with a box of hair dye, a man's change of clothes, and an envelope with wallets and a stack of passports. What rolled out of the last sack got everyone's attention: a velvet envelope and a sunglasses case.

"These are sick! They look military grade." Jaxon grabbed the expensive sunglasses and put them on.

Shim opened the vinyl bag and pulled out binoculars. "Are we supposed to be hunting something?"

"I think we are the hunted ones," I replied, looking in the thick envelope. "*Whoa.*" Everyone turned to look. "It's full of money!" I leafed through the thick wad of twenty and hundred-dollar bills, shocked. I had never seen so much money in one place before.

Breeze was going through the wallets; they all had IDs with the same man but different names and hair styles. Skylar reached into the velvet envelope and pulled out a watch covered in dials. A white tag attached by a string fluttered at the clasp. A second item rolled out of the envelope, and it was met with a gasp from the group.

It was a cuff, wide enough for a man's arm, made of flat-tened bronze with a round reddish-green stone with silver threads set in the center. My eyes widened in recognition. I was very familiar with that stone—it exactly matched the one in my mother's necklace. *How was that possible?*

A dark shadow of suspicion entered my mind. I knew why I was shocked to see the stone, but why had the others reacted as they did?

"That's Dad's cuff. He always has it on. What's it doing here?" Breeze said, her blue eyes troubled as she turned to Skylar. She reached out to touch the metal, like she could reach her father through the bracelet.

"It's the same stone as my mom's necklace," I said, pulling the necklace out from under the collar of my shirt. I pushed a thumb under the stone at the front, angling it to show the others.

"No way!"

"Oh, it's pretty," Breeze cooed. They all leaned in closer. Everyone, except Shim.

"Wait a minute," Jaxon demanded. "That's the rock that's on my mom's ring."

I turned to Jaxon, and Shim swore softly. Pushing up off the floor, he paced away from us.

"Shim?" Jaxon asked with a hint of uncertainty quivering in his voice. "The stones are the same, aren't they?"

Shim cursed again. With a loud exhale, he spun around and dug into his pocket. "Yeah, it's the same as this." He pulled out a ring made of a different metal from the other two pieces of jewelry. The ring's band was studded with chunky, glittering crystals, but the stone set in the center was the same.

"You took her ring?" Jaxon shouted at his brother.

"*Shhhh,*" the twins hissed.

"You..." Words poured out of Jaxon's mouth I had never heard before as he lit into his brother. Without a pause, he launched himself at Shim, knocking the ring out of his hand and punching him in the face.

I scrambled back, shrinking against the wall to stay out of range as legs splayed and arms flying the brothers rolled by.

The ring landed next to me, and I studied it without picking it up. It was interesting that the ring had the same stone—maybe a remarkable coincidence. But the odds that the cuff was made from the same metal as my mom's necklace and the same stone was in all three—that was unreal.

And I couldn't believe that we are on the brink of discovering something that might help us rescue our parents, and these two idiots were fighting.

"We don't have time for this!" I hissed, my voice harsh. "We have to focus...We have to figure out what to do next."

"What do you mean? We have to go back home, of course," Breeze said.

Did this girl not remember what had just happened?

Shim shoved Jaxon off, his clothes now dirty and a new scrape starting to bleed on his arm. Pulling his shirt down where it had ridden up, he came back to our huddled camp around the packs. On his way, he scooped the ring off the floor and held it tight in his fist. Jaxon started at him again, but Shim glared, and something in his dark expression made Jaxon stiffen and back off.

I found my hand on the cold metal at my throat. Unless I was swimming, I was always wearing it. Running my fingers along the necklace, I pulled it out and studied it upside-down, comparing it to the other pieces and logging the differences. After my mom died—went missing—I had become obsessed with researching the necklace. I'd spent a lot of time online reading about gems, geology, metallurgy, and jewelry making; I'd even studied meteorites. That is how I knew that the metal on the necklace was the same as the cuff but different from the ring. My mother's necklace was a torc, a single piece of curved metal that, when I wore it, wrapped around my neck at my collar. Both pieces were smooth with no visible hammer marks, but the surface of each was etched with a pattern of intricate score marks, like a script, that I'd never been able to identify. The metal was aged and darkened in places. Both ends of the pieces terminated with a miniature metal-screened dome. On the necklace, the ends hung in front and were several inches apart, linked by a chain, and in the center, a cabochon-set stone sat in the hollow of my throat.

The cuff, however, would have wrapped around the wrist with the metal folding back and forth and the stone mounted in the center. The stones were identical on all three pieces, a deep reddish-green threaded through with twisting silver lines.

In all my research, I'd never seen anything like this stone.

It raised so many questions. Where did it come from? Why did each of the siblings have one? Well, a piece. They were obviously slices from the same rock. And that led to the most troubling thoughts, the ones I was pointedly avoiding. How were our parents really connected? How could my father have kept all this from me? What really happened to my mother? It made my stomach ache, but this was the path we needed to follow.

"What are they hiding?" Had I said that aloud? *Yes, I had.*

Looking at the four of them, I held up my mother's necklace and repeated, my voice trembling, "What are they hiding? Why were they ready to run?" I yanked gently on the chain, then pointed to the cuff Skylar had put on and the ring in Shim's hand. "These stones are the key."

Shim studied me. He had a smudge on the side of his cheek that took the intensity from his glare. When he nodded, the tension eased in his face.

"Yeah, I think you're right." Shim's gaze lingered on the stone, and he shook his head. "How long do you think they have been on the run?"

"What do you mean?" Skylar looked up from the cuff he was studying on his arm.

"What if they weren't just ready to run?" Shim nodded to the backpacks. "What if they were *already running?*"

"Yeah. All those times mom made us move," Jaxon said.

"All the new schools," Skylar added.

"All the job changes." I thought about how many times my dad dropped a perfectly good job, and we up and left a town in the middle of the night.

"Our dad is a *Locum Tenens* physician."

I raised an eyebrow at Breeze.

"That's a doctor who fills in for other doctors. We only stay in a place for a couple of months, then move on. No friends, no family." Breeze's voice was soft.

"But they did have a family." Skylar made a circle with his finger pointing at each of us.

"Not a real family," I reminded them. "They were pseudo-siblings."

"It was real to them. Whatever they experienced in that foster home bonded them together. *We* might not know each other, but our parents knew about each of *us*. What I don't understand is why they kept us a secret from each other."

I looked from the stones to the bags. "There is some kind of connection here. Between all of us. Something happened that connected our parents, but also frightened them, so they stayed apart."

"Maybe they saw something illegal or a murder," Breeze guessed.

"Oh, like they were in a witness protection program and had to hide who they were." Skylar got excited at the idea. "Maybe they carried guns and went undercover to spy on some mafia-types."

"Man, you watch too much TV." Jaxon's tone was scornful. "My mom wouldn't spy on anyone. She's too smart to get caught up in that."

Shim corroborated with a nod.

"My dad's a marine biologist. I can't imagine who he would spy on," I admitted.

"Your dad's not one of them." Jaxon's blunt tone needled me.

I bristled at the exclusion of my dad from whatever this was —he had been taken too.

"Logan isn't either," Shim reminded his brother. To me, he added, "Logan O'Connell, he's our dad. I bet that was why the Micah dude who visited Kindle last year wanted to know what she had told him. Whatever happened to them must have happened before they married our dads."

"What are you talking about?" I asked.

Jaxon glowered at Shim. They stared each other down like mad dogs, willing the other to blink first. I didn't think Jaxon was going to respond. Then he broke eye contact.

"My mom was pissed after the divorce," Jaxon began,

slowly. "Last year, there was a huge blowup. The police got called." His face scrunched as he dug deep into the memory.

"Afterwards, this stranger turns up; I'd never seen him before, but Kindle knows him. At first, he's comforting her, then this guy demands to know where Amy's diary is and what Kindle had told Logan." I was about to correct the pronunciation of my mother's name to Amé when his eyes widen and he continued his story. "Big mistake. She started yelling at him. Called him 'Micah.' Said she 'hadn't told Logan the truth.' Then they saw me and immediately stopped fighting. It was so weird."

"So, Micah was one of the original five. Who was the fifth?" I asked.

"They mentioned someone else. She had a strange name too. I think it was his wife." Jaxon's face went blank and he shrugged.

Skylar let out a whistle. "And you don't know what it was she might have told your dad?" He looked back and forth between both boys, who were shaking their heads.

"How did they know?" I muttered, shivering as goosebumps raced up my arm and alarm bells went off in my head.

"Know what?" Shim scooted closer to ask.

"Diar—" my voice cracked and I started again, "diary. My mother kept one. It had a green cover, and she always had it on her when I was growing up. We never found it after…" When had I last seen the diary? I pushed back through my memories, swimming backward through the messy ocean of pain. What kind of person couldn't remember something so important? How had Kindle and Micah known about it, and why would Kindle have it?

"Man, this is messed up." Jaxon swore a string of curses as he got up and hitched up his jeans, then walked around the small alcove, kicking at the corners where the wall met the floor.

I would have liked to pace out the frustration that was

making me feel trapped. My knee felt better, but it still twinged as I flexed.

What else had my mom and dad lied about? Why lie to me? What did I do that they didn't trust me? Now my dad was in trouble, all our parents were, and we couldn't call the police because what if they were criminals? I shuddered. This couldn't be real.

How much of my life was a lie? How would I ever know the truth?

"So, now what?"

I wasn't paying attention and didn't hear who asked the question, but I knew what I wanted to say. *Let's go home.* But I didn't have a home anymore...and the van with all our stuff, I couldn't go back to that, I couldn't even drive yet...and my dad was gone...and my mom was gone. I didn't have anything—except this stone.

And just like that, I knew what needed to be done. I looked up at the others.

"It's up to us." I drew in a breath and exhaled shakily. My voice trembled a little when I added, "We can't go to the police, we don't know who to trust, and our parents can't help us...but maybe we can help them."

"How?" Skylar asked. He raked his hands through his hair, the disheveled white-blond strands sticking out at all angles. "How are we supposed to help them when they never told us anything?"

"We find out the truth. We find out what they've been running from and who would want to kidnap them. It's the only way."

They all stared at me, and it was making me nervous. My throat tightened, and I tried to push down my nerves. We had just met today. We were strangers, and these could be the people my dad didn't want me to trust. All I knew about them was that the two blond wannabe child models looked like angels and seemed to plow through trouble like pixies. The foul-mouthed redhead was as volatile as nitroglycerin, and I was pretty sure he hated everything, including me. And the biggest puzzle, the shaggy-haired boy who stole from his mother, whaled on his brother and didn't like to be touched. And what I was asking them to do—maybe it was too much.

"I think Grace is right." I was surprised Shim spoke up first.

Jaxon let out a frustrated growl and stubbornly turned his back.

"You mean, what? That *we* find out the truth? *Ourselves?* Without calling the police?" Breeze's voice wavered as she answered her own question.

"That's exactly what she means." Skylar turned to his twin, and they did this non-verbal eye communication. Then he turned to the rest of us and nodded. "We're in."

Breeze didn't look happy.

Jaxon let out a puff of air as if resigning himself to following us fools. "Fine, whatever." Shim gave me a half smile, one side of his mouth tilting up while the other still looked grim.

"So, what do we do?"

So what do I do? What have I started with these people that I just met? I had no idea where this was going to take us. There was more to our parent's story, and it was finally time to find out what that was, but could I depend on this group to help me search out the truth? Did I have a choice?

Okay, Grace, think it through. First step, we have identified the problem. Now how do we find out the truth? What resources do we have? I thought about the backpacks, the stones, and the watch. Pulling out the watch again, I examined the attached tag. It had a gallery name and address. The watch came from the jewelry bag with the cuff. Could the two items be connected?

"Do you know where this is?" I held the tag out to the twins.

"Yes, it's near here. Should we try and call them?"

Jaxon and Shim thought that was a bad idea and leaned back against the wall of the alcove as I watched the willowy twins stand nose-to-nose with the muscular brothers and debate their opposing points. My mind is spinning with the events of the day. I couldn't get past the thought that my mother might not be dead. It was tearing me up inside. What if she had been kidnapped too? I felt guilty for not trying to find her. I didn't really care that she might have been involved in some kind of illegal activity. She could be in trouble. At the very least, she had been on the run from something. Someone? Maybe the same someone who had my dad and the others? The same someone who had replied to my text earlier, pretending to be my father.

"We can't call." I interrupted Jaxon whose flushed face matched the color of his spiky red hair. He cut off his diatribe on the twin's monumental stupidity.

"What do you mean?" Asked a perma-scowling Shim. Just barely taller than his younger brother, he had been using his muscle and posture to support Jaxon's position.

They all turned to look at me.

"We can't trust any technology." I had held up my phone as an example. "They either had my Dad's phone or hacked it and texted me. We can't trust any messages we get. And, my Dad says that people can track you through your phone." I cringed, gritted my teeth, and with an underhanded throw that would have gotten me kicked off a softball team, I tossed my phone into the fountain.

"She's right," Skylar chimed in with his support. "I read an article that the CIA can track your phone even if it's turned off."

"I doubt the CIA are after us, nerdlet. I'm sure they care more about terrorists and shit." Jaxon pulled his cell phone out of his pocket, gave a little shrug, and tossed it into the fountain.

Breeze gasped, her mouth an "O", and her eyes wide. She watched Skylar pull his shiny blue smartphone out of his pocket and give it a fond caress before lobbing it into the waterfall.

Shim had his eye on me as this all went down. I crossed my arms and glared at him, arching a brow. He shrugged and, with a flick of his wrist, tossed his phone. With the shallow angle, it did a skip, then sank into the pool.

"Argh" Breeze clutched her glittery pink phone to her chest with one hand while petting it with the other. "No, no, no, there must be another way." Her voice sing-songed as she clung to hope, throwing out one ridiculous suggestion after another. "What if they are waiting for us to call them?" she reasoned, eager desperation lit up her face. "This could all be a mistake." The tone of her voice hitched up at the end of each word.

"Come on," Skylar coached, "hand it over."

"Nooooo, please. I'll turn it off. I'll...I'll bury it in the backpack with the other phones."

"You know that's not how it works. And those are burner phones. They're untraceable. You have your whole life mapped out on your phone. Every action you do is trackable." Skylar stroked a calming hand over her hair down from the crown of her head, each stroke reaching farther down her arm and closer to the phone, eventually touching the phone and gently pulling it from her grasp.

"Nooooo. Please, not the fountain. Just leave it here, in the alcove. I'll leave it behind, but don't sink it."

Skylar looked at her big blue eyes pleading with him and caved. "Okay, okaaaay." He tucked the phone up against the wall of the alcove.

"All right." That task done, I turned to the next one. "Let's grab our bags. We are walking to the gallery." I stood, bracing for an ache in my knee and for another debate and was surprised that everyone followed my directions.

Crack! Plunk!

"Noooo." Breeze wailed.

I turned back from picking up my messenger bag in time to see Jaxon's foot returning to the ground. Breeze slid across the floor, landing on her belly with her head leaning over the edge of the pool. A mournful wail issued from her lips as she had said goodbye to her phone.

4

THE DUCHESS

A FLASH SPREAD through the waterfall as twilight triggered the light meters and the fountain's spotlights popped on. Dusk settled, and the howls of the city died into an evening purr.

Slipping out from behind the waterfall, Breeze led our grim-faced group across the lawn. Skylar was next, his eyes nervously searching the shadows, and I followed, limping slightly on my injured knee. I assumed the moody Shim was somewhere behind me with the third backpack. Jaxon had snuck out earlier, checking the grounds and whistling an all clear.

Quickly moving across the lawn, we merged into the pedestrian traffic on Third Street. Crossing in front of the Modern Art Museum, we walked briskly up to Market Street. The enraged horns from the heavy evening traffic echoed off the stone and pavement.

Walls of buildings rose up on either side of Market, stretching up to the sky as we walked the canyon between them. Boxed in and antsy, I watched the unfamiliar streets alternate from thriving businesses and cafés to empty storefronts with boarded-up windows and barred doors, then back to thriving businesses. Heading deeper into the shopping district, we passed a series of trendy clothing boutiques and crossed streets packed with never-ending cars, headlights bouncing off heated surfaces. The pedestrian traffic picked up as we turned onto Post Street. Lamplights popped on as twilight settled in.

The gallery was in a ground-floor shop, and the twins gave furtive glances up and down the street before they shot inside. Jaxon and Shim followed. I paused, taking a nervous, shaky breath. What were we going to do if we didn't find the answers we needed here? It had surprised me when everyone had listened to my ideas earlier. I'm not the kind of girl that inspires a following. What if they all turned to me for the next move?

Reluctantly, I pushed open the gallery door. The sweep of cool air washed over me, bringing a faint trace of oil and something metallic. Stepping over the threshold, I glanced around to make sure we hadn't entered a mechanic's shop by mistake. I was still sniffing the air when an object darted across the floor, heading my direction.

The gizmo stopped in front of me. The rotating collection of cogged wheels and levers intricately laced together was slightly smaller than a basketball. The spinning pile of metal had an undulating row of levers, like a spine, and a small silver head with floppy copper strips on each side. The head looked up at me and then blinked two gorgeous brown marble eyes as a red tongue made of leather lolled in its mouth.

My nervousness disappeared, and I clasped my hands to my checks. The pile of metal was in the shape of a dog, its whole body moving in a mechanical jolt as it tried to jump up and wag its tail at the same time. I smiled as the metal dog pawed at my leg expectantly with a spork-like foot.

"Duchess, down," came from the back of the shop. A tall man rushed forward. "Down, girl." He chided the pile of metal as he pushed the cutlery off my leg so I could enter the shop.

Jaxon, who had missed the mechanical wonder on his way in, turned back.

"It's a dog!" He sank to his knees, and a smile transformed his face as he patted his legs. "Come here, girl." The mechanical dog gave a last jump at me, and with a slinky, 180-degree rotation, Duchess launched herself at the new voice. Her paws had small wheels under them that rolled her across the room then locked as she jumped up and tapped Jaxon on the arm.

The man who had called Duchess back raised an arched brow at Jaxon's laugh. His waxed handlebar mustache twitched. He might have smiled in amusement, but it was hard to see under the facial hair. He was dressed in a long brown military-style coat covered with leather straps and brass buckles. A gold watch fob hung between his jacket pockets. He looked like a refugee from another time, or like he had just returned from Burning Man.

In spite of his twitching mustache, he didn't look happy to see us. He kept glancing behind me as if to check if we had adult supervision.

I looked around the shop, hoping to see someone else we could talk to, but it was just him. The gallery held a selection of oils and watercolors. Paintings of rolling California landscapes and still-life abstracts of wine and cheese were interspersed with elegant stone sculptures and round handmade ceramic bowls. Despite the art, the space felt sterile and didn't match the dog that greeted us or the man who had yet to say hello.

Breeze and Skylar sank to their knees on either side of Jaxon, laughing as they took turns patting Duchess' head.

"We were wondering if the owner was here."

"And who is asking?" The man didn't look up as he replied in a formal diction with a faint accent, somewhere between Harry Potter and Benedict Cumberbatch.

I hesitated. How much should we tell him? "We have...business with him."

"And who would you be?" he asked again. Skylar, Breeze, and Jaxon seemed to remember why we were here and stood up.

"Um, we have an item we need some information on," I said.

"Well, let's see it," the man said. His curled mustache looked friendly, but the set of his mouth and his folded arms screamed skeptic.

Glancing at the twins, I gave Skylar a nod, and he pulled the watch out of his pocket and held it out. The man looked down at the watch but didn't reach for it. His arms stayed wrapped across his chest.

"And where did you pinch that?" He asked coolly.

Skylar hesitated again, so I made up an answer for him. "It was a gift." That was a mistake.

The man looked at each of us, then walked over and opened the door and pointed out. "I think you need to leave, and I will be calling the police."

5

THE SECRET GALLERY

"GET OUT!" The handle-bar mustache dipped over his pursed-lipped demand.

We eyed each other warily. *Now what?*

When we didn't move, the man pulled a phone from one of his many pockets in an angry huff and said, "You are lying." Most of his accent was wiped out by tension, but his words were still formal and clipped. "And I am going to call the officials if you do not leave."

Frantic, I looked back at Shim who gave a *what have we got to lose* shrug. He had quite a command of non-verbal skills—and he was right. At this point, we had lost so much, what could the truth hurt? I didn't want to say who we were, but I could tell him where we got the watch.

"We aren't lying." I glanced at Skylar and Breeze. "Arie gave the watch to us."

The retro-man looked startled at the name. His fingers froze over the phone, and he cocked his head and looked at me. "*You* know Arie?" He drew out his words, imbibing each with a bucket load of sarcasm.

I floundered, trying to come up with a good lie that would explain why we had this watch and not reveal who we were.

Glancing back at the twins, I stuttered out an "uhmm," stalling, when Jaxon interrupted.

"For Stars sake. Arie is their father." He pointed at the twins.

The group gasped. Shim put his hand over his face.

"Oh, come on," Jaxon exclaimed. "He was never going to tell us anything; he thought we jacked the watch."

"Is it true?" The man looked at the twins with narrowed eyes. "Arie is your father?"

They nodded.

"Yes, and we need your help," Breeze whispered.

It took some convincing to get the man to believe we truly did know Arie and hadn't stolen the watch, but the change that came over him was amazing. Stepping in front of a couple entering the store, he cut them off. "We are closed." He shut the door in their faces. He flipped the lock, turned the sign in the window that read, "Shut Happens," and pulled down the blinds.

"Head upstairs, fourth floor, then turn left." He indicated a door in the back. "I'll close up the downstairs gallery and meet you up there." He started to move away, then turned back to us. "My name is Jonas, and Arie is my friend. If you are who you say you are, and you have that watch, then you need my help."

We looked at each other, stunned. What a turnabout. With a cautious glance up, we followed the directions and ascended the shadowed stairs to the fourth floor. At the top, we turned left as instructed and faced a heavy dark-wood door. Shim, in the front, slowly turned the handle and cautiously stepped over the threshold. The oily metallic smell was much stronger here, and there was a whirring sound, like a winding clock.

"Smells like a motocross shop," Jaxon muttered, following him and pushing farther into the room.

We emerged in a gallery very different from the downstairs shop. The space had a retro-futuristic Victorian vibe. The front walls were covered in sheets of riveted metal connected by delicate art deco arches. The remaining walls had exquisitely patterned wallpaper. Floor to ceiling shelves were in the center of the room, each crammed full of mechanical devices and pieces of metal art.

A large painting in the corner showed an ethereal golden planet with metal pavilions floating in the air. Other paintings hanging throughout the room featured futuristic landscapes, human-mechanical hybrids, Victorian era-inspired laboratories, and flying machines.

In the center of the room sat an old-fashioned chrome and leather motorcycle with a keyboard handlebar, elongated body, and tall organ pipes extending vertically from the back. Beside it was a bicycle with treads and cogs instead of wheels and a mannequin head where the seat normally would be. The pieces were amazing, wondrous, bizarre, and in some cases, extremely dangerous. I gave a wide berth to the chainsaw shaving chair.

We dispersed throughout the room, gasps and laughter following each new find. It was sometime later when I heard footsteps coming up the stairs and looked up. Jonas came into the gallery and shut the door behind him.

"Come with me." His shoes tapped on the wood floor, his stride brisk as he swept through the exhibit space and entered a door in the back. We tentatively followed him into a workshop and over to a large wooden partners desk that had been turned into a workstation with spider-like metal arms to which a lamp and magnifying glass were attached. He laid a velvet cloth on the desk and put on cloth gloves.

"Let's take a look at that watch."

Skylar dug it out of the pocket of his jeans and reluctantly handed it over to Jonas. Laying it gently on the cloth, Jonas bent over the magnifying glass, silently studying the piece for several minutes, a metal probe with a rubber tip assisting him with his investigation. Flipping the watch over, he removed the face and examined the inner workings.

"It is Arie's watch," began Jonas, not looking up. "I've cleaned it several times over the years—tried to buy it from him, too, but he never would accept my offer." He flipped it over again and secured the cover on the face of the watch. "It is in perfect condition, the same as the last time I saw it, which was well over a year ago." Jonas paused. "Well, almost the same. This is new." He pointed to the back of the watch where a pattern of dots and lines were inscribed above a line of text that read, "Find your way home."

"This design and the inscription weren't here the last time I examined the watch." He looked up and pursed his lips as he studied us, his brow creased. "Whenever I tried to buy this watch, your father always declined. Said it was an important family heirloom—all he had left."

I eyed the twins. They said their father was in foster care with my mother. How could he have a family heirloom? My family didn't have any. Then again, most people probably didn't move around with everything they owned in the back of a VW van.

The twins looked as poleaxed as I felt. More secrets. How odd it would feel to know this stranger knew more about your father than you did.

I empathized. What kind of family didn't tell you that you had cousins, aunts, uncles, a mother who was still alive? What kind of family hid all the time? Mysterious kidnappings, hidden family heirlooms, cryptic messages. When had life gotten so complicated? None of this new reality matched up with my previous existence.

I searched my memory for any story I could think of from my mom's childhood—real stories, not the ones about fantastic underwater kingdoms and sea monsters that she made up to entertain a child, but a real, historical account of her life.

Nothing.

How could I know so little about my own mother? I knew that water and the ocean were important to her. But I knew nothing about her real life. No grandparents, no hometown, no middle school horror stories. Most kids don't pop into existence, fully formed, at fifteen years old and enter the foster care system. But it seemed my mom had.

I felt cheated. She had stolen something from me that, until this moment, I never knew I was missing. Maybe if she had shared more, filled in some of the gaps, I could have had a family history, something that made sense of what I was learning now. I kept coming back to the idea that there was something they were trying to hide.

Jonas reassembled the watch and settled back into the wooden chair. He gave the twins a speculative look as he stretched his long legs out under the desk. "So, Arie couldn't bear to part with the watch, and now, here you are with it." After a minute of silently studying them, he pushed back from the desk and walked over to the window to look down on the street. As if drawn by a magnet, we all moved into the void for a closer review of the inscription. Jonas turned his back on the window and sat, balancing on the frame. Watching. Calculating.

"Would you like to sell the watch to me?" Jonas inquired, his brow crinkling into a frown. "I'm afraid with it now damaged, it won't be worth what it once was, but I can make you a nice offer. Net you quite a bit of cash."

"It's not for sale." Breeze spoke up, and Skylar and Jaxon moved quickly into a defensive position, shoulder to shoulder, blocking, protecting the watch.

"I could give you a great price," Jonas continued, "more than you might expect for such an insignificant item."

I tilted my head to one side then back, trying to understand what Jonas was doing by pushing us on this.

"No way." Skylar's hand hovered protectively over the watch, like it could be snatched from the table at any minute. "We aren't parting with it."

"I could trade you for Duchess. You seemed quite taken by her. Even swap. What do you say?"

The twin's eyes widened. Jaxon, a gleam in his eyes, started to speak and Shim's palm quickly covered his mouth, silencing him. Breeze gave a sad shake of her head.

"No deal." Skylar was steadfast.

A moment of silence stretched out, tangible friction in the air as they measured each other's resolve. Finally, Jonas brought his hands together with a loud clap, breaking the spell.

"Good." Rubbing his hands together, Jonas's tone instantly changed from guarded to helpful. "Good. Then what do you want to know?"

The twins and Jaxon looked confused.

Jonas had been testing us—and we had passed. My stomach eased for the first time all day. "You wanted to see if we were trying to sell the watch, implying it was stolen before you told us any more about it."

Jonas cracked the first smile I had seen on him. "Yes, and there is more to tell about the watch, but if you were just interested in selling it, it wouldn't matter."

"More to tell?" Shim picked up the watch, examining the face. "Is it about these dials and why they don't tell time?" His face had the eager curiosity of an engineer salivating to take something apart and understand it.

"What do you mean they don't tell time? It's a watch. What else is it supposed to do?" It was impressive how Jaxon could add just the right amount of derision to his tone even when he was confused and asking for information.

Shim pulled the watch closer and examined it. "This outside dial"—he pointed to a lighter gold band that ran around the face of the copper-colored watch—"looks like it might tell time, but it's not set to a twelve- or twenty-four hour clock. It looks like it might be"—he paused to examine the band—"a twenty-eight hour clock?" Shim shook his head in wonder, then sat on the chair and pulled over the looking glass.

"These three smaller dials set inside the larger band, well, two of them look more like altimeters, or something similar, to measure altitude. This third one could be a dial for a calendar, but it's also off. It has thirteen marks around it, so it can't be measuring a twelve-month year," Shim shook the watch gently, "and that, that feels like an off-center mass. It may have a vibration mode," Shim said, eagerly prodding the cover with the rubber-tipped probe.

"But if it isn't a watch, then what is it?" Skylar looked as confused as I felt.

"Oh, it's a watch. It just doesn't track time the way we are used to tracking it. Which is most interesting. And the other dials, they could be for tides or planet orbits. It's hard to tell without the context of where it is from, and I don't know where that would be...It's probably just decorative, but someone went to a lot of trouble to make a watch that isn't meant to tell time anywhere on Earth." Jonas paused and let that sink in before he added, "Why don't you tell me why Arie gave it to you?"

We looked at each other. *Now, what do we do?*

∞

JONAS HAD PEPPERED us with questions about the watch, but none of us said anything. Not that we knew anything. At this point, we had more questions than answers. I was sure he was going to throw us out. Instead, he offered us a place to stay for the night and ordered dinner.

"Atta girl!" Jaxon praised, rolling a ball again for Duchess to chase. Shim and Jonas were leaning over the watch on the desk, deep in discussion on how it was made and what it could be measuring. It was an unexpected side of Shim. Not that I knew him very well.

Jonas's tablet was balanced on my knees. I had told him I wanted to check the weather for tomorrow. My real intention was to research what this "waters" could be and why my dad had sent me a text sending us there. Well, *me* there. Not us. I had to remember, just because we were all together now, it didn't mean we would be sticking together. I may not have any place else to go, but I'm sure the rest of them did. The brothers had a father somewhere, and the twins must have something—A mom? Grandparents? I could pretend we were an "us" all I wanted, but when a storm hit, I knew the only one on the boat I could count on was me.

"I'm asking," Skylar hissed at his sister. Breeze and Skylar had been in another one of their half-whispered, half-telepathic conversations where most of what they said was done with eye rolls and facial expressions. It looked like it was turning into an argument. Skylar pulled away from Breeze. "How did you meet our dad?" he demanded of Jonas.

"We met here at the gallery. Most people in the city with an affinity to the genre find their way here."

"I never knew he liked steampunk stuff." Breeze looked puzzled to learn about this side of her father.

"Arie is the ultimate futurist. His immersion and understanding of the art were immense. It was like he had lived in the worlds he wrote about."

"Wait, he was a writer?"

"Of course. I thought you knew? He had a pseudonym, but surely, his children would know..." Jonas paused for effect. He had a way of speaking that was both condescending and inquisitive. It would be extremely annoying if he wasn't being so nice to us. "No? Well, he has several Gaslamp fantasy short stories—not that he lets anyone know. An extremely private man, your father is." Jonas resumed inspection of the watch.

"I can't believe it. How did we not know he was a writer?" Breeze turned wounded eyes to Skylar.

Was anything we knew about our parents true?

I resumed my internet search on "waters" and was turning up diddly, but I was only half looking. My mind kept spinning on Arie telling Jonas about his watch and having a secret life as a writer. I wasn't the only one whose parents kept secrets. We were all suffering from a baffling lack of information, and what we did know was confusing—the heirloom watch included.

Conflicting emotions of remorse and anger swarmed through me at the thought of my mom. I breathed deep, sinking into the memories.

Warmth. A beautiful, ethereal, pale face with large, silvery eyes. Everyone said I looked like her, but I couldn't see it. Only the hair was similar, and hers was longer and silkier. I buried my face, and the green and ash-brown strands tickled my nose.

"Mom, did you your mother have hair like ours?"

A rich laugh shook through her lean swimmer's build, and strong arms hugged me. "Let me tell you another tale about the Merpeople of the Underwater Land of LaDér."

I sighed. It had been one of my favorite stories. Upon reflection, I realized she used it to distract me whenever I asked for details about her life, a deflection from getting too close.

My sad nostalgia was replaced with a familiar anger and a sense of betrayal. I remember mom being sad. She must have missed her family. What was her life like when she was growing up? Had she had a family? Friends? A dog? I didn't even know if she was American born. She didn't have an accent, but her name was Amé. I could be half French or Canadian.

She had been fifteen years old when she ended up in foster care. That was younger than me. I tried to think of anything I knew about her from before that time. Nothing. By the time she was my age, she was an orphan, and I guess that was when she met up with the rest of her foster siblings: Arie, Kindle, the guy Micah, and the fifth one whose name we didn't know. A few years later, she must have met my dad, and as soon as they were old enough, they had gotten married.

I was about to ask the others what they knew about their parents' pasts when an article caught my eye.

I gasped. I'd found something.

Jonas looked up at the sound. "You okay?"

"Yes, fine." I bared my teeth in an overly enthusiastic smile. Shim gave me an odd look, his eyebrow cocked up as his head tilt to one side. I gave a barely perceptible head shake as Jonas looked back down at the watch. Shim saw the movement and let it go.

Soon afterward, Jonas pulled out inflatable mattresses and piles of blankets and pillows. He laughingly admitted to playing host to a lot of traveling artists in his studio. Saying goodnight, he left us alone, heading up to his apartment on the next floor.

I waited until I heard the door to his apartment close, then yanked the tablet off the desk and quickly brought up the article.

Stars. This part was going to be hard. I took a deep breath and then thought that maybe standing would be a good idea. So I quickly stood and cleared my throat. Here goes nothing. "So, when my dad sent me the text telling me to run, there was a more to the message." The others looked stunned, and I realized I had really messed up by not telling them the full message earlier.

"You know who took them and you didn't tell us?" Jaxon jumped up from where he was playing with Duchess.

"No, look, I wasn't keeping things from you. I had no idea what the message meant, and I forgot about it. I mean, we were being chased, trying not to get kidnapped ourselves." I sighed deep and scrubbed a hand through my hair.

"Grace, can you remember the full text?" Shim said, his tone was encouraging. I tried to remember the exact wording, wishing, not for the first time, that I hadn't tossed my phone in the water fountain.

"The message said, 'the helios are here! Run! Find waters.'"

"That's weird," Jaxon stated.

"Do any of you know what Helios are?" Shim asked the others, who all shook their heads. Then he looked back at me.

"I don't know either." I felt the need to defend myself. "But, well, I did some research, and I think I found something on Waters." I wondered if they were all too mad at me to care. Shim was sitting on an air mattress, his eye narrowed, but he stretched out a hand. I fumbled, handing the pad over to him. Leaning back on one leanly muscled arm, he held the tablet up and read through the article, then looked up at me with a gleam in his amber eyes.

"Do you think this is what your dad meant?"

"It would explain that cryptic message. I was looking for something near the water, like a boat. But what if..."

Shim picked up where I left off. "What if it isn't something on the water? What if Waters is a person?"

"A person?" Skylar cocked his head.

"How can water be a person?" Breeze asked, finishing her brother's thought.

Jaxon came over and crouched next to Shim to read over his shoulder.

Shim pointed back at me.

I excitedly filled them in on my theory and the two-year-old article I had found. "The article says there is a group of homeless people who hang along the Embarcadero, the most notorious being this old veteran named Waters."

"You think that's what, or who, your father texted you about?" Skylar asked.

I nodded, twisting my fingers around the chain on the torc at my neck.

"So now we know who we are searching for." Breeze looked excited.

"And where to look," chimed in Skylar.

Shim handed the tablet back, and I started to close it when Shim grabbed my arm. My skin tingled where he touched me, and I flushed.

"Erase the browser memory."

"I hadn't thought of that. I don't know how." Shim got up and reached around me, his arm rubbing against mine, spreading more tingles, and I nervously thrust the tablet at him. He took it, his fingers flying over the screen.

"You're good with tech," I acknowledged.

"No, I'm not." He sounded offended.

Completely confused, I turned to help the twins organize the mats. We lined them up on the floor, and the twins took the two on the far end. Jaxon grabbed the bed on the opposite side, which left Shim settling in next to me. *Great.*

As I lay on my back in the darkened room, the moon and city lights shone through the window and the heavy weight of the night surrounded me, pressing down. This was my first night on my own, I realized. I tried to convince myself it wasn't a big deal, but my heart thumped rapidly, and I'd never felt so small, so lonely. It had been devastating, crushing, to see Dad taken away, his shoulders slumped in defeat. He truly was my last anchor, and with him gone, I felt adrift. The others all had someone. Skylar and Breeze were like two halves that, together, were whole. I could hear them whispering as they huddled, comforting each other. Jaxon and Shim were fighting over something, shoving and kicking, but they were brothers and always looked out for the other. I was apart from them all. My finger rubbed the stone at my throat.

Maybe there was something defective in me that I was always losing things and people. Our VW van. My mom. My dad. I'd probably lose this group next, and maybe it would be for the best. The twins were clique-ish, Jaxon was kind of violent, and the way Shim stared at me... intense. No, they would probably head their own way soon. And I couldn't blame them.

Suckiest. Day. Ever.

6

____

DOWN THE CHUTE

A LOUD BANGING sound woke us the next morning. I rolled over, confused as to why I was sleeping on a floor that smelled like an auto shop. It took a moment before the events of the previous day rolled through my head. The abduction. Running. The gallery.

Shim crouched down next to me, muscles tight, his face pinched, and I noticed the mintiness of his breath as he whispered, "Grab your stuff. We have to go."

It was good I had slept in my clothes.

On my other side, the twins shot up like they were fired from a canon, scrambling to collect their things. Jaxon was holding the twins' third backpack and his skateboard.

Shim was doing a quick check around the workshop, making sure we hadn't forgotten anything when Jonas stumbled down the stairs from his apartment above. "W-what is that?"

The hair that yesterday had been slicked back and neat now stood on end, and one side of his mustache drooped, having lost its handle. A Wellington pushed up the red-plaid pant leg of his pajama bottoms. The other boot was in his hand. Off-balance, he clopped toward the stairs to answer the door.

"Wait. That might be the people who took our parents. Please, don't let them find us," I pleaded.

"Took your parents?" Jonas tromped over to the window and looked down at the street, then back at us. He hesitated, but when the banging downstairs resumed, he seemed to have made up his mind. He gave a quick nod. "Up the stairs to the back bedroom. There is a window that exits to the fire escape. Go up, not down. Four buildings that way is a red brick under construction." He rattled off directions as he pointed with his hand. Leaning against the wall for balance, he put on the other boot. "You should be able to find your way down from there." He squared his shoulders and paused to tug on his sleep shirt like he was straightening a vest, then pulled fingers through his hair, smoothing it. "Well, what are you waiting for? Go!" he demanded in response to our dumbfounded stares. "I'll hold them off as long as I can. Good luck," he said to our backs as we raced up the stairs.

It took some hunting, but we found the window in the back of the apartment. Jaxon was there first, and he shrugged on one of the backpacks and wrenched open the old window. The painted over frame was slightly warped from water damage. At first, it refused to give, but it seemed that nothing could resist Jaxon's loving care, and it gave with a loud splintering sound.

Shim grabbed his brother's shoulder. "Quiet! They might have people waiting at the back of the building. Give me the bag."

Wordlessly, Jaxon shook his head and shoved Shim back before he slipped his skateboard through the straps between his back and the backpack, flipping it so the grip tape wouldn't shred his shirt. Hanging his head and upper body out the window, he looked down to the street below, then pulled the rest of his body out the window. Crouched on the fire escape, he pointed below, nodded his head, and held up two fingers, then put one to his lips. Then, after a quick glance up, he silently started to climb the fire escape. Breeze and Skylar went next, nimbly clambering up.

Shim nodded to me. I felt a little green as I pulled myself out the window. Now would not be a good time to mention my fear of heights. I bit my lip and tried not to look down.

Yeah, okay, I can do this, I gave myself a pep talk. *Here we go.* I realized I hadn't moved. The grated metal was still biting into my legs as I kneeled on the fire escape platform.

Shim pulled himself out of the window, closing it behind him. He looked at me, and when I tried to smile, his face grew concerned. He reached up and tugged a strand of my green hair forward, studying it, then tucked it behind my ear. He gave a crooked grin and pointed up.

I turned back to the ladder and stretched out a hand, grasping the first rung and pulled myself up, clinging to the metal crosspiece. One rung at a time. I could do this. I unwrapped my arms, pulled myself up, held tight through the tremors and then repeated the action. Every movement brought a swirl of disorientation, and I felt like I was swinging wildly.

"Shhhh," Shim whispered below me.

I didn't even realize I was whispering to myself a sing-song chant. "Just keep climbing, just keep climbing."

It felt like hours before I could finally see the top. My heart beat wildly. Jaxon reached out, but he was too far away. I unwrapped my arms and slowly pulled myself up another rung, my arms aching as they clenched the rung tight through my full body shudder. Goosebumps had broken out on my skin, and sweat was slicking my hands, making the ladder slippery when I finally felt Jaxon's fingers grip my forearm, helping me scale the rough concrete of the ledge.

Hands on my knees, I tried to catch my breath while my

heart pounded its way out of my chest. Somehow, over the corresponding throbbing in my head, I heard Shim behind me and realized I needed to help him. I rose and turned to reach for his arm, and my shaking hand collided with the skateboard on Jaxon's back.

The board slid free, ringing loudly as it hit the metal ladder, followed by a sound like sandpaper rubbing together as the last two wheels slide from the strap and the board dropped. Shim reached out lightning fast, catching the board with one hand before it could fall to the ground.

We froze. Not even breathing.

I listened. It was quiet below.

I let out a sigh of relief as Shim climbed up and over the edge and joined us.

Then there was a shout from the street.

We pushed off from the edge with a new sense of urgency and raced across the gravel rooftop to where the twins were climbing a ladder up to the next roof.

At the ladder, Jaxon shoved his board between the backpack and his back again, and Shim secured it by wrapping and tying one of the loose straps around a wheel. Resenting the help, Jaxon smacked his hand away from his board before he scaled the ladder. Shim reared back but didn't look surprised. Ignoring the rebuff, he pulled me forward and pushed me up behind Jaxon. This ladder was easier as it didn't drop to the ground below.

We landed in a rooftop garden with lounge chairs and a table. After dodging the furniture, we screeched to a halt at the edge of the roof. There was a gap of several feet separating the buildings, and the next roof was a foot lower than the one we were on. Skylar and Breeze stood at the edge, contemplating their options.

Shim did a quick U-turn back to the wooden patio table, picking up one end and dragging it across the roof. Jaxon gave a short laugh and grabbed the other end. The table fit like a ramp between the two buildings. Before anyone could blink, Jaxon jumped up and did a standing slide down the tabletop, across the expanse, to the other building.

My heart stopped.

"You kamikaze moron," Shim hissed in an exaggerated whisper. "Wait for us to help you next time." Jaxon flipped a finger at him but stood at the edge of the table to help the twins.

Breeze and Skylar got up on the edge of the table next. They held hands, and Skylar reached out to Jaxon while Shim held on to the waistband of Breeze's jeans. They slid slowly across the dark void on the improvised ramp. Jaxon pulled them down safely on the other side.

Shim jumped up on the table next. With one foot on the flat building ledge and the other on the sloping table, he reached down to me and stopped at what must have been a look of utter terror on my face. I'm sure my eyes were screaming, *This is crazy.*

And it was. Normal people didn't parkour across rooftops. They didn't run from unknown kidnappers. They played online games, talked on the phone incessantly, and watched too much Netflix. But even before this, I had never felt normal. I had always hated the feeling of being out of sync with the rest of the world. As I felt my blood pump like I was swimming the best race of my life, I decided from now on I was going to be the one to make up the rules for what was normal.

I reached up and grabbed Shim's hand, pulling myself to the top of the ledge. I looked down at our joined hands, but before I could appreciate the zing of awareness that came with the feel of his warm skin, I looked over the edge of the roof. My pep talk faded quickly as I tried not to follow my eyes.

Shim tapped a finger under my chin. "Don't look down." He flipped me a lopsided smile. "And don't fall down," he whispered in my ear.

"You are messed up," I replied, reaching across for Jaxon's hand.

"That has already been proven."

My feet lost traction, and I slipped across the slick surface of the table. My heart stopped, and I opened my mouth in a silent scream. Just as I reached the end, Jaxon halted my slide. Panting softly, I turned back for Shim. He pushed himself off the roof ledge and slid across. As he crashed into me, my feet were snatched out from under me, and we collided into Jaxon, the three of us landing in a heap on the roof.

Thunk. Wham.

"Ow." Jaxon pulled himself out from the bottom of the pile.

"Watch it," Shim growled as Jaxon stomped on his leg getting up.

"Stop playing around and hurry up," Breeze said. She and Skylar had scouted out the roof and were now making their way over the ledge to a hidden ladder. They dropped down two stories to the roof of a red brick building.

Then we discovered Jonas was wrong.

We raced for the access door, and Jaxon grabbed the handle and yanked on it. It was locked. The building was being renovated—the roof was littered with construction material and supplies—but we couldn't get down to the street from here. The next rooftop was at least twenty feet away.

We were trapped.

Jaxon jerked on the knob, growling and kicking the door in frustration. The twins raced up behind him and beat on the door. Shim attacked the hinges, trying to see if he could pry them off. The steel door didn't budge.

Frustration welled up. How could we have come this far

and now be stuck? There had to be another way. I walked around the edge of the roof, looking for a way down. The back of the building had the broken remains of a fire escape ladder, ending abruptly a foot below the ledge. It looked like it had been removed for construction.

A canary yellow construction chute yawned open where the brackets of the fire escape had been. I studied the chute.

"Hey, guys," I said. "What about this?" The others stopped working on the door and came over to where I stood. Shim's mouth gaped open.

Jaxon looked up at me, his eyes wide. "Either you've got guts...or you are one fry short of a Happy Meal." His voice held a note of astonishment and admiration. The commendation was a little worrying coming from him.

"Well, we have two options: wait here until they catch us"—I indicated the edge of the roof—"or use the chute."

"You sure?" Shim's eyes traced the yellow vinyl snake mounted on the side of the building that ran all the way down to the dumpster below. Then he looked back at me. He looked worried after his quick risk assessment.

My resolve wavered. The others probably thought I wasn't the kind of girl who took risks. They would be right. I felt ill at the idea of jumping into that chute, and I hadn't been able to look at the dumpster at the base of the building without the dizziness almost pitching me over the side.

Why was I doing this, besides the fear of being captured? Was I afraid the others would have no reason to keep me around if I didn't?

"I'll go first." Did I say that out loud? I did. *Oh, Stars.* But I couldn't ask the others to do it if I couldn't. I gulped. Taking a jerky breath, I moved to swing a leg over the edge of the ledge.

Shim stopped me. "I'll go first. Grace, you next, then Breeze and Skylar. Jaxon, you go last." Shim climbed onto the edge.

"Wait," said Jaxon, concern in his eyes as he looked at his brother. I wondered if they were going to have a tender brotherly moment together.

"Take my board. I can't carry it and the bag. And don't break it or I'll have to kill you." He pulled the skateboard off his back and handed it to Shim.

"Yeah, I love you too, man," Shim said, giving his brother a playful push back as he launched himself into the chute with a hushed battle cry.

This was a bad idea.

I cringed at the thumps and flailing sounds Shim made as he dropped like a rock to the bottom. Breeze and Skylar held onto the waistband of my pants as I leaned over the edge and into the chute. "Shim?" My voice came out in a nervous squeak. "Shim!" I shouted down.

Silence.

I tried again. "You okay?"

I heard a faint "Oookaaay."

It was enough. I stood up, and before I lost my nerve, I quickly swung a leg over the ledge. The others steadied me as I scooted to the edge and put my feet into the chute. Jaxon slipped the strap of my messenger bag off over my head, and I clutched the bag to my stomach. Squeezing my eyes shut, I took a deep breath and pushed off with an involuntary "whoop" as the air escaped from my lungs.

Instead of the smooth slide like a ride at an amusement park, I banged against the walls, my toes and elbows catching on the edges of each section, my exposed skin scraping on the yellow vinyl walls and leaving burns.

The bump-drop, bump-drop slowed at the end. Then I was dumped out with a cloud of dust and a *crack* into a dumpster. I landed on a stack of drywall that gave way, breaking my fall.

"Ohhh," I groaned, rolling onto my side. Pain. *Pain!* If I was lucky enough to not have broken anything, I was going to have a thousand bruises from this. As the numbness receded, I started to check parts of my body. Feet, legs, ribs, arms, fingers, neck. Nothing broken, but everything hurt.

A figure covered in fine white dust reached down and grabbed my hand. It was a ghostly version of Shim with chunks of chalky debris littering his hair. He pulled on my hand and dragged me out of the exit path for the chute.

Leaning against the wall of the dumpster, I coughed, spitting the bitter dust from my mouth. I heard a sound like a parachute flapping in the breeze and realized it was someone coming down the chute. Then there was a thump and a groan. I looked over, and two round eyes blinked back at me. Breeze was lying, stunned, in a pile of sheetrock. Shim pulled her out of the way, and a second later, Skylar landed with a crunch. The flapping started again, sounding like a thousand birds about to take flight, but this time, it was followed by a ripping sound. Shim quickly reached for Skylar and pulled him free of the path. I looked up in alarm and could see the top of the chute pulling away from the side of the building.

"Watch out," someone shouted. With nowhere to go, we crouched by the inside wall of the dumpster. As the final thump hit the sheetrock, Shim dove over his brother, protecting him the best he could from the falling debris. When the sky stopped raining rubble, the brothers were buried under a mound of yellow vinyl and metal.

Cursing, we scrabbled through the heavy vinyl, pulling the long strips off the brothers. Finally, we cleared enough debris that I could wrap a hand around Shim's arm and pull him shakily to his feet while Breeze and Skylar pulled Jaxon out of the pile.

Jaxon stood with his hands on his knees, spitting out bits of dust and trying to catch his breath. When he could, he turned to me with a look of awe. "You are one Mad Hatter."

The others gave a weak laugh, and the corners of my mouth turned up tentatively. Shim was leaning shakily against the wall, his face apprehensive as he studied me. He didn't return my smile.

7

FINDING WATERS

AFTER LEAVING the alley by the dumpster, we merged into the foot traffic around Union Square and headed north. Our appearance was drawing stares, and passing by a shop window, I saw my reflection and knew why. I looked like I had escaped from a bakery explosion. We were fortunate no one had come running when the chute fell.

Breeze and Skylar were picking debris off each other like monkeys grooming. I leaned over and shook my hair, flecks of white falling like dandruff. Jaxon delighted in slapping Shim hard on the pretense of getting the dust off his clothes. Shim pulled off his shirt and shook it out.

What the... He was lean and muscled, but what had grabbed my attention was his torso striped with scrapes, the side of his ribs a mass of fading black and yellow bruises.

My gasp must have been audible. Shim swung toward me, his eyes narrowed, and with a dark look, he pulled his shirt back on. Our eyes locked in a silent stare. That's why he was flinching when he helped me walk yesterday. I thought it was from having to touch me, but the pain of me leaning against him must have been terrible, and he'd never said anything.

Breeze broke the tension when she wedged between us. "Wet wipe?" She pulled the packet from her bag and offered them around. The first couple swipes smeared the dust around, but eventually, we were able to wipe most of our faces clean. Well, cleaner.

Even tidied up, we were conspicuous walking the streets. Turning a corner, we caught sight of a group of older students heading through a gateway into Chinatown. We quickly caught up to them and merged into the back of the pack. I put the image of the marks on Shim's tan skin behind me and assessed our situation.

Despite the near miss at Jonas' apartment and jumping off the building, everyone was surprisingly optimistic. Finding the lead on Waters and knowing we were just a few hours from getting some answers so we could find our parents and go home had put everyone in a good mood.

Was it just yesterday we had raced off? Escaping twice from kidnappers, racing through malls, sleeping in stranger's shops, jumping across rooftops? I hardly recognized myself.

Skylar and Breeze led the way, swinging their hands together and playfully skipping behind the students. Plunking down his board, Jaxon rolled along in what I was starting to recognize as a happy version of his sullen mood. In the back, I reached forward and pulled a piece of painter's tape off Shim's back. He startled, then saw the tape and shrugged. I didn't get him. Most of the time, he was annoyed at me, and other times, he stared with such intensity, it made me nervous. And what was up with all those bruises he hadn't wanted me to see?

THE SUN WAS STARTING to set when I finally collapsed on a bench at Fisherman's Wharf. We had been at it for hours, under the hot sun, pounding the two-mile stretch of concrete between the large tourist areas anchoring each end of the Embarcadero. This is where the article said Waters spent his time, but that two years ago. He might not even live in the city anymore.

But we had kept at it. We had walked up and down the Embarcadero at least a half-dozen times.

We questioned people in the green parks under enormous art sculptures, the glistening water of the bay in the background.

We talked to people strolling along the sidewalk.

We stopped every homeless person and every street performer we passed and asked if they knew someone named Waters.

At first, we had been subtle, trying to start up conversations. By the third trip down the Embarcadero, people started to avoid us. Skylar and Breeze had been shouting Water's name at people as they passed them, and Jaxon, who had been riding his skateboard all afternoon, wasn't talking anymore and had even started ramming into people in his way. I was surprised we hadn't been arrested. This was *not* the type of attention we needed to be drawing to ourselves.

"I'm so hungry I could eat ABC gum." Breeze declared.

"That's disgusting, but, yeah, I want food now." Jaxon demanded.

Shim sighed, and motioned for them to follow them to follow him into the Sourdough bakery.

I couldn't work up the energy to join them and sank down on a bench.

"Maybe Waters doesn't want to be found." I muttered, knowing I was only talking to myself. Maybe I was losing my mind. I groaned and slipped lower in the seat.

"And what would you do if you found him?" The hair on my arms rose at the whispered drawl. I shivered and glanced around. The evening crowd of tourists was still milling about. Street entertainers had set up a traveling tightrope several yards behind the bench but too far away for the voice to have come from them. Another group, across the street, was blaring hip-hop music and spray-painting team logos and fantasy landscapes on metal license plates for tourists. The music competed with the plastic bucket drums being rhythmically beaten farther down the street.

The only thing close to me was the bronze sculpture of a businessman I was sharing the bench with. I leaned close, squinting as I studied the sculpture's nose. It twitched.

"Holy Sources, you are real." I catapulted off the bench in surprise. Then I realized what he had said and sat back down. Grasping the seat between us, I leaned in close and looked at the face.

"You're kinda making it obvious." The voice was deep, thick with an accent I didn't recognize and cracking with age and humor. His lips barely moved. As I looked closer, I could see the bronze face had pores. What I thought was metal was skin covered with thick coats of metalic makeup.

Oh, he was good.

From the top of the fedora on his head down to a bronze book in his lap, every inch was covered in thick paint hardened to a shiny coat. Except for the faintest glimmer of white in the eyes and the whispered voice, there was no difference between him and the other sculptures scattered around the park. Except, he was real and may have the information we needed.

"Do you know Waters?" I whispered, sitting back down and trying not to be too obvious as I talked to the sculpture, uh, man.

The man chided. "You been asking for Waters all day long. I watched you. What you want with him?" The bronze lips barely moved.

"My dad sent me to find him. Can you help us? Can you

take us to him?" Doubts raced through my head, and I wondered what we would do if he wouldn't help.

"You're cookin' with gas now." Was that a yes? His lips turned up slightly at one corner. I rolled my eyes and sunk down on the bench with a groan of realization.

"You've been sitting here all day watching us make a public menace of ourselves."

"Yep, and I was about to call the police myself." He drew out the word so it sounded like *poe-lease*.

"Please don't," I begged, turning back to him. "How can we find Waters?"

"Well, Waters doesn't like all the attention he's been getting, and he might not be willing to talk to you. What you got for him?" In his gravelly voice the phrase came out "What shoes got for m", but I understood the essence of what he wanted. Money.

I had passed the first test. Now I had to be careful not to make us look too desperate; though, I was pretty sure we had passed the pathetically desperate stage around three o'clock this afternoon.

"What we have for Waters is between him and us," I hedged. "What I have for you is one hundred dollars. Fifty now and fifty when we arrive safely in front of him. And we don't have a lot of money, so don't even try and shake us down for more," I hurriedly added. "I've got a volatile redhead and a hypoglycemic whiner, and I'm not afraid to use them."

"Uh-huh, I'm real scared." The bronze man broke his pose and shook his arms, the fabric of his jacket rattled and scraped together. "Hundred now and another hundred when I take you to him."

"Nope, 50/50, and we will buy you dinner. We're just a bunch of broke kids." I hoped I looked confident, yet humble enough that he believed me. My stomach was swirling in knots, and my breath was all choked up in my chest; I was surprised I could talk. The worst thing possible would be to let him know we had money. That would put us all in danger. But, if he walked, what were we going to do?

"Hmm, you drive a hard bargain lil' girl," he drawled at me. "But since I'm such a givin' spirit—and you are including dinner —I'll take you up on it."

Shim was headed back our way with a bread bowl of soup in each hand. The twins danced in front of him, making faces of enjoyment as they relished their soup, Jaxon trailed behind.

"That my dinner there?" The man rolled his eyes toward Shim.

"It is if you want it. Then, after dinner, will you take us to Waters?" I pleaded.

"I surely will." He smiled.

Before I was able to mention our deal, the bronze man had reached out his hand toward them. Skylar jumped back, alarmed to see the sculpture move. Both of his hands flew up. Fortunately, he had stepped back into Shim, so his soup flew over Shim's head; unfortunately, Jaxon was close behind him. The hot soup drenched his shirt, and the bread bowl hit him on the side of the head. Dripping soup, Jaxon yelled and reached around Shim to give Skylar a one-handed shove and a foul look. This action knocked both soups out of Shim's hands.

Shim clenched his teeth and looked down at the soup on the ground then shot a furious look over his shoulder at Jaxon. At the pointed glare, Jaxon rolled his eyes and handed his soup to me. After a short explanation, the brothers and Skylar returned to the restaurant to clean up and buy more food.

Breeze was thrilled with our new friend. She settled on the ground next to him, peppering him with questions. I handed Jaxon's soup to the bronze man, and as he dug into it with relish, he drawled, "Dinner and entertainment, what a treat."

$$\infty$$

IT WAS full on dark by the time we paid the Bronze Man the fifty-dollar deposit and followed him away from Fisherman's Wharf and deep into the city. He took a twisting, turning route through back alleys, empty buildings, and up long staircases on steep hills. *How did the old man keep going?* Every few minutes, he would stop, turn around, and ask one of us a personal question about our parents. Based on the answer, or non-answer since we refused to give details to anyone but Waters, he would grunt and head off in a different direction. He was obviously taking us on a ride. Jaxon and Shim wanted to ditch him, and we were about to take a vote when he stopped in front of the charred remains of an old Victorian house. The blackened exterior was surrounded by abandoned scaffolding and construction debris. The front door was boarded-up as were all the windows.

One minute, Bronze Man was standing in front of us; the next, he was gone. My heart raced at the idea this could be some kind of trap. Jaxon cursed, Shim growled, I searched the porch, and the others joined in. Suddenly, the boarded-up front door swung open. Shim, who was closest, jumped back, startled. The Bronze Man did a mock bow. "Well, are you coming in?"

Desperation overrode suspicion, and I took a tentative step over the threshold. The others followed. My heart raced as the door swung shut behind us.

We had entered a time warp. The house looked as if it had been abandoned in the middle of the night...twenty years ago. A winged-back armchair, the leather cracked and stuffing pulled out in places, sat sentinel at the dirt-smudged front window. On a little table next to it was a *Readers Digest* held open by a pair of half-moon reading glasses. Another patched fabric chair had an embroidered cloth thing over the back and a side pocket with knitting needles and a ball of yarn sticking out. Faded framed photos on the walls showed children in arrested stages of development, frozen in time, like this house. Everything from the frayed carpets to the stairs leading up to a second story was covered with a fine layer of dust.

"This is my retirement property," Bronze Man over pronounced as he swept a stiff arm around the space. "I'm saving this for my elderly years." It was hard to tell under the layers of metal-colored makeup, but I was pretty sure he was already deep into his elderly years. "My current dwelling is in the back. Come'n."

The back of the house was a surprisingly cozy nest. The dated kitchen had been turned into a living room. There was a misshapen couch and a couple more threadbare wingbacks. A cot was pushed up against the back wall. The tall windows were pasted over with newspaper, making the space dark.

Bronze Man lowered himself to the couch, his knees cracking as he stretched out his legs.

"Okay...what do you want to know?" he asked.

"You're Waters?" I'd thought so, but with confirmation, a wash of excitement came over me.

"Sure am," he drawled.

"How do we know you aren't lying?" Jaxon asked suspiciously.

"You don't. But I know who you are." He smiled slyly at us, his eyes wrinkling up at the corners sending fissures through his makeup. "You're not too smart for all your bravado. You're Jaxon, Kindle's youngest." Then he nodded at Shim "and that would make you Shimmer. Odd name for a boy, but your momma is one strong-headed woman." He smiled fondly as he spoke about Kindle, but I was stuck on Shim's full name. Who names a baby Shimmer?

"You two." He pointed at Breeze and Skylar. "You little

jabber boxes gotta watch your mouths. You don't ever know who is listening in. You told me your father was Arie, that you have too much money, and that he would do anything to get you back. You put a bull's-eye on your back with your loose lips."

The twins were taken aback by both the proclamation of their deficiencies and the identification. When had they mentioned their father?

"And you little lady"—he pointed at me—"why, I'd know you anywhere. You're the spitting image of your momma. You don't talk much, 'cept at the beginning when you told me your Da sent you, but more troublesome is you're holding yourself like you are waiting to get attacked. You can't show fear, girl." He cocked his head. "We gotta toughen you up. You make a good leader, but you need some brass in you."

My brows arched up into my hairline, but most of it was probably true, except the part about me being the leader.

"So, you are Waters. Where did you meet our parents?" Shim asked, suspicion scrunching up his face, or it might have been distaste at being called Shimmer.

"Do you know where they are now?" Skylar asked.

And Breeze butted in. "How can we get them back?"

"Why were they taken?" I added.

"You need to take me to my mom," Jaxon demanded, thumping a fist into his palm.

Waters raised his hands to hold off the questions that came at him. "Whoa there, Nelly," he intoned out slowly. "Don't know where they're at, but if the people who took them are the same ones that was after them years ago, then you are in a heap of danger." With a litany of crackling and popping joints, he got up slowly from the couch and headed for the door.

We stared at him, focused on his every word.

Waters turned at the threshold. "I met 'em about twenty-five years ago. They were in trouble, so scared and all alone—

displaced is the best word I can think of to describe it. They just didn't fit anywhere and didn't know how to get along. I helped them learn to survive." He paused, looking off into the memory. "And that is all you are getting from me until I got a better understanding of what you can do," he finished with a snap.

"What do you mean 'what we can do'?" I challenged.

"They sent you here for a reason. They want you to go to school with me, same as they did." He headed down a hall. "I'm fixin' to peel off a little paint. You discuss amongst yourselves what you're gonna do next. If you decide to stay, you can sleep upstairs. There is probably a bed or something up there." He paused in the hall and added a grave warning. "But you ain't got a second chance at me. You say no now, and you're gone. I know what is chasing you, and you should be very, very afraid."

I shivered. We knew we were in trouble, but was it as bad as Waters was implying? Our parents had been scared. Very scared. And now, I was too.

"You've never been upstairs?" Shim asked. That guy was *so* weird. Of all the things we had to worry about, that is what he decided to ask the old man?

"Nope...that's where the previous tenants died." He gave a deep haunting laugh and disappeared.

8

DEAD MAN'S HOUSE

I ROLLED OVER AND GROANED. If you had told me a month ago that I'd be sleeping where a dead body was found, I would have said you were crazy. Yet here I was. Well, it was a dead man's house anyway. We don't know for sure which room he died in.

But it could be here.

Right where I lay.

Ick!

Not trusting Waters, we had decided to all sleep in the same room on the uncomfortable dirty wood floor. The only thing that would have made it worse was if the room had been furnished and carpeted. My skin itched thinking about what would have been crawling in the upholstery.

I pulled the zipper on my jacket up to my chin, more a gesture for security than cold, though the room was drafty. Night air crept in around the cracks in the walls and streamed in alongside blue moonlight from the holes in the cardboard taped over a broken window. Lying on my back in the dark on the old house's cold floor put me closer to the smell of rot, a witch's brew of mothballs, mold, and something herbal. No wonder I was having trouble sleeping. I shuddered as I stared up at the stained popcorn ceiling. Yellowed with water damage, it sagged in the middle like a stalactite poised to let loose a drip.

I thought about my Dad. Where was he? Is he okay? He wasn't used to taking care of himself. What if he wasn't safe? What if I never saw him again, like my mom? I tried to shut out those thoughts and failed.

And my mother, was she really alive? If so, where was she? Was she hurt? Was she being hurt all this time? Would death have been better? I was so confused; I'd gotten used to the idea of her being dead. For a minute, I lowered the wall of betrayal I felt toward her and reminded myself she may have had no choice in leaving us. Was it selfish to want that? To want her to have to suffer being forced to leave, instead of me suffering her death? My stomach rolled. What kind of person was I that her suffering made me feel closer to her? Heat burned in my face.

Thank Stars the twins and the brothers couldn't read minds. Mine was racing in circles. I'm sure the others already don't like me, don't like the way I've been bossing everyone around. Waters talked about me being the leader—no one would be on board for that. *Did I like them?* I hadn't had much time to think about the others, let alone decide if I liked or disliked any of them. Did it matter? The twins just *expected* life to work out, and the brothers reminded me of all the people who taunted you when it didn't. I guess there was not a lot to like.

In spite of these conflicted feelings, I did fell a strange connection to them—and oddly, through them, I felt closer to my mother. The thought made me angry. We had been lied to. But it also made me sad.

Something about being here with them brought up all these memories of her. They surrounded me like thin slivers of light, flowing as if on a current through the room, winding around us, past and present, and connecting me to my mom again.

It was amazing to think she had gone through Waters' "schooling." Had it helped her? What had happened to her life? What was so horrible that my mom had been driven to work with Waters? The man was highly suspicious. Surely, whatever she had run from couldn't be as bad as what had brought us to Waters. I tried not to think about the mess we were in and some of the decisions I had made.

I can't believe I jumped off a building. In hindsight, not my smartest decision.

My mind wandered to Shim and the way his amber eyes had narrowed, brows lowering in silent judgment after that jump. As if he could feel me thinking about him, I heard him turn over, shifting in his sleep. He was lying on the far side of the room, against the wall. I could hear his slow steady breathing as he slept. Breeze and Skylar were curled up together, Skylar having issues with the dust and wheezing with each breath. Jaxon, in the back corner by the window, had more of a grumpy snore.

My hand strayed up to the necklace balanced on my collarbone, fingers stroking the stone like a talisman. The thoughts still swarmed my head, but I drew comfort from the stone.

Slowly, I became aware of something...no, not something—someone, someone else.

A voice.

There was a very distinct male voice breaking through my brain chatter.

"Hello?" I moved my lips silently in more of a thought than a spoken word. I froze, waiting to hear something back.

Silence.

I was letting my imagination run wild with all the suppositions spinning around in my head. Curling over on my side, I rearranged my messenger bag, which I was using as a pillow. I needed to get some sleep, but my mind wandered on, spinning back over what we had done today and wondering what we would be doing in a few days. I was starting to think that we would not be finding our parents quickly.

Was it right to agree to Waters' form of education? I can't believe I was even considering this. *Who was this girl doing all these crazy things?* I didn't know myself anymore. Could I trust anything I was feeling right now?

"Yeah, you can."

The voice came out of nowhere. Loud and clear and—in my head. I might be losing my mind. That's what it meant, right? When you recognized a voice in your head other than your own? Was this some type of auditory hallucination? Oh, my God. I read somewhere that was a serious mental health issue, hypnagogia or something. Had my mind snapped?

"Stars, you're dramatic!"

Every muscle in my body froze. *"That voice sounded real."*

"I am real...and you could be losing it," the voice conceded.

Silence. Then, like a switch flipping, a million things burst out in my head at once. *"You're real? Who are you? How did you find me? Who else can you talk to? No, wait, how? How can you talk to me? Is this a trick? I'll bet this is a trick."* The mental circus that usually only I heard went flooding out.

"Wow, that's a lot to process."

"Are you a ghost?" I asked.

"I could be a ghost. Wh-o-o-o-o-o, a spirit with unfinished business."

"You're a rather snarky ghost," I thought

"I'm not a ghost. I'm real, Grace." The voice sounded irritated now.

"How do you know my name?" I sat up from the hardwood floor. Terror rocked through me as my fingers clutched at my throat. Across from me in the silent room, I could see Shim sitting up in the darkness. We stared at each other.

"Shim?" I whispered aloud, wondering if he could hear the voice too.

Shim shook his head. I frowned. What was going on? I tried to speak again, and he glared. We stared at each other silently when I heard the voice again.

"Grace."

"Shim?" I thought.

"Yeah."

"How is this possible?" I said loudly. Shim waved a shushing hand in front of his mouth, and I repeated it in my head. *"How is this possible?"*

"I don't know," Shim responded

"But have you, you know, done THIS before?"

"Talked to a girl in the dark? Yes. Talked to someone in my head? Of course not," he replied. *"I'm not crazy..."* The "like you" was implied in the note of laughter in his voice—in my head.

"I heard that!" I narrowed my eyes at him. *"So how is...what is...how long?"* I sputtered out, then thought of something. *"Have you been listening to me all day, 'cause that—that is an invasion of privacy."* I tried to think back to what I'd been thinking about today that I wouldn't want someone else to hear —which would be everything.

"Are you for real?" He glared at me across the room. *"You can talk to someone else in your head and your first thought is 'invasion of privacy'?"* Even through the pale beams of light from the window, I could see his raised eyebrow.

"Right, sorry." I hated to admit it, but he was right.

Shim shrugged. Seconds ticked by, and the silence extended between us.

"So...how do you think we are doing this?" I broke the stalemate.

"What do you have in your hand?" Shim asked.

I realized I was still clutching the stone at my neck, gathering comfort from it. I opened my hand and held the stone in my fingers, angling it toward the light so Shim could see.

He held up a clenched fist bathed in moonlight and slowly unfolded each finger to show me the ring in the center of his palm.

"It's the jewelry?" I asked in my head. There was no response.

I looked at Shim and cocked my head to the side. He held up one finger, then placed it on the stone in the center of the ring.

"Can you hear me now?" The line from an old commercial echoed through my head, loud and clear.

I nodded. *"It's not the jewelry; it's the stones."*

"Apparently."

"And you didn't know this already?" I challenged.

"I told you, no." Intense irritation came through our connection, followed by suspicion. *"Are you saying you just figured it out? You've had your mom's necklace a long time."*

"No! I mean, yes, I've had the necklace since she left, but I never knew it could do this. How did you figure it out?"

"It took me forever to figure out who was having an existential crisis in my head. Once I realized it was you, I had to wait for you to stop talking long enough so I could say something." The voice in my head was droll. My first instinct was to huff and turn my back on him, but this was too momentous.

"You are such a jerk," I responded bitterly.

He ignored my statement. *"It is weird. I'm looking at you and hearing you talk, but your lips aren't moving."* I was a little appeased at the awe in his voice.

"Yeah," I conceded with a smile, but wondered, Now what? *"Do we wake up the others and tell them?"* Maybe they could

help us figure this out. Something occurred to me. *"Hey, do you think the other stone works the same way?"*

"Why wouldn't it?" Shim shrugged.

I thought about my original question. *"Maybe...maybe this is something we should just keep to ourselves, for now."* Honestly, I couldn't say why I didn't want to share this with the rest of them. Maybe I was thinking of the exhausted whimpering sounds the twins had made as they tried to find a comfortable spot to sleep on the hard floor. I was so tired myself, I could barely keep my own eyes open in spite of this amazing discovery. But Shim seemed to get it, and in that minute, something between us synced up. *"They have all been through so much. One more thing might break them."*

"Maybe..." Shim hedged.

"Are you dating anyone?" Oh my Stars, what did I just think? I fell back onto the floor and pulled my messenger bag over my head. How could I ask him that? I wasn't even thinking it. I'm so stupid–stupid–stupid!

"I heard that." Shim chuckled in my head.

"Oh heavens, this is embarrassing." Trying to turn off my thoughts was like telling myself not to think about something—and guaranteeing it's all I could think about.

"It's hard not to communicate through the stones every random thought that enters my head," Shim commiserated, but since I was still buried under my bag, I couldn't tell if his face was serious. *"So tell me something not embarrassing."*

At the odd request, my body relaxed. *"What isn't embarrassing in my life is boring—really boring."*

"Huh, so tell me something about your boring life," he said.

I hesitated. I knew what he was doing, trying to distract me, but it had been a long time since anyone had asked about me. My face flushed, and I pushed the bag off but stayed flat on the floor looking at the distorted ceiling. I did feel less lonely since I had started talking with Shim through the stones. It felt good, and when I closed my eyes, I could almost imagine it wasn't Shim, a complicated guy I was stuck with, that I was speaking to. It was just some guy who thought I was interesting. So, I told him about growing up on a boat, silly things my dad used to say to keep me entertained, and thoughtful gestures my mom made so I wouldn't miss having friends.

Every so often, we would fall into silence. At one point, I looked over at him again. Shim was lying on his back, studying the ring. I could make out the glitter from the cubic zirconia that circled the outside. His thumb was rubbing the dull stone in the middle of the ring, worrying the stone, polishing it.

I understood the pull. I rhythmically smoothed my finger over the worn surface of the stone at my neck, and it seemed to increase the presence of the connection in my mind. I studied the stone. The dullness had faded, the mottled red and green looked richer, and the silver threading brightened and warmed, like it was flowing through the stone.

Somewhere in the middle of my monologuing, Shim started sharing too. He told me about all the "crap" on his mind. His word. He talked about how he usually avoided Logan, his dad. How he hadn't known what to do when he had caught Logan stealing Kindle's ring. He told me about their panicked escape to San Francisco, including sneaking out of their home in Las Vegas in the middle of the night. He told me how hard it was to keep Jaxon out of trouble, that his mom and Logan had always made him feel like it was his responsibility, even punishing Shim when Jaxon got in trouble.

I told him about my slippery slide into being the adult in my household and how I resented that I had become the one to make sure rent was actually paid and we had food.

Finally, I asked Shim about his bruises. He was reluctant to talk about them at first. And in the end, he didn't go into detail, but he said they were football injuries and how much he hated doing team sports, or "man sports," as Logan called them. Shim said he loved extreme sports: bike tricking, freestyle motorcycling, boarding, you name it. But he did whatever he could to prove to his father that he was tough so he would leave him alone.

"And computers?" I asked with a mental yawn. Shim stopped talking.

"I guess we should get some sleep," Shim finally stated after a long silence. I didn't know how long we had been talking, but the room was darker, and the noise of the city had died down.

"Yeah, maybe we should." It felt awkward. After all that talking, I didn't know what to say to him. I still wasn't sure I liked him, and now I had committed myself to sharing another secret.

"Night." That easily, he rolled his back to me and fell asleep.

Huh, that was anticlimactic. Closing my eyes, I willed myself to go to sleep. *Yep...that wasn't working.* Thoughts resumed racing through my head like a deranged scavenger hunt. I was careful to keep my hand off my necklace. I eventually nodded off to bizarre dreams of people drowning who I couldn't rescue and phones ringing I couldn't reach.

9

BOOTCAMP

I WOKE up feeling like something important had happened, but I couldn't remember what it was. Groaning, I sat up and stretched, my back popping.

Jaxon was arguing with the twins, and Shim wasn't in the room. I blinked rapidly as I tried to figure out why I found that unsettling. My hand reached instinctively for my mother's necklace. As my fingers ghosted along my collar bone and connected with the stone hanging at my throat, it flooded back to me.

Oh my Stars. The stones. Why had I never known what they could do? I guess it was because I never knew there were other stones. I always thought there was just the one. Mine.

The thought occurred to me again that maybe this was too big of a secret for us to keep from the others.

A heated argument started across the room. The twins were sitting on the floor with Jaxon, who was holding a small, mechanical dog.

Duchess wagged her tail as Breeze and Skylar tried to wheedle a turn with the steampunk pup. Jaxon refused.

"What the hell is that?" Shim stormed into the room and

headed for Jaxon. "You little shit! After all Jonas did for us, you stole from him?"

Jaxon jumped up and shifted Duchess behind his back. "I didn't do anything. I don't know how she got here. She wanted to come"—he sputtered out excuses then pointed to the twins—"they wanted her too."

Breeze held up her palm and negotiated. "Well, we would support your harmless prank if we got equal time with her..." She trailed off with a little smirk.

"Yeah, 50/50" —Skylar grunted when Breeze elbowed him, and he switched his offer—"make that 30/30/30."

Shim scowled and was about to say something when negotiations were interrupted. *Bang Bang Bang.* Something knocked hard on the wood stairs, and Waters yelled up, "Five minutes."

There was a mad scramble to get out of the room. Duchess was swept up into the backpack.

Shim slapped his hand on the strap over Jaxon's shoulder. "Your responsibility."

"Of course." Jaxon's sneer couldn't hide his smile.

"I mean it. You took her, you take care of her until you can return her. And don't let Waters see her, or she'll be chopped up for parts and sold off before you can whistle."

Jaxon glared at Shim before hustling out the door after the twins.

Shim turned to me. He looked indecisive and said, "Um, ah, morning."

I flushed.

"Hiya." I pushed past him, and his fingers brushed down my arm, leaving a trail of tingles. *Did last night happen, or was it all a dream?*

"Pretty surreal night." He held up his hand, the ring on his big thumb. I guess that answered the question.

It was real.

"Yeah." I took a shallow breath. I didn't know what else to say and didn't have time to think of something as the banging on the banister started up again.

"Class is in session," Waters bellowed, and we darted out of the room and down the stairs.

∞

I'M STILL NOT sure how we ended up staying with Waters. We didn't even discuss it. That first night when Waters left, flinging the ominous warning behind him, the boys had given each other these maniacal grins and headed for the stairs. Breeze and I were left gaping after them. Then, realizing we were about to be left behind, we reluctantly followed. I didn't trust the brothers. I trusted Waters even less. I knew he was playing us, but he wasn't obvious. On the surface, he was helping. He provided a place for us to stay, taught us how to stay safe, didn't snitch on us, though the last was probably a strategic move. He was a master strategist: scouting out info, positioning pieces, building alliances—and we were pawns. He might be fond of us because of our parents, but in the end, pawns were the ones sacrificed.

It was a concern that grew as we spent the next several weeks following his direction.

I'd shared my concerns with the others. The siblings had listened and agreed he was using us. But we needed information, and Waters had it, so we did what he asked. I just wasn't sure he would ever share what he knew.

"Going to school" with Waters wasn't about taking notes and sitting in class. It was like being at a bizarre summer camp, but instead of archery and canoeing—or whatever kids did at camp—we learned boosting, evasion, and breaking and entering.

At first, Shim and Jaxon said there wasn't much he could

teach them and laughed about the whole thing. They got educated pretty quick.

I was nervous about what he expected from us, but since I couldn't think of what else we could do, I went along with it. I knew we had relied on sheer nerves and dumb luck to get us this far. It would be nice to have a few skills to back it up.

Breeze had been adamantly against "school" with Waters from the beginning. She had protested to the point of belligerence, insisting she just wanted to go home. She was even starting to wear thin with Skylar, who had been working as a buffer between her and everyone else.

With all the makeup washed off, Waters was a lighter, duller version of the sculpture he imitated. He had weathered skin, a bald head, and wily brown eyes. By his own proclamation, he was somewhere in his late "older than old, but younger than dirt" years. His hands were calloused, and his face deeply lined, so it was hard to pin it down more than that. He kept his word and showed us all the street survival skills he claimed to have shown our parents. We learned how to blend into a crowd, how to avoid being tailed, and how to procure fake IDs. He also had friends come in and show us self-defense and fighting tricks so dirty even Breeze would be able to take out a full-grown man. I tried to imagine my soft-spoken mother kicking a man in his balls or ripping out armpit hair...Yeah, I couldn't see that happening.

As a procurer and reseller of "specialty items," as Water's liked to call his stock of merchandise, he had a quirky client list. Some were displaced, some were shady, and some were just looking for bargains. Early each morning, he would do his rounds, meeting and selling to clients and searching out the latest news of what was happening on the streets. He sold that too. He seemed to know everything that was happening in his city.

He had a keen eye. He could tell if an area was hot, and he had the uncanny ability to know when a contact had snitched—said it was in their eyes.

In his way, he was a good teacher. As we walked through an alley, he would point out escape paths, threats, and potential financial opportunities. When leaving a new contact, he would whisper under his breath their tells: a wide-eyed stare, gated posture, signs of submission or dominance. At first, he sounded like a first-class bullshit artist, talking like he could read his client's minds, but eventually, I started to see the tells too.

Waters was also a master negotiator. I quickly realized if he hadn't wanted to help us, there was nothing we could have done to persuade him to, not that he would ever acknowledge that. He rarely gave a "yes" or "no." He would turn it into a question or raise his brow and say, "Huh, that so?"

Jaxon was a little too interested in some of the more illegal lessons. Waters labeled him our "heavy." Jaxon fearlessly took on any task that required sheer guts and a lack of tact. Shim could pick any lock and excelled at electronics. I had pegged him as a jock, but I was surprised when taking things apart turned out to be a specialty of his.

Once Breeze let up on the whining, we learned she and Skylar had the ability to sweet talk people into giving them anything they wanted. The twins learned how to procure whatever we needed—by any means possible. They were particularly talented with fake IDs and documents. It reminded me of the stash of wallets with fake IDs we had in our backpacks, and I wondered if it was an inherited skill. We were careful not to mention those or the stack of cash also in the backpack to Waters.

No one was more surprised than me when I turned out to be the best pickpocket. Years of slinking around new schools trying not to be noticed had probably given me the edge in sneaking up on people. Shim made some crack remark about me having a basic credibility. I think he meant I was boring. I was loath to admit to the rest of them, but I was still struggling with the moral aspects of what we were doing. Mostly, we practiced on each other or someone Waters brought in to test us. So far, I'd been getting double the practice by putting the items back, undetected, after I took them. I don't know how long that would fly.

Waters had a series of rules all his lessons tied back into. His basic premise was that people are devious, unpredictable, and not to be trusted. He included himself in this judgment. Maybe I'm soft, but that was kind of sad.

Waters' rules broke down to:

Rule 1: If something looks too good to be true, it probably is.

Rule 2: There is an easy and a hard way to do something. You should choose the smart way.

Rule 3: Everyone has a weakness: look for what they love and what they hate.

Rule 4: Be strategic: people protect what's most precious to them and frequently forget about the rest.

Rule 5: There is always a backdoor. Use it.

And the **Golden Rule:** Always look out for yourself.

In another life—one where he didn't carry a knife in his sock and a gun at the small of his back, sleep in a burned-out shell of an old crack house, and wasn't borderline nuts—Waters would have made an excellent high school teacher. I could picture him all cleaned up in a sweater vest and flannel slacks, standing at a marker board. "Now class, where should the decoy be while the mark is being selected?"

Okay, so sometimes it did seem like he was trying to kill us. Last week, he'd sent us to make a buy of information in the Tenderloin district, not because he wanted what we were buying, though he did use it to help procure our new IDs, but because the area had the reputation of being one of the toughest. Waters was adamant we needed to toughen up and smarten up.

Whatever pants-pissing fear hadn't registered yet from our parent's being kidnapped and running for our lives, well, that fear sunk in as Waters' raw talent for obscenities and life lessons helped to clarify our dire situation.

Oddly, as much as he shared information, he refused to talk about the time our parents had spent with him. All he would say was that when training was over, he would answer our questions.

Were we being set up? Definitely. But for what? And why was Waters helping us? Every so often, he would let something slip, like telling me I reminded him of Amé when she was my age, or when he pegged Jaxon right off as being Kindle's son from his temper. I'm sure it was no accident. He was giving us small encouragements to keep trusting him.

We were probably getting played. And wouldn't *that* be the biggest life lesson Waters taught us?

10

THE STONES

I STRETCHED AND WINCED, my muscles protesting. This time, Waters put a new twist on our training, a much more physical one, and I ached everywhere, but at least I didn't get hit by a car like Shim. Actually, he had hit the car. I imagine it still hurt.

Waters had hooked us up with these parkour guys. The brothers loved it but were still learning to land moves. I had flopped around like a fish out of water and had several painful and embarrassing face plants I was still trying to live down.

At least we were no longer sleeping on the hardwood floor. I swear, I was getting splinters in my backside. When we had realized we were going to be with Waters for a while, the twins had purchased sleeping bags, and we had cleaned out one of the upstairs rooms in the old Victorian. It didn't feel like home, but by piling cheap foam pads on the floor in a nest, we could huddle together in our bags in the illusion of safety.

I heard the mechanical whine of Jaxon squeezing Duchess while he slept. It had been a week before he had stopped guarding her like Shim was going to ship her back, tail between her legs, in the middle of the night. We all still kept her close, worried Waters would find her and sell her off. Jaxon had taken to sleeping with her curled up in his arms, which no one mentioned but everyone had agreed was one step away from having a teddy bear. It made Jaxon happy—well, it made him less grumpy.

As part of my nightly ritual, I reached up to my necklace and fingered the flat metal. I contemplated calling Shim. That didn't sound right. I wasn't dialing up his neurons. Contacting was a better word for it. I pulled my hand back. I was still pretty nervous about some of the things Waters had us doing. True, we were just lifting wallets off each other now, but I knew where it was heading.

Across the room, silhouetted by the moonlight streaming through the window, I saw Shim roll onto his back and slip his hand into his pocket, tugging the ring free of the denim. It glittered as he spun it on his finger, then hooked it onto his thumb and brushed the center stone with his index finger. My hand was already on the necklace, fingers moving to the stone. It was like a magnet drawing my touch.

Before I could say anything, Shim asked, *"So...what happened with your mother?"*

I groaned. Now I had to talk to him.

Every night since "first contact"—communication through the stones seems worthy of a science fiction name—I thought he was going contact me, and I got nothing. At first, I had wanted to talk to him. There were a million questions jumping around in my head, from how the stones worked, to my suspicions of Waters. Whatever he was training us for, I was not okay with it. I thought about leaving, finding my father on my own. But how would I even begin to do that?

So, every night, I would hold onto that damn stone in the necklace and practically glare at Shim across the room. And what would Shim do? Roll over, showing his back, and go to sleep. And during the day, he was completely unapproachable and moodier than Jaxon. Plus, I didn't think we should talk about stuff in front of Waters. It just felt like it would be a mistake.

I'd finally gotten used to the cold shoulder. And now he wanted to talk—about my mother?

"So, what happened to your mother?" He asked again.

I wondered if the stone had a "Do Not Disturb" button. Rolling onto my back, I stared up at the ceiling. Did I want to do this?

"She left." Guess we were doing this.

"When?" Shim asked.

"The accident was last year."

"Accident?"

See, this was why I didn't want to talk about it. It was so much more complicated than most people wanted to hear. People liked clean stories. She died, or she left, I got over it, the end. At least, I thought it was the end. But this story was harder than that. And I never really got over it.

"Tell me," he coaxed.

Closing my eyes, I let go of the fear and concentrated on his voice.

"She was a diver and volunteered on a team documenting the floor of the Monterey Bay. She often went out on her own, though she always let people know when and where she was going."

"Is it safe to go on your own?"

"It is if you are good. It can be safer than going with someone who isn't really experienced. And she was—is—a really good diver and swimmer. She loved—loves—the water. Master swimmer, diver, and sailor. She taught me."

"You can sail?"

"Yeah. My dad sold the sloop a few weeks after she died. We loved that boat. There was a time when the three of us lived on it for several years. It was more home to me than any apartment we

had ever rented. He said we needed the money, which was always true, but I think he couldn't bear to look at it anymore."

"So, what happened? She went out diving and—"

"—and didn't come back. A couple of fishermen found our boat adrift." I paused. This was where the story gets tricky. *"They called in the authorities, who searched for a while and sent down divers. The other members of her team searched for her. They found her gear on the seafloor a couple of miles away."*

"What does that mean?"

"Well, they say that meant something happened after she got back in the boat. Maybe her gear fell in and she jumped in to try and rescue it."

"You said 'they say that.' What do you think happened?"

I was surprised; people never asked me that. They just told me what they thought happened. *"I thought...at first, I didn't believe it. I know she couldn't die in some diving accident. She wouldn't go in after her gear. And even if she had, she was a very strong swimmer. If she didn't die, and she didn't come back. Then..."* I left things hanging.

"Then you thought she left."

"Yeah, at first."

"Anything else to back that up?"

"Well, my dad. He and my mom were very close. But after the accident, I don't know, he changed, checked out. I don't know what to call it."

"He was sad?"

"Profoundly. He sunk into a deep funk. Counselor at my old school said he was depressed. She was going to try and talk to him, but we left that school too. He never speaks about her dying, always about her being gone. He got even more paranoid, and he sold the boat and everything else we had registered. Kept our van, but he got new license plates for the old VW. We moved several times in a row, so many he didn't even try to put me in school,

and we changed our names a couple times." Oddly, I realized even though we moved up and down the coast several times, we still ended up back near Monterey on the Central Coast. Like he couldn't be too far away from where he had last seen her.

"He thought the authorities lied about what had happened to her?"

"He never specifically disagreed with them, and his sadness is real. It oozes from every pore of his body as if she haunts him. I didn't believe for a long time, resisted. I kept making up reasons why she had left us; I was angry. I've heard stories about parents who couldn't take it and just walked away, and our life was crazy. But finally, I gave up and tried to grieve." Before I knew it, my whole miserable life story was spilling out of me—well, the highlights—and to my surprise, he listened, interjecting questions at different parts and laughing at the appropriate places.

Born, constantly moved, homeschooled, Mom died, moved more, bullied at school, took care of Dad, more moving, ended up here. It was a short story when I thought about it.

I'd had enough of talking about me. It made me sad. I started poking questions back at him. *"Why did you steal the ring from your mom?"*

Shim groaned and, after a long pause, confessed, *"I didn't. I caught Logan stealing it, so I took it back from him."*

"Logan is your dad, right?"

There was a long pause before Shim answered, *"That's what they say. But he makes me call him Logan."*

I hesitated. What did he...did he mean... *"What do you mean 'that's what they say?'"*

"I'm being stupid. Ignore that comment." From across the room, I could hear Shim's deep exhalation.

"Well, no. That's a rather important comment. Do you think —" I didn't have the slightest idea how to put into words what I was thinking, and I really didn't want to hurt Shim.

"—don't say it. I can't— just don't say it. I know I don't fit there. I know I'm nothing like him. But I've not even allowed myself to think it, so don't say it...please." Shim trailed off, the last word a faint whisper in my head.

Okay, time to change the subject. *"...So the ring?"*

"Yeah, the ring. Logan doesn't care about things; he cares about control." Shim's voice lost the uncertainty. *"If you do what he wants, you can usually stay off his shit list. If you don't, well, he puts you in your place, usually by taking something you care about and making sure you don't see it again. He knew Kindle cared about the ring because she NEVER takes it off. That's why he took it. If I hadn't seen him, the ring would have been gone forever."*

"What did he do when he caught you?"

Shim didn't respond.

"Are you afraid of him?"

No response.

"Do you think your mom knew what the ring could do?"

"Kindle had the ring a long time. How could she not?" Shim finally responded, then paused. *"Usually, you know everything that's on Kindle's mind—because she is yelling it at you. But she never made a noise about you guys or the others. I think, that is what has me most concerned—her silence."*

11

GRADUATION DAY

THE NEXT MORNING, I woke feeling optimistic. For years, I had stumbled around trying to be as least disruptive as possible to my world and the people around me. In a way, I had been sneaking through life. Now, I'm a proactive part of my own story. I had no idea how we would face what was coming next or how we were going to find our parents, but I was doing something to make it happen.

After unzipping my sleeping bag and crawling out, I neatly folded it, then took my turn in the bathroom. We had figured out an ingenious workaround for no running water that involved different buckets for different task. With my teeth freshly brushed and face still wet, I headed downstairs to join the others, my mom's necklace thunking comfortably against my collarbone. For the last two weeks, Shim and I had been talking every night through the stones. Sometimes, it would be a long discussion, like the night I told him about my mom. Other times, it was just a quick check-in. Maybe those stones messed with the wiring in my head, programming out fear and replacing it with misguided confidence.

Or maybe finally being able to talk about all the things that worried me somehow released them into the universe and allowed me to step back with a fresh perspective and rebalance, instilling new confidence—no, more likely it was the rewiring thing.

My euphoric state burst, like an overfilled water balloon, when Waters announced his plans for our Graduation Day, and all that newfound confidence swished out of me like someone had flushed a functioning toilet.

∞

A COUPLE OF HOURS LATER, we stood on a busy sidewalk and stared up at a large building that looked like it had been turned inside out, all the metal structure exposed around the smooth shell.

Over a breakfast of power bars eaten while squatting on the kitchen floor, Waters declared classes were done, and we were ready to graduate. We had hopped on a Muni bus along the waterfront, then the light rail down Market Street, getting off at Seventh. Staring up at the fortress, he made his big announcement.

"That's it." He had a hard smile on his face, one I now recognized as meaning he had scented money. "In three days, this is where you are going in."

My jaw dropped. The San Francisco Federal Building? He wanted us to break into government property? Fabulous. Petty thieves to felons in just weeks. Really, Waters should write plots for movies. No one else would believe the stuff we did.

I looked around at the others. They were staring up at the building, a little glassy-eyed. My fingers played with my collar bone as I caught myself unconsciously reaching up for the necklace again. All morning, I fought the urge to use the stone to contact Shim, torn between wanting to check in every minute and wanting to keep the stones a secret.

I'm not sure why I thought talking to Shim would help. He was a Jekyll and Hyde roulette. There was the Shim I saw in front of me—bullying his brother, distant, silent, calculating—and the one I knew in my head—funny, smart, insightful, a little too perceptive. Maybe having the Shim I talked to in my head being so very different from the one I saw each day in person was normal. Were all guys like that? I hadn't gotten to know very many to find out.

I glared at Shim, and his eyes widened as he made sure I could see his hand slide into his pocket before he casually turned his back on everyone and walked off a few feet. I ran my finger over the stone at my throat.

"What?" He husked out.

"What?" I replied indignantly. *"What? What do you think?"*

"I know." His shoulders slumped. *"This seems a little crazy."*

"You think?" I knew I was freaking out, but that warm fuzzy feeling of assurance I had woken up with was gone...completely. *"We could go to jail for this."*

"We could," Shim agreed.

"Hard time. Like, they would try us as adults."

"I know." His shoulders sagged, and he turned around. The others were distracted. Breeze and Skylar were deep into their own discussion, and Jaxon was having a staring contest with Waters. *"I don't like this anymore than you do. Do we have a choice?"*

I thought about that. I believed you always had a choice. Beyond right and wrong, good and evil, and all the subtler shades of grey, you always had a choice. Maybe not good ones, maybe not better ones, but every path branched off into choices

—and outcomes. What would we be giving up in information from Waters if we didn't pass his final test?

"I don't know if I can do this."

"I know." The flush of relief hit hard. He didn't have to agree, but he understood.

"I mean, gah, he is such a weasel!" I tried not to let my frustration show as I vented to Shim. *"He gives us a place to stay and knowledge to stay safe on the streets, but on the flip side, I know he is using us, and I see how he eyes our bags."* We had all seen the gleam in Waters' eye when he caught us rooting around in our backpacks for something. And we knew he had noticed we never left the bags behind. Someone was always watching or wearing them. *"He would rob us in a heartbeat."*

"Unless—"

"Unless?"

"Whatever he thinks we can do for him here is more valuable than what he thinks we have in the backpacks? What if this"—Shim's eyes shot up to look at the huge metal structure beside us —*"what if breaking into this building has been his end-game all along?"*

I thought about it. But if that was true, then how do we beat him at this game? Shim must have been reading my face.

"We have to be smarter than him. Whatever he wants from here, we have to make sure he doesn't get it until we have what we want from him." This was the only hope we had of getting the information we needed from Waters, and when I thought about it, there was another problem.

"We have to be ready for anything and ready to run, or else we will never be free." This had been a worry of mine for a while, that Waters might string us along, making us pass test after test, eking out little bits of information to us, piece by piece.

"Should we tell the others?" Shim asked.

"To be ready?"

"Yes, and about our suspicions"—he hesitated—*"and maybe about the stones and how we can talk through them?"*

I thought about it. It would be so easy to screw the whole thing up. *Someone is going to get hurt because of the decision you make.* Every taunt that had ever been thrown at me boiled down to that. *Screwup. Loser. Chicken...*And I was—I was chickenshit. Well, I had been. It was time I changed that. Right or wrong, I was going to take some action to change my future.

"Yes, yes, and no." I declared firmly. *"We tell them our suspicions of Waters, we see what he wants, then we figure out how to beat him. We keep the stones as a backup."* I paused. Was my desire to keep the secret of the stones only to hold on to my connection with this inner Shim—the one so different from the guy I had come to know in real life? Maybe, partially. But it felt like the right decision. It was risky to tell them. Waters might get to one of the others, might get them to talk somehow. The stones were too important to become part of Waters' product line.

"THE SAN FRANCISCO Federal Building offers a frank, contemporary response to its context, but more importantly, it establishes a benchmark for sustainable design in its use of natural energy sources." Breeze read the architect's description of the building aloud as Skylar snapped photos of the lobby.

The self-tour was an ingenious way for us to infiltrate the building. Most Federal buildings were pretty tight with security, but this facility was funded to educate in sustainability, and so it provided greater access to "the people," i.e., us, to view, or scope out, the modern landmark.

Our three days of planning were up, and we were narrowing in on our target, specifically a coin on the desk of some guy who worked on the ninth floor. Waters had a source who claimed the coin had a username and password taped to the bottom.

It was actually more complicated than just a little B&E, and it all started because of Breeze. Weeks ago, while we were watching our parents being abducted, that baby Einstein had been the only one smart enough to snap a photo of the van that took them away and email it to herself. We would never have found out about this, except during one of Waters demos, Breeze got hit by a case of Krispy Kremes that Jaxon and Shim were fighting over and ended up with a fat lip. She was moping about with a bit of ice pressed to the wound, mourning the loss of her phone and the inevitable selfie she would have taken, when she mentioned the last photo she took, real casual like it wasn't the most significant breakthrough we'd had since finding Jonas' shop.

Since we had trashed our phones, which she reminded us she had been against, we couldn't easily access her email and get the photo. After Breeze told Waters about the picture, he had us go clear across town to a copy store, log in on their computers, and download the photo.

With a little research, we were able to identify the license plate and TSP tracking numbers on the van as being Federal. Federal? As in the Feds? Agents?

Why would the government take our parents into custody? Some freaking out occurred at that point: Breeze wanted to call home; Shim and Jaxon fought; and I was pretty sure I was having a heart attack the way my heart tried to pound out of my chest. It might have been a panic attack.

Waters was more helpful, if a little crude, in reminding us we had been sent to him because our parents didn't trust the *bleep, bleep, bleeping* government.

Through various nefarious contacts, Waters picked this

building as the best way to gain access to the government's vehicle tracking program and declared it our final project. Maybe this had been his plan all along, to use our desire to access a system and track the van to get access to something major, like government secrets he could sell.

So here we were, ready to infiltrate. As Breeze continued to play guide, I looked around the lobby. It was straight from a dystopian novel. The open atrium wedged up into the floors above like a grayish wound. Pale green protrusions extended overhead, intensifying the harsh flatness of the concrete walls and balconies.

It was eleven-fifteen in the morning, and the lobby was over-flowing with federal workers escaping for lunch. The office we had targeted would be empty—we hoped—as a Federal employee's day started early and most took an early lunch. Our self-guided tour entry time was eleven-twenty. Knowing we had to go through a full security checkpoint with metal detectors, we had left our bags with Waters. That would have been a big bonus for him, but we had pulled out almost all the cash, and the bracelet, watch, and ring, and left the items in a locker at the Caltrain station. I hoped it didn't turn out to be a mistake.

For two days, I had been tracking the General Services Administration (GSA) workers. They kept federal agencies running and one of them would have the access we needed. The Social Security Administration Offices were at a neighboring entrance, so there were a lot of people hanging around outside the eighteen-story mesh box of a building, and it was easy to fit in with them.

Early that morning, as I swayed on the metal handrail of a downtown bus, Sharron Talsko had taken the seat behind me. Sharron worked for the Office of Transportation, Relocation, and Vehicles, located on the ninth floor of the Federal Building.

Like a well-organized dance, I slid into a seat beside her. It was perfect. A lot of people wore their badges on lanyards or clipped to their pockets. I'd overheard Sharron telling a co-worker that she thought that looked tacky and didn't match her jewelry, so she clipped hers to her purse, which she plunked down on the seat between us—like a big open yard sale. *Easy pickings,* I thought as I palmed the badge. Unfortunately, the badge didn't say what floor her office was on.

It was now eleven thirty-five, and I caught sight of Sharron Talsko leaving the lobby elevators for lunch. She was with a friend and complained about leaving her badge at home and having to wait in the ID line to get back in. We had to hope the rest of her office was as punctual, or we would have to turn to our backup plan.

With the tour leaflet flapping in front of her, Breeze read off details about the sustainability of the building, and we all stared up, pretending to be engrossed in our examination of the futuristic space. Sharron Talsko cleared the lobby, and we smoothly hopped on the elevator. Shim had accessed the building directory and confirmed which floor we needed to get off on. I watched him now as he pushed the button for the ninth floor. I noted how steady his hand was in contrast to mine, which had been shaking from the minute I pulled the badge from Sharron Talsko's purse this morning. Staring up at the numbers, I absently played with the necklace at my throat as I watched each floor tick by and tried to calm my rapid breathing. I must have sounded like a racehorse, air whooshing in and out, my nostrils flaring. But no one else seemed to notice my internal struggle.

This floor was indistinguishable from every other floor. The elevator doors opened on a mini-lobby and, to the left and right sides, doors labeled "Employee Access Only" with a keypad beside them. We got off the elevator in a conspicuous clump, huddled together, eyes wide. A steady vibration told me I wasn't the only one shaking.

Shim is the one who shook us out of it.

"Breeze, point. Jaxon, rear. Skylar, lookout," he hissed. Breeze immediately snapped to and turned right. We all stopped and stared at her. She stopped and sheepishly back-tracked. "Kidding." She gave a weak laugh as she headed to the door on the left that our online research had told us housed the Department of Transportation. Scanning the porthole style window in the door, she gave a thumbs up. Turning, I saw Jaxon and Skylar give a similar sign. Moment of truth. I went to the keypad and swiped the badge. There was a delay, then a green light followed by the click of a mechanism unlocking. Sharron Talsko's badge had worked.

I entered through the door first, followed by Shim, then the twins, and Jaxon bringing up the rear. A wall of windows on one side of the hall and glass front offices on the other made me feel like we were walking a gauntlet, waiting for someone to challenge us with each step. We had backup plan upon backup plan if we got caught, but we would lose this opportunity, and a second attempt would get trickier.

The first room we passed was a kitchenette. The others funneled in, and I did a quick walk down the hall, checking office numbers.

There it was, third from the end. As I U-turned and passed the office again, I did a quick sneak peek.

Oh Stars. There was a big bald mountain of a man spread out in the back. He must have to lift weights every spare moment to stay that jacked. His body was poured into khaki pants, a plaid button-down, and a green tie his neck was exploding out of. He sat hunched over his desk with his knees pulled up under it like it was kindergarten furniture. The guy had an unwrapped sandwich and an open soda laid out in front of him. A novel was propped on his monitor. Daaannnggg it! I moved past the room and headed back to the kitchenette.

"We need the doughnut decoy. Just one guy: big, bald, green tie, plaid shirt."

"On it." Breeze and Skylar headed down the hall toward the office.

I started counting. At thirty, I pinned Sharron's badge to my jacket and left the kitchen, trying to act casual as I passed the big guy in the hall.

"Hey, someone said there is a box of fresh Krispy Kreme Donuts in HR's break room," the Mountain of Man volunteered as he passed me.

I used his massive frame lumbering down the corridor as an excuse to squish up against the window and hide my face as he passed. He was out the security door before I could respond.

With the coast clear, I unclipped the badge and shoved it in my pocket, then called to the brothers, and we darted into the room to start searching. We had calculated it would take someone about twelve minutes to get down to the HR department, realize there were no doughnuts, then get back.

Jaxon groaned when we entered the room. It was a large space that held a dozen desks, utilitarian things with metal sides and wooden tops piled with wire baskets of papers and file folders. Personal items littered the surfaces: photos of family, coffee mugs with cute sayings, stuffed animals, and paperweights of children's handprints. Layered in the mess, every desk had a government printed calendar with the holidays marked in red.

We were looking for a coin amongst all the clutter. Waters' source didn't know what kind of coin it was. I had assumed it was a silver dollar, or maybe one of those Susan B. Anthony coins, if it was big enough to have a password taped to it. I started with Sharron's desk, checking everything metal, then realized it might be inside a drawer or under something. Going back, I rechecked the desk. Shim joined me, flipping over her keyboard and checking under her monitor and mouse pad. Nothing. We moved onto the next desk. Same results. Time was passing, and we still had to access the system once we found the password.

"What's this?" Breeze held up a bronze disk.

"You found it!" Jaxon put up his hand in an enthusiastic fist bump, and she left him hanging as she stared at him.

"A Challenge Coin, of course!" Shim said.

Breeze eyed the metal disc she had found on the Mountain of Man's desk. "What's a Challenge Coin?"

"They give them to you in the military. You are supposed to keep them on you at all times. He is going to miss this if we take it," Jaxon explained.

"Well, Waters wants the coin, so if we just get this one chance, we better get to work." Shim gave a Dr. Evil laugh and rubbed his hands together.

Breeze flipped the coin over and read off the password stuck to the back, and Shim made quick work of logging on while the rest of us clustered around him. "Jaxon, keep lookout."

"Ah man," Jaxon groused and slunk to the door.

"Okay, what are the numbers?" Shim asked when he was ready. I pulled back the sleeve of my jacket and read the license numbers written in marker on my arm. It was a bit dramatic, but I had been worried they would keep something when we went through security. It was hard enough smuggling in Sharron Talsko's badge.

Shim punched at the keyboard, clicked, clicked, clicked his way, navigating the system like a IT veteran.

"It's crazy you can do that with a computer," I spoke without thinking, and Shim stopped typing. His hands slid into his lap. I didn't understand why that comment would throw him off his game

"No, it's a good thing," I protested.

"He gets enough shit about it at home. Leave him alone," Jaxon said over his shoulder, his back to us as he watched the door. Then, to Shim, he added, "Come on, man. We haven't got all day."

Shim quickly raised his hands and started to type again.

"It's been eight minutes," Breeze confirmed.

More typing, a pause, another click, typing. "Winner, winner, chicken dinner." Shim fist pumped the air. "Here we go..."

12

THE FEDERAL BUILDING

COMING AROUND THE DESK, I slid onto the edge of the chair next to Shim. He kept tapping at the keyboard while scooting over and making room for me. As I looked at the computer, I felt his stare, but when I glanced over, he was looking at the screen.

Vehicle Check Out
Agents: James Hart, Roy Peters, Paul Colson, Anna Bailey

Vehicle Returned
Agents: James Hart, Roy Peters, Paul Colson, Anna Bailey

Civilians:
Subject: Arie Galen
Sex: Male / Age: approx. 41
Birthplace: Unknown
Status: In custody, suspicion of espionage, violation of
Foreign Agents Registration Act
Location: NSD Interned, undisclosed

Subject: Noah Thompson
Sex: Male / Age: 40
Birthplace: Monterey, California, USA, Earth
Status: In custody, suspicion of espionage
Location: NSD Interned, undisclosed

Subject: Kindle Hunt
Sex: Female / Age: approx. 41
Birthplace: Unknown
Status: In custody, suspicion of espionage, violation of
Foreign Agents Registration Act
Location: NSD Interned, undisclosed

Note: See related case #40593

My legs grew weak, and I collapsed with a thunk to the floor. "Suspicion of espionage?"

The whites of Breeze eyes showed as she asked, "What is the Foreign Agents thing?"

"It means the government thinks they are spies. At least we know for sure they have them." Shim's voice was tight. Only I could see the slight shake to his hands as he hit print, and across the room, a printer whirled and churned out pages.

"NSD? Is that the National Security D....agency-something? Aren't those the guys that can take you out of the US and torture you?" Skylar's panic was infectious, and I felt nauseous as my stomach dropped.

"We don't know that. We don't know anything for sure," Shim rushed to reassure us, but I could see he shared my fear and confusion. This had all been a waste. There wasn't anything to follow up on to find where they were.

I was chewing on my nail, so I used my elbow to point at the screen. "What's with the related case note at the bottom?"

"I'll look it up." More clicking and clacking followed his response. "Hmmm..."

Case #40593
Subject: Micah Pujari
Sex: Male / Age: approx. 42
Birthplace: Unknown
Status: In custody, suspicion of espionage, violation of
Foreign Agents Registration Act
Location: NSD Interned, undisclosed

Subject: Trystal Pujari
Sex: Female / Age: approx. 42
Birthplace: Unknown
Status: In custody, suspicion of espionage, violation of
Foreign Agents Registration Act
Location: NSD Interned, undisclosed

Subject: Amber Pujari
Sex: Female / Age: 18
Birthplace: Los Angeles, California, USA, Earth
Status: In custody
Location: NSD Interned, undisclosed

Subject: Jada Pujari
Sex: Male / Age: 15
Birthplace: Los Angeles, California, USA, Earth
Status: In custody
Location: NSD Interned, undisclosed

Subject: Gemma Pujari
Sex: Female / Age: 4
Birthplace: Los Angeles, California, USA, Earth

Status: In custody

Location: NSD Interned, undisclosed

Note: See related case #21376

"Weird. The kids all have birthplace listed as Earth." Shim chortled.

"Why does Arie, Kindle, Micah, and Tyrstal's records say 'birthplace unknown'? Wouldn't foster records or a TPR, termination of parental rights, show where they were born?" I asked.

Shim shrugged. "It's the government. I thought they had access to all the 'rents records since they were in the system."

"So this is the Micah that visited your mom? Is he one of them? Do you think this Trystal person is too? If they are foster siblings, does that mean he married his sister?"

"Gross." Skylar curled up his lip, then pointed to the screen. "Look at the dates. The government must have taken them into custody first, then picked up Noah, Kindle, and Arie...and then tried to pick us up."

"Two minutes!" Jaxon's harsh warning whispered from the door startled me. "He just got off the elevator. Breeze, Skylar, do the next decoy." The twins raced out of the room. Shim hit print and started to rise from the seat.

"Wait. There is another related case."

"There's no time."

"Please," I said. We had hit a dead end and had more questions than answers. We had to push a little further.

Shim shrugged and sat back down, quickly tapping in the new case numbers.

Vsheewww. Click, click, click. I jumped at a whirling and ticking sound. I felt the adrenaline injecting into my heart, making it race, even as I realized it was the building's automated systems opening the windows.

"Grace." Shim grabbed my hand. His tone was serious, and my adrenaline spiked again. When he pointed to the screen, I followed his gaze.

"What—" All sound and motion stopped as my vision tunneled in on what was on the screen.

Case #21376

Subject: Amé Thompson

Sex: Female / Age: approx. 39 (deceased)

Birthplace: Unknown

Status: captured, terminated by Helios Kratos, suspicion of espionage, violation of Foreign Agents Registration Act

Last Known Location: Monterey, California

Note: See related case #00045

My vision blurred. Shim was shaking my hand—no, I was trembling and shaking his hand, which was the only thing keeping me from a total meltdown.

"I don't understand."

Shim tugged his hand loose, and I felt myself free fall into a black hole. There was a buzzing in my ears. I barely registered a whirling sound in the background and more clacking.

"Wait," I protested as he started a new search. The word "terminated" kept repeating in my head. I didn't realize I was saying it out loud. Shim had a vice grip on my face, his hazel eyes were staring into mine, and he was saying something— repeating the words over and over.

"Grace, Grace," he repeated in a loud whisper, "Shhhh. Grace, come on, come back, Grace." When I blinked, his grip loosened, and I registered the contrast of his warm dry hands with the clammy iciness of my skin. I had beads of perspiration on my forehead, and I had to keep blinking to focus. Was I going to pass out?

"Grace," Shim repeated. "Grace, look at me," he hissed. He shook me roughly. "If you ever want to find out what happened to your mother, you need to pull it together, and we need to get out of here."

I stiffened at his words, and a bit more focus came back. Shim let go and returned to the screen. His last search had come up. Barely looking at it, he hit print.

"I'm okay. I'm okay." I pushed Shim away from me and back toward the computer. I felt wobbly without his hands on me, but I tried to shake it off. "I'm okay, keep going...find out what that means."

It was good I was already on the floor. I lowered my head to my knees. I didn't feel much better down there, but it wasn't a bad idea to be closer to the floor anyway, just in case I passed out.

"Here is the last case note." I rose up on my knees, and my head craned up, looking up over his shoulder at the screen, my hands braced on his thigh, fingers biting into his skin. He flinched but didn't move away.

Case #00045
Subject: Tar Xanon
Sex: Male / Age: approx. 64 (1995)
Birthplace: Unknown
Last Known Location: Gypsum Cave, Las Vegas, Nevada
Status: suspicion of espionage, violation of Foreign Agents
Registration Act. Terminated by Helios Kratos,

Subject: Unknown
Sex: Male / Age: approx. 14 (1995)
Birthplace: Unknown

Location: Las Vegas, Nevada
Status: Terminated by Helios Kratos

"I don't know what this means. The status..." I couldn't say the word. "That's the same as my mom..." My voice trailed off, and I didn't finish the thought.

"Who the hell is this Helios Kratos?" Shim asked, his voice menacing. He hit a key, and the printer in the corner whirled as he started a new search.

There was a shrill whistle from Jaxon, followed by voices coming down the hall.

Leaping up, I ran to the printer and grabbed the pages quickly folding and shoving them into my back pocket. Shim was scanning the screen up until the last second, then leaped up just as sandwich guy lumbered back into the room.

The printer whirled one last time.

"Hey, what are you kids doing in here?"

"Where are the bathrooms?" Shim motioned to me.

"We got lost." I stepped in front of sandwich guy, pulling his attention away from Shim, who was still standing close to his desk.

"How did you get access to this floor?" The guy eyed us both suspiciously.

"Well." I shook off my earlier daze and launched into Plan B, a dramatic explanation of our mother bringing us to work today and, in an effort to get us out of her hair, sending us off to get doughnuts. However, trying to find a restroom, we got off on the wrong floor and followed someone through the door, ending up lost and...Shim, who was over by the printer now, interjected colorful side comments on our trek. Slowly, we both backed out of the room. Still eyeing us suspiciously, sandwich guy pointed down the hall to a sign that read, "Employee Bathrooms." "That way. Don't wander around without a badge."

With an apologetic thanks, we took off.

Skylar, Breeze, and Jaxon were waiting at the elevators. I remained silent for the ride down to the lobby.

Breeze resumed her narrative from the self-tour of the building's features. Skylar responded. I could see Shim keeping a worried eye on me.

∞

"GWALD SLOOW GLOOD!" Skylar had his mouth full of an Indian curry wrap and was taunting Jaxon who had turned his nose up at the truck.

After our escape from the labyrinth of the Federal Building, we had circled the block, stopping to regroup at United Nations Plaza. Several groups of protesters holding banners and shouting slogans took up one end of the plaza. In the middle, *Off the Grid* food trucks circled like an old wagon train around clusters of office workers eating their lunches while they baked in the sun on rickety white folding chairs. Shadowing the plaza was the hulking mesh building we had been in earlier.

Slowly, the heat ate at the white fog in my mind until it just resided at the edges of my vision. I was dying to ask Shim if he had found out anymore, but I was loath to break the spell that fused this moment to the earlier moment—the moment when I still held hope Mom had left us and could come back at any time.

"Why are we sitting here in these crappy chairs under the sun instead of over there in the grass under the trees?" Skylar asked. The invasion of the food trucks and office workers had pushed the plaza's regular residents into the edges.

"Since we arrived, I've seen three drug deals over there," Jaxon muttered under his breath.

Wide-eyed, Skylar and Breeze mouthed "oh" and continued to shovel in food.

"Aren't you eating?" Breeze's voice sounded faint as if I was hearing her underwater. I looked down at the food in my hand. I had tried to eat a fry when we first sat down, but it had tasted like wood chips. When I swallowed, my throat seized, a lump blocking the path, and fearing it would involuntarily go the other way, I had made the choice to spit it out. My mind was still churning through the white static, numbed. I wasn't aware of my arms and legs moving or brain processing. I'd felt the same once before when they told me about my mother's accident—only now I knew it hadn't been an accident. *Sources*, I'd been so angry at her for leaving, for not sticking. But now I felt like I was the one that had given up on her.

"Grace." I registered Shim's tentative touch on my shoulder. "Hold on. We will get somewhere soon where you can let it all out." He grabbed up his boxed lunch. "Guys, come on. Let's try and find a little privacy." I saw the others wrap up their remaining lunch and follow along. Walking deeper into the park, away from the Federal Building and toward City Hall, we settled on an open bench along the plaza.

Shim told the others everything we had found in our search of the Federal government computers, including what his last search on the word "helios" had found—which was nothing. Well, not nothing. It had come up with a security block and a request to reenter username and password. Then denied him access.

I perked up. Surely, if the government had a name for them, Helios or whatever, then they had more information. But if it required a higher level of security, then it couldn't be good.

Somewhere in the middle of the recitation, I had handed over the pages from my back pocket. When they started a discussion over who Tar Xanon and the unknown fourteen-year-old male had been, I stood up. I couldn't sit still anymore.

"At least we know they are all together, somewhere," Breeze said, her tone consoling.

"I don't understand why they didn't know their birthplace. I guess I never realized that even I don't know where Dad was born. Do you?" Skylar asked Breeze. She shook her head.

"Yeah, that is weird. Shim, did Kindle ever tell you where she was born?" Jaxon looked at his brother.

"No, Grace and I noticed that and"—he pointed down at the papers—"this is the second search. Micah and Trystal also had birthplace listed as unknown, but their kids, Jada and Gemma, have Earth listed. Who says that?" His voice rose with incredulity.

Then there was the third search.

"Grace." Shim looked up from the page. "Did you want to talk about this?"

"Nothing to talk about." I jumped up, walking ten steps up, then back. Repeat. "They were right all those years ago. I was wrong." The words seem to scream off the page. Captured. Terminated.

"What do you mean?" Breeze asked. With a quick nod of permission to Shim, I turned away while he explained I had never believed my mom had been killed in the diving accident and had just learned I was wrong. All those years, I had been blaming her for leaving...

I felt hysteria bubbling up, and I wanted to let loose with a yell to rival the protestors on the other side of the plaza. No...I didn't want to scream. I wanted to punch something. Oh, what I would give to be in one of Waters' dirty fighting classes and get to whale on something. Just hit and hit until it crushed under me. In the back of my mind, the aggression frightened me, but I was too wound up to care.

"You said 'Helo-krat-something' before, but I don't know what that is. Do you?" Breeze looked at the others who all shook their heads. Shim muttered something, and I strained to hear.

Seeing my face, Shim cleared his throat and, looking uncomfortable, mumbled, "Helios Kratos were Greek gods of sun and war."

"You speak Greek?" The twin's gaped at him.

Sheepishly, Shim ducked his head. "No, I just remember reading it somewhere."

"Nerd." Jaxon made a scoffing noise, but the corner of his mouth turned up, gentling his face as he said it.

My mind settled into a white-hot anger. Resolve burned in me, rushing out, taking over. "We have to find out more. We need to do everything we can to find out what the 'helios' in those reports is." *Or die trying.*

13

WATERS' STORY

ARRIVING BACK AT WATERS' Victorian burnout, I was ready to hand over our ill-gotten gains and get out of there. I was tired of games.

The others did not share my view.

With a congratulatory chant of "Pomp and Circumstance" that carried a hip-hop rhythm and a lot of foot stamping and clapping, Waters presided over our unofficial graduation—which consisted of a sly wink and a slap on the back for each of us.

I thought Waters would want to know what we had learned about our parents today, but he brushed it aside, said he didn't need or want to know—in fact, the less he knew about it, the better. He was, however, very interested in the username and password we had acquired. We had decided it was too risky to take the coin, so we left it. Hopefully, the Mountain of Man would think the password that Shim now had in his hand had fallen off.

Shim was about to hand the password over to Waters when he paused. He pulled back his hand and tucked the paper back into his pocket. "After you give us the information we want," Shim told Waters.

"Then I guess y'all will be buy'n me some dinner, as this story takes a bit to digest."

We placed an order at Waters' favorite nearby takeout. The brothers went and picked it up. Breeze and Skylar wanted to make an occasion out of graduation dinner. I went through the motions of helping them out, but my head wasn't in it. In the wake of the emotional tsunami, my brain had spun to exhaustion in a what-ifs teacup ride, and now I wanted to curl up and sleep for a week. Instead, I trudged along behind the party planners as they "Martha-upped" Waters' kitchen.

The twins took an old door and spread it across a couple of buckets, then pulled in all the remnant chairs from the house to finish off the shabby-chic dining room set. Add in a couple of cans with candles in them and an old painter's tarp for a tablecloth, and I had to admit, it looked good.

Waters sat back in his chair in the kitchen, watching us while we worked. As loath as I was to emerge from my furious funk, they made dinner fun.

After dinner, the atmosphere changed. Waters pushed out from the table, leaning back in his chair as he got comfortable, thoughtfully chewing on the toothpick between his teeth.

Eventually, we noticed the change in his demeanor and quieted. Waited. After a couple of minutes of silence, Waters launched into his story.

"Your parents came to me through a mutual acquaintance —his name's Lincoln. We were in the army together a lifetime ago. Survived the jungle. You're young and don't know what war's like. It changes you. Many of us...well, we never really came home." He paused. He had a faraway look in his eyes, and his voice was thick, like his story came from a wild place inside him, a deep place that didn't see much light. After a while, he continued, "People get real uncomfortable to be around. Family expecting things you just can't give anymore. Sometimes, you get lost. Sometimes, it's better to...disappear. Lincoln, he was a true friend. He had it rough, and his own demons to fight, but he always kept tabs on me, and he never let me disappear." Waters looked down at the toothpick he had been working on. "So, when he sent y'alls parents to me, he said two things: they needed help, and they had saved his life." Water shook his head. "That's all I needed to know. I helped."

I was caught up in the story, and it took me a minute to shake out of the spell his voice had woven. "Did he ever tell you how he met them or how they saved his life?"

"Nope. Didn't know where they came from or where they was going. Didn't need to know. I set them up with some good learning, the same ways I set you up." He hesitated.

Shim latched on to that and asked, "But?"

"I learned some things about them while they was here."

We sat up in our chairs, full attention on Waters. He nodded to the five of us. "You all know about modern things. You're like them typical teenagers: drama, drama, drama, and lots a dumbness." I suppose we should have been insulted, but we'd grown accustomed to Waters telling us we didn't know jack. He continued, "But your folks weren't nothin' like that. They were truly clueless. They were like refugees, misfits. Smart kids, but they knew nothing about the world. And so very homesick, almost broken.

"They weren't family, but they were thick, and they took care of each other as if their lives depended on it." He nodded. "That's what it was—like something had happen'd and they knew their lives were at stake." He shook his head at us, his gaze serious. "You, you're just playing. I mean, you're scared, but you ain't nearly scared enough yet for what you've got ahead. You really want to find your folks, then you need to get a lot more scared and a lot more smarts."

A chill went through me at his words.

It was the most Waters had ever spoken to us—well, the most that wasn't related to B&E—and he had never said this much about our parents before. He kept his time with them shrouded in mystery. We had asked him questions, but he was always evasive, acting like he wasn't sure we were ready to hear the truth.

And he was right.

I was coming to realize—to *know*—our parents weren't who we had grown up believing them to be. They hadn't just met in a foster home and become friends; they had lived a hard life on the streets, and they had been afraid and had to make difficult choices. How did you prepare yourself for this kind of truth? We needed to know more.

"Do you know who was after them?" Shim asked.

Waters shook his head.

"Please...I want to understand. Can you tell me more about what my mom..." I stumbled through the words, choking on them. Remembering that each piece we learned was part of a larger puzzle, I added, "...what all our parents were like back then?"

Waters hesitated. Was it loyalty to our parents or his inability to give anything away for free that was holding him back?

Shim pulled the slip of paper out of his pocket and waved it in front of Waters. "It's part of the deal," he reminded him.

Waters' face hardened. His black eyes drilled into Shim. "All right, I'll tell you a little something about them and then answer one question from each from ya," he said grudgingly.

"How do we know you won't lie?" Jaxon asked.

Anger flared in Waters' eyes. "You don't." His harsh retort

was a reminder this man was very dangerous. Just because our parents had sent us to him didn't mean he could be trusted.

"Deal," I quickly interrupted the harsh response Jaxon was poised to deliver. Shim gave Jaxon a glare that said if he didn't shut his mouth, Shim would shut it for him.

Mollified, Waters looked at me as he started. "They was a funny-looking group. Called themselves family, like they were all born together, but you got them two older Indian kids, a golden boy, a pretty young Black girl, and your momma, about the palest white girl I'd ever seen with that odd green hair—just like yours." He laughed. "A real kaleidoscope of a family." He paused, searching for the words. "They were all still getting to know each other, like they'd only met a little while back." Waters eyes turned soft as he remembered. "Micah was in charge, and he took their safety real serious. That boy was green. They'd been running for months, and he'd learned a little, but you could tell he had lived a privileged life, all book smarts, but didn't know a thing about how to survive on the streets."

"He was closest to Trystal. He would talk to her and confide in her." Waters gave a fake shiver. "Cold girl, but she was always there for him. Got to say, after she left, never saw her again. All the rest would come and visit, stop and say 'hello,' drop stuff off, but not Trystal. She had moved on."

I shifted impatiently. I didn't know who these people were, and while the context was interesting, I was impatient for him to get to the important people. Waters shifted his gaze to Breeze and Skylar.

"Now your papa, Arie, he was one of them kids everyone was just drawn to. Nice-looking boy, more confidence and charm than was good for him. Girls loved him. He was what they call a 'well-bred' type, but he never looking down his nose at a body. All these years later, he still comes by and checks in, seeing if I need anything. Real class act. He was kinda Micah's unofficial lieutenant. A problem-solver. And oh, boy, did Micah need him, 'cause I ain't never seen so much trouble as your Momma." He turned and looked at Shim and Jaxon.

"Kindle was well named, 'cause she started more fires than a loose cigarette in a dry grass. She just couldn't help herself. If someone said the sky was blue, she would argue it was red, just for the sake of arguing. She fought it, but she was a pretty girl with an ugly temper. She was clever and a survivor. Of all of them, she the one coulda made it on her own. But she stuck with them."

Shim shifted, looking uncomfortable with Waters' description, and Jaxon looked ready to tear into the old man, and that wouldn't get us anywhere. Waters was watching Shim and Jaxon, reading their reactions.

"Yep." He eyed Jaxon. "You got that same fire in your belly, but you're not as likable." He laughed fondly at a memory. "We was talking about it when she was here last summer."

The brothers both leaned back, surprised, and the anger in Jaxon's face diffused. I thought the brothers lived in Las Vegas. That was a long way for Kindle to come to visit.

"And you"—he turned his attention to Shim, studying him for a minute—"you look like your father." Shim's brows screwed up like he had eaten something that made him sick. He started to break into Waters' monologue.

"What—"

"Nope, no questions until the end, and I won't answer that one anyway." He quickly shot down Shim and turned to me.

"Now your mother, Amé." He pulled out the last syllable of her name like it was a sigh. "Ahhh, she was the sweetest little thing." His mouth turned down in the corners. "I'm so sorry she gone. I sure do miss her terribly." He had trouble meeting my eyes, like it was uncomfortable for him to acknowledge pain. My chest ached at reopening the wound. "Amé was so scared and homesick when I met her. She hid it, but everyone knew she cried herself to sleep most nights. Still, she gave everything she had to the family, and they were very protective of her..." He paused. "Something bad had happened, I don't know what, but there wasn't any one in that group that wouldn't have done anything for her. It was almost like she was their talisman. She brought out the best in each of them and gave them something to be strong for."

I sniffled and swiped at the tears running down my chin, surreptitiously brushing them away. I was crushed at how vulnerable she had been, relieved to know she had friends and family that cared for her, and surprised that Waters knew her the way I remembered her, as bringing out the best in everyone.

Waters nodded, a faint smile on his lips as he talked. He grew silent and repositioned his head on the chair behind him, sighing deeply, his wrinkled face a scuffed leather stretch over his domed head. The lines on his face deepened like all the years had suddenly snuck up on him. He looked tired, old, and sad. He half closed his eyes, resigned, but not completely trusting.

"All right, one question each. Think about it before you ask. No take backs."

Jaxon blurted out his question first, "What the hell you got against our mother? What'd she ever do to you?" he demanded.

"Nothin'. She's my favorite. I love her visits. Kindle's a real firecracker. One minute she is cracking balls and taking no prisoners, the next she is smooth talkin' someone around to her point of view. Tough as nails and not afraid to show it. In fact, there ain't much she is afraid of, and if something scares her, you should really ask yourself"—his feet hit the floor as he leaned forward, hands to his knees, eyes flying open and drilling into Jaxon, "—*why?*"

Jaxon tried to say more, but Waters shook his head. "Uh, uh, you had your one question." As Jaxon sputtered, Waters gave a dark chuckle. In any other situation, Jaxon would have protested, but some sense of goal preservation held him back.

"You said our parents were homesick and like refugees. How so? And refugees from where?" Breeze's question was tentative and worded carefully.

Waters twisted his face up. "Don't know where they came from. They never said anything about their family or their home. Nothing. Think about it, what young kid says *nothin'* about their family? Or home? Just wasn't right. Then there were little things, like them knowing nothing about any holidays, Christmas, Easter, and the like. I thought maybe they were from overseas. They had funny accents. But one day, a plane went overhead, and Kindle asked me what it was. How did they get here and not know about planes? Your parents, they were just —odd."

Okay, that was weird. I glanced around, and the others looked as perplexed as I felt.

Skylar went next. "What were they scared of, and what did you mean we aren't nearly scared enough?"

"Your parents were scared spitless." He pinned us with an intense stare. "I think they were rich kids, well-educated at least, probably all kind of resources at home, but they weren't going home for help. Made me think they *couldn't* go home.

"They came to me because they needed skills to survive. They weren't on some adventure. They had something real ugly chasing them." He hesitated, and the room throbbed with silence until, finally, brow tight, he spoke in a hushed whisper, "One night, Micah was upset. He was talking more than he usually did, so I asked him why they all just didn't go back to their parents. He said it was impossible. They had tried. There was a person who might have been able to help, but what was chasing them got there first and had killed him."

The air sucked out of the room, and the fear that had kept us running since the kidnapping amped back up, along with a blistering case of anxiety with a chaser of panic. Looking around, I saw the emotion mirrored in the other's eyes. *What was chasing them?*

Finally, Shim ask his question. "What was the real reason our parents sent us to you? And this man, Lincoln, how can we find him?"

"Two questions"—Waters looked at each of the siblings—"but I'll answer both of yours, too, because I think they are connected, as the others were."

"Your parents sheltered you. They wanted you safe—but not paranoid. I think they kept secret what they were scared of to keep you safe. Now, all that has changed. Now, they need you to know how to take care of yourselves, and they need you to learn their secret. That's why they send you to me. That's why I'm going to tell you how to contact Lincoln."

I sat back, surprised.

I hadn't expected Waters to agree to connect us with Lincoln. Shim leaned forward, elbows on his knees, looking pleased with Waters' answer to his question. It was a relief, but I didn't know why he was as committed to pursuing this as I was. I just wished there was someplace safe we could drop off the twins before we dove down the rabbit hole. It was funny. Jaxon was the youngest, but I was the least worried about him.

"You're up, sugar."

Surprised, I looked away from my contemplation of the twins to see Waters watching me.

My mind raced with all the things I wanted to know. *What had happened to my Mom? Where had she come from? Where did he think our parents were now? Who was Helios? What should we do next?* But Waters couldn't answer any of those questions. We couldn't even trust that the story he had told us about our parents was true. I thought for a moment. This was a chess game. With Waters, it was always some type of game, and you had to think strategically.

"What are you not telling us?" Waters cocked an eyebrow, and I fingered the metal at my throat. "For example, you know something about my necklace. I've caught you looking at it several times, but you haven't mentioned it or tried to steal it."

Waters chuckled. "What I'm not telling you could fill a library." Then he got serious. "I will tell you something your parents don't know that I know. I overheard them talking one night about a stone, just like the one in your necklace." He pointed to the vivid reddish-green rock with silver veins that sat at the center of my mother's necklace "They called it the 'Keystone.' Mentioned a real fancy geologist they had just met who had told them all about it. He had been helping them, but then something happened, don't know what, and they ran—again. Always on the run." Waters snorted out an exasperated breath. "Remember that. They have always been on the run.

"This happened when they was up in the Pacific Northwest. That's where they met Lincoln and saved his life." Waters finished talking and pushed back from the makeshift table, standing, joints popping and creaking. That was it. He was done talking. It was the most he had ever said to us, and it opened up a whole new world of questions.

He held out his hand, and Shim put the piece of paper with the username and password in it. "I'll get a word out to Lincoln to expect you." And without another word, he headed out the front door and left us behind.

$$\infty$$

MY MIND RACED, stuck in neutral with the tires spinning. So much had happened to us in the last few weeks, I felt like I was crossing through a cyclone in a foundering ship, with no time to contemplate what the right or safest thing to do next was, each course change sailing us into a new set of uncertainties.

With Waters' answers, even more questions were piling up in my head. I wanted to reach up to my necklace and talk to Shim to sort them all out. I don't know why I felt I could do that through the link between the stones but I couldn't do it in person.

The stones, we had a name for them now—Keystone.

One answer, but still, I was swimming in questions, questions, questions. The race from the apartment as our parents were arrested. *Why were they arrested? Why was the government holding them? How could we find them?* Finding Jonas and learning about this strange watch. *Where had it come from? What did it do? Why did Arie have it?* The rooftop escape from the gallery. *Who was chasing us? Was it the Helios? Was it the government? What would they do if they caught us?* Water's training program. *Why did he feel we were in so much more danger than we knew? What had our parents been running from? Was it just the Helios, or were there others? Who were our parents?*

And crammed down at the bottom of the list, stuffed into the back of my subconsciousness with a "not the right time to examine" sign posted on the front were the questions: *Who was I? Who was I becoming? A girl that jumps down construction escape chutes, picks pockets, and sneaks into buildings?* Yeah, that's something I would have to wait to have a heart-to-heart with myself about.

There was one thing I was sure about—it was time to come clean.

I cleared my throat.

Since Waters had left, we had been going over everything we now knew. Turns out that what Waters told us was new to everyone. I wondered if my dad had known. He must have. He had mentioned the Helios and sent me to Waters.

"I don't know about you guys, but I feel—" I started.

Jaxon burst out, cutting in, "—like my mom should have told us. She owed us." There was a lot of nodding from the others.

"Betrayed," Shim supplied the word. More nods.

"Lied to," Skylar whispered. Heads bobbed.

"My family used to be so close," I continued, "but when it comes down to it, what do I really know about them?" I shrugged my shoulders like it was nothing, but really, it was everything.

"Me too." Breeze sniffed. "I was kinda angry with Dad after we got the info this afternoon. Then, talking to Waters and hearing how scared they must have been, I just wonder, why didn't he tell us? We could have been more prepared. We could have helped."

"Yeah. All the secrets suck," Jaxon agreed.

I nodded to Shim. "That's why I think we shouldn't have any between us." When Shim nodded back, I continued, "So, in the spirit of a day full of 'startling discoveries,' Shim and I have to tell you something *else* we discovered."

The other's eyes were curious as they waited.

Shim pulled the ring out of his pocket and turned to face his brother and the twins. "It's about this."

I put a thumb under the stone on my mother's necklace. "And this."

The others looked confused, and Jaxon swiped the ring out of Shim's hand. "Give me that. What are you talking about?"

"Put your finger on the stone in the center," Shim directed. Jaxon rolled his eyes, then reluctantly complied, his lips twisted in a sneer.

I touched the stone at my neck. *"Hi, Jaxon."*

"What the..." Jaxon snatched his finger back, accidentally flinging the ring across the room. I folded forward, trying to hold back a laugh. It was nice to have the mood lightened.

Chuckling, Shim walked over and picked the ring up off the floor. He blew off the dust and rubbed it on his shirt before holding it out to Jaxon. "Try again."

Jaxon eyed him with a lot more suspicion this time, but in the end, his curiosity won out. Reaching for the ring, he put his finger on the stone.

"Hi, Jaxon," I repeated. *"It's okay. We were really freaked out the first time too."*

"Hello?" Jaxon responded loudly. I winced at his volume.

"Try again. This time, just think it." I encouraged.

"Hello?"

"That's it."

"Holy Sources, is this for real?

"Yeah, it's real."

"How did you figure this out?" Jaxon asked. I tried to explain.

Breeze and Skylar were watching us stare at each other.

"What's going on?" Skylar looked confused at Jaxon, then me.

"They are talking to each other."

"No way," Breeze gasped out.

"Let me try." Skylar reached out for the ring. Reluctantly, Jaxon handed it over.

"Hi, Skylar."

"This is sooooo amazing," Skylar shouted in my head.

I cringed at the volume. Unhooking the necklace, I gently unwrapped it from my neck and handed it over to Breeze. She hesitated, then took it, making an exaggerated motion of putting her finger on the stone.

"Like this?" she asked.

I nodded.

She let out a loud squeal. I was glad I hadn't heard that in my head. After a couple of silent minutes while the twins talked to each other, she started to cry. "I always knew that's what you would sound like in my head." Skylar got up and hugged her. They handed back the stones and sat close. Being as they could practically read each other's minds, I guess they didn't really need stones to talk to each other.

"How is this possible?" Jaxon asked.

"I have absolutely no idea," Shim responded.

We debated the scientific to the fantastic options for how the stones worked, but no one had an answer.

"All right." Shim sat down. "Now the secrets are out of the way, what are we going to do about the others? What are we going to do next?" They all turned and looked at me. *Oh shit!*

In school, I had studied math, science, history, the regular stuff. Wouldn't it have been nice if they could have focused on a something more useful, like Critical Decision Making in Crisis Situations 101? Now, that class would have been helpful.

Was our priority to take the next step and find Lincoln? Or should we keep trying to find our parents—at the risk of getting captured ourselves? Would finding out the truth of our parents' past help us find them? Maybe we should just find a place to hide until this all went away. But I knew that wouldn't work.

Taking a deep breath, I told them what I thought should happen next.

14

FINDING LINCOLN

"I GOT SOMETHING." Jaxon punched my arm, jostling the white mug in my hand, and burning pain followed the trail of scalding tea that slopped over the edge, soaking my arm and shirt. Quickly, I put down the mug and hooked my thumbs through the holes I had worried into the ends of the sleeve, rubbing the hot liquid off my skin. Shaking the dripping tea off my hands, I took the wad of napkins Jaxon handed me and tried to clean up the mess.

"I think I found one of them." Jaxon skipped the punch this time. I summoned a smile, which I suspected looked more like a grimace.

Three days ago, we took the forty-five minute bus ride from San Francisco, across the Golden Gate Bridge, to Sausalito. We wanted to take a ferry, which would have been half the time, but we were concerned they would require ID. The fewer people that knew we had left the city, the better.

Since then, we had been sitting in Sausalito, staring out this window, watching the Vina Del Mar Park.

Waiting.

Waiting for something to happen. For someone to contact us.

Waiting.

Did I mention waiting? I was about to lose my mind. We all were.

Of course, the time hadn't been completely wasted. While we watched the park, we also searched for the geologist Waters told us about, the one in the Pacific Northwest who had examined the rock—the Keystone—for our parents.

At least we knew a little more about the rock than Waters did. While we didn't know where it came from, we knew there were at least three pieces: I was wearing my mother's necklace with the stone mounted on the front; Breeze had Arie's cuff with the stone set in it; Shim had Kindle's ring. I wonder it Trystal and Micah each had pieces?

I checked the park across the street. Still no change.

While Jaxon had hunted for the geologists like a bulldog, the rest of us had been focused on finding Lincoln. Waters had set up a meeting place but hadn't given us a time. We had staked out the place and set up patrols. Shim had organized us. While one person sat in the park waiting for Lincoln to turn up, two people would watch the sitter, and the other two would scout the town. Currently, Jaxon and I were on patrol, and he had talked me into taking a break in the coffee shop so he could use their computers to do more research. Breeze was in the park, and Shim and Skylar were across the street in our hotel room where they could take turns watching her from the window.

It wasn't really a park, just a triangle of green space carved out of the expensive real estate of the trendy, waterfront tourist mecca. In the center, there was an enormous fountain dedicated to the city's Chilean sister city that was surrounded by a few yards of grass and trimmed squat palm trees. The whole park was ringed by a dense growth of finely manicured, shoulder-high bushes. The street behind the park had been closed off to provide an enormous bike parking lot and, behind that, a one-way shuttle bus stop. All this was done to accommodate the large number of visitors the city received thanks to its California charm and panoramic views across the San Francisco Bay. The crowds worked in our favor, helping us to blend in and distracting from our loitering during our long vigil.

When Waters had given us Lincoln's name, I thought, great, we would contact this guy and, bam, have what we needed, right? Not right. Waters only had a number to leave messages on and a meeting place. He had called and explained who we were and set up a meet. That was how the men usually connected.

That had been three days ago.

"Time to switch," Shim's voice came into my head. I hadn't even realized I was rubbing the stone.

After the first day of sitting in the park waiting for something to happen—that never did—we realized we needed a strategy. We dug into our envelope of bills and checked in to the Hotel Sausalito, getting a room with a park view. That was when we discovered that cash goes a long way to ease concerns over minors checking in on their own. Splitting up, we set up an irregular rotation schedule so none of the locals would get suspicious seeing any one of us for too long. Waters' training was turning out to be very useful.

"You're clear," Shim announced in my head. At his signal, I nudged Jaxon, and he quickly logged off the computer. We grabbed our bags and walked out into the fresh summer air. We had done this many times before.

After leaving the coffee shop, Jaxon headed across the street to the park to relieve Breeze, who I had seen a minute ago in the back by the trees, singing to herself. I headed down the street. Most of the stores in the center were two or three stories high and had expensive, bohemian-style shops on the ground floor with huge front windows.

Walking the well cared for sidewalk, I wove around benches with colorful cushions and tables set for fine dining with glass stemware. The dense pedestrian traffic was distracted today, wandering lazily. Everyone got a little sun-shock when the temperature rose, and the warmth of the afternoon put a hiatus on the biting wind.

I hadn't gotten very far when the back of my neck started to tickle. Was I sensing someone behind me? Uneasy, I stifled the urge to look behind me and stopped in front of a shop window instead, using the reflection of the glass like a mirror to scan the people strolling up the street. A couple in workout gear, pushing a stroller. A tall skinny guy in rolled up jeans with his arm wrapped around a girl, his hands sliding up the edge of her tank top as he whispered in her ear and she laughed. An older woman in loose flowing clothes and brightly colored shoes walked a small, white dog with a large orange bow. None of them raised any alarm bells, but the feeling didn't ease, so I headed back to the park. When I got closer, I heard Jaxon.

"Breeze?" It wasn't a shout, but it was close and sounded very panicked. I grabbed onto the necklace.

"What's Jaxon doing? Where is Breeze?" Shim sounded stressed.

"Isn't she in the park?"

"I don't see her, and Jaxon is tearing the place apart. He must be looking for her." From the room, Shim could see the whole park. How could we have lost her?

My first instinct was to step across the street and help Jaxon. But that prickly feeling had me stepping back into a narrow alley and taking a minute to look around. I glanced behind me. Stairs led up the steep hill to the expensive homes above. I turned back. Jaxon was headed toward me. Off to the right, I saw Shim and Skylar leaving the hotel and moving toward the park, their bags on their backs. No one paid attention to us, and I didn't see Breeze anywhere.

"She isn't here." Jaxon's voice was angry.

Suddenly, Skylar's panicked voice filled my head. *"Did Jaxon find her? Has anyone seen her?"* He must have wrestled the ring away from Shim.

"No, Jaxon checked the whole park and didn't see her. I'm down here, too, and I haven't seen her for several minutes," I responded to Skylar. "She must be here somewhere. Do a loop around the outside of the park," I ordered Jaxon. He took off.

"Skylar..."

"It's Shim. I got the ring back from him. He's...upset."

"Keep Skylar with you and check out the coffee and the ice cream shops." Best not to send Skylar out on his own.

After scouring the area, we came up with nothing. Where had she gone? Okay, now maybe we should start panicking. Skylar and Shim were double-checking the park while Jaxon and I re-checked every shop.

"Hello?" Breeze's voice was tentative over the stones. She hadn't spent as much time talking through them as the rest of us had.

"Breeze..." Shim started, then was interrupted.

"BZ?" Skylar breathed in relief. *"Where are you?"*

Breeze ignored the question. *"Follow these directions quickly, and try not to be noticed,"* she said. *"Go to the base of the park and follow Bridgeway north."* She sounded rushed. Was she running or scared? *"Take the second right onto Bay Street."*

"Breeze, are you okay?" Skylar sounded desperate.

Breeze ignored her brother and firmly repeated, *"Take the second right onto Bay Street."*

Shim and Skylar emerged from the park ahead of me. They

were walking at a brisk pace, and Shim had a hand on Skylar's bag, holding him back from running.

"At the corner of Bay and Humboldt, cross the street to Marotta Yachts of Sausalito. Take the wooden walkway down to the Spinnaker Restaurant," Breeze instructed.

To my relief, Jaxon walked up beside me. Now, we didn't have to worry about two people being lost. I gave him a quick summary of what was going on, he scowled, and we quickly followed the directions while keeping a safe distance from Shim and Skylar.

The wooden walkway ran along the harbor, giving access to boat berths. Cars, nose in, were parked along one side of the walkway: a couple of Porsches, a SAAB, a Maserati, two Hummers, not a hoopty in sight. On the other side of the walkway, large, expensive yachts were lounging in berths, like grand racehorses that rarely left the barn, bobbing up and down in the water, their ropes groaning and squeaking. Acoustic guitar music reached across the water, mixing with clinking glasses and accompanied by the cries of seagull.

Our shoes clacked on the wooden boards like an out of tune xylophone as we raced to the waterfront restaurant at the end of the path.

Just before reaching the building, I heard, *"Look left."* Shim and I turned, pulling Jaxon and Skylar with us. Down a wooden gangplank, a white motorboat was idling. Breeze sat in the boat, waving. She wore an orange life vest and a big smile.

Traipsing down the gangway to the pier, we were not happy campers. Skylar stomped down first.

"Are you okay?" He hissed at Breeze, who still hadn't answered the question.

"Yes, of course! Sorry I scared you." Breeze nodded to the man behind the wheel and the woman on deck casting off the ropes. "These are Lincoln's children, Linda and Herb."

Herb nodded, his face serious. Linda gave a tight smile and tugged nervously at the front of her windbreaker.

"I don't mean to rush you, but we need to get out of here before someone sees us." She glanced around the marina. "Would you mind coming with us? We have some important information to tell you, and it's not safe here."

Something was off. Why send Linda and Herb to meet us instead of Lincoln coming himself? Why the rush through town? Why not tell us what was going on now instead of having us go out on their boat? It's about this point in most mystery shows where everyone is yelling, "Don't get onto the boat."

But we did anyway. Stars, we must be stupid.

15

LINDA AND HERB

A MIX of emotions rolled off the pair of older siblings. They appeared to genuinely want to help, but they were holding something back, some secret, that made me uneasy. Sorrow blanketed the air around them like a thick San Francisco Bay fog. They seemed desperate to talk to us, but we could tell our appearance disturbed them.

Linda looked like she should be drinking a glass of wine as she invited us on board for cheese and crackers. She was in her mid-fifties. Her chin-length blond hair had faded to gray streaks, and lines creased at the corners of her eyes and mouth. She looked comfortably wealthy, dressed in white capris, blue boat shoes, and a blue windshirt with white detailing. An enormous ring glittered on her finger, and ropes of diamonds jangled at her wrist as she fretted, wringing her hands.

Herb had on brown Birkenstock sandals, faded jeans, and a bright red Hawaiian shirt that showed under his half-zipped windbreaker. His fine blond hair was graying and showed most prominently in his sideburns. As the wind blew, thin patches showed on top.

Herb and Linda kept shooting nervous glances around, unsettled. They wanted to talk but were holding back.

Skylar had already moved toward the boat; he wasn't going to be parted from Breeze again. Jaxon and Shim both looked at me.

"What do you think?" Shim asked.

I watched Linda help Skylar into the boat. "If we want answers, we are going to need to go."

The brothers nodded. None of us were smiling as we climbed aboard.

Once we were settled, Herb revved the engine and pulled away from the berth. The wind whipped up as we were leaving the shelter of the marina. Linda shuddered. "It's absolutely honking out here today," she shouted to Herb over the sound of the engine. Shim pursed his lips and raised one questioning eyebrow at me.

"It's windy," I explained.

Linda cocked her head at my response. "Do you sail?"

"I used to, with my parents." I frowned at the memory. Linda waited expectantly, so I reluctantly continued. "My dad's a marine biologist, so we spent a lot of time on the water, and my mom is—was—an expert sailor. She taught me." My voice trailed off, sucked into the wind as I looked out over the water.

When I looked back, Shim was watching Jaxon white knuckling the seat as he fought the waves and bounced around like a bobble head.

The bay seemed to never end, long fingers reaching back into the land creating hidden nooks and crannies that Herb seemed intent on exploring. The water was surrounded by low hills with racks of houses descending until they floated on the water. I wondered where Herb was going as he zigzagged through several course changes. It was a long while of bouncing around in the swells before I realized Herb was making sure we weren't being followed.

Finally, Herb pulled up to a boat anchored in the middle of the bay out from the marina where we had started. We climbed aboard.

"Welcome to the *Fly to Blue*. This was our Dad's boat."

"Lincoln?" Shim clarified.

"Yes."

"Can we see him?" I pushed, tired of the subterfuge.

Linda looked sad as she rubbed her hand on the wheel. "He died three days ago." There was a whoosh of air, gasps. Now, the solemn faces made sense. The excitement that had been building in me deflated like a popped life raft.

Shim leaned in closer. "I'm so sorry. Our parents will be upset to hear he—um, passed."

"He didn't pass," Herb growled out, his mood dark. "He was murdered."

"Now, Herb, don't scare the kids. It's not their fault." Linda leaned forward and squeezed Shim's hand "Thank you, dear. It was a random, senseless. Someone broke into my house to rob it. He had an apartment in our basement where he stayed when he wasn't here on his boat or on my boat, the *Fly to Blue Too*—I named it after his boat.

"He came home unexpectedly and caught the robbers. They shot him. It was...horrible." Her story ended with a sigh, then a little hiccup.

There was something so, so...wrong about this. The timing was too coincidental. I wasn't convinced this break-in was random. *Three days ago.* That was when Waters first called Lincoln. My stomach clenched at the idea our search might have harmed someone important to our parents. It seemed Herb didn't think it was coincidental either. With fists shoved deep into his jean pockets, his lips were pursed and his face pinched.

"What was taken?" Shim asked.

"My dad interrupted them. They left an awful mess. We don't think they had time to take anything—" Linda stopped, and tears welled up in her eyes. Blinking quickly, she waved her hands by her head and closed her eyes as she continued, "The whole house was torn apart. Especially his apartment. He was..." she choked off.

"Linda, why don't you grab us something to drink?" Herb offered. She gave her brother a watery smile at the reprieve and headed below deck.

"Look, this wasn't your run-of-the-mill breaking and entering." Herb's tone was low and grim, barely audible over the lapping of the water on the hull. "Our dad lived on the streets most of our lives; he knew how to handle himself. And the whole place was torn apart, nothing of ours or his was taken—" He glanced at the stairs that went below deck. "Dad was worried after he got Waters' message that you wanted to see him. He told me he called your parents to check on you, and he couldn't get through to anyone. He also said he had something of Amé's." He turned angry eyes on me.

"What was it?" I whispered.

"I don't know for sure..." With a deep sigh, Herb's face crashed, and he surrendered his secret. "Several times this last year, I caught him reading from a book I'd never seen before. When he saw me, he always hurried and hid it, like he was worried about getting caught with it. It had a greenish cover, and the one time I saw the pages, they were handwritten, like a diary. He carried it everywhere. The longer he had it, the more and more paranoid he became...Well, I guess he wasn't paranoid after all." Herb squatted down next to me, his face a mass of conflicting emotions. "I think that's what they were after. After it happened, I looked everywhere for the book, and I couldn't find it. I don't even know for sure what it was."

I did.

It was my mother's diary.

Growing up, she always had it on her. Leaving the boat, she would check her purse for her keys, her wallet, and her diary. It was just as much an appendage as her green hair. I looked for it after she left. I was convinced that if she had taken it, then she had left because she wanted to, and when I didn't find it, I knew I was right. She was very private about it. I couldn't imagine her sending it to someone else, letting someone else read it.

Herb interrupted my musings. "Dad was devastated when he heard about your mother's accident. She meant a lot to him." He looked at each of us. "All your families were so important to him, and I can't tell you how much what they did for him meant to our family." He choked up and had to stop talking.

"What did they do?" Shim leaned towards him.

"They gave him back to us." Herb gave a miserable shrug. "Our dad left when we were young. Even though it had been horrible living with his PTSD, his leaving destroyed our family. I grew up feeling like I didn't have a father...just emotional baggage." He cleared his throat before he continued. "He had a lot of problems from the war. He was raw. Messed up for a long time. Lived on the streets most of that time. When my grandparents died, they left him their boat. It didn't change him, but it got him off the streets, and he was always calmer when he was on the water. Then he met your parents. They saved him—not just his life, but his soul. They changed...*everything*. I don't even know how they did it, but they brought my father back and gave us a second chance to have him in our lives."

Linda climbed back onto the deck. She had forgotten the drinks. With a sad smile, she sat down and put a hand on Breeze and Shim's arms, who were closest to her. Herb did the same, putting a heavy hand on Skylar's and my shoulders. "We are so thankful for the time that your parents gave us with our dad. We would do anything for them to thank them—and that means helping you. No questions asked. Just let us know what you need."

Their story was amazing and confusing. I couldn't wrap my head around Lincoln having my mother's diary, and I didn't want to even imagine what it meant if the Helios or the government had murdered him and had it now. It made me want to hurl when I thought of those people touching something so personal of my mother's.

Herb and Linda's offer to help was kind but useless. It was Lincoln who had the information we needed, and with him gone, I wasn't sure what we would do. We hadn't thought further than locating Lincoln and getting his story, then maybe calling or emailing the geologists our parents had worked with, if we could track them down.

We needed to talk together and figure this out.

"Thanks for your offer to help. This does change things for us, and we need to decide what we should do next." The sun was starting to set behind them as I spoke to the older siblings. "We are staying at the hotel in town." At Herb and Linda's looks of alarm, I added, "Maybe we shouldn't go back?"

The older siblings had a quiet discussion. There was no way to escape overhearing the whispers in a boat this small. "They could... but what if... it's not safe for us... cost a lot...what he wanted."

Trying to ignore them, we checked out the other vehicles anchored out in Richardson Bay. Shim filled in the awkward silence. "What are all these boats doing out here? Why aren't they in the marina?"

I nodded to the bobbing chucks of floating wood and fiberglass around us. "Marinas are safe, but expensive. There is a maritime tradition that it is free to anchor offshore. It attracts a combination of freewheeling sailors and drifters." I pointed out a couple of the boats around us. Some had tarps used for water-proofing and debris piled on deck, and weathered hulls that, by some miracle, still sported a mast and canoes or battered row boats tied behind. Beyond the floating bits of boat rubble, nicer boats, some like *Fly to Blue*, weathered but well-maintained, were anchored with motorized dinghies tied to the back. Lights were starting to twinkle in some of the boat windows, and beyond that, further out across the bay, huge plate glass windows glowed in pastel houses terraced up the hills, each vying for the best view of the bay and sparkling city beyond. "We lived like this for years." I sighed, content to be back on the water.

"Which were you, freewheeler or drifter?" Shim asked, watching me.

I tilted my head to consider my response. A long strand of mottled ash and green hair caught the wind and repeatedly slapped me in the face. Shim reached out and pulled it away, seeming reluctant to let the soft strands go as they slid through his fingers.

"Both, I guess. It certainly felt like we were drifting most of the time. I guess my parents were trying to get lost." Subconsciously, I had been leaning in closer since he pulled on my hair. It might have been just to hear him better. "But we would never"—I pointed out to a boat that had tarps covering most of the roofs and windows and was still taking on water—"ever let our boat get in that condition. Even with no money, daily care can go a long way in the maintenance of your boat."

"Okay," Linda announced loudly. "We think it's best if you sleep here tonight. The pantry is fully stocked, and there's plenty of diesel and water." She looked to me. "You know about boats, right?"

I nodded, uncertain where this was going.

"But do you know how to sail?" Linda asked insistently.

"Yes." I blushed. It was one thing in my life I could honestly say I was really good at. "It's been a while, but I've crewed with my parents since I was a baby in a life vest. We lived on board for several years. I've also solo sailed frequently. We had a smaller sloop than this but very similar."

"Good"—Linda breathed deep—"then you should consider using this boat to get to wherever you want to go next."

What? My eyes bugged. This was not what we were expecting.

"We couldn't," Shim protested.

I knew I was a good sailor, and it felt wonderful to be home on a boat again, but this was too much. Plus, we really didn't even know where we were going next, especially now that Lincoln couldn't provide answers. We needed to regroup and figure it out.

"Just think about it. We don't need to know where you are going, and this way, you would have complete freedom to leave the city without anyone noticing. You could call us and tell us where to pick up the boat after you docked."

"We don't have a phone."

"How did Breeze call you?" Linda looked puzzled.

Breeze panicked. "I...uh..."

"Never mind, we don't want to know," Herb interrupted. "I left a burner phone for you on the counter. I programmed my number into it for emergencies, and I'm the only one with its number."

Herb and Linda climbed into the motorboat. "Don't decide now. We will be back in the morning, and we can talk about it. Sleep well."

I numbly nodded thanks and waved goodbye as the brother and sister motored away from the sailboat.

We were left alone to sort out our future.

As Linda and Herb's motorboat sped farther away, I sat down cross-legged next to Jaxon, feeling as lost as he looked.

Jaxon groaned and stretched out on the back of the boat "F-ing great. Now we're stranded on this floating toothpick"

I sighed.

16

THE EXPLOSION

THE SHOCK WAVE WOKE ME. It shook the boat, and before I could even remember where I was, it was followed by a whooshing noise. Amplified by the water, the explosion sounded like it was happening right outside.

Someone screamed, and panicked shouts responded.

Punching up, I leaped from the bunk.

Within seconds of the sound, I was rushing out of the companionway onto the deck. Shim was already at the stern. Sunrise was hours away, but a red pre-dawn light was taking over the darkness.

"What happened?" I blinked, trying see through the cloak of night. For a minute, I couldn't remember why I was on a boat. It all flooded back as Shim grabbed my arm and turned me around. Off in the distance, a ball of fire sat on the water. It wasn't the dawn that brought the red glow. Flames licked up toward a giant cloud of grey smoke hovering over the marina.

"Something blew up!"

We stood in shock, watching the flames leap as they consumed what we could see was the glowing remnants of a yacht. I'm not sure when everyone else joined us, but Jaxon was the first to speak. "I think it was a boat. What are the odds that a boat would blow up here? Now?"

Dread filled me. The same thought had been on my mind.

"Stars, this is getting dangerous." Skylar sounded grim.

"When hasn't it been?" Shim challenged.

Last night had been one of the best evenings we had in weeks. At Waters' place, our time was all about training. In Sausalito, we had been stressed about making the connection with Lincoln. Here, even with the bewildering loss of Lincoln, we had finally felt safe, like we had a secure place and time to consider our options and make a smart move next.

A stationary boat was a great hideout. But sailing a boat you didn't know up a dangerous coast, that wasn't smart.

Last night, I had tried explaining this to everyone after Linda and Herb left. But the twins had found nautical charts, and they'd laid out their trophy on the galley table and looked at me expectantly. Surprised, I asked what they wanted me to do. With perfectly straight faces, they told me they expected me to sail us to where we were going next. I laughed. I thought they were kidding, but they weren't. Instead of explaining the intricacies of sailing, I humored them while they cooked us dinner, checking the boat's resources and looking at options. It had been comfortable below deck, the heat from the galley warming the space.

The cabin was a pretty sweet setup. The thirty-five-foot boat made the most of its space. The galley on the right had a full kitchen with a stove and oven and an itty-bitty fridge. It was fully stocked. Beyond the galley, there was a table surrounded by cushioned benches that could seat at least six. Directly left was a small desk at the end of a long bench that functioned as a sofa with throw pillows. At the end, an open door led to the main sleeping cabin, which was really a trapezoid-shaped mattress on a box with room to stand only by the door. On the opposite end of the galley and on either side of the stairs leading down from the deck were doors. The right one, with better access, was the bathroom. The left one, behind the galley, was a small space for sleeping or storage.

Watching the twins in the galley had been like watching synchronized swimmers or highly trained surgeons. They moved harmoniously as they passed off knives, bowls, and opened cabinet doors for each other, keeping up the nonstop chatter during their fluid dance around the confined space.

I dug around in the seat pocket, found a copy of the *Pacific Coast Pilot*, and sat down at the table. "So where are we going?" I had asked with a humoring grin.

"Washington," Jaxon blurted out.

Surprised, we all stared at him. Unfazed by the silence, he pulled papers out of the bag he, Shim, and Duchess were sharing. "I've been doing some research. We need to go to Seattle and then Portland." He pushed the papers across the table to us. "I've narrowed it down to these geologists. I thought we could email them, but how do you put that in an email? 'Hey, do happen to remember meeting five kids with a weird rock about twenty-five to thirty years ago?'" He paused for effect. "Come on, that's not going to work. We have to go meet these guys and question them."

"But Washington?" Shim asked. "Waters just said they had been in the Pacific Northwest."

"Yeah, I know, but I researched the crap out of it, and there are only a few schools that have geology programs with mineralogists that would specialize in something like this."

"Guys"—Breeze stopped what she was doing to stare at us— "twenty-five years is a lonnnnnngggg time. How do we even know they are still alive?"

"Yeah, yeah, I thought of that," Jaxon responded. He was

irritated. "Look, this is where we need to go. You either believe me or not."

"Calm down. We believe you. We just want to understand your research," Breeze negotiated. "That's a long way to sail."

"Hey, whoa! Why sail? I'm not sure you guys understand how difficult sailing from here to there would be. The water would be really rough. You're already seasick, and we're parked in the bay. Do you really think you could take open water?"

They needed a hard reality check.

"Maybe we should take a bus up," Shim supplied. He had been researching ways out of the city. "We could catch a ride, maybe with Herb or Linda, up to Santa Rosa and get a bus. They might not be watching the stations there."

"Good idea." I supported Shim's plan. There was no way I was sailing an unfamiliar boat up to the Pacific Northwest. That would be the worst trip ever, if we survived it.

A ringing sound pulled me from the memory of last night. The flames had died down, but the hull of the boat still glowed like a morbid nightlight.

"Where is that ringing coming from?" Breeze headed back down into the cabin of the boat. "Hello?" She came up the companionway a moment later with Herb's burner phone held to her ear. Eyes wide, she nodded several times, forgetting the person on the other end of the line couldn't see her. "Uh huh, I got it. Thanks, Linda. I'll tell them." She was silent and, with a sad smile, finished, "Thank Herb for us. Good luck to you too."

Hanging up, she pulled back her arm and threw the phone over the side of the boat.

"What are you doing?" I rushed to the edge.

"Hey," Jaxon shouted, his body following the arc of the phone.

Confused, we turned to Breeze while Skylar slid up next to his sister. "What is it, BZ?"

"That"—Breeze pointed, her pale arm lit by the bloom of fire—"is all that remains of *Fly to Blue Too*. Linda's boat." Shocked, we turned to the glowing horizon. "Linda and Herb weren't on board when it went up, but they are at the marina talking to the firemen who say it looks like a bomb went off."

"Thank the Stars they weren't on the boat," I whispered. Wide awake now, we huddled in the stern, listening to Breeze recall her conversation with Linda.

"Linda said that Herb thinks whoever killed Lincoln tracked us to the marina, and when we didn't leave, assumed we were staying on her boat"—she pointed again—"and blew up the one registered under her name at the marina." Eyes wide, I tried to absorb our most recent brush with death. "Herb says we should get out of here tonight and never contact them again. Wherever the boat gets left, they will eventually contact him as Lincoln's trustee. He figures if we leave now, we should have a solid week before anyone can track us."

"Come on, let's go!" Skylar grabbed my hand and pulled me forward. "Make it move!" He demanded, like sailing a boat was magic.

"No!" I yanked my hand back. "Not like this. We can't leave in the middle of the night with no planning."

But we also couldn't stay.

I hummed under my breath as I quickly tried to think of a way to make it work. "It's too dangerous to sail off on an unknown boat without a plan. But," I added as Skylar and Jaxon both tried to interrupt me, "if you all help me, we can get the boat moved to a different location so they will have a harder time tracking us. Then we can make a plan and leave at first light."

Everyone jumped in to help, following my directions to pull up anchor and start the engine. Could we pull this off? Sail up the coast on a strange boat with a novice crew? It's not just any coast. The Pacific Northwest with its highly unpredictable weather patterns was treacherous for even a seasoned crew, but if it worked, this could be a real break for us, to be able to disappear from one city and turn up in a new one with no one the wiser. I itched to talk to Shim about it, the Shim I knew from conversations in my head, not the in person one. I still hadn't reconciled the two Shims.

Sighing as I stared at the still burning hull, I realized we were stuck between a rock and a hard place once again.

17

SETTING SAIL

A SPRAY of water splashed high over the boat, giving me a hard, salty slap. I swiped at my face, then adjusted the course slightly. In spite of my misgivings, we had headed out early this morning.

After the explosion the night before, we had changed anchor locations and found a new spot, still in Richardson Bay, but out of view of the marina. I had spent hours pouring over the charts and books and decided to take it one leg at a time. The first priority was to get us out of San Francisco and into a safe harbor somewhere else.

I hadn't been bragging earlier. I had a lot of experience on the water. My solo sailing had given me confidence I could handle most situations that would come up, and I accepted the risk to myself. I wasn't comfortable with the risk to the others. In my opinion, they didn't understand the peril.

Then, there was Jaxon. It was obvious Jaxon hated boats; he had gotten sick looking at the Personal Flotation Device when I'd walked the others around showing them the safety features on board. It had been a big surprise when Jaxon had opted in for sailing. He said he would handle it because we needed to try and get out of the city clean. He had guts. I just hoped they wouldn't be all over the bottom of the boat by the time we got to Seattle.

After plotting a course for the next day, I grabbed a few hours of sleep and rose at first light to start checking over the sloop. This was the moment of truth.

I had decided I wasn't taking the boat anywhere if it wasn't seaworthy. Turning the radio to channel fourteen, I listened to the San Francisco Vessel Traffic Service while checking the sloops' body and seeing how she sat in the water. I turned on all the electronics one by one, then all at once to see if the electrical system could handle it. I started the engine, checked the condition of the oil, and ran the pump, which woke everyone up. I went through every compartment, every locker, every bilge space, hunting down where the tools, fire extinguishers, and flares were stored and found them all and a six-man life raft—which I hoped we would never need but was glad to have. Same for the water maker I found in a locker.

By now, the twins had breakfast ready, and they were sitting with Jaxon, wide-eyed, watching me. I think they were finally getting how serious this was.

Shim had stood with them at first, but when he started following me around and helping, I explained what I was doing and what to do with what we found. By the time I was checking the condition of the sails and lines, everyone was following me, so I gave a quick tutorial on how to behave when the sails were up. The in-mast furling sail with vertical battens was brilliant, similar to the system on our old boat.

I was impressed. *Fly to Blue* was in primo condition. Lincoln had done an excellent job of maintaining her, and she was all prepped and ready to sail.

∞

"WHAT DO YOU THINK?" Shim came up the companionway as another spray of droplets rained down.

"I think—" I paused, wiping water off my face and bracing for the rolling of the sloop. I was trying to think with my gut and my head and not let the adrenaline from the explosion influence me. "I think we can make it, but I'll need a lot of help."

"You got it. But honestly, I don't know anything about boats. Why don't you explain what you are planning?" He offered up.

I couldn't believe his faith in me. I guess I was waiting for someone to point out I had no idea what I was doing and they would all leave me. After everything that had happened, everything that led us to this point, I was still constantly surprised any of them were still listening to me. They didn't need me. They had each other. I couldn't explain how much their faith in me meant to me and confused me. I didn't have all the answers. I didn't have any answers. And it burned me to think of all the times my mother could have told me the truth—and hadn't.

"I wish..."

"It is what it is." Shim interrupted my thought as if he was reading my mind. That was a disturbing thought. "I just mean you can't make it perfect. We just have to focus on what we can do to get the best possible outcome with what we have."

"Yeah, you're right. And we are lucky. The sloops' a real sweetheart."

"That's this boat? A sloop?" I smiled when Shim stumbled over the word.

"Yes. The *Fly to Blue* is a beauty. A Catalina sloop, thirty-five-footer, well-maintained and well-used from the looks of it."

"Huh, you do know a lot about boats."

"It's on the registration papers I found inside." He gave a

crooked smile at my admission. "So, from my review of the conditions and the notes I found in the *Pacific Coast Pilot,* we'll need to motor sail up the coast." At his confused look, I explained, "That means to use both the sail and the four-cylinder diesel engine the whole way. It will be faster. The trick will be to not run out of diesel. We will have to do some harbor hopping. It will add a lot of time to our journey, but it will be safer since I can't man the helm twenty-four hours a day, and with the lack of wind, we will need to refuel more frequently. Plus, the evening harbor stops will give Jaxon a break."

Shim nodded. "That makes sense. Can you teach me to sail-motor-drive-whatever, so I can help you?"

"Sure, I can show you the basics. It will be good to have backup."

"Cool." The muscles bunched in his arms as he plunged his hands into the pockets of his jeans, legs spread to balance on the moving boat.

"I wish I could look online and get more information about what we are sailing into."

"If wishes were fishes..." Shim said.

"You have a lot of those sayings." Shim's face relaxed into a laugh at my response.

"Nah, it just sounds like something you would say." He smirked.

I laughed. "I suppose I can hit up the locals for advice as we go along. Ready for your first lesson?"

"*Now?*" The smile wiped from his face, and he pulled his hands out his pockets and waved them frantically.

With the city at our back, we were motoring along at four knots and about to pass under the Golden Gate Bridge. The sun was out, burning off the fog and showing the burnt orange struts of the suspension bridge in contrast to the brilliant turquoise sky. The rugged headlands in multi-hued shades of green stretched down on each side of the bridge to sandy beaches. Off our port, a harbor porpoise jumped out of the water, then shyly swam off when he heard us.

"Now," I confirmed with a smile. "Come here." I showed Shim where to stand and gave him the basics of how to take the helm. Standing behind Shim, I reached around and realized even though we were close in height, his shoulders were much broader. I had to stretch to make the course correction.

We quickly put the gleaming windows of the city of San Francisco behind us and turned toward the sparkling water of the ocean, pushing past the mouth and out into open water. The weather was good, and my heart sang a happy tune as the long swells rocked the boat in a familiar rhythm.

As I kept a lookout for the coastal markers, Jaxon settled into one of the side seats in the back of the boat, a life vest strapped on and a waterproof blanket protecting him from the spray. He stretched out with his head turned to watch the receding shore with a look of yearning.

Shim stayed with me all morning. Soon, I was even able to turn the helm over to him for bathroom breaks. By afternoon, he was getting more confident, and I took a nap on the bench across from Jaxon.

We made it to Bodega Bay and anchored out in the protected harbor before dark. It was a great place to stop, something we wouldn't have most nights—there weren't a lot of harbor options heading north, and most were rough to get into—so we needed to take the opportunity where we could.

Breeze and Skylar made a simple meal and tried to tempt Jaxon into eating. This first day at sea had been awful for him. I slid on to the bench across from him and pulled out the charts and books to double check the route. A while later, Shim finished up on top and joined the rest of us in the cabin, sliding in next to me. For once, I didn't reach up to touch my necklace.

The subconscious gesture had come to represent my desire to talk to the Shim in my head, but now I was finding the real-life Shim equally easy to talk to. The two were starting to merge into one.

Shim said, "It's strange the way the motion of the water hits Jax. I've seen him do backflips on his bike and roll in circles for hours on his skateboard. But put him on water, and he turns Kermit-green until he hits land again."

I smiled. "He did great today." I then raised my voice so everyone could hear me. "So, I wanted to explain the plan."

"You have a plan?" Jaxon challenged me, a small spark of his old self returning.

"Well, sort of." I tapped the book confidently. "I didn't want to push too hard today to give us a chance to adjust. We need to make sure we get a lot of rest tonight and pray to the Stars the weather holds. It's going to be a real grind heading north against the prevailing northwest wind."

"Are we going to stop at a place like this each night?" Breeze asked.

"I'll try. I'm thinking with a hard day tomorrow, we can make Fort Bragg, next Humboldt Bay, then Brookings, maybe Coos Bay or Newport, and so on. We'll need to fill up on fuel at each stop too. We'll go through a lot motor sailing like we are. It's going to be tricky, trying not to be spotted. We just need to keep moving and stay ahead of whoever might be following us."

"Was this the hardest day?" Jaxon perked up, voice full of hope.

"Dude," Skylar cut in before I could break the news, "This was probably the easiest day." He looked up at me, and I nodded.

"We need to rest up the next few days while it's relatively easy and get ready for the rough weather we will get into around

Mendocino. That's also the longest leg of the trip. There are no safe harbors, so we will sail overnight."

"Argh," Jaxon groaned. "I'm gonna be skin and bones by the time we get to Seattle."

"If we even survive," Skylar added.

"Don't be a downer!" Breeze admonished him. Flicking on the radio, she started to clean up the galley. The only station they could get in played 70s dance music. Skylar jumped up and helped her, and before long, they were both singing along.

Shim and Jaxon groaned at the music. After a couple of songs, Jaxon pulled out a deck of cards he had found and started to shuffle.

Shim pulled me over and whispered in my ear, "I've been wanting to ask you something. The book that Lincoln had, was that your mother's diary?"

After a sharp inhale, I collapsed down, suddenly exhausted in a way the day at sea couldn't match. "It had to be. She always had it on her, and she never let me look at it." I felt so stupid admitting it, but he needed to know. "I have no idea what was so important in the diary that someone would kill for it."

Shim studied me silently, then nodded. "Do you know why Micah thought she had sent it to Kindle?"

"No—it's so strange. She never would have parted with it. I don't know how Lincoln got it." A horrible suspicion had been floating through my thoughts since Herb mentioned seeing Lincoln with the book. "What—what if he hurt her to get it? What if he took it from her?"

Shim cocked his head to the side and stared off into the pitch blackness outside the round window beside us. "That seems unlikely from everything we heard about the relationship from Waters, and Herb and Linda. But I'd like to see what's in that diary."

Me too!

He wrapped an arm around me and gave a squeeze. Something in my body responded to the comfort and the touch, waking up. Too soon, it ended. Jaxon called us over to join the others as he played out the rules for poker.

Inside, I knew everything had changed.

18

———————

CALM WATER

IT WAS STILL DARK out when I heard a noise in one of the cabins. I was in the galley pulling on one of the wind jackets we had found on board when I caught sight of Shim exiting the berth he and Jaxon had claimed. I hoped I hadn't woken him. I raised a brow as he started to pull on a jacket. He shrugged. I smiled and headed up the stairs. He followed.

"How's Jaxon?" I whispered once we were above deck.

"Passed out, thank Stars. He's pretty amazing. Sick as a dog, but all in. Solid," Shim whispered back. The two of us worked quietly in the darkness with whispered directions when needed. When we finally powered out of the bay, I had us head south of Bodega Rock before turning north. The boat's navigation lights cut through the inky blackness, illuminating the ocean's merge with a moonless sky.

I showed Shim how to do the watcher's job, keeping an eye out for obstacles and traffic. He sat at the front of the boat, his back against the mast, his attention on the surrounding area.

When we were farther from land, I tilted my head back and looked up at the sky. The moonlight was a sailor's beacon, cutting through midnight blue fabric that was popping with stars and the thick band of the Milky Way.

I walked up next to Shim, locked in the sky's exquisite spell. "This is one of my favorite times of the day. We're lucky the fog lifted." I whispered. Shim jumped at the sound of my voice next to him. Surprised, he slipped off his perch.

"How can you be here?" He questioned, pushing himself back into his seat and then looking back at the empty helm.

"AP." At his blank look, I explained, "Autopilot. I wish there was a wind vane, but this will do. It's good for short breaks."

"Ah. Didn't even know boats had that. Makes sense." After a quick scan of the water, he glanced back at me and stared.

I looked down. My skin was glowing, almost luminescent, in the moon's radiance. I was so pale, I could be a lighthouse. I sighed and ducked my head, but Shim caught my chin with his thumb and rubbed lightly at my skin, studying my face before letting go. He had a faint smile on his mouth when he turned forward again. I hid my grin.

Something had been bothering me, and now that I had Shim alone, it seemed a good time to ask about it. Maybe.

"Shim?"

Shim sat and waited for me to say more. It was something he was good at. Most people thought they were good listeners, but actually, they were good at nodding until it was their turn to talk. Shim was a good listener because he was good at waiting.

"I wanted to ask about the stones. Do you think...Well, did you feel...I mean, I—" I stumbled, paused, and tried to collect my thoughts. I started again and seemed to find my footing. "I felt, when we were talking through the stones, like I got to know this one guy, then later, in person, you were different. Colder or tougher, totally someone else. You know?"

"You saying I'm not tough?" He growled like it was a sensitive subject.

"No, Stars, you're one of the strongest people I've ever met." I was careful not to use the word tough, since it seemed to mean something different to him than it did to me. He was silent, waiting, so I continued, "Did you feel that way?" My voice shrank down at the end until it trailed off.

"Like there were two different Graces?" Shim questioned. "One Grace totally decisive and confident, and one that was conflicted and confused?" he challenged.

"Yes!" Did I come across that way? I was disappointed. I thought I'd done a better job faking my confidence. "Once I realized I was talking to you, I started to worry what you thought of me in real life."

"You didn't have to put on a front." He paused and tilted his head. "Maybe it's good you did. We didn't know each other. But how could you not have doubts about everything that was going on? None of us know what we're doing. You know, in motocross, you have a course, a direction, but every second, you're making decisions. Sometimes, you're going so fast you make decisions and commit to them on pure instinct. You have to have confidence in what you've decided and move on to the next thing. You do that. I've seen it time and again."

"Me?" The sky was growing lighter, and I could see it reflected in his amber eyes.

"Yeah," Shim said.

We let that settle, sitting in silence for several minutes.

"I want to ask you something else, but I have to check the helm."

I grabbed the guideline and headed to the back, immediately missing his warmth. I could feel him watch me for a minute, then he left his perch and took the bench on one side of the helm as he waited.

After making a few minor adjustments to the controls, I settled in on the bench across from him.

My voice was more confident now. "So after we fell in the dumpster, and you pulled up your shirt to clean off, I saw the scars and bruises on your side and back."

His eyebrows rose.

I was silent, watching him. This time, I was the one waiting.

"And you were wondering what? If I was the poster child for abuse?" He scoffed. My brows drew together, but I stayed silent. Finally, he relented. "It's not what you think. Not exactly, anyway." He raked a hand through his hair, blowing out a puff of air that held for a second in the cold morning.

I got the impression it was ingrained in him to keep his mouth shut about anything personal. Maybe I shouldn't have asked him. But I felt like he knew about my mother and other things I'd never shared with anyone. I wanted to know about him.

"It's complicated," he finally said.

"I'm not asking your dating status."

He smirked, then grew serious. "I don't talk about this, about Logan—my dad," he explained, and then shrugged. "He doesn't like me."

"And...he hits you?" An angry flush spread across my skin.

"What? No! Not what I meant at all, and that would be really bad since he's a former boxer. No, he is just very...difficult to live around, especially if his expectations aren't met. Football, motocross, boarding, just about every sport there is, he expects me to be the best or die bloody on the side of the field trying. There isn't any room for second place. Most of those scars are road rash, a couple of broken ribs, a wrist, that kind of thing."

"And it's the same for Jaxon?"

"Oh no, he loves Jaxon." Shim looked down, his finger tapping a strap on the seat cushion. "Jaxon can do no wrong. I can do no right."

"That is not fair," I said.

"Facts of life." He looked over my shoulder, his eyes distant. We sat in silence for a minute.

"Shim, why doesn't your dad like you?"

Shim was silent a long time before he answered. "I was born three months after they got married."

"Oh, wow."

"Yeah, guess he felt like I trapped him," Shim said.

"Not you. Kindle," I reminded him.

"Doesn't really matter."

"What Waters said, about who your dad was—have you ever asked her?" I groaned in my head. I wasn't going to ask him this —ever.

He didn't look confused or ask me what I was talking about. He knew. Shim stared out into the ocean, away from the shore and into the vast inky darkness. The silence stretched out like the water ahead of us, and I wondered if I'd damaged the fragile link that was growing between us, a connection I was just starting to recognize and appreciate.

"Don't want to ask. I've always suspected Logan wasn't..." he hesitated. His voice trembled, and in the wind, I strained to hear him "...my father. But if I ask her, then I'll know, and knowing—that's different."

We sat in silence for a few minutes more before Shim cleared his throat. "You, um, want a hot drink?"

I studied him. I don't know if he was expecting pity and maybe a little remorse for bringing up the topic. Instead, I met his eyes and held them. I hope I came across as understanding, maybe a little angry on his behalf. I gave a brisk nod. "A hot chocolate would be good."

Shim quickly made his escape.

I AWOKE WITH A START, completely disoriented until I felt the boat rock and I remembered where I was. We were being tossed roughly by the wind, and I was surprised I had fallen asleep. Shim was at the helm, feet braced, riding the waves. He was humming a soundtrack, guns rat-a-tatting, great bangs of explosions, whooshing of aircraft landing. It sounded like he was building his own *World of Warcraft* battle in his head, the noise competing with the crashing ocean's roar.

When he had offered to take control for a while, I had forced myself to sit down, thinking I would just rest a minute. Shaking my arms to wake up, I looked out at the water. It had gotten rougher while I slept, but we were making steady progress, keeping the coast on our right.

I pushed up off the bench and headed to the cabin. I made a quick trip to the head, then grabbed a cold sandwich. The twins had prepared a truckload of them two days ago in Fort Bragg, where we had spent the night, stocked up, and refueled.

Grabbing a bottle of water, I headed back up to relieve Shim. This was our fourth day at sea, and the clear weather had lasted till late this morning. By early afternoon, it turned, and sticking close to the shore meant we were frequently in thick, disorienting fog, riding up and down on swells that rarely broke for calm water.

We had spent last night at Humboldt Bay. It was the first time we'd had any problems on shore. While the others had gone to reload supplies, I had gotten updated tide and current data from the Coast Guard. The information was essential, and because of the projected bad weather, I decided we should skip the channel and go outside the St. George Reef. It would get us out of the fog, but the tradeoff made for a rougher ride. The problem came when we went to top off the fuel; they had required boat registration info. So far, we had avoided having to produce anything that would get us tracked. Concerned, we had backed off and not refueled. The fear of running out and the bad weather made for a miserable day, so we were all looking forward to pulling into the harbor at Brookings.

"You sleep?" Shim's voice was hoarse. A curl of cocoa hair was plastered to his forehead below the rim of his hat. His cheeks and lips were rosy from the wind. He was alert, coiled, ready to spring into action. Shim made an excellent sailor.

"Yeah. I can't believe I was knocked out for a good two hours. Crazy, huh?"

"You needed it," he acknowledged, and he was right.

I'd been pulling a lot of hours above deck and spending a lot of time below deck mapping a course and stressing about everyone and everything. I couldn't stop myself from asking, "How do you think everyone else is doing?" I indicated with my head the twins who were playing word games while acting as the watchers for Shim.

"Tight. Good sailors." The ultimate compliment.

"Jaxon?"

"Napping," said Shim. That's what I'd expected. Jaxon had been taking the Dramamine we had found in the emergency kit, knocking himself out during the day, and trying to help in the evenings.

"He's doing great. I can't imagine being sick like him whenever I was on the water." I leaned over him and made a slight adjustment at the helm.

"How long have you been sailing?" Shim asked.

I thought back. "Always. One of my earliest memories is from when we were living on our boat. We followed my dad's job. Marine biologists get around, and my mom homeschooled me. I helped with everything: repairs, cleaning, piloting, plotting the course."

"That must have been an amazing way to grow up."

We swapped positions, me taking the helm and Shim

stretching out on the bench for a break, his coiled body relaxing. "It was. We lived and breathed the sea: sailed, swam, dove... until my mom died."

"You dive?" he exclaimed.

"Certified Junior Open Water Diver." I smiled. "That's just a certification. I was diving with my mom for years before I was certified."

"Bold!" He laughed. I liked talking to him like this. It reminded me of before, when we would talk through the stones. We hadn't used them since we left Sausalito. His face grew serious.

"I gotta go to the bathroom," a female voice wailed from the bow. Breeze darted below, leaving Skylar on watch. With Skylar's hair hidden in the hood of his windbreaker, he looked so different: serious, older, more mature. Maybe it wasn't the hood; maybe it was the absence of Breeze. You almost never saw one of them alone.

Shim was silently studying me as I checked the nav lights were all on, then looked over the other equipment, including the VHF radio, the chart plotter, and the radar. We had to top off our fuel at the next stop. Motor sailing consumed a lot of power. Worrying about the fuel levels, I almost missed his question.

"So, how do you feel about her now?" Shim asked.

"Who?" Leaving one hand on the wheel that was being tugged around by the wind, I used the other to stretch up, then switched, stamping my foot as I shook off the last of the sleep. We just had to get past this truly gnarly stretch of coast to Brookings tonight. Then, if the weather held, two more days of harbor-hopping before we would have to face the Columbia River to get into the port at Astoria. I hadn't told everyone yet that we didn't need to go all the way up to Seattle.

"Your mom." Shim spoke quietly, but the question boomed, overpowering the storm. I stared at him. His face was serious.

"You were angry at her for leaving you, Waters tells you how he met her and how scared she was, then you find out she was killed by these Helios guys."

I had been trying not to think about it, thank you very much. But here was Shim, pushing me. Wind knocked me sideways, and I caught myself and braced.

"How do you think I feel?" I lashed out at him.

"It doesn't matter what I 'think,' it matters what you feel," he shot back.

"Is this because I asked you about your father? Are you getting even?" I was deliberately misreading his intentions, I knew it, but I was angry he was forcing me to think about this. Especially now.

Rain started to fall in thin razor-sharp drops, and the wind whipped it around us, adding to the cacophony and beating against the side of the boat, plastering our rain pants and jackets to our skin.

"I'm going below," Skylar yelled at us as he slipped down the companionway, his hands white knuckling the railing as he went.

"No, of course I'm not trying to get even." Shim jumped up, his face stern. He put a knee on the bench and a hand on a railing to steady himself as he glared at me. "And I'm not going all touchy-feely on you." He made a disdainful face. "I'm trying to get you to stop bottling it up and *think* about what you feel. Grace, you found out your mother, who you love and thought had left you, was dead, and she had been murdered. And you immediately had to put it aside to deal with Waters. Then you found out more about her life from Waters, and you had to put it aside to try and find Lincoln. Now, we are finally the ones pursuing the truth about all our parents instead of being pursued. We are going to find out more, I know it. I can feel it, can't you?" He beat his chest with his free fist and carried on without a response, shouting above the accelerating storm, "And I just..." he stalled in the face of the hurricane of emotion he had generated, and he suddenly stilled. "I'm just worried about you. The same way you were worried about me when you thought Logan was hurting me."

We were only a few miles out from the Port Brookings harbor, motoring along, but suddenly, I felt as if I was adrift without an anchor. I staggered back. The pain in my chest radiated up like the mushroom cloud of smoke we had seen above the burning *Fly to Blue Too,* and quick on the heels of the pain came a furious rush of emotion.

"I'm angry," burst out of me on a yell. "Is that what you want to hear?" I forgot about our course, the boat, the lives of the people depending on me, and I let myself feel. I didn't even notice Shim coming closer or reaching around me and flipping on the AP.

He stared down into my eyes, and the rest gushed out of me.

"I don't even know what this emotion is. Anger is not enough of a word for it, and I'm not sure if it's directed at her, the Helios, or myself."

"Why would you be angry at yourself?" His voice was cautious, the way people speak around wild animals they are trying not to spook.

"For not believing she was gone. For feeling relief she hadn't voluntarily left me. I'm awful." I finished the last in a soft voice that couldn't have carried the inches between us, but he seemed to have heard anyway. He shook his head.

"It's not awful to not want someone to hurt you. I've felt if many times. And it hurt you when she was suddenly gone."

"I should be mad at the Helios. And I think I will be someday when the rest of me doesn't feel so confused."

"You can't 'should' yourself into feeling something."

"Do you do that?" I deflected. Being the focus of attention

was uncomfortable. I'd rather be solving someone else's problems than focusing on problems I didn't even know I had.

"Sure, I've always thought I 'should' love Logan, but I just..." Shim sighed. "Well, it's hard when he has no love for me."

"I miss her." My inappropriate timing made it sound like I was comparing my loving mother to Shim's unloving father.

"She sounds amazing." He was leaning into me, protecting me from the wind as I shivered. "I bet my mom and Arie and those other two, Trystal and Micah, have good stories about your mom."

"I'd like to hear them," I said.

He nodded. "But Grace, we might find the Helios before we find the parents. Are you prepared for that to happen?" I was clinging to his arm now like a wet blanket, pulling his warmth from him. I shuddered at the thought of meeting up with whatever the Helios were.

"Do you think that will happen?"

He was thoughtful. "We know the government has our parents. I don't think they would have killed Lincoln or blown up his boat, so we don't know who has the diary. Waters said we should be very afraid of what was chasing our parents. Maybe it's the Helios. I think, whoever that is, they are now chasing us."

"Somehow, they knew we were headed to Lincoln's."

"Yes," he said.

"And we are on his boat now."

"Yes," he said.

"We have to get off this boat."

"True, but so far, we haven't had to leave any registration information anywhere."

"That won't matter. They can track us through the GPS. The only thing that might slow them down is them thinking they got us when the other boat blew up." I breathed in deep. I felt stronger, more determined from having talked this out, almost like a saline cleanse of an old wound. Painful, but healing. I pulled away from him and stood up straighter. "I've been thinking about not going all the way to Seattle." Shim's brows pinched together.

"If Portland is one of our destinations, then we only need to go as far as Astoria, then take a bus to the city. It would get us off the boat at least two days earlier, and we could go to Seattle afterwards."

"That would be good."

"The only problem is as soon as they find the boat in Astoria, they are going to assume we went to Portland. And I'm afraid they will quickly realize what we are doing there. Jaxon needs to be ready to meet with his professors, and they can't know when to expect us."

"That would be bad," he said.

"Yeah," I agreed. *Real bad.*

19

INTO ASTORIA

DAYS LATER, fatigue was wearing on me and so was the theme song to *Gilligan's Island* that was looping through my head at a frenetic pace.

To get into Astoria, we had to deal with the Columbia River and its infamous sandbar. We were also encountering the most shipping traffic we'd seen since San Francisco. Not wanting to alarm everyone, I didn't mention the area we were entering was known as the "Graveyard of the Pacific."

I'd timed our arrival to use the currents and winds to get us over the bar and past the normally strong seaward current. We made it, and the sun was setting as I switched our radio to channel sixteen and kept an eye out for freighters stacked high with lumber and logs.

Finally, we came to a large bridge spanning the waterway, and I headed to the south shore, pulling into a marina in the bridge's shadow. Down shore, huge freighters were being loaded. Further up the shore, rotting piers and docks were smothered in thick moss, but the marina was quiet and had a lot of open spaces.

After docking in a guest berth, I secured the boat. Shim

chatted up a local who, with a little cash incentive, was willing to sign for our spot at the marina so we didn't have to show registration or proof of insurance.

Jaxon hauled himself off the boat. Unsteady, he stumbled up the pier. Our guest berth was at the end of the marina, close to a paved walking trail. He stumbled along until he was on solid ground, then, with a groan, collapsed, molding his body to the pavement.

It was pretty late in the evening by the time everything was secure, and the rest of us fell into beds in the cabin. The last thing I remembered was the sound of water lapping against the hull.

When I woke up, the sun was starting to climb into the sky. I was curled up in a ball on a seat cushion; I hadn't even made it into one of the beds. Familiar now with Breeze's soft snores and Skylar's wheezing, I could tell they were knocked out in the forward sleeping cabin. I sat up and looked in. Sure enough, they were piled up like puppies on top of each other. I eased off the bench and grabbed my bag, heading to the bathroom. After a spit shower and a change into fresher clothes, I peeked into the aft cabin. Empty. Puzzled, I headed up on deck.

Nothing above deck. Where were they? I looked on shore, and on the walking trail, there were two lumps covered in sleeping bags. I approached the pile, treading softly down the pier and up the walk, trying not to disturb them. Shim had covered his brother up and was camping out next to him so he wouldn't be alone. They were covered in dew, and I was surprised they hadn't gotten rained on. Luckily, the sky looked clear this morning. Sleepy eyes opened at my approach.

Putting a finger to my lips, I whispered to Shim, "Shhh, I'm going to get real food."

"You got your necklace?"

I pulled it out from under my collar and put my finger on

the stone. He held up his hand, the large gaudy ring on his thumb.

"Keep an open channel and let me know if you see anything. They may know we've landed here," he said.

I nodded. I hoped we were a few days ahead of the Helios and the government, but knew now wasn't the time to take anything for granted.

I noted the berth number, then wound my way out of the marina. An enormous bridge dominated the sky to the east. It floated hundreds of feet off the ground and loomed over the town. At the edge of the marina, an access ramp stretched up to the bridge with homes and businesses tucked under the shadow of the slope. The bridge's tall supports were wrapped in construction tarps, and the constant scraping and blowing of sandblasting accompanied the contractor's banging and knocking on the metal bridge. The cacophony echoed and mingled with the horns of traffic, the blasts of seafaring vessels headed out to sea, and the seagulls cawing to each other. I suddenly realized it was just Monday morning. Weird. It felt like we had been on the water much longer.

I headed up the trail. A family of ducks was paddling around a calm patch of water under a rotted pier, oblivious to the massive tankers across the way that loaded handfuls of logs with winches like a mechanical arm at an arcade picking up pencils. Rows of tankers dotted the bay, waiting for their turn. *Sources! This place was raw.*

I skirted the fish cleaning station where a captain with a ruddy complexion was scrubbing down her passenger's catch from the weekend. Scrub. Wash. Filet.

I was about to turn into town when I caught sight of the sign on the building behind the captain that read. "Fresh Salmon." A menu was stapled to the left of the rectangular door cut in the wall and covered with plastic flaps. Oh yeah, the kitchen was open.

After picking up food and a newspaper, I headed back to the boat. It was strange, but after a week, the boat felt like home. Maybe it was the people waiting there more than the boat itself. I'd started this journey with four strangers, but from our time together, trying to unravel this mystery, we had become friends. Yeah, I would call them friends, even Jaxon.

When I got back, Shim was sitting up on deck, waiting for me. "Everything okay?"

"Yep, got fresh seafood and some crackers for Jax. How is he?"

"He's in the head." My eyebrows shot up. "No, no, he's back in the mix. He got some Zs. And since we docked, he hasn't..." He pretended to cover his mouth as he made a barfing motion. I cringed and handed over a bag with crackers and Gatorade. Shim nodded. "Thanks, this should help."

The soft, salty air was surprisingly warm and fresh, and we decided to eat up on deck. The morning sun was drying and warming the wood. Shim helped spread out the food, then dug into the newspaper. In a matter of minutes, he was absorbed in the news, the paper spread in layers across the deck, anchored by the shoes he had taken off.

Jaxon climbed up from the cabin, still pale but moving better. He groaned at the food. "Fish? Why didn't you just stab me with a harpoon?" He pinched his nose against what I thought was a delicious smell. Breeze and Skylar must have agreed with me, because when they came up on deck, they fell upon the food like starving animals. The four of us ate with relish.

Shim motioned for him to sit behind him, away from the food, and handed over the Gatorade and crackers. It was several minutes before anyone said anything.

"Slwe fround slomthing," Skylar said with a mouth full of food. He chewed for a minute, as we watched—and waited—and then he repeated, "We found something. Down below. There's a photo of our parents."

"What?" Everyone stopped eating but Skylar.

"Photo, in a frame. It's wedged under the edge of the bed next to the hull. Can't get it out. Breeze found it when she fell out of bed."

"Got shoved out, you mean." Breeze feigned anger. Skylar shrugged and crammed in another mouthful of crab cake.

"Show us."

Jaxon stayed on deck as Shim and I followed the twins below. Jumping on the bed, Breeze and Skylar pulled up the edge of the blanket and pointed below the mattress. Shim and I got down on our hands and knees in the tight space and twisted awkwardly to look up at the underside of the mattress to the spot the twins pointed at.

There it was. The raised blankets revealed a wooden picture frame stuck between the mattress box and the hull. The pressure had cracked the frame. The photo was of people sitting on a boat, but from this angle, you couldn't see any more. Shim gave it a pull. It was wedged in tight. The twins pushed on the mattress box while Shim and I pulled on corners of the frame. At first, it wouldn't budge, then, with a scraping sound, it slowly moved. Giving a hard pull, there was a crack and Shim jerked it free. With the abrupt release, his momentum had nowhere to go, and he fell on top of me. In the tight space, there was a scramble, and we somehow reversed our positions, me now on top, just as Shim knocked me in the solar plexus with his elbow.

I yelped. One hand went protectively to the wounded area, and the other braced on the hard muscles of his chest. Shim stilled at the impact, as if afraid by moving, he might hurt me more.

"I'm so sorry. Are you okay?" He put his hands on either side of my face, and my breath caught. I could feel his body down the full length of mine, every inch, every muscle. Staring down into his honey-colored eyes, my brain took a little vacation. I could feel the heat rushing through my checks, heck, my whole body. I inhaled and struggled to remember how finish the breath.

"Grace, are you okay? Are you hurt?" Shim shook me slightly, and my brain returned from its trip, unpacked, and picked up where it had left off.

"Oh, yeah, I mean, no. I'm okay, just got the wind knocked out of me." I tried to crawl off of him but was backed up to the mattress box. Unconvinced, Shim slid out from under me into a crouch on the cabin floor. I landed in a sprawl. Somehow, we managed to back into the main cabin and rise to stand.

"Uh, what's on the photo?" The twins had that saucer-eyes thing going again: Breeze's mouth was gaping open, and Skylar was sporting a smirk.

Shim hesitated self-consciously, then looked down at the photo in his hand. He put it down on the table in the main cabin and pulled back so we could all see. The color photo was faded, but the image still clear. Five kids were sitting on the deck of this very boat, and in the middle of the group sat a man that must be Lincoln. They looked our age. I recognized my mom next to Lincoln. She was so young compared to the rest of them. The two that looked Indian must have been Micah and Trystal; they were the oldest of the group, and Micah had a wrinkle of tension between his eyes.

"That's Dad," Breeze pointed to a teenager sporting a golden tan and sitting with an arm casually hooked over a leg.

"That's Kindle." Shim gestured to the dark-haired girl sitting so close to Arie, she was nearly in his lap.

"Geez." Skylar touched the heavy wooden frame. "Look

how young Dad was." His finger traced the face in the photo. I was thinking the same thing looking at my mother's bright, innocent smile. She would have been younger than Breeze when the photo was taken.

"You were right; your mom has the same green streaks in her hair," Breeze remarked. "You look really similar to her."

"Except she was much prettier," I clarified. Shim snorted, but he didn't say anything. My eyes were glued to the image in the photo.

"I wonder if they wrote anything on the back," Skylar injected into the somber silence. "They used to do that back then. Write about the people in the photo. Break open the frame."

Shim flipped the frame over. The back of the frame was completely carved. The top was engraved with an intricate design, and around the edges were the carved names of all the people in the photo. I reached out to touch my mother's name. Shim ran his finger over the design at the top.

"This design is the same as the one from the watch." That got everyone's attention. He had spent a lot of time studying the watch, so he would know. Under the frame's design, the words "finding home, July 1995" had been engraved.

"Hey, where is everyone? Dudes," Jaxon yelled down from the deck. "You need to check this out." We all followed the sound of his voice up the stairs.

Up on deck, Jaxon was clutching the edges of the newspaper. His skin was still grey, but he had an intensity in his eyes that got everyone's attention.

"You know all the research I did to try and find which geologist they might have met with? Well, that was one of them." He punched the paper. "Looks like someone else was doing research too...and they got there faster." He held a fistful of newspaper out. Shim pulled it from him and read aloud:.

*Friday, prominent geologist Carl Stringham died at the
age of 82. Winner of the prestigious Vetlesen Prize for
scientific achievement, his passing is a loss to the entire
scientific community.*

*Well-known for his controversial theories of life on other
planets and Earth's role in the universe, he was adamant
in his support of the use of meteoritics, the study of meteorites, to explain Earth's geologic history.*

*"His research did more to further our understanding of
the planet than any other discovery in the last 100 years.
The theories he put forth revolutionized our thinking of
our place in the universe," said his research partner, Sid
Cambridge.*

*The last surviving member of his family, Stringham is
mourned by his colleagues at the Clarkton University
and his research partner, Sid Cambridge.*

*While no foul play is suspected, the cause of death is not
being released by the coroner at this time.*

Jaxon pointed to Stringham's portrait. "I have a list of dudes
in the right place in the 1990s and with the right specialties. But
he was the one I was betting my money on." Waves of frustration rolled off Jaxon, and in spite of the gray pallor, he looked
like he wanted to punch something again.

"Are you sure? The guy was eighty years old. He probably
just died of natural causes," Shim said.

"Of course I'm sure. And after Lincoln, do you still believe
in coincidences?" Furious, Jaxon grabbed the paper back. We
had all been surprised with how passionate Jaxon had become

in tracking down the geologists that had met with our parents and had been happy to turn the research over to him; the search kept him distracted while we were waiting for Lincoln to contact us. I hadn't thought he would find anything after all this time. But Jaxon had dived into it like he was possessed. He spent hours on the coffee shop's computers and working late into the night on our borrowed tablet. He memorized the names of all the prominent geologists in the Pacific Northwest and knew most of their bios.

"This guy, Sid Cambridge, he was one too. I know you will think I'm just trying to get off this damn boat, but I think we should start with him...now."

"Where is he?"

"Clarkton University, in Portland."

"Well, that's why we are in Astoria. It certainly wasn't the easiest harbor to get to, but it's about two and a half hours inland to Portland from here. You said there were people on your list from Seattle to Portland. But the longer we stay on this boat, the better chance someone will connect it to Lincoln and catch up to us."

"So what are we waiting for? Let's go to Portland," Jaxon exclaimed.

20

STUMPTOWN

I WOKE with the fuzzy-headed disorientation I always got when I took a nap. Yawning, I stretched my arms over my head. A "Welcome to Portland" sign on the side of a building slid by the window as the bus pulled in and stopped. We disembarked onto the bricks of Pioneer Courthouse Square. As the passengers started to spread out and disperse, the twins immediately rushed to share intel they had gotten from the Clarkton University alumni they had met on the bus. The former student had suggested we hop on another bus that would cross the Willamette River and take us up to the University.

We started for the pickup spot when Jaxon put a hold on everything.

He snapped our burner phone shut. "The prof called in sick today. They say it isn't unusual on days he doesn't have classes." His lip curled up in disgust, and he stamped his foot in anger. When that didn't help, he kicked a trash can, barely noticing when the older man next to it jumped in surprised and scowled at him. "He's scheduled for classes tomorrow. We just have to try again then."

"We should find a place to stay," Shim suggested

Simultaneously, Skylar and Breeze said, "We should hit Voodoo Doughnuts." The three stared at each other. "Jinx! We win. Let's get directions." The twins raced off to the Visitor's Information kiosk.

"This isn't a vacation," I protested weakly to their backs.

"I don't care if we sleep in a tree or eat doughnuts till we hurl, as long as it doesn't involve water or a boat," Jaxon growled and followed them.

"Give me a minute. I'll meet you back here." Shim turned around and headed to the opposite side of the plaza where a couple of guys were skateboarding. When Shim returned, he had found us a room for the night. It was dive-y, but they liked cash and didn't ask for ID.

The twins took over the rest of our "vacation" day, and I relished not being in a charge for a change. We followed them through the city, people watching, checking out fountains, and stopping at the brightly colored food carts at Fifth Ave and Oak Street. This was a kind of a surreal vacation from our "real life" of evading kidnappers and investigating our parents' disappearance. Or was this real, and the running-for-our-lives the surreal? We had been on this journey long enough that I wasn't sure anymore. But having something normal for a few days, even a few hours, felt good.

I remembered when I was nine and we stayed on land for the first time in ages. While the boat was being repaired, we had moved into an apartment for a month. It was supposed to be a glorious time. I had it all planned out in my head: no moving from berth to berth, a huge, green field in the back to roam through, and there would be other kids there. Living on a boat, I rarely got to meet other kids. I was looking forward to making friends. But the reality was much different. The neighborhood had already formed its own cliques, and I was most definitely not a part of them. My mom had always homeschooled me, but now, she had to get a job to help pay for the boat repairs. I was on my own. And since we were on land, she wanted me outside as much as possible. I spent most of that summer month sitting on a broken piece of sidewalk while a group of kids mocked me for my funny hair, odd accent, and any other weird thing they could think up. It was really just a warm-up for high school. When the repairs on the boat were delayed, meaning dad couldn't pay for them, my misery was extended. I began to wonder—was this neighborhood my reality and life on the boat a surreal dream, or was it the reverse?

THE SKY WAS GREY OVERHEAD, and a fine mist of rain started to fall. I pulled up the hood of my jacket. Sky and Breeze did the same. Shim and Jaxon left theirs down, the water soaking into their hair. I caught myself watching Shim time and again as the rain hit his head, soaking into his hair, the dampness tightening the curls at his nap. My eyes traced a drop of water coalescing at the end of a dark curl before dropping down to his nutmeg skin and into the collar of his shirt.

I somehow missed the unicycle pulling out in front of us, causing Shim to stop suddenly. I plowed into his back, hard, pushing him into Breeze, who knocked into Jaxon. Jaxon scowled. Breeze yelped.

"Sorry." My face heated. I ducked my head and waited for them to start walking again when I realized we were at the back of a line of twenty people waiting under a pink sign reading, "Voodoo Doughnuts."

The rain stopped while we waited. Breeze and Skylar

tutored us on the doughnut selection; it was obvious they had done a lot of research as they kept up a discussion on the merits of our options, each word more animated, as if they were getting a high from the sugary air wafting from the vents above us. Instead of looking at the tourists in line, I watched the locals on the street. Mutton chops and handlebar mustaches. Rolled cuffs and layered jackets. Cyclists with helmets and slick jerseys. Each person had their own unique style of dress complemented by creative tattoos, makeup, and retro hair. Their backdrop was the wall mural across the street that read, "Keep Portland Weird."

"Not that I don't love seeing the city, but why aren't we looking into one of the other scientists? Why are we waiting around for this one?" Breeze posed the question while keeping her eyes glued to the sugary display case.

"This is the only one in Portland. We would have to leave the city, go north to the next one, and then the next one, and come back to this one at the end if none of the others pan out," Shim explained.

"No, man," Jaxon exclaimed. "This is the one. I'm telling you." He pulled off his bag and shoved his skateboard out of the way. Unzipping the top, he pulled out a handful of surprisingly tidy papers.

"This is a list of all the universities and institutions that would have had geologists on staff. There are a couple of private companies in there too. Waters said they saw a 'fancy school' geologist so I've been focusing on the universities, and they are easier to track. I found every university, college, and certificate program in the region that had a geology program, found their staff lists online, matched them up with the dates we are talking about. Some of the old geezers are long gone. Can't do nothing about that. But a few of them, based on the info I've found, fit what we are looking for. And Stringham, he was it, I'm sure of it. And we just missed him." He fell back against the wall behind him and slapped a hand on the sparkly bricks. "I can't believe we missed him."

Shim took the papers and shuffled through, pulling out one. "So, we are waiting to see his assistant, Sid Cambridge?"

"Yeah, it's worth it. I swear," Jaxon said, his face earnest.

"So what are we going to do with the rest of our day?" I asked.

"You know, since we have the time, we could go check out Burnside." Jaxon's face lit up.

"Of course." Shim snorted.

"It's on the schedule." Breeze wiggled her eyebrows and refused to give our more details about the day's itinerary.

Jaxon was a puzzle. He usually wore his angry nonchalance like a protective cloak. But he was an excellent investigator and had dug into the research like a bulldog. This was my first trip to Portland, and the city—like the doughnuts—was a revelation. From prim and proper to weird, pristine to gritty—all the elements fit together as if they required the other to come into their own fully. Kind of like our group. I was starting to understand how my mother could learn to call strangers family.

We had long since licked the sugar off our fingers by the time we made it into the huge concrete box with an enormous red and white striped "Powell's Books" sign on the front. Inside, it was a reader's wonderland. A multi-level, multi-floor smorgasbord of all things print. My head did a happy dance the minute we walked through the doors, and the smell of ink and paper hit. We pushed farther into the store, past the subdued chaos of the checkout to the inner sanctum. It was quieter here, with only hushed voices and the *wisp, wisp, flip* of pages being turned. My pulse sped up. So many stories to read.

As I wandered around, floor after floor, I quickly and willingly lost myself and the others.

"How the hell long are we going to stay here?" With a dramatic collapse, Jaxon was suddenly lying prone on the floor with a martyred expression on his face, uttering exaggerated moans. "I've read all the good manga and magazines they have, had two drinks, and walked every floor. We've been here forever." I checked the clock. Forty-five minutes had passed since we arrived.

"Knock it off." I smirked.

"That's what I'm trying to do," Jaxon countered, pretending to pull his head off his neck and throw it like a bowling ball. Then he chased after it and disappeared.

Shim found me next. I was in the last row of the Science and Mathematics area. I had taken off my jacket and wadded my long hair into a messy ball on my head and was digging through books on astronomy.

"There you are." Strands of hair flew loose when I spun around at the sound of his voice. He smiled and lowered his voice before he added, "Jaxon's going apeshit, and I promised him a stop at Burnside."

"He found me too."

Shim had reached my side now, and suddenly, I felt self-conscious being alone with him in the narrow space, which was an odd reaction since the five of us had been crammed on the sailboat for so long. He was chewing on his lip when he spied something over my shoulder. "Hey, that's what I came here to find." He pointed up to a shelf at least three feet over my head to a copy of *The Practical Encyclopedia of Rocks & Minerals.* Shrugging out of his backpack, he dropped it to the floor and grabbed a footstool. Dragging it over, he stepped up, stretching as he reached for the book. He just missed it. "Damn."

"Maybe I can reach it," I offered.

"No way. Besides, you aren't as tall as me," Shim said.

"Excuse me?" I tilted my head and stared.

"Yeah, alright, you're the same height as me." I shook my head at his silliness. I was at least a half inch taller than him. He punched up and grabbed the book with the tips of his fingers, going Odell Beckham Jr. on the book. He latched on and held. Then the footstool tilted. He flailed, windmilling his other arm as he started to fall. I grabbed him from behind. My arm was wrapped low around his hips, his shirt riding up and my hand splaying across his stomach. He grabbed at my arm for support, and I could feel his stomach muscles clenching. I was fascinated with the contrast of his caramel skin against the pale skin of my arm. It looked like I'd never seen the sun he'd been blessed by.

He stood there, catching his breath. I suspect he was trying to get his cool back, muscles flexing as he held my arm in place longer than it needed to be. There was something comforting about Shim, grounding. I took a minute to appreciate the sensation. Before I knew what I was doing, my head dropped against his back. He smelled like fresh mint mixed with the ink and paper smells of the store. Color rose in my cheeks when I realized I was sniffing him. *Oh Stars,* how embarrassing. I let go.

He held on.

"You trying to save me?" He sounded teasing, but his voice was husky. "You should know I don't go in for that white horse crap."

I laughed. With his arm holding tight to mine, I was pressed against his hard back. The rumble of his voice in his chest sent my mind reeling.

He cleared his throat and pulled away, stepping down he said, "To be fair, I should probably tell you..."

At the same time as I asked, "So, what have you got there?" I stepped back, uncertain.

He looked like he was going to say something else, then

changed his mind. "Geology." He raised the book in his hand. "I thought maybe we could find the stone in here somewhere. It might give us an idea of where it could be from."

"Clever! That would give us an advantage when we talked to the professors. But I should let you know, I've been researching that stone for years, and I've never seen anything like it." I stepped back further, giving Shim room.

Shim balanced the book on an empty shelf and turned to the specimens section. I pressed in closer, and we bent our heads over the pages as he flipped through them. I pushed past the awareness of his warm body next to mine and tried to focus. Gradually, we both got lost in the book with me slapping his hand if he turned a page too quickly.

"There you are." From down the book stacks, Jaxon stuck his head into the aisle. "It's time. Let's go," he demanded. He looked suspiciously between the two of us sitting closely together, before stalking off, turning back, his eyes bulged. "Come on."

Shim stretched his back, looping his arm behind his head and massaging his stiff neck. "Wow, how long were we reading that book?"

"I lost track of time." I stretched beside him. "As I expected, we didn't find anything even close to what we are looking for."

I watched Shim shake himself as he considered my words. "Yeah, nothing seemed like it was even in the same classification. The closest was Bloodstone, but it doesn't have the silver." I thought about our stones. The reddish-green color was common, but nothing had the silver threads, let alone the ability to let people talk to each other's mind, though I'm not sure they would put that feature in a book.

"Maybe we are looking in the wrong section." I examined the bookstore's list of sections on a nearby sign.

"What do you mean?" Shim closed the book and climbed

the step to reshelve it. This time, he managed a more graceful dismount.

"Well, maybe we should have been looking in Astrology or something in Electrical Engineering."

"Yeah, maybe. Let's check that next time," Shim readily agreed. I hid my smile as Jaxon dragged us out of the bookstore.

21

BURNSIDE

BURNSIDE SKATE PARK was a series of concrete pits lovingly crafted under a bridge. Graffitied covered every inch that wasn't skateable. The community-maintained skate park was colorful and tidy.

Jaxon blindly handed his bag to Shim. He grabbed his board and stood on a flat slab of concrete at the edge, just off the parking lot, watching for several minutes before he rode his board down, then up the slope to where the locals hung out by the chain link fence that circled the park and introduced himself. A few minutes later, he was in the rotation, taking turns dropping into the large bowl.

Knowing we were going to be here a while, we settled onto a wide concrete ledge to the left of the concrete observation slab, out of the way, but with a great view. This was most definitely not a park for the inexperienced. There were no signs listing pad requirements or supervision, which I had seen at other parks. There were other differences too. Everyone here was in their late teens or older. We were by far the youngest. A hand-made sign said, "No Bikes, No Scooters, No Booze."

The local guys looked edgy, wearing faded T-shirts and with

holes torn in their jeans—the kind of holes you get from wear, not from the mall. The girls were hardcore in tight jeans and tanks. One had a muscle shirt with the sides ripped out, showing a lace bra and a tattoo down the side of her ribs. There wasn't a lot of talking; they weren't unfriendly, just intensely focused.

Breeze and Skylar sat leaning against each other, back-to-back, Breeze with her nose in a book, facing out to the parking lot and Skylar with his eyes tracking each skater. Shim stood down on the observation slab, also watching the skaters.

Crack! A skater hit the wall hard, slipping off his board, which slid down the slope without him. Popping up, he chased after it, jumping on and immediately trying the same trick again.

I settled in next to Breeze and Skylar, meaning to watch the skaters, but my gaze kept landing on Shim. I found myself studying him as if we had just met. Plain gray T-shirt—I had never seen him wear anything with a logo—blue jeans low on his hips, looking good without being too tight or loose; and plain black kicks. He had his arms comfortably hanging at his side. I considered his face. He winced when the guy wiped out again. His jaw was set, his tiger-eyes alert. He wanted to be out there, too, but was holding back from asking Jaxon for his board. Eventually, Shim sat down on the slab of concrete, his back to me. I thought I was safe in my observations, then he glanced over his shoulder and caught me staring. My eyes widened as he stared at me, unsmiling, his eyes intense.

Oh Stars. Unnerved by the steady way he held my gaze, I wondered what he was thinking. I was confused by what I had felt in the bookstore, and I didn't like the feeling. This would be a good time for a distraction, to focus on anything other than thinking about what had happened at the bookstore.

"What do you think we will find at the University tomorrow?" Breeze interrupted my thoughts.

"I hope this dude will give us an easy answer to what is going on so we can be done with this. Like it was all a misunderstanding, and the parents are at a rock and mineral show and just forgot to tell us," Skylar grumbled, his eyes not leaving the skaters.

"Hmph, you think it's that easy? Besides wearing the cuff, do you ever remember Dad showing any interest in rocks?" Breeze turned slightly to look over her shoulder at Skylar.

"No," Skylar admitted. "I just said that's what I hoped would happen."

"Honestly, I can't imagine our dad doing any of these things: living in the streets with Waters, sailing a boat down the coast with Lincoln, even being close to any foster siblings. He never mentioned any of it." Breeze shrugged her shoulders in frustration.

"Maybe we never asked," Skylar whispered, then cleared his throat. "Grace, what about your mother? She ever mention something like this? Is she a daredevil?"

"Stars, no." I thought about the best way to explain it. "My dad always called her a 'gentle soul.' I can't even imagine her living with Waters. Music and the ocean were her things. Not rocks. She could sail down the coast, no problem." I thought a moment. "I don't know why she never mentioned having brothers and sisters of her heart. That's what she used to call people she loved. I was always daughter of her heart, and there was this one old guy that came around when I was young that she called father of her heart. But she was always adamant she had no family. Neither of my parents did. I was homeschooled, and I wasn't around other kids, so I didn't know it was strange, and I guess I never thought to ask." How could I have never asked?

"Shim, do you have any other family? Does anything we've learned seemed like something your mom would do?" Breeze asked Shim, who was leaning back on his elbows, keeping one eye on the bowl and the other on our conversation.

After a long pause, Shim shrugged. "Nope, no family, just a psycho dad and a slightly less crazy brother." He sat up and stretched, looking like a big cat as he gazed out at Jaxon taking a turn in the bowl. "Even the rock is odd. It's obviously a rare stone, which just doesn't fit. Kindle is very particular about her look."

"What about Waters or the boat?"

"Waters—yeah, I guess I could see that. When she loves you, she is very protective." He looked across the park at Jaxon, then back at us. "The boat? Well, she loves water about as much as Jaxon." We were all happy to be able to laugh now Jaxon wasn't green and hurling over the side of the sloop.

"I'm hungry." Breeze pouted. A new skater climbed up on the slab next to Shim and overheard.

"You from 'round here?" the new guy asked. We shook our heads cautiously, but he didn't seem put off by our reserve. "You should try Big-Ass Sandwiches. They got a trailer parked about three blocks that way." He pointed off the opposite side of the park, then launched his board over the rise to the others, our muttered thanks getting lost in his departure.

We took his advice. When Breeze and I got back about thirty minutes later, the brothers and Skylar were the only ones left in the park.

Jaxon was giving Skylar a lesson, whose previous experience was apparently acquired on flat land. Jaxon showed him how to drop in and then how to fall without hurting himself.

Breeze kept yelling out for him to be careful. After a couple tries, Skylar was able to drop in and attempt a trick. A second later, he was lying prone at the bottom of the bowl.

Skylar took Jaxon's offered hand.

"You didn't do it. You were right on the edge, as close as you could get without grinding. Just got to practice a clean ollie, then you'll get the 50/50. Give it another try." Skylar tried several more times and finally got the move just as more people arrived at the park. "See, you found your groove." They exchanged a fist bump as he handed Jaxon back the board and headed over to where the rest of us were eating enormous sandwiches. He had a huge grin, a split lip, and a bruise coming up on his cheek, but he kept smiling, even through Breeze's fussing.

A misty rain started again, but the bowl stayed dry, tucked up under the bridge. The newcomers spent a lot of time stomping and sliding their feet on the concrete to dry their soles. This group was more experienced, and they started running different areas at the same time. One of them had a professional video camera and was recording tricks while he chomped on a thin cigar. Their boards were like Jaxon's—scraped-up, and not light on design and stickers. Jaxon took a couple more runs, then stopped for a break.

Shim asked to borrow his board, and when Jaxon handed it over, Shim quickly dropped with a "Hoo-wah" into the bowl. He took a few slow runs to get a feel for things, then slid up on a perch on the other side to see where he wanted to go next. He was amazing to watch. He flowed gracefully up the side to land on his feet and grab the board, I was reminded of a bird, flying high for visibility and speed and then swooping low for prey. He dropped in and popped over a lip. I took the guilt-free chance to run my eyes over his lean muscles. Every so often, I would hear a whoosh of air escape on the harder tricks.

As he arced high into the air, tossing a handplant, I heard a feminine voice next to me say "nice." I looked over.

A girl in a long tank, high-cut jean shorts, with legs up to her arm pits was watching Shim. She had dark eyeliner, and her hair was pulled back into a loose ponytail. She looked about eighteen, and she was smiling with more than athletic appreciation.

After watching Shim grind along an edge sprayed neon green, she turned to me. "Is that badass your boyfriend?"

I was surprised by how much I wanted to say "yes," but it wasn't true, and I couldn't get it out.

"We're just friends," Breeze volunteered. I wasn't sure if I should hit her or hug her for saving me from saying anything.

"Excellent." Her response drifted back to us as Tank-Top did her drop-in and headed right over to Shim, pulling up on the ledge next to where he was catching his breath. As she started chatting him up, Shim pulled his shirt up and used the hem to wipe sweat off his face, showing off rock-hard abs and tawny skin. I muffled a groan and decided it was time to get my head together.

"BZ, is your book good?" I half listened as Breeze enthusiastically described the storyline of her book, but nothing registered until sometime later, when Shim dropped back in and came over to where we sat. Landing beside us, Shim handed the board back to Jaxon, who had wadded up his sandwich wrapper and was ready for more airtime.

I didn't have to say anything. Skylar dove right in. "Wow, you were flying! Hey, what'd that girl want?"

Shim shrugged quickly, he became extremely interested in eating his sandwich. I suspected he was avoiding the question. Skylar nudged him and asked again, "What'd that girl want? She was cute. Did she ask you out?"

I kept my eyes glued on the guy with the cut-off pants doing a frontside flip.

"Invite to a party," Shim said reluctantly.

"Cool, when is it? Are we all invited?" Skylar was excited.

"Uh, no, just me," Shim muttered.

Skylar made an "oh" with his mouth. "A priiiiivate party. I get it." He gave a squeaky chuckle. "You going?"

"Of course not." I think he shot a look sideways at me, but I was concentrating on the skaters, pretending not to listen. "I got better things to do."

I realized I was holding my breath. Taking a stuttering breath, I turned and gave him a little smile, not much, but he saw it. The corner of his mouth ticked up as he bit into his sandwich.

"I'm tapped out." Jaxon landed next to us, throwing himself down onto his back on the concrete.

"What's next?" Skylar asked.

"We should leave for the University early tomorrow." Shim rapped his knuckles fondly on the concrete. We were all smiling as we headed to the room Shim had found for us.

22

CLARKTON UNIVERSITY

THE NEXT MORNING, the city bus dropped us along with a handful of students at Clarkton University's rolling green lawn. The grass was crisscrossed with white paved paths and surrounded by monumental redbrick buildings hidden in patches of Douglas-fir.

Following our campus map, we headed for the last building on the right at the back of the mall. Its brick wings spread out from a huge white central rotunda. A sign on the side of one wing read, "The School of Earth Sciences."

"This department is really prestigious, second only to Stanford School of Earth and something—I don't remember the rest of the name—in California," Jaxon filled us in.

"Grace." Shim pointed to my necklace, and I remembered I was going to remove it so the professor wouldn't recognize the stone until we were ready. I unlatched the chain and slipped off, tucking it into my messenger bag.

As we entered the hall, we left the tangy smell of pine behind. I thought, not for the first time, it would have been nice to have some advice from our parents as we went into a situation. But if any of our parents had talked to us about this, then we wouldn't need to be here now. This would definitely be a topic for discussion next time I saw my dad—if I ever got the chance to see him again. *When,* I corrected myself, *when* I saw him again.

The student population on campus was low for the summer semester. I imagined the laid-back uniform of jeans and T-shirts was distinguished from every other college campus in the country only by the color of their T-shirts, a bright yellow or blue with "Clarkton University" on the front.

Jaxon had confirmed with the department that Professor Sid Cambridge had classes today. Not wanting to risk making an appointment under our own names, Jaxon had pretended to be a high school science teacher scheduling a campus tour and visit with the professor for several of his honor students.

Passing classrooms and small offices, we followed the signs to a reception area and checked in. After a few minutes' wait, a student greeter pointed us to a set of double doors.

As department head, Sid Cambridge had a spacious office. One side was lined with bookshelves and display cases, and floor to ceiling windows covered another. A sturdy oak desk was stationed in front of a wall of degrees and award plaques.

When his assistant announced us, a charismatic man in his late fifties waved a greeting from the corner of the desk, a casual posture you could tell he often assumed from the multiple circular impressions his butt had left in the piles of term papers and dissertations on the surface. Tall and lean, with a full head of gray hair pulled back into a low, rakish ponytail, he wore a fitted western shirt with pearl buttons tucked into faded, field-worn jeans. Ankle-high cowboy boots with pointed toes swung against the edge of the desk. He posed for a moment on his desk, then stood, and, with a wide, toothy grin, reached out a hand to shake each of ours as we came closer.

If this was the university our parents had come to, then

Cambridge would have been an assistant professor at the time, working with his mentor, the legendary—according to Jaxon— Carl Stringham. Jaxon's research had shown that over their careers, the two of them had promoted some revolutionary and controversial ideas in planetary geology.

We introduced ourselves, using one of the fake identities the twins had put together. Shim and I were seventeen-year-olds, Shane and Gwen, looking for colleges to apply to and the others were our younger siblings. After the pleasantries, Cambridge broke into a history of the department and the importance of its culture and philosophy in influencing geology at an international level. To keep myself awake, I studied the plaques and photos on the wall. Several showed Sid and an older man together, presenting at conferences, shaking people's hands, or digging in desert locations.

Cambridge asked about Shim's and my background in science. What classes had we taken? *None.* Where did we see ourselves in the future? *Hopefully not dead.* Were we aware of the different types of programs available? *Couldn't care less.* He gave a casual glance at the watch on his wrist while we both gave plausible, rehearsed answers. At one point, he asked, "So Shane, what other universities are you looking at?"

Shim had been studying a photo showing Cambridge and Stringham digging at a meteor crash site. Covered in dust and sweat, they had victorious smiles and were holding a pock-marked grey rock between them the size of a baseball.

"Yeah, *Shane.*" Jaxon gave an aggressive kick to Shim's chair to get his attention. "What other universities have you checked out?"

Stiffening and turning back to us, Shim floundered. "Uh, we've just started looking."

A smirking Jaxon took the opportunity to re-direct the conversation as we had planned.

"I read an article you and Professor Stringham co-wrote," Jaxon started. "Can you tell me where you got some of your ideas on meteorites as conduits for energy?"

We tuned in and tried to follow Cambridge as he pontificated on his theories and the many conferences where he had presented his ideas.

"But," Jaxon drilled down, "you stated you and Professor Stringham had found proof meteorites were conductors. Where's the proof?"

Cambridge paused in the recitation of his list of most recently published articles and the prestige they brought to the university. Clearly, he was not accustomed to being interrupted.

"We are just such big fans of your work. So many people don't understand the contributions you and Professor Stringham made to the field," Shim followed up. "It would make our whole trip if we could see the evidence you found."

Cambridge rose up from the desk edge and paced around to the back, using the desk as a barrier to shut us down.

"The meteorites we have collected have all been extensively studied by experts, and their properties and chemical structure included in our published work. They are far too valuable to keep around the office." He wound back up to continue his recitation of his contributions to the field.

While Cambridge went on for another twenty minutes, I looked at Jaxon, taking his lead on what to do next. His eyes were narrowed, his freckled face tight in concentration. Finally, his reddish-brown head bobbed as he nodded at me. Waiting until Cambridge had turned away to point at several of his framed photos, I pulled the necklace from my bag sitting on the floor, slipped it around my neck, and pulled my collar up to cover it.

Apparently, the professor didn't need to breathe like normal people. He could probably have talked about himself for days, so when he finally paused for air, Shim quickly stepped in, praising his work and feigning an interest in following in his footsteps.

"You know, I've never seen an actual meteor," Jaxon chimed in.

"Would you like to see one?" This was the introduction we were waiting for.

"That would be great." Skylar and Breeze, who had been silent through the meeting, chimed in that they also would like to see a meteor.

"Well, now I do have a few small ones I can show you." At our vigorous nods, he went over to one of the old wooden cabinets against the far wall and started pulling out flat file drawers. He went through four before he found the one he was looking for. He motioned us to join him at the waist-high drawer. "We finished testing these a long time ago. I use them for teaching purposes now. All of these samples are from asteroid collisions, and the pieces were found in the Southwest over the last fifty years or so."

We crowded around him, *ohhh*-ing and *ahhh*-ing at the collection. Breeze and Skylar were laying it on thick while Jaxon remarked on the different colors and textures of the stones.

On cue, I faked a revelation "Hey, these look like the rock in that necklace I bought in the antique store yesterday." It didn't really, and when Cambridge didn't appear very interested, Shim shook his head at me.

"Forget it, Gwen. These are real meteors, not some fake plastic."

"Hey, mine could be real." I pulled back my collar, showing off the necklace. "What do you think, Professor? Have I got a real meteor?" I gave my best wide-eyed and innocent look. It had to look completely fake.

We watched Cambridge's face as he glanced at the necklace. There was a flicker of emotion on his face, a widening of his eyes. It had only lasted a second before it was covered up. But I saw it. Then, with a patronizing air and an exasperated sigh, he put his hand on my shoulder and another on Jaxon's head and tousled his spiky hair. We froze, and Jaxon's cheeks flushed. The grip was loose, but the intent to patronize could not be missed.

"Well, young lady, I'd be happy to look at it for you." I held my breath, waiting to see if Jaxon would keep it together, or if he was going to go ape-shit at being manhandled. Plastering a huge fake smile on his face, Jaxon ground his teeth until I could hear his molars crashing together. My smile was more of a grimace, but I slipped off the torc and handed it over. Fortunately, Cambridge was so busy pretending nonchalance and fronting a casual interest he didn't notice, but I had seen the gleam in his eye the minute he touched the jewelry.

Cambridge turned his back on us and went over to his desk. He pulled out a cloth and a pair of gloves. Spreading the cloth out on the desk, he gently lay the necklace on top. He put on the gloves and pulled the swivel lamp over. After several minutes of examining the stone, he turned off the light and stood up.

"Sorry, dear, it's just your garden variety jasper." His gloves snapped as he removed them and threw them in the trash. "It's found all over the western coast of the United States. It's a nice piece, and the setting is attractive, but I hope you didn't pay too much for it." He chuckled.

"Told you." Shim's shoulders tensed, and he turned to look at a picture on the wall. The twins were staring at their shoes, and it looked like Skylar might have bitten his tongue.

I tried to look disappointed and faked a laugh as I responded to Cambridge. "It sure does look like one of those pallasite meteorites you showed us. Are you sure it's not valuable? Have you ever seen anything like it before?"

"Well, sure, I've seen lots of jasper before. It frequently gets mistaken for meteorites." He gave a sympathetic nod. "If it makes you feel better, I can hold on to it for a few days and show a colleague."

"Oh, no, that's okay, I don't want to put you out." I said. Cambridge had been shuffling us towards the door, essentially ending our appointment. "Professor, can I have my necklace back?"

"Hum?"

"The necklace, I'd like it back." I indicated the jewelry that was still on his desk as he was shoving us out the door.

Cambridge's smile was brittle. He went back to the desk and gently picked up the piece of metal, his fingers lingering on the stone. When he turned back to us, his big smile was back in place. He handed over the necklace, wished us well, and closed the door behind us.

We were on our way out of the department when Cambridge, slightly out of breath, caught up with us again. "I forgot to ask, are you going on a campus tour next?" At our nod, he seemed to relax, puffed out a breath, and rubbed his hands together. "Excellent. Where are you and your folks staying while you are in town? Hope you are getting to see a few of the sites."

Shim was evasive. "It sure is a great town. We are staying out in the suburbs with friends who have been showing us around." At his inquiring look, we declined to add any information and said our goodbyes as we hurried down the hall.

Cambridge trailed behind us until just outside a classroom door where he was overrun by a group of undergraduate students waiting to see him.

We were silent as we left the the School of Earth Sciences and walked briskly up the sidewalk. Jaxon started to say something, and Shim made a shushing sound. We walked for several more minutes until we cleared the building. Going off the path, we walked for a while before we lost sight of campus buildings. Squeezing between two trees, we finally stopped in the center of a cleared space.

"Damn it," Jaxon burst out. "That was some next level bullshit the bastard was spewing. I knew it. I just knew it."

"He was lying," Shim concurred.

Skylar nodded.

Breeze shook her head. "Are you sure? Maybe he has never seen it before or just forgot what the stone looked like."

"He remembers something. Did you see his face? He played it off, but he recognized the stone." I was pacing back and forth in the clearing. The slippery needles crunched under my shoes, releasing the earthy scent of pine.

Shim hit right at the center of it. "But why? Why lie to us?"

"Jaxon, you said Cambridge worked with the one that died, Carl Stringham. Did he live near here?"

Jaxon nodded. "Yeah, just off campus."

My senses were all screaming at me something was wrong. Some previously dormant threat had been triggered, but I couldn't see what it was. There were times when you reflect back and think, *If I hadn't turned that corner, made that discovery, would the lack of knowledge in my life have made any difference? Would we look back to this day and question whether or not we should have turned the corner?*

I said, "I think we need to check out Stringham's house."

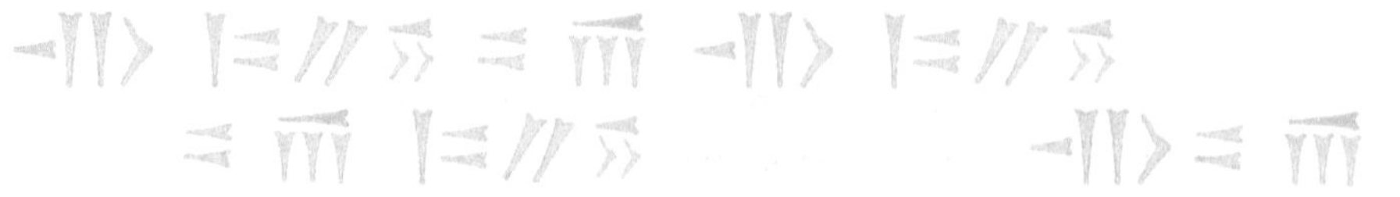

23

____

STRINGHAM'S HOUSE

THERE WAS NOTHING HERE. We had spent the last couple hours searching the two-story Victorian house and hadn't found anything connected to our parents or the stone. Frustration was high, and patience was running out. The twins were tired. Shim was still methodically searching each room, and Jaxon was flat out pissed.

Breaking into the home had been easy. The search wasn't. After nearly fifty years of scientific exploration and study, Stringham's house was like a museum. Every inch of the walls were either covered with large glass-front antique cases full of rocks and mineral samples or floor to ceiling bookcases loaded with books. We had focused the search in Stringham's study. In addition to eight shelves full of personal journals with small, cramped writing, it had twelve full-sized filing cabinets and four multi-drawer flat files. Thick rugs, overstuffed leather chairs, and antique-looking end tables filled the interior rooms.

"What are we missing?" I muttered as I walked by Shim back into the entryway. Spinning in a circle, I looked at every room leading off the entry. "Stop a second," I called out. Wearily, everyone looked up at me.

"What?" Jaxon complained.

"What are we missing?"

"We have checked everything." Jaxon slammed the door of the cabinet he had been searching. The glass panel made a loud crack, and a thin line raced up from the edge of the glass. "Damn it." The wall received a frustrated kick.

"Watch it, Jax!" Shim warned. He sank into a leather chair and looked over at me. "Not knowing what we are looking for doesn't help. It could be buried deep in these notebooks; we don't have time to read through them all."

"Not to mention it might not even be in this room." Skylar slid to the floor and sat crossed legged.

"If it was something secret, would he hide it here? Other people must have gone through here since he died—they might have taken 'it' with them." Breeze crooked her fingers on either side of her head.

Scanning the shelves, Shim sounded very thoughtful when he agreed, "There are years and years' worth of work piled up in here...wait a minute. Wait, that's it. Year." He pulled a couple of notebooks off the shelf, flipping them to the front covers. "These are all dated...but they aren't in order. What was the date our parents visited?"

"The photo was dated July 1995, so some time around then." It wasn't much, but at least it was something to go on. I was relieved. "I'll help Shim look for the notebook. You guys start at the attic and work your way down to the basement again." The twins and Jaxon groaned at having to retrace their steps for the third time. Climbing the short library ladder, I ignored them and started pulling down volumes from a different shelf.

It seemed like an eternity but was probably only thirty minutes before Shim spoke.

"Got it." Balanced with one foot on a shelf and the other on the desk, Shim had pulled down a softbound journal from the middle of the top shelf. The date was etched in pencil on the cover: *January 1995 – March 1996.*

"We've got something too." The other three burst back into the room. "Sky found it." Breeze was so excited, she started bouncing from foot to foot. "Well, we almost found something."

"It's the windows; one is missing." Shim and I exchanged a puzzled looked.

"Huh, what?"

"From the front of the house, you can see a roundish stained-glass window between the second and third floors. I remember seeing it and thinking it was a really small window for a room, but from the inside, there aren't any windows that size. I think there is a hidden room."

"That's incredible!" I said.

"And another damn thing to find." Jaxon plopped down onto the couch and put his feet on the coffee table. Pulling the lid off a crystal candy dish on the table, he sorted through and took a peppermint.

"Hey, that's a dead dude's candy," Shim protested.

"Yeah, and he ain't gonna need it since he is—you know, *dead.*"

While Shim and Jaxon argued the etiquette for eating dead people's food, Breeze and Skylar were pacing, murmuring to each other. "Must be something here." "Maybe a fake panel." "The walls don't make sense." Skylar stared at the main staircase, then, with a rush, ran up all the way up the stairs to the top floor and back again. He repeated the journey. By the time he made his third trip up and back, stopping to hop on each stair, he was out of breath, and we were all standing, wide-eyed, at the bottom waiting for him.

"I think it's time for an intervention," Jaxon muttered out of the side of his mouth, only half joking.

"Ohhhhh, I get it." And there went the other twin racing up the stairs. The rest of us stood stunned at the bottom.

When the twins didn't come down from their last trip, we went up to them. They were on the landing of the third floor, running their hands over every inch of the banister and up and down the walls. Breeze was pushing on the railing, using the light sconce on the wall next to the stairs for balance, when we all heard the loud *click*. The twins jumped off the steps.

Someone gasped, and there were a couple of "Holy Sources" uttered, as the steps rose into the air.

Without a gold pan, we had found the mother lode.

In the gap under the main steps was an opening with a narrow set of stairs down that led to a spacious L-shaped room. It was more of an archive than a workspace. Faint light trickled in through an octagon shaped stained-glass window covered in dust. Everything else in the room, with the exception of a pair of very old cabinets, was relatively clear of dust, neat and tidy. Shim reached over and turned on the light switch. Several accent lights set in the ceiling came on. Like the downstairs rooms, the walls were lined with filing cabinets and the shelves were full of journals and artifacts. Unlike the downstairs, most of the items on the shelves were, well, odd. There were pieces of clothing in sealed bags, like crime scene evidence, biohazard stickers across the front of fire-safe lock boxes, locked glass and steel cases with what looked like artifacts crafted of clay, bronze, and maybe silver, and row after row of red leather-bound journals.

I flipped open a journal that read: *June - August 1994*. "Hey, I saw this one downstairs. There must be a duplicate set of journals. I wonder if one matches the dates of our parent's visit." I continued to search the journals.

The filing cabinets were all locked. Shim examined the

locks to see if there was any way to pick the lock on them while Breeze and Skylar disappeared around the corner of the room.

"Wow...you guys have to see this." Jaxon was trying to jimmy open the lock on a glass front cabinet with a letter opener. The lock finally broke, and he flipped open the case. He reached inside and lifted out a bronze necklace that had been lying on a cushion. The center of the beaten gold medallion was set with a small cabochon, a weathered reddish-green stone with dull silver threads at its center. It was less than half the size of our stones and strung on a sturdy cord with modern gold beads.

Skylar pushed back his jacket sleeve, and he and Jaxon compared the rock in the medallion to Arie's cuff. It matched.

"That's...how is that possible?" Jaxon asked.

"Shhh..." Shim whispered, his head tilted, and we all heard the sound of a car door slamming. "Someone is here." Shim shut off the light in the ceiling. In the faint glow from the octagon window, we stared at each other until we heard the house's front door opening.

Great Source! We left our bags in the study downstairs. Whoever it was would see the bags, and we couldn't leave without them.

"Quiet." My voice was barely a whisper as I spoke to the others.

"Get ready to run," Shim added when he saw me put my mother's necklace back on and hide it under my shirt.

The twins headed up the secret stairs, and Jaxon followed, sliding the ancient-looking bronze necklace with the gold medallion into his back pocket. Silently, Shim and I pulled journals off the shelf, urgently flipped to the cover page, then discarded them until we found the one with the right date. Shim slid it into the back waistband of his jeans.

As we emerged from the hidden room, I heard a voice I recognized as Cambridge's carry up the stairs. The man was talking on the phone to someone. My chest seized as Shim stepped out of the room and leaned over the banister to hear better. Closing the hidden passage door, I quietly followed him.

"Damn it, Dawes, your men were supposed to track them...I don't give a shit about Helios' creed, this supersedes everything...listen to me: THEY HAVE A KEYSTONE. Do you understand what that means...Positive. It's an exact match to ours... I'm there trying to find it...No, I don't know where they got theirs from. They lied about buying it in some antique store..." He muttered something I could barely hear—"Teenagers ...awash in dopamine...reckless" —before he was back shouting into the phone, "Yes, I think they are connected to the original set—somehow." The conversation was muffled, and it hard to catch what was said next. Then the voice came back loud and clear. "...it takes, whoever you have to kill, find them...Yes, I'll join you in Gypsum Friday. Has Smith found anything in the diary? What?...lazy, incompetence...she's had it for weeks." There was a muffled curse, then the tone of his voice changed to a shout. "They are here—at the house—send people now!"

Something slammed against a hard surface, splintering and shattering into pieces that hit the floor, then there was the fast tread of footsteps on the stairs.

"We've got to rush him," Shim whispered, "grab our bags and head out the back. Ready?"

The twin's faces were white but resolute. Jaxon's teeth were pulled back into a mean grin, like bowling people was his favorite game and he was ready to roll. I nodded. Shim darted ahead to take the lead down the stairs.

In a crouched run, Shim plowed a path and the rest of us followed. I saw him reach Sid Cambridge first.

"What the hell—" the man exclaimed.

Cambridge fumbled with something behind his back, and

Shim added an extra shove as he pushed past him, causing the man to lose his footing. Something metal dropped. "He's got a gun," Shim shouted just as I saw the black metal object bouncing down the stairs, hitting each with a thud. Jaxon gave a head butt to the professor as he passed, then kicked the gun. It skittered down the next set of stairs and slid across the wood floor of the landing. The twins hurtled past without stopping. I brought up the rear. As I passed Cambridge, he caught my arm, and before I could block him, he wrenched me forward.

"Where do you think you are going?" With a cruel look and a sharp twist, he cranked my arm behind my back. I screamed in pain.

I was trapped precariously dangling at the edge of the step held there by my arm, my face twisting as sharp stabs of agony shot through my shoulder socket. Cambridge shoved me forward after the others, following them down the stairs, his eyes frantically searching for the gun.

"Keep going," Shim urged the others. As he turned to help me, he kicked the gun down the next flight of stairs.

A growl of rage shook from Cambridge, spittle from his mouth flying over my shoulder. But in spite of the pain, the minute my feet were on the ground, I took advantage of his distraction chasing the gun and, using Waters' self-defense training, stomped down hard on his instep. Howling in pain, he released my arm. I slammed my head back into his face, hearing an unpleasant crunch as it made contact. I rammed the elbow of my good arm into his stomach and pushed myself away from his body.

At the base of the stairs, Shim was waiting for me. I weaved toward him, and he grabbed my good arm, guiding me down the last set of stairs. In the library, Shim snatched both our bags off the floor without stopping. We shot out the back door. As our feet pounded across the lawn, the cover of trees looked miles away but was probably only a couple dozen yards. The others were at the tree line waiting for us and took off as soon as we reached them.

"A couple of cars just pulled up in front of the house," Jaxon relayed, looping back to sprint behind us.

I grimaced in pain with each step. I wouldn't be able to keep up for long.

"Jax, when is the next bus?" Shim asked. Jaxon had written the schedule on his arm that morning. But it wasn't needed as we saw the bus at the shelter.

"Now," Jaxon said, his voice grim. It looked miles away. Could I make it?

"If we catch that bus before they see us, maybe we can lose them. Jax, hold it for us. Go!"

We increased our pace, but Jaxon shot ahead. As it was, the bus had already pulled away and was trying to merge into traffic. Jaxon raced past the twins and across the street, between two cars, and over the hood of another. He jumped up and banged on the window of the bus as it tried to fill in a gap in traffic. The driver slammed on the brakes and opened the side doors to yell at him to get off. The twins jumped on board. Arguing with the driver, they held the doors open while Jaxon got on and joined the argument, delaying the departure long enough for Shim to help me wobble on board. The twins immediately paid the fair and urged the man to go. We took seats in the back while the angry driver continued to shout at us in the rear view mirror, but the bus was moving, and eventually, he turned his attention back to his route.

I lost track of who was shouting at who as I tried to breathe through my nose and slow down the pain. Shim's gaze was glued to the street behind the bus, waiting for a black car to appear or someone to race out of the woods behind us. The bus took off with a lurch. We had made it. I pushed my face into my good arm that was braced on the seat in front me. My breathing was shaky from the adrenaline rush, and I kept my injured arm cradled against my stomach. I felt Shim slide into the seat next to me. He was breathing hard. When I finally looked up, the twins and Jaxon had found seats behind us. We all sat in stunned silence for the trip back to downtown Portland. The noise of the city and the automatic inhalations and exhalations of the bus as it let people on and off muted as we got lost in our thoughts.

24

ON THE RUN, AGAIN

THE BUS DROPPED us off after the Steel Bridge on the west bank of the Willamette River. We walked around for a while so we could check for tails. Shim kept trying to get me to stop so he could check my arm. Since I didn't feel the need to throw up anymore, I told him it was getting better; the throbbing was nonstop, but the pain only radiated through my body when I moved.

Shim pulled me down an alley and behind a building.

Handing off our bags to Jaxon, he turned to me and demanded, "Take off your top."

I arched a brow at him. "Excuse me? A bit forward." I tried for a laugh, but it came out more as whimper.

Shim flushed. "I need to look at your shoulder joint. I've dislocated my arm twice. Jaxon's done it once. If that's what happened, it needs to be treated."

"No way." I stepped back.

"Raise your arm above your head, Grace." He put his hands on his hips and waited with fake patience.

I blew out an exasperated breath and stretched up my arm all the way, gritting my teeth. It raised two inches. "Arghhhh.

Oh..." I gasped, and tears burned out of my tightly clenched eyes as I clutched my arm to my chest. *Stars* above, that hurt, and it hadn't worked out as I had hoped.

"Now that you've proven you're not fine—take off your shirt."

I was panting and trying not to pass out. I managed to say through clenched teeth, "Even if I wanted to, I can't." Beads of sweat had broken out on my forehead.

"I can help," Breeze volunteered. "Grace, you have that button up shirt you wore yesterday in your bag?" At my weak nod, she instructed Skylar, "Pull out the scissors from the first aid kit."

"Might was well grab tape, the ace, and an ice pack too," Shim added, his concerned eyes staying fixed on my face as he took the items without looking and handed them off to Jaxon.

Breeze cut my shirt from neck to arm, then on each side, then she held the modified halter top in place while Shim took over, probing my shoulder and elbow and checking the joints and red welts on my wrist. I squeaked and shrilled at each touch like a cat caught under a rocker.

"Well, doc"—I panted, the pain sharp now—"how is it... owwwwie." I cringed and tried not to completely break down like a baby as he probed a tender spot.

"Not a doctor." He looked grim. "Just going off my own experience, I think it's very badly bruised but not dislocated. The joints seem okay, but you are starting to swell up. Do you think if I tape it you can keep going?"

"Yes, yes, I'll be fine. Tape it up, coach. I'll be good to go." I bragged like an injured sports hero and managed to muster a weak smile, not sure if it was convincing.

Shim gave me a measured look—one I was starting to associate with him trying to read my mind—then he nodded. He reviewed the selection Skylar had found in the kit and picked up a roll of blue tape. He took the scissors from Breeze and proceeded to cut several lengths. He had Skylar help me move my arm as he applied the tape in a complicated pattern across my arm, shoulder, and down my side. Then he took the white roll and taped the ice pack to my shoulder and used the ace to immobilize the injured arm to my side. Instead of feeling trapped, my injured arm felt supported, and I immediately felt some relief from the pain.

Breeze had the guys turn away again and she helped me get my one good arm into a new button-up shirt and my jacket. With the empty sleeve flapping around, I looked ridiculous, like I was smuggling something under my shirt on one side, but having it taped and iced helped the pain, and the other arm was a fully functional, so it would have to do.

"Okay, let's talk about the call Cambridge was making," Shim said, first handing me two pain killers from the kit, then the water to wash them down. In between swallows, I recounted the part of the phone conversation I had heard. Shim had caught the bits of it I'd missed, and we were able to piece together a pretty clear picture. Actually, it was a muddy, foggy, completely incomprehensible picture.

"So, we know Cambridge recognized the stone and reported us to someone at Helios," Jaxon summarized, and my blood ran cold at hearing the name tied to my mother's death.

"And he is working with at least two people, Dawes and Smith, and he is meeting them in a place called Gypsum on Friday," Shim added.

"He called the rocks keystones." Breeze looked thoughtful as she fingered the cuff Skylar had brought out of his bag. "That's the same word Waters used."

I didn't know what it meant that Cambridge used the same name, but it wasn't good.

"I bet Cambridge or Stringham stole a piece of the stone

from our parents," Jaxon proposed, holding perfectly still as Breeze continued to finger the cuff on his wrist.

"Or our parents stole the stones from Cambridge and Stringham. Maybe that is why they were being chased." Shim flipped the statement around, and it was an unpleasant thought.

"That doesn't sound like my mom at all," I protested.

"What do we have in our pockets now? Stolen journal, rocks, and an ancient artifact. What if the professors had already collected that old necklace and the stones, and our parents snatched the stones and made them into jewelry?" Shim replied.

Oh, Stars.

"Listen," Jaxon demanded. "I don't know why we are debating this when the important bit of the conversation was where Cambridge was ordering that we be caught or killed. Did you somehow miss *that?*"

Yes, that part we had all heard, and it added an even greater sense of urgency to find out what on Earth our parents were up to. But that wasn't the most important bit to me.

"No, the most important bit was that this Smith woman has my mother's diary. The Helios has the diary. And if they have that, then they killed Lincoln."

The grim conclusion was unsettling and prioritized our next actions. First, stay alive. Second, find Gypsum.

Jaxon didn't believe in downtime, so he had used the time Shim was wrapping my arm to hop online and look up the location of Gypsum. At this point, we were only using the burner phones for internet searches and the stones for confidential conversations. He found one place in Nevada called Gypsum Cave and another place called Gypsum in Colorado.

"Let's try Nevada first since its closer. We have resources in Vegas."

"Your da– Logan?" I quickly switched at Shim's wince.

"Yeah, we can stay at his place. He's gone on business all summer." I thought it odd the brothers hadn't thought to call Logan O'Connell earlier for help. I mean, he is their dad, and I mentioned as much.

"No, we might be in trouble now, but Logan *is* trouble."

"Calling Dad would be like calling in a volcano to fight off a tiger. He doesn't care about collateral damage," Jaxon agreed without looking at us, his eyes glued to the screen. Jaxon perked up. "There is a bus every morning and evening. We just need to get our stuff and another burner phone, then we can head out in the morning."

We had the essentials with us. The twins had their backpacks with Duchess tucked away in the third one that Jaxon was wearing. He said it was to hold his board, but he didn't like it when someone else carried Duchess. Jaxon also had my messenger bag strung across his shoulders and hanging in front.

With a goal in mind, the twins lead us as we headed to the room we were staying in. Shim positioned himself on my side by the swinging empty sleeve, and Jaxon brought up the rear.

We had covered most of the distance to the room when a huge man with gold-rimmed sunglasses, a Euro-style blue suit, and a yellow tie stepped out of an alley a few yards ahead of us. He couldn't have looked more out of place on the Portland streets. A few seconds later, I spotted another one in a charcoal grey suit with a messy do that spoke of hours in front of a mirror. Both had tattoos creeping out from their shirt collars. My gut started to churn.

The bus had dropped us off on Glisan Street. After Shim bandaged me up, we had headed south. We had planned to spend the night going through the material we had found and, after a good night's sleep, catch a bus to Las Vegas.

But those plans changed quickly.

When the third fitted suit turned up, I whispered to Shim,

"Either we have wandered into a European fashion show, or these suits are following us." Shim gave a barely imperceptible nod.

"Jax, get ready to grab BZ and Sky."

We turned a corner, out of view of the suits, and took off at a run. Jaxon snagged the twins by their arms and pulled them along as he filled them in.

"I thought it was starting to trend Italian," Skylar huffed out as he was dragged along.

After a quick dash down a side alley and two more streets, we ducked into a dark shadow beside a dumpster. Cold dread settled into my stomach as a shiny black car crawled by. Behind dark glasses, the driver scanned the crowd.

"We're being chased by the Matrix." Breeze panted as she bent over, hands on her knees, catching her breath.

We abandoned the idea of returning to the room—everything there was disposable—

and decided to take the bus out tonight. We just had to kill a few hours and not get nabbed in the process.

A man walking backwards near us caught my attention. He had a microphone and was telling the history of the area to a group of camera-wielding tourists that followed.

"Come on." I grabbed Shim with my good arm, and we all merged into the middle of the group of tourists. Perfect. Ten minutes later, when it started to mist, the tour members opened up umbrellas. Even better! Nothing says "I'm not local" like an umbrella in Portland.

The group entered a building, and each person waited their turn to descend a flight of stairs to the basement. There was another group at the entry of the building and a third already underground. In the jostle of people, cameras, and bags, I tried not to slip on the wet concrete floor. Shim gently tucked an arm around my waist, being careful not to bang into my injured arm.

At the bottom of the stairs, we followed our group through a basement as the tour guide went on about underground Portland's Shanghai tunnels. It was only as the people thinned that we realized we had lost the twins and Jaxon.

There was a moment of panic as we covertly searched the group, trying not to tip off anyone that we weren't supposed to be there.

"He isn't here." Shim's voice was tense, the way he always got when he lost Jaxon.

"I'm sure they are together, and he and the twins will turn up at the Greyhound station in two hours."

It was early afternoon, but it had been a busy day: being lied to, breaking and entering, almost getting shot at, being man-handled—or was that girl-handled?—chased, and the whole topless in an alley thing—in front of Shim. Yeah, except for all that, the tour would have been extremely interesting. But the adrenaline spike I had been running on crashed down around me in the dark, and suddenly, I was exhausted. We moved slower and slower until we finally fell to the back of the group.

"Do you think we could just stop and rest for a bit?" I asked. I could see Shim in the light from the small penlight he had pulled from his pocket.

"Sure, might as well kill those two hours here. It's cold but dry." He pulled us away from the group and into a side room. As the light of the group got farther away, the darkness closed in, and I could only see what the penlight illuminated. "Here, sit down." He shined the light on a low crumbling concrete ledge in front of a wall. After he helped me sit down, I heard the sound of fabric sliding next to me. Suddenly, arms pulled me back until I landed on muscle. Shim had slid until his back was against the wall and pulled me against him. Cushioned, it only took a minute before my eyes started to close. "This okay?" he asked. I nodded against his shirt, struggling to keep my eyes open, but the fatigue from the pain and the dark won over, and I drifted off.

I woke up sometime later in the dark with that disorienting sense of being lost in time and space. My nose was cold. Some cloth, a jacket, was draped over my shoulders, and the soft cushion under me was warm. "Where am I?"

I felt a rumble under my ear and smelled mint. More importantly, how had I ended up sleeping on Shim?

"Chased by suits, underground tunnel, you fell asleep?" Oh, that's right, I thought as my brain started to wake up, followed by a moment of all-out hyper-awareness as the rest of my senses kicked in. I felt his hand stroking my hair, and hard, warm chest muscles under my check as I curled up on my uninjured side. I squeezed my hand to move—oh crap, I quickly moved it off his thigh.

"Um, sorry, I didn't mean to fall asleep on you."

"Don't mind." Typical Shim, brief and to the point.

In the silence that followed, he flicked on the penlight. I could see his arm and the side of his chest in the glow from the beam. He had brought one of his feet up onto the concrete ledge, probably to support me better while I slept. My brain exited the post-sleep mush and started to whirl, and words just fell out of my mouth. "I miss my bag. I know Jaxon will take care of it, but, you know how you get used to having something all the time around you, and then when it's gone, you feel like something is missing?" My brain wasn't awake, but my mouth was, and I rambled on about the bag, unable to shut off my mouth or my nerves from being this close to Shim. "Have you ever noticed how disorientating it is to wake up in a strange place?" I kept my head on his chest, my cheek rubbing against his soft shirt while I spoke.

"Grace." Shim chuckled softly. I stopped speaking. "Grace." He tugged at my chin, his hand steady as he pulled my face up to look at him. The glow from the flashlight gave a harsh shadow to his features: round cheeks, straight nose, strong jaw. My good arm was trapped under me, or I would have reached up and pushed his dark brown curls aside so I could see if his amber eyes glowed like a cat's in the dark. With a slight smile, he shook his head, a little bashfully, and the hair fell back. They didn't, but even in the darkness, I could see the intensity in his eyes.

"I need to tell..." Before he could finish, I pushed up on my good arm, and my mouth touched his, my breath catching his words. His lips were soft with just the right amount of fullness as I pressed into them. He held back, surprised at first, then surrendered and returned the pressure. I loved the feeling of warmth and the tingle that went through me. He turned his head slightly for a better angle. There was an awkward moment where I tried to find an angle that worked, then we clicked into place with the satisfaction of putting in a lost puzzle piece. His mouth opened on mine and our tongues tangled, tentative, brief, before Shim pulled back.

Moment of silence, then, "You okay?"

I bit my lower lip, smiled, and nodded. "Uh huh." I said, then my lips returned to his. He met me. We were better this time, his sigh vibrating into the friction of our mouths moving against each other. His lips parted, catching my moan and deepening the kiss. I didn't remember doing it, but my good arm braced on the concrete under me, pushing me closer to him, closer to his lips. *Holy Sources, this was a kiss!*

He parted my lips and tugged on the bottom one with his teeth, then licked the spot. I chased his tongue, and we met in a heated open mouth kiss that made something deep in my stomach ache. His hand gently rubbed along my back, sliding up into my hair and cupping the back of my head, pulling me gently closer, before he seemed to remember he had wanted to talk and tried to pull back.

"Grace, really, I need to tell you..."

"No." I shook my head, then snuggled down on his chest. "I'm so done with talking and bad news and chaos." All the craziness could just go to H-E-double hockey sticks. I wanted one thing in my life to stay simple. "It doesn't have to mean anything. It doesn't have to be anything. It just is. No talk."

"But..."

"What did I say?" I challenged, refusing to leave my perch on his chest and look up at him again. I wasn't hurting. Actually, I felt great. We weren't being chased, for the moment, and we were alone.

He snorted a laugh. "Okay." He leaned back in.

A while later, it was the sound of shuffling feet and talking that broke us apart. Shim switched off the penlight, and we froze, breathing heavily, and listened. The glow of flashlights coming down into the basement broke the darkness.

"We really need to go meet the twins and Jaxon. We should join this group," Shim voiced reluctantly.

"How long was I asleep?"

"About an hour. I used your necklace to contact Jax. They are safe." I'm glad he had thought to do that. With the pain in my arm, I had completely forgotten. I was a terrible leader. Good thing I wasn't in charge. "They are getting food, but we need to get to the station and buy the tickets. How is your arm?"

"Better, actually. The tape and the ice pack really helped." I sat up.

Before the tour group caught up with us, he took back his jacket and handed me the remaining two painkillers from the package in his pocket and what was left in our bottle of water to chug them down. Switching off the light, we moved to the front of the storage room and positioned ourselves behind a wall. As the tour group passed, we switched our light back on and joined them.

As we followed the group, I found myself smiling. I couldn't help it. I tried to wipe it off my face, but it persisted. After all, I was the stupid one that came up the whole "it doesn't mean anything." I drank more water and concentrated on listening to the tour guide's narration. Nope, still there. My lips seemed permanently curled up at the edges. As I felt Shim's arm around my back, pulling me close, I looked over at him. He was grinning too. That just made my smile bigger.

25

BUS TO VEGAS

SHIM WAS STRESSED. The minute we arrived at the bus station, he started pacing back and forth across the dirt-brown tiles, eyes inspecting everyone that came close while searching for the familiar face of Jaxon. He had the necklace and kept checking in to see if they were trying to contact us. I tried to get him to stop moving. His nervous energy was starting to attract the type of attention we didn't want. But, he couldn't stay still.

The bus station was red brick, not the historic style that adds value to a building, but the industrial kind they use to make post offices and police stations. Conveniently located next to the train station, it was the convergence of people in flux between where they were coming from and where they were going, between old lives and new ones, people with baggage just waiting. Like us.

Shim started another loop. I could tell he was on his last nerve when Jaxon, Breeze, and Skylar finally arrived. There was no time for explanation. They had announced our bus's last call, and the end of the line was boarding when we rushed to the door. There was an anxious moment as Shim showed our tickets, his fake ID, and the parental permission papers he had forged for Jaxon and the twins. Then they let us on. Few seats were left. Shim found two together in the middle of the vehicle. Jaxon looked surprised when Shim ushered me into one of them and put his bag on the other. He grumbled but found a seat across from us. Skylar and Breeze had to split up into consecutive window seats, Breeze directly behind me.

It was still light out as the bus pulled away from the terminal. I was struggling to get my jacket off; Shim took his seat and turned to help me.

Once settled, Breeze handed sandwiches and sodas forward through the crack between the seats. I was starving. While we inhaled the food, Jaxon leaned across the aisle and filled us in on what had happened after we split, with Breeze injecting details he omitted.

Caught up in the other tour group, the twins and Jaxon had left the underground tunnels. Once on the street, they bumped into the suits again. They had spent the better part of an hour racing through back alleys, up fire escapes, over fences, and finally hid hanging off the side of a bridge incline.

"Sources, Jax." Shim groaned at how close they had come to getting caught. He reached for his brother like he needed some connection, a pat on the arm something to confirm Jaxon was okay. The concern was shoved right back at him, and the pushing ended with an unpleasant word from Jaxon's seatmate.

I reached my good arm between the seats, back to Breeze and squeezed her hand. When Breeze asked what we had done, I blushed and hemmed, and Shim choked on his sandwich. "Uh, ducked off the tour while we were underground, and, uh... we stayed there for a while. Grace needed to rest her arm, so she, uh...took a nap."

"I can't believe we are going to be on the bus for twenty-five hours." Breeze groaned. "I already have to pee."

"There are twenty-six stops and two transfers. You'll have

plenty of breaks," Jaxon assured her with a roll of his eyes, "and there is a bathroom in the back." She wrinkled her nose at the idea.

Even though it was early evening, the rhythmic *thud, thud, thud* of the wheels on the freeway and the steady side-to-side rocking lulled me into a fretful sleep. Time passed in unknown chunks, and I barely registered the frequent stops with a half-conscious head nod and then flopped back into sleep again.

Once I woke, and I was leaning against the window with Shim's jacket under my head. I had a fuzzy memory of the woman next to Breeze leaving and Skylar moving up. I woke up another time to arguing. Jaxon was getting testy with his seatmate, and I was leaning against Shim, the armrest gone and his arm around my shoulders.

When I finally fully regained consciousness, Shim was gone.

Panic. *Did they leave me?*

I sat up fast. The pain immediately returned to my shoulder, but the throbbing had lessened. I looked around me. The bus had stopped, and most of the seats were empty. I glanced behind me and relief washed over me when I saw the twins. Breeze was curled up in the seat with her head in Skylar's lap. He was reading something on the phone. Passengers started loading, and I glanced back to the front of the bus in time to see Jaxon and Shim jumping on with bags in hand. A minute later, the bus took off again. Plucking packets of chips and cans of sodas from his bag, Shim handed them off to Skylar. He passed a magazine over to Jaxon, then pulled out a box of icepacks, took one out of the box and popping the pack to activate it; the cold was seeping through the pack when he handed it to me.

"Aw, you shouldn't have. What, no flowers? Chocolates?"

"Nah, not my style."

I smiled and slid the pack inside my shirt against my shoulder, sighing with relief at the coolness. Looking up, I caught a glimpse of my reflection in the window and cringed. I looked like an owl, my eyes blinking with sleep, hair all tufted up. Horrified, I tried to smooth it down with my good hand. One side of Shim's mouth rocked up, and he slid his hands down either side of my head, pretending to smooth out my hair for me, but just messing it up more. He laughed and pulled more painkillers and a bottle of water out of the bag. "Here are your chocolates."

As he opened the bottle, he teased, "Love what you've done with your hair." I bit back a laugh. With his curly hair and buttery-colored eyes, he was just the right combo of tough badass and sensitive, caring guy. I was afraid I was hooked.

"It took hours to get my bus do. Don't hate," I teased him back. We laughed and kept whispering back and forth in the intimate space between the two bus seats. I was an idiot for saying I didn't want to define this, to keep it simple. Something was opening up between us that was more than just friends, not defined, but fragile and beautiful in its infancy. And as much as it made my heart race, it also scared me to death.

I tried to ignore the measured look Jaxon was giving us. His eyes narrowed to slits, and his lips pursed. He punched his elbow back into his seat, pissing off his seatmate again, and they started another nasty argument. Shim told him to knock it off or we were going to get kicked off the bus, to which Jaxon demanded Shim switch seats with him. Shim refused with a glare of his eyes.

"I'll do it," Skylar volunteered with a sigh. Groggy and half-asleep, Breeze had lifted her head at all the noise, and Skylar slipped out of his seat and switched with Jaxon. Holding herself up on one arm, Breeze stared as he slid into the seat next to her, her face confused, lids blinking like fast-action windshield wipers. Jaxon rolled his eyes, then put his jacket in his lap and told her to lie back down. She complied instantly, her head knocking with a thud on his knee. The impact must not have hurt because she closed her eyes immediately.

Out of courtesy to Breeze, Jaxon used his "indoor whisper" to demand Sky swap the phone for his magazine, declaring it made the most sense for him to research Gypsum since he knew the Las Vegas area. Skylar made the swap. Relieved it was all settled, I leaned into the window and let the painkillers and ice pack do their stuff.

Later, when I woke, the bus was bouncing around in the dark. Occasionally, yellow beams of light strobed through the windows from passing headlights. Everyone was asleep, even Shim, who had his head back on the seat, his lips parted. I felt suspended in the rhythmic sound of wheels on the road, enveloped in the darkness. The glow from the LED lights running along the floor illuminated Shim's profile. I reached out to touch his full lower lip, just managing to stop myself, my hand hovering close to his face. As if sensing me, his lids half opened, and one brow cocked inquiring. Silently, I shook my head and, as best as I could while sitting up, snuggled in next to him. As my hand slid across his stomach, I felt warm skin where his shirt had ridden up. His arm went over my shoulders, pulling me in tight.

THE SUN WAS CRACKING the horizon when the bus pulled into the Sacramento station. With the vehicle stopping every hour, none of us had a restful night. We were happy to get out and stretch, shaking limbs to wake up during the bus transfer. There was a fast-food stand open near the station, and while we waited for our to-go breakfast, Breeze and I went to use the bathrooms. When we returned, Jaxon was having a stare down with Shim. They looked like they had been arguing.

We ate while waiting in line for the next bus. Our early positioning was rewarded with first pick of seats, and we grouped together in the back of the bus for better privacy and less jostling as people got on and off.

The very back row had three seats across, and I went in first, then Shim. I expected Jaxon to sit next to Shim after all the fuss from the night before, but he snubbed his brother and sat in the seat in front of us, causing Breeze and Skylar to have to split up. Breeze settled in next to Jaxon and proceeded to tease him into a better mood.

Breeze had that ability with everyone, but it was a little awe-inspiring to watch her use that magic on Jaxon. His face was relaxed, and he even had the hint of a smile curling the corners as he listened to her talk with her exaggerated hand gestures.

"Harumph," Shim grumbled and shook his head at Jaxon. He reached into his bag and pulled out the two journals we had "borrowed" from Stringham. He handed the paperback journal we had found in the library to Skylar, and he opened the red leather journal from the secret room. I listened while they started making a date-by-date comparison of the entries in Carl Stringham's parallel journals. They had been at it for at least an hour and several stops, and my attention had drifted as I tried to puzzle out in my head our next steps once we arrived in Vegas, when Shim bolted up.

"There, that's it." He pulled on Skylar's arm. "Go back and read that again."

Skylar reread the entry.

June 13, 1995 – Referral appointment to review meteor from Clark Warren. Stone turned out to be an unimportant jasper specimen.

"What's so important about that?" Jaxon and Breeze had flipped around in their seats and were hanging over the backs.

"Now listen to this." Shim started to read from the red journal.

June 13, 1995 – Today, I have made the most important discovery of my life. The stone was brought in by five students, children really, a referral to me from Clark Warren. He thought they had a meteor. This is no object fallen from the sky; this specimen is a transformative catalyst in our understanding of planetary geology. With not a single marker to indicate it breached the atmosphere, as a meteor would have to do, it has all the elements of alien origins.

Much more research is needed. However, the students will not sell me the specimen. They appear to be without means, so I have invited them to stay at my home while we continue with this research. It is a small concession to have access to this boundary-shattering discovery. This could be the missing link, so to speak, that ties the work of geologists to that of astronomers.

Over the next week, we will be doing the customary chemical testing and photomicrograph but also using mass spectrometry, and I'm even going to attempt to book time for an ultrasound.

"Wow," I said, my hand on my neck, touching the stone on my mother's necklace.

"Keep reading," Breeze encouraged.

"The next entry in the phony journal is..." Skylar flipped the page and started to read.

June 14, 1995 – I have hired one of my students, a young man named Sid Cambridge, to assist with my research. While only a graduate student, he has been resourceful and found an anonymous donor to fund my work. I look forward to working with such an eager assistant.

"At least we know Cambridge was around then," Breeze said.

Shim turned the page of the red journal. "This one has a lot more between those two dates, pages and pages. It's mostly technical jargon and chemical data from the research. I wish we had a geologist we could trust to explain this. Let me see what I can pick out..." He flipped through a few pages, back and forth. "Okay, it says here the silver veins are 'high energy conductors.'" I pulled off the necklace and examined it. Skylar had pulled up his sleeve and was looking at the stone on his dad's cuff, which, at some point, he had gotten back from Jaxon. "Something about the potential for conducting unlimited energy...that's pretty amazing..." He flipped a few more pages. "They didn't seem to know what triggers it. Apparently, while it has all the properties to conduct, when they tested it, nothing happened. So, they think there is an activator missing."

"What's an activator?" Jaxon asked.

"It's a catalyst. Something that turns it on," Shim replied.

"So what turns it on?" Jaxon asked.

"Don't know," Shim said, nose still buried in the journal.

"Activate to do what?" Jaxon persisted.

"Don't know," Shim drew the words out.

"Well, what do you know?" Jaxon jutted out his jaw.

"I know I'm going to lock you in the bus bathroom if you don't shut it," Shim returned without looking up from the book.

"We must be activators," Breeze postulated. "How else could we talk to each other through the stones?" She had a good point. We hadn't talked through the stones often, but we were all able to do it.

"Ew," Jaxon said. "That kind of freaks me out. What if using it does something bad, like Bilbo's ring?"

"It's not like Bilbo's ring," Shim insisted, nose still in the book.

"How do you know?" Jaxon challenged.

Shim looked up. "Because, unfortunately, you have not disappeared." He smirked at Jaxon's scowl. The look turned speculative. "But it's true we haven't spent much time testing the stones."

"I feel like I've stared at them forever," Breeze complained.

"Yeah, we've looked at them," Shim replied, "but in all this time, we've never tested their range, or if you could connect more than two people at the same time, or if the stones are more than just communicators."

"More?" I said. It was stunning to imagine what else they could do.

"Oh, here is something interesting." Jaxon had been reading upside down. I didn't know he could do that. "Turn it around." He grabbed at the journal and summarized, "Stringham talked our parents into letting Cambridge cut up the stone. That is why each of our parents have a piece. And it mentions Cambridge betraying them and cutting an extra slice for himself."

"Really?" Shim exclaimed. Pulling the journal back, he read aloud:

I've had this image in the back of my mind I was unable to place. I felt like I had seen something similar to this stone before, but not in the context of a meteor. Late last night, I realized where it was from. I had to hunt around but finally found the old issue of the African Archaeological Review

Journal. It had museum photos displaying a unique stone originally found on an archeological dig at Wadi Halfa in Sudan in 1907. The excavation had discovered several unremarkable ceramic bowls and wooden implements at the site, dating them to 4000 B.C., then made the find of a lifetime, discovering beads and two metal disks. There is a great deal of controversy over these necklaces because the quality of the finds and the material used is not consistent with the stratigraphy of the layer being excavated.

The description of the necklace was brief: bronze beaded necklace and a central disk with cabochon set stone in the lower half of the disk. They cited several iconographic references that refer to the necklace as a 'keystone,' but I've not seen any support for this. The other necklace was a plain gold disk with raised markings and a hole in the top. The material it was hung on had long since disintegrated. There was a photograph of the two pieces. The stone has a remarkable resemblance to the one I am studying.

I will have to pursue the private owners of these pieces and obtain permission to study them. If this rock is the same as the one in the 'keystone' necklace, the scientific implications could be staggering.

Wide-eyed, Jaxon had pulled the bronze beaded necklace out of his back pocket. "Whoa, whoa, whoa, hold it there. Is he saying my ass has been sitting on a 4000-year-old thing since Portland?" He held it out, away from his body, like he was scared it would bite him.

"No." Shim placed the journal in my lap and gently cupped the dangling necklace in his hands. "More like 6000-year-old thing." He studied the bronze disk. "Keystone—that's what Waters heard our parents say."

"Yeah, about that. Just what is a keystone?" Jaxon asked.

"In architecture, it's a center stone that locks all the other pieces together," Shim replied.

"So what does our keystone have to do with that?" Jaxon asked.

"Don't know," Shim said.

"Well, what do you...?" Jaxon started to challenge again but broke off when Shim glared at him, then eyed the bus bathroom door and raised an eyebrow.

Breeze gently took the ancient necklace from Shim's hand. "Do you think this stone works like ours?"

"One way to find out." I put my finger on my necklace. Breeze did the same with the ancient stone, and Skylar reached up to his cuff.

"Hi Skylar," said Breeze.

"Hi Skylar," I mimicked.

Skylar shouted out, "No way!" Several passengers stared back at us, and he lowered his voice. I smirked, and Skylar confirmed with an embarrassed grumble, "I heard you, Breeze, and you, too, Grace. It works."

"Which is amazing." I reached out my finger and tentatively touched the ancient necklace. "This is prehistory, from the Bronze Age—before the US was established, before Europe was a power, way before the Romans and the Greeks."

"How do you know all that?" Breeze's voice was full of wonder.

I looked up and blushed. "I, um, read a lot." I ducked my head to study the ancient necklace again. "I just don't understand how our parents got a stone a renowned geologist had never seen before that matches an ancient necklace."

Shim pulled the red journal back to his lap and flipped a few pages back and forth. "Listen to this."

June 17, 1995 – Against my better judgment, I have been coerced into taking on Sid Cambridge as my research partner. I knew his proposal of an anonymous donor to fund our work sounded too good to be true. It is through a group called Helios Funding. He says they sought him out based on inquiries he made—against my recommendation and advice—to colleagues on the chemical results from our test on the students' rock.

True, we have unlimited funding now. However, none of our work can be published except through Helios' permission structure and much of what we are expected to do, like spy on the students that brought us this specimen and do material testing on clothes the Helios send us—some of those articles of clothing had dried blood stains, the poor souls—is distasteful. The Helios group wished to speak with the students, and I am most relieved they seem to have disappeared with the rest of the sections from the rock. We still have the one piece Sidney cut illicitly for us. Our work will continue using this specimen, and we will find the truth. I don't know if the world will ever know of the discoveries we have made.

"I wonder if they ever got the stones to communicate?"

"So far, it's not mentioned in the journal, but they probably studied them for years after our parents left."

"I wonder who this Clark Warren is and how he know our parents? Where'd he meet them? How did he know to refer them to Stringham?" I asked. More puzzles to solve.

"You know, it's odd he never says our parents' names," Breeze pointed out.

"Who, Stringham? Maybe that was his way of protecting them. He hid the journals because he knew the Helios were dangerous," Shim theorized.

"Maybe," Breeze replied.

"Is anyone else feeling like we got a raw deal from our parents?" Jaxon interjected sourly. The thought had occurred to me, and from the other's faces, they had been thinking it too. We were expecting to find our parents and maybe some truth about my mother's death when this investigation started. Now it seemed the bigger mystery was surrounding her life and all our parents' lives.

"Maybe our folks were just really scared, like Waters said, and didn't think it was safe to tell us," Breeze offered.

"Maybe they didn't trust us," Skylar whispered heatedly, mindful of keeping his voice down in the bus. "Did Dad think we couldn't handle the truth?"

The others looked as upset as I felt.

Shim shrugged. "It makes sense to me. I've always felt locked out, separated by secrets from Kindle and Logan. That's just standard operating procedure for Kindle. And Logan, he just doesn't care. Even if he knew something, he wouldn't tell me." Shim looked relieved to say the truth that he had always known out loud. He glanced at his brother. "But he would talk to you. Did he ever say anything?"

Jaxon made to protest, but he dropped his head "No. I don't think he knows anything."

"We still don't know anything. That's the problem! And these journals—the more we read, the more questions I have. And they only tell us the professor's point of view. If we really want to know what happened, we need to find my mother's diary."

I felt betrayed. I had been lied to about something so monumental that it resulted in my mother's death, Shim being neglected by his father, and our parents' kidnapping. We all needed to know the truth. We needed to know where they were and what this Helios Funding Kratos thing was. We deserved that truth.

We spent the rest of the trip researching the Helios Funding group and reading through the journals. Unfortunately, there wasn't a lot more about our parents. The remaining entries were about the research Stringham and Cambridge did on the piece of the stone they had kept, and there were several entries discussing the dissatisfaction with the almost Mafia-like exclusivity of the Helios arrangement, along with a few descriptions of some of the more terrifying ways the Helios would discipline you if you disappointed them.

There was an entry dated a couple months after our parents would have left listing a male's personal effects that had been sent for study from the Las Vegas area. Those items had included clothing items, a plaid shirt and jeans, and a ring with markings similar to the gold disk from the Wadi Halfa site. Stringham had been very excited when he noted it, but he said they were unable to find a reason for the similarity.

As Shim studied the detailed drawing of the ring in the journal, he had a eureka moment. He got so excited he could hardly speak. Sitting up, he had pointed a hand at Breeze while he caught his breath.

"Holy Sources, Breeze, give me your dad's watch." Breeze dug through her bag and handed it over the seat to Shim. We all stared as he lay the journal in his lap, then flipped the watch over and compared the engraving to the drawing in the journal. There was no denying the marks on both pieces were a similar style. Jaxon laid the ancient necklace next to the watch, and Shim rummaged in his bag, pulling out the picture frame, flipping it face down next to the other three items on his lap. The marks on the ancient disk were faint. We hadn't even noticed them before, however, when laid beside the others, the similarities had been too close to dismiss.

"You know, this kinda looks like something I've seen before." Breeze said, scrunching up her face in thought. "Maybe on a rock or in a book."

"Like a petroglyph?" I asked her. Breeze shrugged.

"Like a language—" Shim said, his voice thoughtful.

But what did this mean? Was it even connected to our parents?

26

NATIONAL ATOMIC TESTING MUSEUM

ANOTHER TRANSFER and twelve hours later, we finally arrived in Vegas. I peeled myself off the seats, convinced I would find the pattern of the fabric engraved on the backs of my thighs. The smothering heat enveloped us when we left the terminal to catch a local bus. We got off the bus on the strip. The traffic noise was jarring, and the bubble of introspection I'd been in since we started reading the journals broke. I felt like one of the bugs on our bus' windshield. I was trying to adjust to the shocking differences between this city and Portland, and I desperately needed a bath and several hours without the hypnotic vibration of movement.

Shim said his father, Logan, was a developer who played with real estate like monopoly pieces. They were always moving into his newest project. When Logan had completed a place called The Vine Towers, he moved the family into a posh five-bedroom condo that took up half of the top floor. Later, they moved to a complex he was developing in Summerlin. After their parents divorced, Logan had moved back into the condo, which he had been unable to sell once the market had crashed. Shim and Jaxon split time between their parents. They sounded rich, but Shim assured me it was all other people's money. Whatever, it still sounded nicer than sleeping in a broken-down old VeeDub called Van Ekman, but I didn't tell him that.

I tried not to gawk as we entered the modern building right off the strip and rode an exclusive elevator to the top floor. But I had to scrape my jaw off the floor when I saw the apartment. Just from the door I could see a balcony large enough to host a football game, a patio spa pool, and floor to ceiling glass windows that, frankly, freaked me out. I was going to stay away from those and their view down.

"Won't your dad be upset we're barging in on him?" I had to ask. I was still standing in the expansive entryway. Jaxon described Logan O'Connell as a foul-mouth force of nature, and that was when he was saying nice things about him.

"Nah, he's spending the summer in L.A. working on some deal," Shim assured me.

"Probably shaking down an old folks home," Jaxon muttered.

For everyone else, as soon as we had entered the apartment, their behavior had changed. Weeks of tension from being chased eased away, and they quickly relaxed. Except me. I was still trying to figure out if I should take off my shoes. I finally decided to kick them off and try to get past the entry way.

"Dude, stop messing with the channels." Jaxon said. I had finally talked myself into entering the sunken living room, and Jaxon had the massive wall-mounted TV on. Skylar was trying to wrestle control of the remote from him. "We need to see the weather."

"There's no food." Breeze came in through an arch on the opposite side of the room. Behind her was a sea of granite and stainless steel. "All he's got is protein powder, eggs, and beer."

"My dad still lifts weights, and he tends to stick to the basic food groups," Shim responded loudly from somewhere else in the condo.

"Come on, this show is boring," Skylar whined, trying to pull the remote from Jaxon's hands, who then stood on the coffee table and held it over his head. Skylar tackled him, driving him into the sofa.

"Skylar," Breeze shouted at her twin to stop and, when that didn't work, grabbed a sofa pillow and started beating him over the head. I was surprised at her defense of Jaxon, and so was Skylar, who launched himself at her next with a bout of laughter. Jaxon didn't realize Skylar had pulled back his tackle of Breeze and retaliated. Limbs flying, he hit the back of my leg and brought me down into the mix.

"Stop." Shim waded into the limbs. "Watch out for Grace's arm." Jaxon gave him a half-hearted sucker punch in the gut, and Skylar grabbed his arm and pulled him down into a headlock, trying to give him a noogie. Okay, maybe twenty-five hours on a bus was too long for anyone to not lose their minds a little.

"Quiet. This is what I was waiting for." Jaxon shushed everyone as the weatherman came on and confirmed a weather front was moving into the county. High winds and dust storms were expected for the next twenty-four hours. "Well, that's it then. We can't go to Gypsum tomorrow. Too dangerous in a dust storm."

"Woo hoo! sleeping in." Skylar had pulled himself out from under Jaxon, who was trying to detangle his limbs from Breeze's.

He snatched the remote out of Jaxon's hand. "Victory!" Skylar crowed.

"YOU WANT TO GO WHERE?" I walked into the room. The twins were looking at Shim like an alien had invaded his body and started speaking in pig Latin.

"Oh, not that old museum again." Jaxon groaned. "I'm not going. Besides, the X Games are on."

We had slept in, ate leftover pizza from the night before for breakfast, and now we were lounging around the living room. Jaxon had Duchess out and was letting her wander around the apartment and explore.

After being trapped on the bus for so long, I thought I just needed to clean up and sleep, then I would feel more comfortable here. I had investigated the spectacular bathroom and slept on the softest sheets I had ever felt. But no matter how I tried, I couldn't get as comfortable in this apartment as Duchess was. I kept expecting the owner to come barging in, and I was worried about touching anything since it all seemed so expensive—which was ridiculous. I could sail a $100,000 boat, but I was nervous about sitting on a ten-thousand-dollar couch? But no matter what I did, my muscles just got tighter and tighter.

"Need some company?" I blurted out "I mean, I like museums."

Shim looked surprised but recovered quickly. "Sure. Anyone else want to go?"

Skylar shook his head and rooted himself deeper into the couch.

"Um, I was hoping I could try out the patio pool?" Breeze asked Jaxon. Jaxon nodded enthusiastically, and Skylar tried to sneak the remote away while he was distracted.

"Well, I guess it's you and me." Shim gave a weak smile. I immediately regretted begging to join his trip. He had been weird since we arrived. "Jax, maybe you can check on the bikes and make sure they are ready for whenever the weather lets up."

Jaxon grunted an affirmative.

"Okay, we will leave in about thirty minutes," Shim said.

I nodded. Shim nodded back then spun around and disappeared.

∞

"YOU'RE KIDDING, RIGHT?" We stopped walking in front of a huge concrete block of a building, an anomaly in Las Vegas. The sign out front said, "National Atomic Testing Museum." This was Shim's favorite place in Vegas?

"What?" he defended sheepishly. "It's fascinating, and they have a new exhibit I wanted to check out." He didn't say it, but his eyes begged, Please. "They close in two hours, so we won't be long."

"Okay, okay," I conceded.

Even though I had protested and declared I didn't want to define it, I had thought Shim and I were getting closer in Portland and then on the bus. That had all changed the minute we arrived in Vegas. With his strange mood, I had been worried about spending time alone with him today. But he was begging.

I grabbed his arm and led him into the museum. Maybe this could be our ground zero.

∞

"THAT IS SO GNARLY," Shim exclaimed as we left the Ground Zero Theater. Replicating a test-site detonation, the experience made me feel displaced. The detached voice counting down, then the mushroom cloud and the chairs shaking like a real bomb had gone off. Shim tugged at my good arm, pulling me deeper into the museum.

The lights were low, shadowing the concrete walls and rock and metal surfaces. Newsreels of test bombs were rolling around us; glass cases displayed Geiger counters, canned crackers, and a million other minutia of nuclear history.

Shim dragged me over to a poster sporting an image of a man in a HAZMAT suit with a camera. The text read: "How to photograph a nuclear bomb." It was next to the exhibit he was here to see: "Area 51 – Myth or Reality."

We stepped into a dark room with rows of bench seating. A video introduction was nearing the end of its loop, and Shim headed to the front to wait for the next cycle, but I balked, shivering from the chilled air blasting from the vent at the front of the room. I grabbed a seat in the back corner so I could lean against the wall. Shim reluctantly relocated but made sure as he took a seat next to me where he still had a good view of the screen.

He was kind of a nerd.

I liked it.

As the opening credits of the video started, Shim kept his eyes on the screen, and I kept my eyes on him. I squirmed on the hard bench. Leaning against the wall at this angle was hard, so I pulled my legs up and laid them on his lap. I was sitting perpendicular to him, leaning against the sidewall of the room, waiting to see what he would do.

"Um, excuse me, docent, but there seem to be two people behaving inappropriately in the back of the theater," Shim whispered out of the side of his mouth. It was nice to see his mischievous smile again, even if his eyes stayed on the screen. After a minute of my legs being there, he raised his hand and put it on the bare skin of my ankle, his thumb rubbing circles on the skin. The tingly shivers that went through me had nothing to do with the AC. His hand slid up higher, to my knees, sliding under the fabric of my jeans. His hand roamed from knee to ankle like he was drunk on my skin. The touch of his warm fingers and palms left a trail of sparks under my skin.

Suddenly, a loud blast of music punctured the room, followed by the detached voice of a narrator over black and white images of men in uniform.

In the flickering light, my eyes traced Shim's profile. Reaching out a finger, I hesitated, then slid it down his cheek, a light brush. Shim turned his head from the screen, his cheek curving into my palm, his lips nuzzling into the heel of my hand. His lips were so soft, so full. He had a classically beautiful mouth, like it had been sculpted, and a faint blush darkened his skin, still a little chapped from the days we had spent sailing. In the dim light, his amber eyes met mine, the lids heavy. The brows pulled together in a worried frown. I smoothed my finger over the line, trying the ease the marks. He hesitated and then a look of resignation I didn't understand crossed his face, and he leaned toward me. My fingers slid comfortably from his cheek into the soft hair at the nape of his neck, the strands curling around my fingers.

He held back, so close. I used the arm around his neck to close the gap. Our lips met, and a soft gasp escaped from one of us. The last kiss had been a surprise for both of us, I think. This one was an exploration, an expedition to see where we could go next. He pressed soft kisses first to the right, then to the left corner of my mouth, pulling back to look at my lips before diving in again with more pressure. This felt different, more serious, and I was melting into the feeling. I suspected he had far more experience at this than me. What was his experience? I snapped my mind back to the present. There was no way I was going to miss this moment by giving into a nattering mind.

Just as he tilted his head the opposite direction and started to repeat the kiss, there was a sound at the front of the theater. Glancing up, Shim noted it, dismissed it, and glanced at the screen before turning back to me.

He froze.

Every muscle I was touching turned rock hard, and his hands dropped from me. He pushed my legs off his lap and jumped up, racing for the door. He found a docent, a small man in his late seventies with a VFW hat and a brilliant yellow blazer, and, grabbing onto his lapels, demanded, "Can you rewind the video?" The docent was as shocked as I was. His response was haughty as he informed us that if we found it so interesting, we could stay in the theater, and it would loop back and restart again in twelve minutes.

What just happened?

Not explaining, Shim spent the time pacing back and forth in the front of the theater. The video continued to run. The images projected on him made him look like he was wrapped in newsprint. The movie ended, restarted, and finally, the segment of the video he had been waiting for came up again. He pulled me to a bench at the front of the theater. His grip on my hand was uncomfortably tight. "Watch—watch, here it comes," he whispered.

I turned my worried gaze from Shim to the screen. The segment was showing interviews taken over a period of several decades with self-proclaimed abductees recounting their abduction stories. Shim squeezed my hand tighter.

There was a man with thick salt and pepper hair and tan skin so wrinkled and cracked from the sun, it was hard to get an exact bead on his age. He was dressed in a buttoned-up plaid shirt and his callused hands were folded calmly in front of him as he spoke.

"I'm not from Earth, and I wasn't abducted. I was brought here accidentally through a passage while I was working in a mine on my home planet. I was digging in one of the oldest levels of the mine when a blinding light opened a passage in front of me. The gravitational pull

from the threshold dragged me in, and when I fell out of the passage on the other side, I was on Earth. I've been trying to find my way home ever since."

The graphics at the bottom of the screen said he was Terrance Shanon from Gypsum Cave, Nevada. The show moved on to the next interview.

"Did you see?" Shim asked, pulling me off the bench. As he grabbed my shoulders and practically shook me, I shrugged him off and grabbed his hands, holding on.

"I'm not tracking. You need to tell me what you are seeing."

"Does Terrance Shanon from Gypsum, Nevada sound familiar?"

I shook my head.

"What if the interviewer got his name wrong? 'Terrance' could have sounded like the long form of 'Tar' and 'Shanon' could be a misspelling of Xanon. Tar Xanon."

Understanding dawned.

"That was the name from the Federal files on the last case linked to my mother's case. How did you even see that?"

"It was the Gypsum that caught my eye. Now we have a lead on who he was." Shim was right. I was stunned, speechless, and I understood his bizarre behavior now. It was almost inconceivable we could have stumbled on this lead and, based on the past behavior of this Helios Kratos group, not surprising that Tar Xanon might have been killed for telling his story.

We watched the video through again, and again. The docent stuck his head in the room and informed us the museum was closing. Shim used the video mode on the burner phone he was carrying to record the brief interview, then switched to the camera and snapped still shots. We scoured the credits for more information but didn't find anything else useful.

Eventually, the fuming docent slapped on the lights and

forced us out of the room. He trailed us to the front of the museum, pushing us out the front door with a look of triumph. I barely registered the lock on the large glass doors clicking into place behind us. All I could think about was getting back to the condo and showing the others what Shim had found.

27

GYPSUM CAVE

JAXON CAUGHT big air as he jumped a dune. Standing up on the bike, he easily absorbed the impact of landing. Clouds of dust puffed up from the wheels of his dual sport bike as they sank back into the sand on the trail. With Skylar on the back of Shim's bike, he took the dune slower and stayed grounded. I followed at a snail's pace with Breeze riding behind me. I was pretty comfortable on the bike after Shim gave me a crash course on how to ride two-person but was being extra cautious in deference to my nervous passenger.

We had gotten up early to beat the heat and were anxious to hit the trail after waiting out yesterday's windstorm. Shim's video and pictures from the museum of Tar Xanon, a.k.a. Terrance Shanon, his supposed abduction by aliens—unlikely—and connection with our parents—much more likely—had stiffened our resolve. None of us knew what to make from the information, but now we were even more curious and cautious as to what we would find out at Gypsum.

The cave was located twelve miles outside of Las Vegas with the last few being off-road miles, so motorbikes were the perfect form of transportation for the day trip. Though the brothers' bikes were street legal, we took back roads to avoid the police and circled around a lot to make sure we weren't being followed. The extended trip had taken us a of couple hours.

The transition to sand from off the dirt road had been rough for all but Jaxon, who let loose a whoop and yelled, "Come on, you squids," before he belted out across the desert like he had been set free. After a few jumps and spins, leaning over the front tire for maximum traction, he headed back toward us. His face was masked behind his helmet, and he held a straight line from his wrist to his shoulders as he stood on the bike, his knees slightly bent, absorbing the impact and loving the ride.

Shim, a natural on a bike, too, was toning down his cruise to accommodate Skylar.

My bike got a little squirrelly in the deep sand, the handlebars wobbling.

"Remember, accelerate to even it out, and don't use your front brake," Shim shouted over the noise of the engines.

Skylar yelled out, "Relax." I thought he was talking to Breeze, but it might have been for me. My concentration was fierce as I tried to keep loose and not muscle the bike.

Thirty minutes later, we slowed to a stop. Shim hopped off, kicking down the stand and taking off his helmet, grinning as he turned to help us.

I was floundering. Fully supporting both the bike and Breeze's weight, I struggled to keep balanced in the sand. Shim and Skylar rushed to get Breeze, who had surgically adhered herself to my back.

They tried pulling off her hands. Breeze seemed reluctant to let go of her death grip and kept repeating, "Okay...I'm okay... okay...I'm okay." Shim pried up each finger, one by one, and helped her to dismount. Skylar took over, leading Breeze on wobbly knees over to a shaded area to sit down. He fussed over her, helping her peel off Jaxon's old protective jacket.

I sighed with relief, pulling off the helmet and unzipping the jacket, an old one of Shim's. Grit coated my face and had seeped under the protective layer. I itched, and my body was still humming from the memory of the bike's vibration. Shim chuckled as I tried to get off the bike too fast and my legs turned to jelly. I caught myself as Shim kicked down the stand on the bike and offered me an arm of support.

We had discovered online that the cave was an important paleontological and archeological site. I didn't know what to make of that. How could that be a secret base or laboratory? Since the cave was only a dozen miles outside Vegas, you would think the place would get a lot of visitors. But the historic markers had all been removed, and we had only found it based on GPS tracking and an old dirt road that lad up the east side of Sunrise Mountain. It would seem the area had been made deliberately hard to find, maybe by the owner of the land, who, we had learned online, was a private mining company that discouraged visitors.

Jaxon took off to patrol the area on his bike, spraying sand behind him while Breeze lay back on her elbows in the shade of a rock, trying to get her wind back. I was still a little wobbly, but insisted I was okay, so the three of us, Shim, Skylar and myself, dropped into the mouth of the cave.

"Remind me to carry a better flashlight for the next time we are in a cave," Shim remarked. I laughed, like this would happen again.

Once we were past the entrance, it got dark fast, the thready beam of our flashlights bouncing around and every so often trailing across the glittery walls. There was a gypsum mine nearby, which was probably the substance making the walls sparkle. We picked our way past the entrance, examining every nook and cranny we came across.

"How big is this cave?" Skylar inquired as he dipped down to look at a low crevice.

"Three hundred feet." Shim's disembodied voice floated around us. "They found a really old, like 30,000 years old, animal in here, and a basket that was 10,000 years old."

"Wow. Where? This place is empty...eck." Skylar's voice trailed off with the sound of sliding rock. Shim and I flipped our lights around until we found him, jumping up from the ground. "I'm good." He slapped at the back of his pants. We kept searching the cave and found it disappointingly empty. Not sure what we were looking for anyway, we headed back toward the entrance, defeated.

Skylar and I hunkered down in the shade next to Breeze and relayed what we had, or rather hadn't, found. Shim joined us, pulling out bottles of water and power bars.

It was another twenty minutes before Jaxon came screaming back, pulled his rear brake and sliding sideways into a stop, spraying rocks and sand in an arc away from us.

Jaxon ripped off his helmet. "I found something," he said, breathless with excitement. He waited on his bike while we quickly put our bottles away and mounted up to follow him up the hill.

The view from the top was spectacular. Spread out as far as the eye could see was a gigantic quilt of land in shades of taupe, beige, sand, camel, umber, tan, and sienna, sewn together by rust colored hills and low, dark, mountains. Down at the base of the hill was an enormous warehouse surrounded by a field of solar panels, positioned like soldiers guarding the building. They were angled to catch the sun, and the glare bouncing off the acres of shiny plates was blinding.

We hid the bikes behind a large rock formation and crawled to the edge of the summit to study the find.

Shim reached into the bag on Skylar's back and pulled out

Arie's binoculars. "There's no branding, no company name anywhere, just a giant picture of a sun on the front."

"This has got to be it," Jaxon exclaimed.

"Well, solar panels, sun, Helios, it would make sense. Plus, with this many solar panels, they could do some major manufacturing and still be off the grid," Skylar added.

Jaxon's interest in the building increased, and a gleam entered his eye.

"Jaxon, it's just a warehouse. What does it have to do with our parents?" Breeze wasn't sold yet.

"This is what we are looking for. I know it," Jaxon assured her.

"You think our parents are in there?" Breeze asked doubtfully.

"I don't know, but it must be where Cambridge was heading. It sure isn't the cave back there, and there is nothing else here for miles," Jaxon said.

I agreed, but I was starting to get cold feet about our plan. I wanted my mom's diary but were we sure it was here? And, even if we got into this building, how would we find it?

"What do you think Cambridge is going to do here?" Skylar asked.

Jaxon shrugged.

"Look at all the guards. It looks dangerous." Breeze said, still sounding doubtful as she shaded her eyes against the sun to get a better view of the building.

While Jaxon and the twins debated what to do next. I slid closer to Shim, who had been studying the site with binoculars. "What do you think?"

"I think I can get in," he said without taking his eyes from the building.

"Are you kidding?" Skylar asked, incredulous.

"No. Jaxon is right; this is what we were looking for. We

need to know what's inside, and there's only one way to find out. Shim lowered the binocular. "I've been watching them. It looks like they are on a timed schedule. With a little planning, I can slip by them."

"What? We are going in? Are you crazy?" Breeze asked.

"Not we…just me. The rest of you need to stay out here and keep a watch out."

Shim pulled Kindle's ring out of his pocket and put it on, turning the stone inward. He flexed his hand making sure he could touch the stone when he fisted his hand. "I'll keep an open channel, and you can tell me what is going on."

"Not us. Them. They can keep watch." Jaxon pointed to the twins. "I'm going with you."

"So am I," I added. I pulled off my bag and handed it over to Breeze, then ran my fingers along the stone in Amé's necklace at my collar. I didn't trust that anyone else was as invested in finding the diary as me.

Jaxon pulled the ancient necklace out of his pocket and slipped the strand of shiny beads around his neck. His thumb lingered on the weathered surface of the stone.

Shim threw his hands up. He seemed to realize the futility of protesting. "Okay, Fine. Let's do a communication check."

After we all checked in, Shim and Jaxon handed over their bags to the twins.

"*I hope using these things doesn't give us cancer or something,*" Jaxon contributed dourly.

Breeze, who had her finger on the cuff on Skylar's wrist, cut in, "*WHY would you say that?*" Her voice echoed through our heads as Breeze shook her other hand angrily at Jaxon. Her emotion cut through the connection almost as clearly as her words, leaving a sour feeling in the pit of my stomach. Wow, was it my imagination, or did these stones connect us deeper the longer we used them?

"Yuck, I can taste how mad you are at me," Jaxon spit onto the sand.

"It is kind of gross. We will have to watch the emotions while we are using the stones," I concurred.

"Sources, we are actually going to do this?" Shim accidentally transmitted.

"Well, yeah, big bro, it was your idea," Jaxon said.

I took my finger off the stone, so I wouldn't make the same mistake as Shim. I didn't want the others to know how nervous and worried I was about us getting caught. But Shim was right. This was the only way. I took a deep breath and, without touching the stone, said, "Okay, let's figure out how we are getting in."

28

INTO THE SUN

ALMOST IMMEDIATELY, our plan to infiltrate the building started to unravel.

We watched the warehouse from the cover of the hill for several hours until Shim figured out the pattern of the guards patrolling the perimeter. When the timing was right, Shim, Jaxon, and I slinked down the hill. It was difficult crawling on my belly through the sand and shrub brush. Prickly needles penetrated my jeans. I would be picking out the points threaded in the fabric for a while. And I had sand in my bra—but that would have to wait. We slithered into a crouch at the bottom of the hill and, grasping our stones, waited for the twins' "go ahead." When the call came, we raced for the side of the building, weaving through the forest of solar panel stands. With a soft slide into the side of the building, we had yanked on the door the guards had been entering and leaving through.

It was locked. Of course it was. Why wouldn't it be? But now, we had to find another way in.

Shim and Jaxon headed in opposite directions to see if they could find another door, leaving me stranded in the middle. They had been gone forever when I heard a scratch on the opposite side of the door. Frantic, I looked for a hiding place. Behind me, the smooth white wall offered no nook to hide in, and in front of me, the solar stands were too slender for even my scrawny frame to hide behind. Desperate, I raced for the corner of the building, hoping to make the edge before the door opened. I had a dream like this once, where I was running in sand and no matter how hard I ran, my destination was always just out of reach.

"Grace, run faster," Breeze urged in my head. *"Shim, Jaxon, stay where you are. The door is opening."*

I panted. The corner still seemed yards away. In the quiet of the desert, I could hear the metal creak of the door swinging open behind me. My fingers reached out toward the edge.

"Two people in uniform coming out. Guards—they're early." Of course they were. Why hadn't I been brave enough to go with Shim or Jaxon to search for another opening? Instead, I'd stood frozen in indecision.

I finally caught the corner, and with little concern about what could be on the other side, I grasped the edge and pulled, whipping myself around and into the unknown.

"You're clear!" Skylar crowed.

My heart pounded as I hunched over, hands on my knees, sweat dripping into my eyes, as I tried to catch my breath.

"Grace, they are heading your direction. You might want to find a place to hide."

I groaned and stood up. This side of the building was cut in half by a huge loading dock, open and exposed like a large gaping wound. I felt small and vulnerable standing there. What did they ship from here? I only had a minute to puzzle on this before Skylar's warning urged me forward. I didn't see Jaxon anywhere, so he must have made the next corner, but I never would. I had to find a place to hide, and the loading dock was the only option.

A gravel road led out of the loading area, and as my shoes left the hard dirt and raced across road, stones flew up, hitting the backs of my pumping legs. Sweat poured down my back and into the waistband of the jeans I was seriously regretting wearing. My hands burned as they scraped across the concrete when I hauled myself up onto the ledge. I pulled on the dock's rolling door. It was locked. I hadn't expected it to be open, but I had hoped. Jumping down, I did a quick visual exam of the rest of the doors, which all looked locked. Frustrated, I slammed my hand down on the concrete, scraping my skin once again. The only break from all the bays was a set of metal stairs leading up to another security door. I ran for it. The stairs rattled as I bolted up them to the door and pulled on the knob. It was locked too.

"Grace, they are turning the corner. Hide," Breeze beseeched me.

At a loss for what else to do, I slid under the railing and crouched beneath the stairs. It felt like I was crawling into an oven, with the reflective metal hot from the sun and the heat radiating up from the concrete as I pushed as far back as I could into the dark recess of the stairs. I hissed and muffled a cry as my back touched the stairs and burned like I'd been branded.

"That's good, Grace," Breeze's voice whispered in my head as if she was afraid thinking loudly would be overheard. *"They are headed your way, but I don't think they see you. Stay there."* The tense muscles in my body screamed as I locked them, legs trembling, trying not to move. I grasped tighter to my necklace, desperate for the link.

It seemed like a lifetime before I heard the tread of footfalls in the gravel.

Plunk, plunk. I watched sweat drip off my forehead to the concrete. I was afraid to move, even to wipe my brow. My heart beat faster, almost choking me as the sound grew closer and closer.

"Grace, don't move. They are coming right toward you."

"Grace, stay calm. I'm heading your way," Shim reassured me.

"Me too," Jaxon chimed in. I couldn't even think, let alone respond to stop them.

In spite of the pounding in my chest, I tried to still myself even more till my breathing almost stopped. If I survived this, I was racing back up that hill and insisting we head home. Whatever was in this building just wasn't worth it. The footsteps stopped at the base of the stairs and a radio squawked.

"Control One, G-423 and G-442 here. Perimeter's clear. We are taking our break. Over," said one of the booted guards.

The radio squawked back, "Received, G-423. You are both clear to take your lunch breaks. Be back for the greeting. Control One, out."

Heavy steps climbed the stairs. One guard muttered something about the heat, the words lost in the pounding of rubber treads grinding into metal anti-slip spikes. There was a whirling and pulling sound, followed by a beep, swish, and clank. A door-shaped shadow appeared on the concrete next to me, followed by a blissful wave of cold air. I found myself leaning into the coolness and was half out from under the stairs before I realized I'd moved. I could see the back of one guard holding the door. Thankfully, the second guard had already entered the building. As the first guard moved to follow, I got a glimpse of a grey security card, the cord caught up on the guard's radio. Quickly, before I had time to think, I reached up and grabbed the card. There was a tug and the guard followed through the door, the cord stretched, and the card was yanked from my hand as the door slammed behind the guard, blocking off the flow of cool. I collapsed on the concrete in relief, then quickly pulled myself back up and away from the burning surface. Something fluttered and fell down to lay flat in front of me. A grey rectangle about the size of a playing card with a broken reel attached to it.

"Uh, guys. I think I found our way in." I picked up the security card and clutched it to my chest. Would the guard come back for it? I was still sitting there, stunned, waiting for the guard to return as Shim and Jaxon raced up.

"You okay?" Shim approached me cautiously, hands up in a gesture of peace. He and Jaxon crouched on the concrete on either side of the stairs.

I gave a trembling nod, then held up the badge with a weak smile. "I nominate today to be 'Waters Appreciation Day.'"

Shim snorted. "Let's get inside."

AFTER THE BLINDING brightness of the sun outside, it took a moment for my eyes to adjust to the interior of the building. I kept blinking until the dark spots disappeared from my vision, but still, all I could see was white. White walls, white ceiling, white floors. Goose bumps spread in waves across my body as the fridge air conditioning hit my sweat-soaked skin and clothes.

Shim tucked the badge in his back pocket, and we proceeded down the wide, white hall. The hall terminated at a door. We cautiously entered. The door opened up into a large space, a storage room or warehouse of some type. The walls were lined with huge crates on pallets, some stacked double and triple high. One side of the room terminated at a loading bay and the other a glass-walled room. The space was eerily quiet. Maybe it was the combination of it being a weekend and lunch time.

We entered the glass-walled booth and gravitated toward the bank of computer monitors lining two walls. They were security monitors covering dozens of doors, halls, and rooms.

"Where are the guards?" I asked.

"Don't know, but look around for plans of the building so we can get an idea of the size of this place." Jaxon started flipping piles of papers.

"Careful." Shim gave him a shove. "We don't want them to know we were here." Jaxon rolled his eyes and poked at the papers.

While the brothers searched for plans, I studied the monitors. Each had a label with a number and a room or person's name listed. Several were labeled by function: "laboratory," "hall," "door," "break room." There were private offices and conference rooms with cameras, and a disturbing number of monitors devoted to small observation rooms, some set-up with chairs and desks, others just a bed. Four monitors on the right were blank.

"This is odd," I observed. I'm not sure why I was whispering, as we hadn't seen anyone yet, but everything about this place felt wrong.

"What is it?" Shim kept working but glanced up at me.

I pointed to the bottom three-quarters of the screens. "Most of these screens show empty rooms, except for these ones in the top row. It looks like everyone in the building is clustered at a large entry door and in this big conference room. But there are a couple of monitors that aren't working."

"Let me see what I can do." Shim stopped his search for plans and started examining the control panel near the wall instead. "I think they just aren't turned on." He walked along the wall and pushed the buttons under the blank screens. I held my breath. I knew my dad probably wasn't here—they were being held by the government—but this place, those rooms, could have been where my mother was held—where she died. The monitors lit up. Nothing. They showed empty, dark rooms. I released my breath.

"Hello, hello, can you guys hear us?" Skylar's voice broke into my head, and I realized I was the only one touching a stone.

"Yeah, sorry, we got distracted." To the brothers, I raised my hand and gestured to my necklace. They hopped on with their stones.

"There is something big going on out here," Skylar reported. *"One car just arrived, and I think it's Cambridge."*

"There's a lot of dust, so I think more cars are coming," Breeze broke in.

"We should be okay. We are in the back, in the warehouse area. We found a bunch of monitors, and it shows all the activity happening up front," Shim relayed to the twins.

"Ha, I found plans," Jaxon crowed and shoulder slammed Shim.

I frowned and tilted my head. "Does it look like they are preparing that conference room for a meeting?" I said aloud. Shim studied the monitor and agreed. "Now that would be something to hear. Do any of these monitors give sound?"

Shim played with a few of the screens and tried typing in a few commands. "No, these are only video. Probably to give some level of privacy while maintaining security."

"Too bad." Jaxon sank into a chair and pulled out plans on a lower shelf. "We could look forever through this building and never find anything, but if we overheard a meeting with Cambridge, we could learn a lot."

"Well, I know one place we could look." I pointed up to the monitor on the top row labeled "Smith 206," then turned to Shim. "Can you find that room?"

∞

"DOWN THE HALL." Shim and I followed Jaxon's instructions. He had found the room on the maps and was trying to track us using the monitors in the control room. Every so often, he would tell us to duck into a side room. Fortunately, they had been unlocked so far. *"Okay, room 206 should be the third door on your left."* We walked farther down the hall, and I reached for a plain door. "Nope, make that on your right." I eyed Shim. He shrugged, and we turned to the door on the opposite side of the hall. Restricted signs covered the door, and a security pad was by the handle. Pulling out the badge, I swiped it across the pad and held my breath. My heart pounded as the longest seconds of my life ticked by before there was a click and a green light appear on the pad. I breathed a sigh of relief and opened the door.

Inside was a laboratory with shelves and tables full of testing equipment. The surfaces were clear, and one full wall was lined with locked metal cabinets. Shim immediately went to work on the locks of the closest set of cabinets. I headed for the workstation with the computer set up in the corner. It held the only personal items in the room, a photo taped to the wall, and a chair with a lab coat draped over it. I folded back the lapel, hoping it would say "Smith," but it was blank. A quick survey of the desk showed nothing, so I pulled out the top drawer and rooted around. Nothing, at first, but shoved in the back was a box. Business cards! I picked one out and ignored everything but the name at the top: Agent Erica Smith. That was the name Cambridge had mentioned.

"Bingo. Shim, it's the right office." I turned in time to see him crack the lock on the first cabinet. He looked up and noted the card I held up with a nod, then turned back to his work. Shoving the card into my back pocket, I turned to the second, then the third drawer. Nothing jumped out at me, so I yanked on the bottom drawer. It was locked. "Shim, can you get this?" I could pick it, but he was faster, so we swapped spots and I resumed his search through the first cabinet. It was depressing.

More bags of clothing and other matter I didn't even want to think about. Some shelves held jars of liquid with body parts floating in them. Cringing, I stooped to check the wooden boxes on the bottom shelf. They all contained carefully labeled reddish-green rocks that looked very similar to our stone but lacked the silver threads.

"Grace." The tone of Shim's voice called to me more than the sound. I looked over. He wasn't smiling. In his hand, he held a small green book—my mother's diary. Gasping, I stumbled toward the diary, barely aware of my feet moving, hands out. Shim placed it gently in my hands, and I held it like a sacred object. The cover was worn, there was a scratch I didn't remember, and the pages were warping. The sealed plastic bag it was wrapped in, like a piece of evidence, angered me, and I was going to rip it off when Shim tugged on my hand and indicated Jaxon wanted to speak to us. It was just as well. If I opened the diary, I'm not sure I would have been able to stop reading it. I gently tucked the book in the detestable plastic bag into the back waistband of my jeans and tucked my shirt in over it to secure it.

"How bad do you want to hear what's going on?" Jaxon's voice was tense as he efficiently laid out his plan. *"It looks like a ventilation access crawl space leads over the conference room."*

"He wants to climb through the ventilation shafts?" I asked to Shim, then repeated the question in my head for Jaxon.

"Ha, you're funny. I'm not going. I need to stay here and watch the monitors and direct you." I could hear his evil smile *"Have a nice trip."*

29

EAVESDROPPING

FOR THE SECOND time in less than an hour, I was absolutely terrified to even breathe. I was in a metal duct the size of a small oven with my arms pinned to my sides. But instead of baking, I was being flash frozen as the AC blasted cold air around us and into the room. We could only move by making a snake-like wiggle accomplished by our shoeless feet pushing us through the duct. There was no room to turn around, but Shim, who was in the front, found a way to back-up into a t-bend we passed through earlier, so now he was facing me, and we could both press our ears to the vent. We had to maintain absolute silence as we looked down through the vent slats onto the top of the conference room table. Fortunately, the ceilings were high, and it was unlikely the people in the meeting would look up.

We were fortunate that G-423 seemed to have full access, and that the absence of the badge hadn't been noticed yet. With the building plans and from watching the monitors, Jaxon had kept us from being seen as he guided us through the warehouse, past laboratories and open workspaces, and into a secure area that contained sealed observation rooms. Let's hope no one comes back from break and finds him.

There were just two people in the room. One was a huge, slick-looking guy in a suit stretched to capacity. He looked like he had eaten the team of suited operatives we saw in Portland for breakfast. I couldn't see his face, but the top of his head was trimmed into a tight military-style cut, and the back of one hand had a vicious scar in the shape of a circle. The only other person in the room was Cambridge. I shuddered, and my shoulder started to ache just seeing him again. I'm not sure if that was an emotional response or because of the tight fit, but I tried to move my elbow a little to relieve the pressure on my arm. Shim watched me, and I remembered I was supposed to be holding onto my necklace too.

"Okay?" He asked through the stones.

"Yep, never better," I replied through the stones.

"Did you guys make it?" The twins piped into our heads.

"We did," I responded for both of us.

"What's going on?" Skylar asked.

"Cambridge is in the room with a suit—like the Portland gang but bigger. They seem to be waiting for something else. But the suit keeps telling Cambridge what he did wrong, and Cambridge keeps whining excuses...and he has a broken nose. Way to go, Grace!" Shim laughed, and we felt the amusement through the stones.

A phone rang. "The director is on the line for you now," a disembodied male voice spoke out of the conference phone in the center of the table.

"Yes," drawled the suit, "we're ready for her. Patch us in."

"Why are you wasting my time?" The original speaker was replaced by an older female voice.

"Director Koch, thank you for taking our call. Something

completely amazing has happened and..." The suit cut Cambridge off and pushed him back from the console.

"Apologies, Director. This idiot has created a complete cluster, and he requested the agency to come in and clean up for him."

"Explain." The female voice was dry and unemotional.

Cambridge pushed his way back to the table and leaned into the phone console. "As I told your man here, they have a stone. I wasn't able to get my hands on it for more than a few minutes, but I can assure you it's one of the cuts I did years ago from the original rock." His excited voice sounded nasally through the broken nose.

"And you don't have possession of it now?"

"Well, no," Cambridge explained. "The kids took it with them."

"There were five of them. We searched the area when he contacted us, but they were already gone," the agent injected calmly.

"So, you lost the stone and the children," the cool voice said.

"Well, yes, but I was able to verify it was one of the stones we were looking for."

"Cambridge, what do you think we really do?"

"Excuse me?"

"Do you think we are really a solar manufacturer?"

"Well, n-no," the professor stammered.

"Exactly. We need those kids, their stone, and anything else connected to them. The safety of our *planet* depends on it."

Shim and I stared at each other; his eyes had bugged out at the word "planet."

I put my hand up to my necklace.

"What do you think she means?" I asked Shim.

"What did you hear?" the others chimed in, and Shim replayed the conversation.

"*Ssshhh. There's more.*" I signaled to Shim.

"Those kids must be tied to the original children somehow. One of them even had green hair—maybe it was genetic," Cambridge supplied, like the idea had just occurred to him.

"You just figured that out?" The suit leaned back in his chair full of sarcasm.

"Yes," Director Koch responded dryly, "the children are most likely their offspring. We can't access the originals—the government has them locked up tight. We think they are at Gitmo, but our contact can't confirm—that's what makes these kids that much more important...and you lost them."

My thoughts exploded out to Shim, "*What's Gitmo?*" He didn't respond, and I looked up at him. The alarm on his face had me reaching out, awkwardly, trying not to bang my elbow in the tight space, trying to calm him. This was no place for a panic attack. "*What is it?*"

"*They can't mean Gitmo. That's what they call Guantanamo Bay.*" He carried on with his explanation even as I felt the ice race through my veins, "*It's a detention center they send people to disappear.*"

"*A detention center? Why? What are they doing to them? We have to get them out.*" I felt so helpless. We had focused all our energy on evading the people that had taken our parents and trying to unravel their secret, hoping that would help us find them. A small part of me even thought that we might find our parents here, that maybe the government agency that had taken them was tied to the Helios somehow. But all along, they were at a secret government base. Would we ever see them again?

"*Grace, we don't know for sure our parents are there. These Helios guys don't know where they are, and it looks like they aren't tied to the government, even if they have spies there,*" Shim returned. Frustrated, I returned my attention to the conference room while Shim relayed the conversation to the others.

"It wasn't my fault!" Cambridge exclaimed. "I called Dawes, I followed procedure. It's not my fault he wasn't quick enough and gave them time to break into Stringham's house and find the journals."

"Excuse me?" Agent Dawes grabbed Cambridge's upper arms and pulled him out of his seat. His feet dangled while Dawes got right up into his face. "They found the journals? The ones you were supposed to find? And you didn't mention it until now?"

"But... well... yes...but not my fault," Cambridge sputtered and yelled. "I didn't know Stringham had a secret room in his home."

"All these weeks since you killed Stringham, you have been looking for the artifacts and the journals, and these children found them in a couple of hours," the man in the suit ground out.

"Agent Dawes." The voice over the phone had turned icy. "An invasion could be imminent. Those kids must know something. They just don't understand the potential of the stone yet. We need to get to them quickly, before the government does. When you get them, find out what they know, then do the same with them as you did with Amé Thompson. And Dawes"—she paused— "take care of Cambridge."

"With pleasure," the agent replied.

I WAS HANGING half out of the vent when a piercing siren blasted through the sheet metal. I had spent the last twenty minutes trying to move quietly backward through the duct when I heard the alarm and Shim's whispered, "Hurry, go faster!" Wriggling the last few feet, I birthed myself into the room and landed in a sprawl. Shim slid more gracefully out but landed face first on the epoxy floor.

"Get your shoes on fast. We need to get out of here." I had one shoe on and grabbed the other off the floor.

"*Jaxon? What is happening?*" Shim shouted through the stones. He worked to get his shoes on, awkwardly lacing them while keeping his one hand clenched around the stone.

"*Don't know. They are searching for something, maybe the badge? I don't think they know where you are.*"

"Okay, you need to get out of there," Shim encouraged.

"*I'm not leaving you.*" Jaxon was outraged.

"You have to," Shim explained. "*Do you want them to catch us all? You have to go quick and help get Breeze and Skylar out of the area before they start looking outside.*"

"*Damn it,*" Jaxon shouted. "*All right, but you better make it out, Shim, or I'm coming back to kick your ass.*"

I missed the rest of the conversation. I pulled my hand off the stone and grabbed the knot of laces Shim had made trying to tie his shoe one-handed and quickly unraveled and tied them correctly.

Finishing, I rose and approached the door. "Did they find us?"

"Wait," Shim whispered. I heard a pair of footsteps passing outside of the door, heading the direction we had originally entered. "Okay, it should be clear now. Jaxon's not sure what's going on, but he gave me an alternate route out. We need to hurry. If our access card still works, we might make it."

"Is he going?"

"Yes." Shim looked grim. "I just hope it's not too late."

We exited the room in a cautious run. I kept an eye out behind us while Shim followed a set of intricate instructions Jaxon had given him, cutting through rooms and down empty halls. We finally came to a door that required the badge.

"Here goes nothing." Shim pulled the badge out of his pocket and swiped it. We both waited.

Click! Shim looked shocked when the light blinked green and the mechanism on the door unlatched. I turned the handle and opened the door.

Thump, thump, thump. Footsteps pounded down the hall toward us. Shim shoved me through and pushed in behind me, shutting the door. Automatic lights blinked on as they had in every room we had entered. But this was no room. It was huge, about the size of a high school gym with the same tall ceilings. The walls were the stark white cleanroom plastic we had found in the rest of the building, and it reflected row after row after row of metal racks stacking the full length of the room and towering above us. Crates filled the racks, most sealed, but a few on their sides with the contents on display.

"Are these..." I drew closer, reluctant to touch the rack but curious to categorize what I was looking at, "...guns?" I examined something that looked like a shotgun nestled in a fitted foam pad. It was the right shape, except for the bulbous head at the beginning of the muzzle and it was all white. "I don't know anything about weapons, but aren't they usually black?" Shim hadn't heard me. He had wandered down another row, and I hurried to catch up.

"Logan used to take Jaxon and me out shooting. He had a friend who was a big collector. Had a little bit of everything. None of it looked anything like this. These are like a cross between a handgun and—a Star Trek phaser?" He was leaning in to examine the object but, like me, not touching it.

"Do you think all these crates hold weapons like these?"

"Yeah, I do. There must be thousands of them." He pulled out the burner phone and started taking photos.

"Should you be doing that?" I asked. It felt dangerous.

"If we get caught, we are in trouble either way, and this is something. I don't know what, but it's important."

We walked aisle after aisle.

Shim pried the lid off one of the larger crates that took up a whole pallet. I peeked over the rim. "Whoa." It was full of neatly stacked hand-sized weapons. Using his elevated position, Shim took a couple photos of the inside of the crate, then one along the row to show the dozens of similar boxes.

"Look at this." He spread his arms and waved at the room. "It's huge. If these are some type of hybrid weapon, why do they have so many?"

I thought back to the conversation we had overheard. "Director Koch said an invasion could be imminent. Maybe they're preparing to repel an invasion?"

"Or preparing to invade," Shim added.

I shuddered. My stomach felt ill, and the AC was giving me the chills. I was ready to be done with this place. Instinctively clutching at my necklace, I pulled him along. "Come on. We need to get out of here."

Shim snapped a few more photos as we crossed the room quickly and swiped the badge on the other side to exit. As we left the room, I touched the stone at my throat and heard Breeze's shaky voice.

"*Grace, Shim, Stars, will someone answer! Grace, Shim.*" Over and over again, it went through my head. The stones! We hadn't checked in. Maybe they got caught.

"*We are here. Are you okay? Did you get away?*"

"*GRACE! Yeah, we are gone. Back up by the cave and heading out the way we came.*" Breeze's voice was shaky.

Shim saw what I was doing and tuned in. "*Is Jaxon with you? Did he make it?*

"*Yeah, he is here.*"

Shim sagged beside me. *"Make sure you aren't being followed."*

"Look, the guys can't respond. They are driving. I'm behind Jax. Before we left, he took your bike down and left it by the original door you tried to get in. He says that's where you should exit. He didn't know if you would be able to make it up the hill."

I heard footsteps approaching on the epoxy floor. Shim grabbed my hand and pulled me several yards along the hall to a door. Shoving it open, we exited the sterile environment and were engulfed in heat and a blinding light. It took a minute for my eyes to adjust, and when they did, I saw Shim's bike propped up next to the door.

"Got it!" Shim pulled on the jacket, slammed the helmet on his head, and jumped on. I clambered on behind him, struggling to pull my arms through the sleeves and just getting the zipper half-way up before squeezing into the second helmet. As he started up the bike, I tried to figure out where to put my arms. *"I have to let you go. I can't hold onto Shim and the stone...wait. If something happens, if we get lost or something, we will try and contact you on the hour. Okay?"*

"Okay." Her voice sounded like a sob in my head. *"Grace, be careful. You and Shim...just be safe."*

I was going to respond, but Shim took off like a shot. I flailed on the back of the bike, then grappled for a hold, clutching fabric, and finally got my arms locked tightly around his chest.

We wove through the legs of the solar stands, wheels sinking into the soft sand as we started up the embankment. When I heard a shout behind me, I didn't dare look back. I didn't think my heart could race any faster. Then, near the top, there was a loud *pop*, and the sand flew up beside us. I was wrong.

"Shim," I shouted in his ear, my scream muffled by the helmet. "They are shooting at us!" He put on a burst of speed, and we soared over the top of the ridge. The bike landed with a hard thud, knocking the air out of me. Shim immediately leaned into a hard turn to follow the path we had taken earlier back to the cave. I glanced over my shoulder and could see guards on foot chasing us up the hill. Just as the mammoth white building disappeared from view, I saw a vehicle race around the corner to follow us.

"Jeee-e-e-e-eep." We hit a series of bumps, and the word vibrated out of my mouth. I tried again. "Jeep, there is a Jeep following us." I felt Shim stiffen under my hands, then he relaxed back into his form and put on another burst of speed. He'd heard me.

30

ROAD RACE

WHEN I SAW THE JEEP, my stomach bottomed out. I knew, alone on the bike, Shim could out race a Jeep, even a rig set-up for dune bashing. But with me on the bike, using the passenger pegs, we were going to be slower.

Shim pushed the bike harder, roaring through the turnoff we had taken earlier that day to the cave. The tires broke through a crusty patch of dirt and sank to the soft sand below, spinning and spewing a spray of it out behind us. As we started our descent, Shim looked back. The dunes probably blocked his view of our pursuers, but over the high-pitched buzz of his engine, even I could hear a faint roar. With momentum carrying the bike down, he whipped his head back forward, pushing for the dirt road.

As soon as his tires cleared the shrub lining the track, he lit it up. Leaning forward, he laid on more power and picked up speed. I followed his example, plastering myself to his back as he made tight turns on the switch backs to keep our speed up. I winced as we hit a hard bounce, and my stomach flew up through my head then slammed back down on my tail bone.

The dirt path ended at a paved mine road, and Shim made a

sharp turn onto it, heading toward the city. At the turn, we could see the Jeep exiting the dunes and hitting the dirt road, tearing it up as it roared toward us. It was an off roader, and it looked fast. I bet it would be hard to beat in the sand and even harder on the highway.

The engine screamed as Shim revved it, pouring on even more speed. He fought to keep the bike stable and pushed it to its limit. Soon, we came to the freeway and turned toward the city. Shim flew past a car, the first we had seen on the road. Other cars began to pass us going the opposite direction as people exited the city, probably heading for the lake. The cityscape came into view, like a mirage in the distance, floating on the sizzling waves of heat. The road picked up more traffic, and Shim zoomed past cars, weaving in and out.

I was a mess of rolling emotions. I could feel the Jeep behind us. It made every inch of my skin crawl like live wires were attached. My hands cramped as I clenched at Shim's abs and risked a look back. The Jeep was about two-hundred yards aft, weaving through the cars and growing closer. *Oh Stars.* I screamed, "They are coming," in Shim's ear. The sound was probably faint through the noise and the helmets.

He heard. Shim risked a quick glance back, then revved the engine.

The two lanes turned into four, and the desert gave way to cement and suburbs. Concrete barriers lined the freeway, blocking avenues of escape. An engine roared behind us, and I glanced back again in time to see the Jeep edge around an SUV, cutting it off. When the SUV pushed back, the Jeep rammed it. The driver of the SUV lost control, and his vehicle pinwheeled, its tires leaving a circle of black tread marks. Surrounding cars weaved, some slamming on brakes, some crashing into the center barrier. The wave of chaos briefly pinned in the Jeep until it started ramming the car blocking it.

"Faster, Shim!" I screamed in his ear. I could hear the feral cry of the engine and the steady hiss of tread tearing up the road at our back. Unable to resist, I looked behind me. I met the eyes of the Jeep driver, and he bared his teeth and accelerated. Just before the Jeep smashed into us, Shim swerved. I swung my head forward, nauseous, and decided I'd rather not know when it was going to happen. The bike vibrated as he crossed the rumble strip.

Fifty yards further, and Shim slammed on the breaks. The Jeep shot past us.

What was he doing? We slowed to a roll, and Shim put his feet down. There was a two-foot wide break in the concert barriers of the center divide. He stopped completely and threaded his front wheel through the break.

We emerged on the other side—facing oncoming traffic. I beat at his chest and screamed as a double semi-trailer truck flew just inches past us, a roar of hot air pushing us back.

Shim's feet slid, and he bore down until we stopped.

We were blasted with a symphony of horns. Mindless of the sounds, Shim picked his feet up again and rode slowly up the median strip, against the stream of oncoming cars, being careful to not brush them. It was several tense minutes of cautious driving, my hands clamped to his chest so tight I'm sure I was cutting off his breathing. Suddenly, there was a break in the traffic. Shim pointed the bike into the road and pushed to the opposite side of the freeway.

Shim screamed a roar the whole way across, and I helpfully screeched along with him. When we reached the other side, he laughed like a lunatic. Loosening my grip, I started beating him on the chest, cursing when I heard his laughter. Still racing against the grain, it felt oddly safer on this side.

On the opposite side of the freeway, running parallel to us, the Jeep was still ramming its way through traffic, staying even with, but unable to reach us.

"Grace," Shim shouted. "Watch for another opening in the barrier, we need to get off the freeway." I nodded against his back. Shim watched the road while I looked for our escape route. We were drawing closer to the city, and I worried, once in the city, without the divided freeway, the Jeep would be able to catch up with us. Suddenly, I saw it. I tapped his chest and pointed up ahead to the left. There was the gap in the concrete barrier we needed.

Shim slowed to a stop and indicated I should jump off. I did, and my legs collapsed under me. I clung to the barrier while Shim jumped off the bike and pushed through the narrow gap. I tested my jelly legs and decided I didn't have time to adjust. I let go and, with trembling muscles, helped. We were getting off the freeway, but there was no frontage road on the other side, just a narrow shoulder before a steep pitch drop down a gravel bank. Shim flipped up his visor.

"You doing okay?"

I nodded. "Breeze contacted me as we were leaving, I let her know we got out okay. Shim, we can't lead them back to the others."

"I know. I have an idea...you aren't going to like it." Shim snapped down the visor and hopped back on the bike. When I was safely fitted behind him again, he gunned the engine and sped up the freeway shoulder, still heading for the city.

31

THE TUNNELS

I ALWAYS WONDERED about the idiom "my life passed before my eyes." I mean, really, it's the middle of a crisis and you're going to sit back and watch a movie of your life? As Shim crossed into oncoming traffic, I had a sudden flash, and things that were important clarified: my mom, my dad, my newfound family of Breeze and Skylar, Jaxon, and Shim. Shim. Shim, Shim, Shim, Shim. Things that weren't important: my insecurities, self-doubt, body image, fears—they just faded. And the things I hadn't done created a pang of sadness and regret, along with a promise I would do them all if I just had the chance.

My hands hurt, cramping from holding tight to Shim. But his plan worked. The Jeep could see us, but there was no way it could reach us. Shim traveled up the gravel shoulder, dodging the posts for road signs. We had entered the outskirts of the city, and the area was a mix of desert brush, abandoned concrete pads, low flat buildings, and miles of blacktop.

I glanced back onto the freeway. The jeep was running parallel to us on the opposite side. Looking forward again, I screamed.

"SHIM!"

Shim slammed on the breaks. We skidded for several yards, the back tire sliding sideways until we came to a stop perpendicular to the freeway, inches from a drop off. I swung sideways, almost off the back of the bike, and was staring down into the wide, empty, concrete canal fifteen feet below. I screamed again, beating him on the shoulders. Even though I knew there was nothing else he could have done, the adrenaline coursing through me demanded a release.

Shim grunted and dropped back his head as he sagged in the seat.

I spotted the Jeep as it exited the freeway, crossed an overpass, then diverted down a service road that took them to the opposite side of the canal from us.

"They're coming," I cried.

"Hold on," Shim shouted back. "We are going down there." He pointed to the bottom of the dry canal, then torqued the throttle. We took off with a jolt. The bank of the canal was deeply angled and way too steep to descend. That left us traveling away from the freeway and along the top of the sloped embankment with the Jeep racing parallel to us on the opposite side of the canal. The Jeep pulled ahead as the angle of the decline flattened out. It jumped the edge and crossed toward us. At the same time, Shim slammed on the brakes. I held on tight as the back of the bike spun 180 degrees, then he jumped the embankment too. Riding at an angle down the side of the canal, he headed back the direction we had come and toward two great gaping holes under the freeway.

The tires of the bike chewed up the concrete, but the Jeep was faster, eating up the advantage Shim's stunt had given us. The Jeep roared behind me, then I felt a bump. We wobbled, and I clutched onto Shim harder as he struggled to control the bike. I didn't think it would be possible to be more terrified than I had been when we were on the freeway. The synapses in my brain narrowed down into two thoughts: hold on tight to Shim and don't die.

I heard the engine roar again. Shim hunched down farther, and I followed him till we were lying flat on the body of the bike. With the bike going all out, we pulled ahead of the Jeep.

The great black holes at the end of the canal grew larger. It looked like Shim was headed directly to them. I didn't see any light on the other side. It wasn't an overpass or a bridge. It was a tunnel. Surely, he wasn't planning on going in there—we would be trapped.

But as the entrances grew bigger, he didn't slow. The Jeep roared again behind us. Faster! I mentally urged Shim, committing to his plan, whatever it was. The high-pitched whine of our engine almost blocked it out, but I could still hear the Jeep's roar coming closer. "Faster," I screamed.

A series of things happened all at once: the sun was suddenly eclipsed, everything going dark as the entrance to the tunnel swallowed us up, which was followed by the sound of a loud crash and a horrific scrapping of metal on concrete as the Jeep tried to follow us. They had made a tragic navigational error. Our speed took us down the tunnel away from the accident and the danger behind us.

We were slowing, riding along with the momentum, the bike lamp the only source of light as it bounced off the smooth concrete walls, floor, and ceiling. I was surprised to see no trash, no dirt. The whole tunnel looked like it had been swept clean. We glided for a while until the engine started to sputter. Now that we had slowed, I felt the vibration of something on the back of the bike rubbing against the tire and smelled burnt rubber.

Shim slowed to a crawl, putting his feet down on either side for balance. Up ahead in the glow of the lamp, I could see a thin line crossing from one side of the tunnel wall to the other. Shim must have seen it too. He slowed and quickly stopped.

I hopped off the bike, and my legs almost buckled under me. Wobbling over, I touched the wall for balance while I pulled off my helmet, then I continued to approach the line. It was a metal cord pulled tight. At about shoulder height, it would have decapitated us if we had ridden through it.

I shuddered.

The line had an old blanket hung over it like a curtain. One side was pushed back, and I stuck my head around to see what was on the other side. I could make out eerie shadows and a harsh smell that caused me to blanch and step back. Shim came up behind me, pushing the bike, the light sputtering along with the engine.

"I think someone lives here." Shim grunted in reply. Then the engine started to sputter again, the light fading and coming back on.

Shim pulled off his helmet and swore. "They cracked the gas tank when they hit us." I could smell it now, the fumes of gas mixing with the potpourri of smells from the tunnel.

"What does that mean?"

"It means we have miles of tunnel to go through on foot with no light."

Miles? My mouth gapped open. We have to walk through this place in the dark? I wish I had my bag! I always carried it, stocked full of emergency items, including a flashlight. Here we were, in an emergency with no bag. A thought occurred to me, and I frantically patted the back of my waistband, feeling for the diary.

It was there. *Thank Stars!* It felt secure so I decided to leave it where it was.

"Do you have your pen light or the burner phone?"

"I have the burner, but the battery is almost dead, and I have my pen light." He pulled it out and flicked it on, the faint light barely lit from one side of the tunnel to the other. "Wait, I have an idea. Hold on, it's going to get dark." He turned off the engine, and we were left in the faint glow of the pen light. Shim handed it to me, then leaned the bike against the wall. I pointed the pen to where he was working. It looked like he was stripping something from the bike. He yanked out a bunch of wires, then pulled out a key ring from his pocket and used a screwdriver-shaped fob on the ring to unscrew the bike's light. Once released, he started working on something else. Clutching the light close, I tried not to let the thought of the dark creeping in on us, or the knowledge that something might move behind the impromptu drapes, freak me out.

I was doing a terrible job.

My mind wandered, and I was completely caught off guard when the space suddenly lit up. Blinking like an owl, I looked directly into the light, trying to figure out what it was.

Shim turned the light away and held it up. Once my eyes had adjusted, I saw he had pulled the battery and the headlamp from the bike and wired them together. He'd stuffed them into his helmet with the light shining out the visor. He was using the chin guard as a handle.

"Clever," I complemented him grimly, my face still pulled tight with worry.

"Turn off the pen light. Let's stick with this and hope it lasts long enough."

Long enough for what? Just how far did this tunnel go? There was noise behind us. Shim and I froze. I had no idea what that sound was, but I wasn't taking any chances. With my helmet in one hand, I grabbed Shim's arm with the other. "Come on."

Shim gave a last longing look at his bike before he left it behind and followed me around the curtain. The bright light pushed the creeping shadows away, and I could see a bed of blankets stacked on a wooden pallet up against the wall. A wall of crates and boxes surrounded the bed on one side, and a makeshift table looked like it was trying to be a kitchen with food stores stacked on top.f

I wanted to ask questions. *How could someone live down here? Why?* But there was no time. We cleared the room and pushed farther down the tunnel at a run.

We had been running for a while. My legs were still like jelly, and even with a hand on Shim's arm, I was having trouble keeping up. It occurred to me we hadn't checked in with the others. Would the stones even work underground?

"Stop." Shim halted, and I immediately dropped my helmet and leaned over, putting my hands on my knees. Swimming, I could have kept this up for hours, but not running—I needed a break. Shim paced around me, eager to keep moving. "Do you think they are still behind us?"

Shim stopped and listened, then slowly shook his head. "I don't know what we heard before. It could have been the Helios, or maybe it was an animal, or the person whose home we found. Just in case, we need to keep going. We won't be safe until we are back at the condo, and we can't lead Helios back there."

"We need to try and contact the others and tell them where we are. So...where are we?"

Shim sighed and gave a frustrated scratch to his hair, which was still matted with sweat from the helmet. "I don't know exactly. There are hundreds of miles of these tunnels under the city..."

"Hundreds? Are you serious?"

"Yeah, most were built in the '90s. They're a giant storm drain for the city when it floods. Even a little bit of rain can make them dangerous."

A flood? Rain! "Shim, that was on the forecast. It's going to rain tonight."

"I know," he said grimly. "We have to get out of the tunnels as fast as we can."

"What about the others? I don't know what time it is. We were supposed to contact them on the hour."

"Can you try while we are moving?"

I nodded. It wasn't needed, but Shim grabbed my hand to pull me up. His fingers lingered on mine, and he squeezed before letting go.

"Here, give me the other helmet. I'll carry it while you try."

We resumed a slow jog, and I reached up to my mother's necklace. *"Hello? Breeze, Skylar, Jaxon, are you there? Hello?"* Silence. I tried again and again. No one responded. When Shim looked back, I shook my head. "I'll try again in a couple minutes." Our pace quickened. Five minutes later, I repeated my attempt to reach the others, then again five minutes after that.

"Argh." I was growing frustrated.

"Grace, it doesn't matter." He sounded frustrated too. "They can't help us. Even if they had a map for the tunnels and could tell us where to go, we don't know where we are to start from. We just need to keep going until we hit light. But we have to hurry."

I agreed, and we picked up the pace. I stayed with it as long as I could, but soon I was winded and had a stitch in my side. I needed another break. We had passed several more encampments. Most looked abandoned. That didn't seem good. We were in a clear patch now, and I begged Shim to stop again. We slowed to a trot. I had to sit down for a minute. I moved to a wall and started to slide down it.

"Stop!" Shim said, his voice harsh.

"What? I'm tired," I wailed back. I'd tried to be tough, but my shoulder ached and patches on my back throbbed from what I suspected were burns from the metal stairs I'd hidden under at the warehouse. My lower back ached from bumping along on the bike, and now I had blisters from the sand caught up in my sneakers rubbing me raw as we ran. When the Helios were chasing us, I could forget all of this, but now, I felt like crap.

"Just hold on a second." Shim shined the light down to the floor where I was about to sit, and I heard a quiet scraping as something scurried away.

"What was that?" I asked, jumping straight up and away. My eyes, already owl-like in the dark, widened more.

"Scorpion. Always good to check first. You are in a desert."

I looked down in horror. I'd almost sat on a scorpion? Shuddering, I gave up on the idea of sitting and leaned against the wall instead. "Thanks." Shim leaned next to me. "Where is everyone? We have seen all these encampments, but no people. And why do they live down here?"

"They are probably up in the casinos now, hustling credits. And as for why they live here—why does any city have homeless people? Lack of affordable housing? Addictions? Bad luck? Neglect? It's a complex question."

"But why live in a tunnel? Isn't it dangerous if it floods?"

"Yeah, the water comes in fast when it starts to rise. Plus, there are other dangers to living here. I've heard most of the homeless won't even come into these tunnels." He pushed off the wall. "Grace, we really have to keep moving."

I sighed. He was right. But there was something I needed to say to him first. "Shim, I'm sorry."

"For?" He looked confused, and I couldn't blame him. Just because I'd been obsessing about this didn't mean he had even given it another thought.

"I've been thinking about family. How I didn't understand the pressure my parents were under. How I didn't understand the pressure you are under to take care of Jaxon, and I'm sorry for mentioning your father, putting doubts into your head about him. I should never have done that. You are both so different—"

"Grace, you didn't say anything about Logan I hadn't thought before. I've just never had the guts to ask Kindle about it. She's going to have a lot to answer for if I ever see her again."

"They all will, *when* we see them again."

Shim took my hand and squeezed. We rested in silence for a few more minutes, then, without speaking, headed out again. He went a little slower but still kept up a steady pace. The tunnels changed shape and branched off a few times, but Shim kept us moving roughly in the same direction, passing up off shoots that headed out left and right.

It felt like hours later when I slowed again. "Shim, wait. Shine the light there."

The light swung around and illuminated a section of concrete with writing on it. It was a poem. A little further down, there was more writing. We kept moving. Verse after verse of poems lined the walls, some good, some bad, some just crude curses and dirty rhymes. Most spoke of pain, loneliness, and loss.

"So sad," I murmured. Shim yanked on my arm. "What—" I realized my feet were splashing in water. It must have started raining.

Shim ripped the helmet out of my hands, threw it to the ground, and grabbed my hand. "Grace, run. RUN!"

My heart was thudding in my chest. Water splashed as we ran, soaking my lower legs. I found myself clutching my mother's necklace, the touch giving me comfort as fear ate at me. It took a minute to hear the voice. *"Grace, Shim, are you there?"* It was Breeze.

"We are here!" I screamed into the connection, pouring all my fear into my response. The emotion must have come through a little strong because she responded back in a sob.

"Grace, what is it? What is wrong? Did the Helios get you?" Her voice in my head whimpered.

"We escaped the Helios, but we are in tunnels under the city." There was a pause. I imagine she was relaying the information to the others.

"Grace, you have to get out of there. Jaxon says they flood when it rains, and it's been raining above ground for about an hour."

"I know. Shim and I are lost," I said, screaming as I stepped into a hole and stumbled. The water was up to my ankles now, and I was getting anxious. *"We have been trying to find our way out for hours. I have to go. The water is rising too fast, and I can't...I have to go."*

"Gra—" I let go of the necklace. I couldn't listen anymore and focus on keeping on my feet. The water was rising.

The water was up to my calves when I saw the graffiti. Just a tag of names, then a portrait of a young boy, big eyes staring beseechingly out with a dimpled grin, the words "In Memory" written above it. The walls on both sides of us exploded with color in a gallery of art that we ran past as the water rose.

By the time it reached my knees, I was starting to panic. It has only been a few minutes since I had spoken to Breeze. It was rising unbelievably fast, and there was a current. Shim grabbed my hand, and we steadied each other as we tried to lift our legs above the water line to move faster.

My heart raced. I was lifting my leg when I realized the level was so high, mid-thigh now, that it was faster to walk in the water then to try to stay above it. Bottles and debris floated by us, and the current pulled at my feet with each step.

The water was at my waist when up ahead I could make out a larger room. It took me a minute to understand what that meant.

"Shim, there's a light." The current dragged us toward the

source, and we struggled to stay upright. Several tunnels emptied into the room, and above it was the most beautiful thing I had ever seen—an enormous grate open to the sky.

Rain fell from the center and water gushed in from all sides of the grate, glistening like a crystal waterfall in the yellow light of the streetlamp. The water was chest high as we were swept into the room and we almost kept going, the current rushing us to its next destination. I managed to grab onto the side of a round drain shoulder high in the wall. Shim flew past, and I dug in and reached out for him. I caught his arm and held.

The helmet ripped out of his hand. The light bobbed and swirled as it rushed through the tunnel and disappeared.

The strain of holding Shim pulled on my shoulder that had only just begun to heal from Cambridge's abuse days ago. Was that only days? I felt like I had aged a lifetime since then, and I wondered if I would have the chance to age more. But one of the many surprising things I learned about myself this summer was that I didn't quit. I refused to let go of this pipe, and I refused to let go of Shim. Agony shot up my arm as I pulled him closer.

"Grace—" Shim gasped, fumbling and finally latching onto the pipe next to me. We clung there for a minute, catching our breath and gazing up at the grate so tantalizingly close but just out of reach. Then I noticed the ladder rungs embedded in the wall next to the drainpipe. We had swept right by them. They were only three feet away, but with the current yanking on us, rushing water coming from the drainpipe, and the deluge pouring in from the grate above, it might as well have been a mile.

Shim saw the ladder too. "You're going to have to try and reach for them. Hold on." He adjusted his grip on the drain, wedging one leg inside. "You've got one chance. I'll give you a push on three. Ready?"

I nodded. "One," I said.

"Two," he said.

"Three," we said together, and with an amazing amount of upper body strength, he pushed as I shoved off from the drain and launched myself at the closest rung. One hand slipped on the wet metal, but the other caught. It was my weak arm, but I was able to hold on. I latched on with both hands and wrapped my arms and legs around the rungs. *Yes!*

Repositioning, I reached out for Shim. I could almost reach him, but he would need to let go of the drain to reach my hand.

"Ready?" he shouted. The water roared. The water was above our shoulders now, and we could no longer trust that we could keep our footing. We were running out of time.

"Ready," I shouted back. Keeping a leg wedge in the drain, he let go of the rim of the pipe and reached out. The current pushed him away, but he fought it, and our hands grappled for a second, then locked. I pulled, and he muscled his way over to the rung. His leg slipped out of the drain and he floated on the surface of the water, only his hands anchoring him to the ladder. Pulling, he curled himself in and got one foot, then the other, on the rungs below the water.

We both paused in relief and caught our breath.

"Up," I panted, not able to stand another second longer in the water. The source of my greatest joy in life, water, had become the enemy.

"Up," Shim agreed and steadied me as I climbed the rungs to the top, and he quickly followed. We puzzled over how to get the grate open. Tugging at it, it didn't budge. I tried again, putting my good shoulder to the grate and pushing up with the one leg I had braced on the ladder. The grate moved and then slammed back down. I teetered for a moment on my perch before catching my balance.

"Grace, we will both have to do it," Shim said.

Even though we were out of the flood below, I was getting a

face full of run-off water coming in from the grate, making the rungs slick. Shim crowded next to me. We wouldn't be able to stay like this much longer.

"Move up as high as you can," Shim said. I was awkwardly hunched over with my head pushed up against the metal.

"Okay, I'm going to push the grate up, and you need to get whatever you can through the opening. Ready?" I grunted, and Shim pushed. The grate cracked upwards, and I got a better grip and pushed my good hand through, fingers first, then my hand, and finally my whole arm and head. As soon as my upper body was in the opening, providing leverage, Shim started to worm his way through too. With our legs still on the ladder, we stretched as far as we could, the heavy grate on our backs helping to hold us in place long enough for us to worm the rest of the way out.

I allowed the first moment of hope to flood me. We were going to make it! The struggle was brutal, but inch by inch, we crawled out of the drain, clutching at each other in case one fell back in, until we finally we lay face down on the pavement in a stream of water.

I flipped over onto my back to avoid breathing in the water as I panted. But I couldn't move an inch more. The rain beat down on us. We had made it. Shim groaned beside me.

We were alive!

32

THE DIARY

"AS SOON AS I can move, remind me to call Breeze." Water was flowing around me as it made an escape down the grate, and the hard concrete was cold under my check, but I couldn't find the energy to move. My clothes were already saturated so there wasn't a rush.

"Okay...why?" Shim lay face-up next to me.

"She got through to me when the water first started to rise, and I told her where we were. If we never turned up, I wanted them to know where to look for our bodies."

"That's a morbid thought." Shim turned his head toward me. "Wait, they knew we were in the tunnels and the water was rising?"

"Yes."

"Shit, I better call Jaxon now before he does something stupid," Shim responded. "Oh no!"

I quickly flipped over and dragged myself into a sitting position. "What?"

"The ring, it's gone."

I immediately reached up and reassured myself my mother's necklace was still around my neck, and then, in a panic, slapped the back of my pants. I breathed a sigh when I felt the bulk of the book and pulled it out. That plastic evidence bag had done its job, and the diary was the only thing on us not soaked.

"It must have slipped off my finger in the water. It was a little loose and so much stuff was hitting me I didn't notice. *Oh, Stars.*" His fingers were so bruised and cut up, I was wondering if we should go to the hospital. Shim groaned. "Kindle is going to kill me."

"I'm sure she'll be happy you are alive."

"No, no, she won't." He flopped back into the water.

The corner of my mouth crooked down wearily. I didn't understand that. But there was only one thing I could do to help. I tugged on the stone on my necklace.

"Hello, anyone there?" I said in my head.

"Grace!" It was Jaxon. *"Is that you? Are you and Shim alive?"*

"Grace! Are you okay?" Breeze's voice chimed in.

"Yes, both alive, barely. We could really use a ride."

"Where are you?"

I looked around. We were remarkably close to the strip. It was shocking to think we could have died this close to the heart of Las Vegas. *"I see a castle."* Out loud, I said to Shim, "They want to know where we are."

Shim rolled over closer to me and added his finger to the stone. I could hear him in my head as he gave Jaxon a series of cross streets. We hauled ourselves over to the side of the road and huddled under the streetlamp that had been our beacon of hope in the tunnel. I hugged it and whispered, "Thank you."

I think I fell asleep or passed out. I woke up shivering as a car pulled up next to us.

∞

IT WAS a long time later when I woke with a start. My mouth felt like I'd filtered all of Las Vegas through it. Yuck. I groaned and tried to get up. Everything hurt.

Eventually, I stumbled out of the bedroom and into the bathroom. Sometime later, I finally made it to the living room and collapsed on the couch.

I heard a noise behind me, and Shim grunted in greeting as he passed me. Jaxon promptly razzed his brother. "How you feeling? Feel like heading out on bikes again?"

Shim groaned again. "My head feels like I've been through the spin, rinse, and wash cycle. And don't remind me that my bike is probably under a ten-foot pile of trash at the end of a drain. Not that there was much to salvage after they hit us. Caffeine, I need some caffeine." He started rummaging through the kitchen cabinets. We all followed. I was interested in the results of his search.

"You got hit?" Jaxon exclaimed.

We had given them the short version last night before we collapsed. Now that we were rested, everyone wanted to hear more details of what had happened.

"We can make you breakfast while you tell us," Breeze volunteered eagerly. "We bought some food." That sounded good. Both Shim and I agreed. Breeze and Skylar busied themselves cooking while Shim made coffee, and we filled them in on the details from the day before, the twins and Jaxon adding in bits of info from their point of view. No one knew what to make of the warehouse full of weapons. An invasion? Terrorists? What had we stumbled upon?

"Hand me that." I pointed to the plastic-wrapped diary I'd left on the kitchen island last night to dry out.

Breeze passed it to me. "You really found a room full of weapons?" Her voice was a mix of awe and confusion.

"Hybrid weapons," Shim concurred. "At least, they weren't like anything I've seen before."

The others' chatter around me faded as I pulled off the despised plastic wrap that had saved the diary from destruction. With a deep breath, I centered myself, bracing to see my mother's handwriting. I flipped open the small hardbound green book. The binding wiggled, loose with wear.

I looked down at the title page of the book and read my mother's name. A tear welled up, and I blinked it away with a sniff, not wanting to cry on the diary after all it had been through. I flipped to the next page and my eyes bugged. I stood up. *"HOLY SOURCES!"*

The first line was gibberish, a series of marks that made no sense, but the translation written underneath it read: *It was April 1, 1995, when we arrived on Earth.*

33

DIARY: STRANDED

ON THE BACK of the front cover was a letter to Lincoln, so I started reading aloud to the others there.

Dear Lincoln,
Years ago, I promised to tell you everything—someday. I had hoped it would be on my way home, but I've come to accept that will never happen. My diary is the best way to tell you our story. I originally started writing in my native language, but I have translated those sections so I can share it with you. You always said we saved you, but you will see it was really you that saved us.
Love always, Amé

(Translated) It was Saturday, April 1, 1995, when we arrived on Earth. Back home, it was the 20 > 4th cycle on the day of Earden in the year of 5104.

I want to go home. This place is frightening. Micah suggested I write down my feelings. He thinks it will help me process them. I'm not supposed to write what happened, just how I feel. But how will that help when what I feel is because of what happened?

This is how it started. I was on a one-day field trip to Nadun —and now I'm stranded on Earth. Sources sake, my mata is going to be furious with me! She didn't want to send me to the program this summer, said at thirteen I was too young, but I wanted to go, and my Uncle L'To talked her into it.

We were on a tour of the deep mines with fifty other students from various programs around the Federation. A scientist told us the mine level we were visiting had been recently reopened by special request from the authorities and would usually be off limits, but because a couple of students in our group had permission to see the restricted area, our whole tour was granted access. The scientist was very excited about the discovery of a rare rock. While showing us the rock, the ground started to shake with one of the moon's frequent quakes.

But it didn't stop, and everyone was pushing and screaming. I was hit and I fell, scraping my face. It hurt and was bleeding a lot. Large rocks were falling, and the ceiling was moving like it was going to collapse.

An older boy and a girl helped me up (that was the first time I met Micah and Trystal). When they grabbed my arm, Micah handed me the rock everyone had been looking at and told me to hold onto it. They took me with them down a side tunnel. Several other students were behind us.

I thought we were safe. Micah stopped running. Then a wind surrounded us. It circled faster, and a ball of light appeared in front of us. It started as a pin prick and quickly grew. The light pulled on me; the suction was so strong, my feet slid along the dirt floor into a whirlpool of brightness.

Inside, I was moving, sliding through a bright passage strobing with beams of light. The motion and the flashing lights made me ill. I grabbed at the walls and tried to stop, but they burned and blistered the tips of my fingers. The heat was so intense, it was hard to breathe.

Somehow, I held onto the rock.

Just as I thought I was going to burn to death, it started to cool, and I realized I was slowing. The light changed to a continuous bright yellow, and I hit something hard.

When I could see again, I was lying outside. Micah and Trystal were there. Three others who I didn't know also came through the passage. One was Arie, who checked to make sure I wasn't hurt and then went to help a girl named Kindle, who hurt her wrist. Another boy, named M'er, was helping Trystal up. They all have more years than me—I'm the youngest.

As I lay on the ground and looked up at the sky, I felt numb and tingly. Everything felt wrong.
I heard music off in the distance. I remember it playing, then I distinctly heard, "This is Donna and Leila here with the morning show to free your minds on 101.3FM, your freak radio in Santa Cruz."

And that is how we arrived on Earth.

"Are you shitting me?" Jaxon exclaimed. The others were staring at me. Eyes wide, the twin's mouths gaped, and even Shim looked thunderstruck as he sat down hard beside me.

"Keep reading," Breeze encouraged, and I turned back to the diary.

The first few weeks on Earth were a blur of fear and confusion. Some people helped us and became our closest friends, and some people hurt us in ways we will never recover from. There is a kind of loneliness in keeping secrets. And this one chokes us. None of us know how we got here, and none of us have been able to figure out how to return.

We know nothing about this planet or, really, about life. We fear discovery. What if this planet's government finds us and splits us up? And there are much worse people who hunt us. But by far, what scares us the most is never finding the way home.

We have tried. Oh, we have tried so many, many times and ways, I can't even relate them all. Micah kept a log of our experiments. Holy Source, I would give up anything to find the way back.

"Wait a minute." Jaxon yanked the diary out of my hands. "This can't be right." He had settled on the other side of me on the couch. "You must be reading it wrong." I gave him an incredulous look, and Shim reached around me and simultaneously shoved Jaxon and pulled the book from his hands.

"Don't be an ass, Jax," Shim said. "Let Grace read...whoa!" The journal had flipped forward several pages, and Shim started to read aloud.

I finally asked Micah to explain to me where we were. Micah says that on Teran, that's the planet that Micah and Tyrstal come from, there are old, secret stories—legends really— about Earth. He read about them when working with his uncle, who is a political historian. He says our two planets used to be connected by a passage through the sun. Our home in the Federation of Elements is on one side of the sun, exactly opposite on the same orbit is Earth. He says it is a closely guarded secret among the academics in the Feder- ation. Maybe some of the wiser scientists of Earth will remember the Federation and be able to help us get home.

I wish now I had not asked Micah about it. Now I have to admit I really am on another planet. I can't believe I'm this far away from home without my mother's permission.

"That is insane," Breeze exclaimed, reading over Shim's shoulder. "Oh, Grace, this is about you." She read aloud.

It is strange that none of the water people here have green streaks in their hair as I do and as most citizens on LaDér do. My hair gets many stares. Fortunately, I have seen a few people on the street with many other colors in their hair, so maybe it is not too odd.

Breeze giggled. "She thought anyone with colored hair had it naturally like you do." She hunched over laughing. I didn't find it as humorous as Breeze. Skylar took the opportunity to snatch the book from her and skipped ahead a few pages.

"Oh, this is about the rock." Skylar read aloud.

We were staying with some religious men called monks when we met Robert. He is a professor. Micah and Trystal talk to him for hours every evening. Arie joins them too. I was really surprised when they showed him the rock. He was very excited and wanted to know where we had found it. They would not tell him anything specific—like the fact that we were from another planet. He suggested we take it to a specialist in San Francisco. He really wants to study it and even suggested postponing his sabbatical in India if he could take it for a while. Micah refused and said we would bring it to him when he got back. I don't understand what the rock has to do with us coming through the passage, but obviously, Micah thinks it is important.

I'm really glad I'm not here alone and that I have M'er, Arie, Micah, and Trystal with me, and sometimes, I'm even glad for Kindle.

"Wait a minute." I pulled back the diary and silently read the last line. "Who is this M'er? She mentioned him before too. Have any of you heard of him?" Everyone shook their heads, faces somber. What happened to M'er?

We continued to read the diary, passing it back and forth and stopping over sections to discuss. Most of it was the regular day-to-day observations of any thirteen-year-old. Only, it wasn't any thirteen-year-old. It was my mother. And everything we read sank me deeper into confusion and concern. Even though these events happened decades ago, I grew more terrified for her and had to pass off the diary frequently for someone else to read.

"Wait," Shim interrupted Skylar who was reading, "go back." Skylar reread a section that was from six weeks after they arrived on Earth. *Arrived on Earth.* It was hard to conceive of.

Chinatown is like bubbles up your suit, an unexpected

surprise. I love it. Lots of yummy food of the ocean, and old
ladies cackle, cackle with each other. Of course, we have our
translators, so they are always surprised when I understand
them. Arie found a place that sells herbs, and we…

"Stop, that was it!" Shim exclaimed, looking puzzled. "They had translators. I wonder where they got them from?" Shim was always doing that. Stopping over some detail and clicking the puzzle piece in place.

Skylar continued to read.

We went to a gem and mineral show and met a nice man
named Clark. He is a material scientist, and he likes to TALK!
We learned a lot and eventually felt comfortable showing him
our rock. After all that time of having to listen to him, he
didn't even know what our rock was. But he did offer to take
us to a Vegas in his vehicle for recreation to an even larger
gem and mineral show. He says all the leading scientists will
be there. We don't have any other leads…so Micah is
considering it.

"Anyone else think it's weird that this Micah guy is in charge all the time?" Jaxon said with a grumble.

"Hum," Shim grunted, and nodded at Skylar to keep reading.

(Translated) June 2, 1995.
Clark is a religious leader, and he carries a sacred black book
everywhere with him. He says his recreation vehicle, an RV, is
a vessel of faith, and that is why he painted it green and
wrote "Jesus Saves" on the back. I know this Jesus is a lot
like the Source 'cause I hear people say his name all the
time, especially if they are angry.

I was cleaning the RV today, and I found a map that shows the whole of Earth. It is amazing. All its resources are combined on one planet and shared among its inhabitants fairly and in harmony.

(Lincoln, in the Federation, where we are from, a single element is the major domain of each world: the planet Teran is the scientific center all the moons were colonized from, and has the only farmable landmass. My home, LaDér, is actually a moon, and its surface is completely covered in water and ocean resources. The moon Mirah has no habitable landmass but has an atmosphere that houses a floating civilization and fields of turbines to power the whole system. And the barren moon Nadun provides supercritical heating power and rich mineral resources. Each is key to the system's survival.)

"Wow, she really didn't understand Earth," Jaxon remarked sarcastically. "'Sharing fairly and in harmony.' Yeah, right."

"I don't think I believed it until she described all the planets. Well, planet and moons. It's incredible." Shim shook his head.

(Translated) We are famous! Micah is not happy about it.

On the second day, Clark talked Micah into letting him put our rock on display. Micah insisted it had to be in a locked case, and one of us stayed with it at all times. One man, a scientist from some place in the northwestern land, says he teaches in a program that studies rocks and offered to run tests to learn what it is and what properties it may hold. Micah was very interested in that.

On the last day of the show, someone tried to steal the rock!

I saw a strange man staring at our booth and me. Then the stranger seized the whole case with the rock still locked inside. I was so surprised, I screamed. Kindle heard and grabbed the man's legs (she is really strong). He fell on the box, cutting himself on the broken glass, and when the people in authority came, he ran off.

Micah wanted me to record what the man looked like. I only remember that he had a dark marking on his neck and a circular scar on the back of his hand.

Breeze stopped reading, and we were all silent for a minute.

"That description is the similar to Dawes. Do you think that's when the Helios first noticed them?" I whispered.

"Maybe," Shim muttered. Looking over his notes, he sighed. "They were so careful up until then, but they also hadn't made any progress in finding out about the stone."

Breeze sighed. "How sad for them."

Skylar was flipping the pages of the diary as we talked. "Guys, I think I found out what happened to them, why there were so afraid." He started to read.

(Translated) I don't know how things went so wrong so fast. I've never seen anyone die before, and now I can't stop thinking about what happened and how trapped we are.

The closing of the show was a relief, and it changed every-thing. While helping Clark pack up, we realized we were being watched. Across the hall, Arie saw the authorities of the show coming for us, with several law keepers. Clark said they were trouble for us, and we needed to leave. He gave each of us a hug and a handful of paper money to Micah.

Since the attempted theft, Micah kept the rock hidden and had us bring our bags with us so we could leave at any time. It was easy to slip under the tables and crawl out of view of the authorities. Then we ran.

I thought we were clear as we reached the large doors leading out of the showroom, but the back of the hall filled with dozens of men and women in black suits. The man who had tried to steal the rock was with them. He shouted at us to stop. We escaped out the doors and kept running.

Outside the convention center, a man drove up in a white vehicle with big tires. He yelled at us to jump in. Micah recognized him as one of the people he had spoken with at the show, but we didn't know if he was one of the people chasing us. When we hesitated, the van driver said, "I'm Tar Xanon of Nadun!"

"Tar Xanon, the guy from the video," Shim exclaimed when Skylar paused in reading.

(Translated) We scrambled into his van. There were no seats, so we crouched on the floor. The law keeper vehicles chased us, and Tar ignored the road and drove over any barriers in his way. I remember as we raced through the city, I didn't care about the people chasing us; I wanted Tar to answer my questions: How did he get here? Did he know how to get home?

Tar drove up and OVER a law keeper's vehicle. There were loud pops, metal pings, and a window in the van exploded glass. Tar was driving the wrong way down a road. M'er was sitting next to me, squeezing my hand.

A truck even bigger than ours came at us. A horn was sounding. Tar spun the van, and I fell over. Pinned to the wall, I missed what happened next. But, somehow, we didn't crash. Then Tar was on a side street, and it looked like he had lost the chasers.

As he drove, Tar shouted out his story to us. It was hard to hear, and some of it didn't make sense at the time. But I talked to the others later, and this is what we remembered: Tar had worked the mines of Nadun. His assignment was to clean out debris from cave-ins on the oldest levels. The tunnels were deep and hot, mostly abandoned centuries earlier, but occasionally, they would re-open one to follow a new vein of minerals. There were certain specimens all miners knew to be on the lookout for. One day, the tunnel he was working on collapsed. He thought he was going to die there. Injured and scared, he tried to dig his way out. That's when he found a rock so rare, they didn't even have a sample of it, just a description. Before he could dig the rest of way out of the tunnel, a bright light flashed. A passage opened up, and he landed on Earth, but he had lost the rock. Over the years, he tried everything to get home. He knew the rare rock was the key, so he had been mining for a new stone ever since.

Tar's story was so amazing. At first, I didn't realize M'er had stopped holding my hand. When I looked at him to see what he thought of Tar's story, his face was sweaty and pale, and he was panting. I remember asking him what was wrong and looking down. There was red all over his shirt. I must have made some noise. Trystal pulled me back, and Micah and Arie tried to help M'er.

It happened so fast. In all the books I have read, you have time to say goodbye or think about the things you wish you had done. M'er whispered something to Micah, then he was gone. Arie wanted to take him to healers, but it was too late, and Tar said it would jeopardize the rest of us.

Tar told us about the two groups who were chasing us. One was the government, which he had learned the hard way were dangerous, and the other was a private group called Helios Kratos—they were more dangerous.

I realized there is no place for us here. We are lost in this strange world. My mata use to say our paths are laid out for us; we just make one step at a time in Faith. She believes in Faith, and the Source, and the Stars. My pata says we each create our path by the steps we take.

I do not think this was M'er's path. His was stolen from him, and I weep inside for all that might have been in his life.

It felt wrong when Tar dropped us at the bus station. I didn't want to leave M'er or Tar. They were fragile connections to home.

Tar insisted it was too dangerous for us to stay. He said he would do the death rituals. Micah asked how we could find him again so we could try and find a way home. Tar's words shattered me. "I have been trapped here for thirty-five years. There is no going home, there is only survival."

34

DIARY: FINDING HOME

I CHOKED BACK a sob as Skylar kept reading my mother's diary.

(Translated) I don't remember what happened after M'er died. I woke on a bus feeling empty. Deep in my soul, I knew I was never going to see my home again, never have my pata hold me, my pata sing to me, see my cherished grandperes. I was lost. And I'm ashamed to say I envied M'er his quick escape.

"Stop," I choked out, rushing from the room.
"Grace?"
I escaped into the bathroom. Crouching down, I rested my wrists on the cool porcelain of the sink edge, my head dropped between my arms and tried to breathe. My chest was tight and achy. All I could hear was the pounding in my ears and my mind raced over and over those last words: quick escape.

Stars, I'd thought she was a coward. In the back of my mind, I'd thought she had run from us. Maybe living with me was too much work, maybe she had wanted to follow her own dreams and not have to take care of us, maybe...I don't know that I had a good reason, but I always thought it was something I had done. And that hurt. So I got mad at her instead. But now...now I find out she was running for her life. She ran to keep us safe. *Sources,* she was so brave to have survived. She didn't forge a new life in a new land—planet—by choice. She did it because she had to. She was so strong, and I was such a jerk to her.

"Grace." Shim's muffled voice came through the door. I didn't want anyone to see me like this, but Shim and the others in that living room might be the only people on the planet that could understand what I was feeling.

"Come on, open up," he whispered through the door.

Waiting until I could draw a stuttering breath, I turned the handle and studied him through the small slit. He was hunched down on the floor, face pushed to the opening. Concern pooled in his amber eyes.

"She..." I choked, and his face went wavy and blurry.

"I know. I...I know. Do you want to quit reading for the night?"

"Yes...maybe." I thought about it. Was learning about what happened one sad, scary tale at a time better, or should we rip the Band-Aid off? I closed my eyes, suddenly exhausted. "No, let's finish it." My eyes opened.

Shim's mouth tugged up at one corner, and he stood up and held out his hand.

When we returned to the living room, the others looked up.

"Are we still reading?" Jaxon asked with uncharacteristic sensitivity. At Shim's nod, he sighed in relief. "Good, because I've been reading ahead. They must have met and followed Stringham to Portland. You are going to want to hear this."

(Translated) 19>7th 5104, June 13, 1995

Clark had told Micah that most of the people we met at the show were enthusiastic amateurs with a few seasoned experts, and it was rare to meet a true professional planetary geologist. Learner Stringham is one of those rare few, and we tracked him down at his home in Portland.

Learner Stringham was thrilled to see our rock, but he, Micah, and Trystal disagree on what to do. The Learner would like to cut into the rock to examine it more closely. He wants to cut it into five pieces. Micah can't figure out what else to do, so he has agreed. But Trystal is very upset about it, something about the resistance being proportional…something…I had no idea what she was saying. I've been in a program for many years, but my favorite studies are art and music, not science. Most of us leave that up to the Terans—which is why they are usually in charge.

It's risky either way, since we don't know if or how the stone got us here, so we would never know if it has been damaged.

(Translated) 21>7th 5104 (June 15, 1995) For the last two days, Micah and Trystal have been working nonstop with Learner Stringham; they also make sure one of them is always with the rock.

Last night, Trystal told us they had discovered that the silver veins in the rock are high energy conductors. Learner Stringham suggested there is an activator or trigger for this. This is where it got dangerous, and Micah got excited. This activator could be what we need to get the passage back, but we can't tell Learner Stringham that.

"Do you think that learner—professor—whatever, told them the whole truth about what he had discovered?" Skylar asked.

"Maybe, but..." Shim had brought the red journal into the living room and started flipping through the pages while we read from the diary. He held his place and went back a few pages in the journal to check something, then returned to the original page. "This is the section that matches the dates we have been reading. It does look like he recorded the same information in his personal journal as what Amé wrote. She might not have been a scientist, but she recorded the important information, at least what they told her."

"Uh oh." Skylar made a tutting sound. "Here is where they ran into trouble." He read over Jaxon's shoulder.

(Translated) 22>7th 5104, June 16, 1995
Well, they did it! Learner Stringham had his assistant Sidney
cut the stone up into five pieces. They tested each and
Micah was proved right, the individual pieces had the same
amount of power, or conductivity, or whatever, to them.

But when Sidney got involved, he started to ask a lot of
questions we didn't want to answer. He also became very
possessive of the rock pieces and kept trying to conduct
experiments without Micah or Trystal around.

(Translated) 23>7th 5104, June 17, 1995
So we are running AGAIN!

Yesterday, after leaving for the Learner's workplace to do the
additional power tests, Kindle spotted a black car watching
the house. We grabbed our things and ran out the back door.
Arie called into the office and left a message for Micah and
Trystal.

*I was worried we wouldn't see them again. I didn't know they
had set up a place to meet if something happened. They
have to start including me in these decisions. I'm not a baby;
I can help!*

"I know how she feels." Breeze pouted, holding out her
hand to Jaxon. "Let me have a turn." Jaxon huffed and handed
over the green diary, and while she found her place, he shoved
Skylar off his shoulder. Skylar grabbed at him, managing to
unseat him as he toppled to the floor.

Absently, Shim lifted his legs and continued flipping
through the red journal as the other boys knocked each other
about.

"Oh, this is a good part! And it doesn't have a section in
those gibberish marks, just English," Shim said.

Skylar and Jaxon ceased struggling and, helping each other
up, settled on opposite corners of the coffee table as Breeze
started to read.

*June 18, 1995
I finally got to do something helpful today…I saved a man's
life!*

*After escaping again, we were wandering around the water-
front while we decided what to do next. Since I never get
asked my opinion, I left the others, and I walked past the
beach and farther out onto the marina around the docks,
following the pull of the ocean.*

*That is when I saw a man floating face down in the water. The
moon where I was born is covered in water, so I'd learned
rescue training when we are young. I yelled for the others to*

help and grabbed a rope with a float and jumped in. I wrapped the rope around him, pushing the float under his chest, then got back out and used the rope to pull him over. By that time, the others showed up, and together, we were able to pull him out.

Arie told me back home he had chosen the path to be a healer, so I know he has resuscitation training, and after a lot of work, we got him to breathe again. He had a cut on his forehead. It went from his temple all the way down to his cheek. He also smelled similar to my mata's brother L'To when he would get melancholy and starts sucking down the palliatives. Blech!

When the man became aware, we told him what had happened. He pointed to a vessel called Fly to Blue, *then lost consciousness again. Since we were not eager to come to the attention of the authorities, we dragged him on board and cared for him.*

June 19, 1995
The man woke up today long enough to tell us his name was Lincoln and to yell at us to get off his boat. Then he fell back to sleep. He was so angry and didn't thank us for saving him. Arie says I need to be careful around him. But I saved him, so he is mine, and I've been taking good care of him. He obviously loves the water, too, since he lives on it. I think we have much in common. Except for the love of palliatives. He has bottles of the stinky drink everywhere on his boat. We tried to use the oven and discovered three in there, several stuffed under cushions and bedding, and even one curled up in a sail.

"So that is how they met Lincoln and why Herb and Linda said they saved his life. It's nice," Breeze said.

"It's boring, and it's on a boat. Get to a good part," Jaxon grumbled.

"Okay, okay." Breeze flipped pages, talking to herself. "Skipping over them taking care of Lincoln, him offering to take them to San Francisco, Amé and Lincoln becoming friends, Kindle getting seasick on the trip—oh, wow, this is good…"

June 29, 1995

Lincoln was very quiet all day. I thought maybe I did something wrong. But then I saw he was the same way with the others. As we were pulling the sail in at the end of the day, the others were inside making dinner. He motioned me to the front of the boat and asked me if there was anything I wanted to talk about. Then he told me he had overheard us talking about another planet. Lincoln watched me sputter and spin as I tried to make up a lie he would believe. I'm such a bad liar.

He sat me down beside him, and he told me about his daughter and son. About the war he had been in. That he had done things to survive he wasn't proud of. He told me about coming back home and how he felt he didn't fit anywhere. How he had tried to be a good father but had turned to drink to escape himself. And he was afraid for his kids when he drank, so he left. Now the guilt over leaving his kids keeps him from going home. He told me a lot about what fear and guilt and sadness can do to a person.

And that is when I told him the truth: who we were, where we were from, and what had happened to M'er. He was quiet when I finished talking. We sat and looked out at the harbor, watching the ocean rise and fall. Then he told me he believed me.

I cried. To tell our story and have someone believe it that didn't chase us, or want to hurt us, was such a relief. A huge weight lifted, and I took my first full breath since we had arrived on Earth.

Breeze sniffed and rubbed a tear from her check. "That was so sweet."

"So stupid. He could have turned them in," Jaxon exclaimed even as I saw he was absently rubbing Breeze's back.

"But he didn't, and he helped them. There are good people on Earth," Breeze exclaimed.

That struck me as odd. We had only just discovered our parents were from another place, and we were already thinking in terms of an "other world" and "Earth."

"Grace, you want to read again?" Breeze offered with a watery smile. I shook my head.

"I'll read." Picking up the diary, Jaxon muttered, "...Of course my mom gets seasick. Okay, blah, blah, they had to tell the others Lincoln knew, blah, blah, more sailing..."

"Hey," Shim interrupted. "If you are going to read, read it, or pass it off to someone else."

"Yeah, okay—Well, this is interesting."

June 30, 1995

Lincoln was full of questions today. He and I chatted while the others glared. Eventually, Arie started answering a few of Lincoln's questions too. Trystal liked his idea that we needed to adopt Earth names. He suggested second names fitting different regions based on our race. That was a little hard to understand, but I guess because everyone is on Earth instead of spread across moons, each region developed distinctive characteristic, like each moon did back home. He did mention there was no place on Earth where people had green streaks in their hair, so I'd have to tell people I dyed mine or I had a genetic disorder. He also told us about foster families, where an adult would care for children who had no parents and that would be a good way to explain a family as mixed as ours.

From then on, we told everyone we were foster siblings.

Lincoln had so many ideas on how we could blend in and not get discovered that even Kindle was talking to him. Micah was still cautious.

July 4, 1995
It's Independence Day! Lincoln says there will be fire in the sky tonight to celebrate. I can't wait! We pulled into San Francisco yesterday and rented a place to tie up the boat. It took a long time to sail from Seattle. But now, Micah has gotten to know Lincoln better and is starting to trust him.

July 8, 1995
Micah and Arie went with Lincoln today to meet a friend of his named Waters. This friend is going to help us get identifi-cation papers so it will be easier for us to travel and live. Lincoln also wants us to meet Waters because he thinks we need to spend some time with him learning his rules, which are apparently different from the ones the authorities use.

Lincoln cautioned us to not tell Waters about our past.

I will miss my friend. We took a photo together, and I

promised to send him my journal when we left Earth so he could see the rest of our journey.

We skimmed over the section on Waters, which was hauntingly familiar to our own training. Reading through our parents return to Santa Cruz where they spent months trying, again and again, to get the stones to open a passage was depressing, and it was even sadder as, over time, we could tell they were giving up hope. But they gained other things as they went along.

I volunteered to read again.

June 1996.

I guess we really are a family since we now have a foster parent. Robert is a professor of mathematics at Stanford University, and he and Micah get along really well. Robert wanted to foster Micah and sponsor him to attend the University, but Micah said we had to come with him—and Robert agreed! Robert is trying to line up sponsors for Trystal to go to university too. Before we came to Earth, Micah and Trystal were in the year of decision making and studying hard to become academics. They are now studying even harder to adapt to Earth's knowledge of things (I doubt they will get into a university here based on their knowledge of Teran's history). Since Lincoln, we have never told another soul where we are from. And after working with Waters, I doubt we ever will. It is far too dangerous.

Robert said he "pulled strings" and found places for Kindle, Arie, and me at a local program, but we have to live away from Trystal and Micah. From what I've read about Earth high schools, the experience will be terrifying, but I'm looking forward to making new friends.

Once a week, we take a bus and all meet at the spot we arrived on Earth and try to open the passage. We do the same thing each time. It never works. But Micah won't let it go.

October 1996
Kindle hates our high school. I love it! It is right on the ocean and so easy for Noah and me to get to the beach every day. Noah is my new friend. Micah has warned me to not say anything about our past, so when Noah asks, I have to pretend it's too painful to talk about. I think I will tell him someday, but now, we have so much else to discuss it doesn't matter. Noah showed me how to surf on a board. He is really smart and loves the ocean too.

I still go up and visit Lincoln once a month.

Even though Micah is now in classes all the time, he keeps dragging us up to the Mystery Spot to try and open a passage. It's hard for me to explain to Noah where I disappear to each week, and every time, Kindle refuses to go and Arie has to talk her into it.

June 1997.
Kindle and Arie graduated high school! They did it a year early—if you consider our real ages—but we have been using our fake IDs so long, I think they forgot and just thought it was time to be done. They decided to go to college in Southern California. Micah is having a fit at how far away they will be. But he will let them go. Both he and Trystal are almost through their college degrees, and we hardly see them anymore, except for the pilgrimage every other month to the spot.

I'm so glad I still have Noah here at school. Since he took the year off before I met him to study marine biology on a science vessel, his schedule has been messed up, and this year, he has been taking college classes while finishing high school. But we will both graduate next year. I haven't told him I'm only fifteen.

June 1998.
Today we graduated from high school!
Noah and I decided we wanted to go to school in Southern California. Trystal and Micah are starting their PhDs, so I'm glad I'll be close to Arie and Kindle. It will be nice to see them more often, but they are busy too. Arie has decided he is going to become a medical doctor, and Kindle is studying business. She is really good at managing money. She also wants to be Mrs. Arie.

I've decided to end this journal. It has served its purpose, and now, it's time to let go and start something new. I'll take it up to my dear friend Lincoln to read next time I see him. I always promised I would send it to him when we left Earth, but I don't think that's ever going to happen.

As much as I still miss my family on LaDér, there are now people here I would miss if I left. Earth feels like home. So, I guess I was right when I told Lincoln I would send him my journal when we found our way home.

35
____

THE TRUTH

WHEN I CLOSED THE JOURNAL, the sun was high in the sky, pouring in through the condo's wall of windows, blinding me as it flashed off the sea of glass and the gold details of the city. The light was as brazen as the truth I had just read: my mother was from another place...*another planet?*

Planet. I still couldn't wrap my head around it.

In the living room, the silence was a presence, an entity taking up the air in the room, making it hard to breathe. Sinking back into the shelter of the leather sofa, I closed my eyes against the glare. I guess, normally, you would think, What could be more boring than reading your parent's diary? Ick! But each page had been even more mind-blowing than the last.

Could this be real?

Of course, it wasn't...was it?

The fragments of my life were puzzle pieces that now made a strange kind of sense. The nomadic lifestyle. The secrets. One revelation after another flashed through my head, ridiculous, insane, unbelievable. Believable? Maybe this diary was a fake? Half-baked excuses popped into my head, attempting to discredit everything we had read.

I tried to calm the spinning teacup ride my thoughts were on, to latch onto one of the life-changing brain explosions bombarding me and start to process it. The only anchor that steadied me was the bittersweetness of hearing my mother's voice through her words in the diary.

It wasn't a fake. This was real. This diary was a gift, a piece of my mother that I could hold on to. In those written words, I recognized her tone and expressions. In her story of fear and courage in this new place, I heard her confusion, pain, and strength. She was so strong.

And it changed everything.

"How could they keep all of this from us?" Skylar asked.

"Holy Sources, are we—" Breeze sat up, eyes huge.

"Don't say it," Jaxon yelled.

"Are we—" Breeze continued.

"Shut up." Skylar lunged for his sister.

"Are we aliens?" Breeze finally got out.

"No," I scoffed. "Aliens are..." I faltered. Aliens are... people from other planets—which our parents were, which meant...

"Yes," Shim croaked. He looked stunned, and his mouth opened and closed a few times before he added, "Well, at least half."

Skylar got up and looked at himself in the large mirror on the wall. He turned his head from side to side as if he was searching for antennas. "I don't feel like an alien," he concluded. "Nothing has changed. I don't feel any different."

But he was wrong. *This. Changed. Everything.*

Brrrrrringgg. At the sudden intrusion of the ringing phone, we all jumped, muscles tensing. The sound was coming from right beside me. Without thinking, I reached down, fumbling with the extension on the side table and answered the call. "Hello?"

The voice on the other end punched me up to a standing position. My attention snapped to the receiver in my hand.

"Yes, Agent Bailey, this is Grace Thompson. Now, maybe you can tell me where our parents are?"

∞

I PUSHED OPEN the heavy metal door and moved out onto the building's rooftop patio. The smell of rain was still in the air.

"Did you talk to her?" I asked.

Shim shook his head, a quick abrupt movement.

"Did you talk to him?" I asked. Shim looked over at me. Maybe he didn't realize how obvious it was to everyone else. Once the lie was removed, the truth was plain to see. "Did you talk to Arie, your father?"

He snorted and shook his head. "No. They've locked themselves in the master bedroom to yell at each other. I tried to go in, but they ignored my knock."

From the minute the key had gone into the lock this morning and our parents had rushed in, we had been swept up in the chaos of panicked family, protective government agents, and emotional explanations.

Especially when our parents found out that we had found Amé's diary and read it. They hadn't gotten around to asking where it was yet, so I had time to make up a story on how I had lost it again, along with Stringham's journals. Or maybe I would tell them the truth—that I'd traded the diary and journals for their freedom.

Micah, the tall Indian man who had entered with the others, had requested the agents wait outside while we got reacquainted, and even after they had reluctantly agreed, Micah wouldn't let us start talking. We waited as he and the other adults walked through the condo, checking each room. When he was satisfied we were alone, he held up a finger for silence, then pulled a brooch out of his pocket. He turned over the enameled piece of jewelry to show a reddish-green stone nestled in the back. I had reached up to my necklace and fingered the stone at my throat. Dad smiled faintly at me and rested his palm on my collar bone as he put a finger next to mine. I looked over. Skylar had pushed up the sleeve on his shirt and he, Breeze, and their father each laid a hand on the cuff's stone. Jaxon shocked our parents by pulling out the ancient necklace, and he, Shim, and Kindle touched the stone in the center.

The parents had been surprised we knew about the stones, and, as Shim had predicted, Kindle had been furious when she learned her ring was lost.

They started firing questions at us, but we quickly put a stop to that, demanding to know where they had been. But they didn't know. As soon as they were picked up, they had been separated and flown to an undisclosed location, where they were held in solitary confinement when they weren't being questioned. They never saw each other or anyone else. In spite of their relief at seeing us again, they looked exhausted and broken.

Micah was especially disheartened. He had been spying on the government for some time, working for them, not letting them know who he was while he secretly kept tabs on what they knew. He thought they were unaware of his status, but while he watched them, they had been watching him, thinking at first that he was working for the Helios group. When they realized he was not from Earth, they moved to pick him and his family up. Micah got off a warning to our parents, and that had given them the time to make the calls that put us on the run. They were appalled to learn it had ended up redirecting the Helios attention to us.

Then I had to share the worst of it. When Noah learned my

mother's death hadn't been an accident and the government had known the Helios held her, he had been heartbroken. The rest of the parents looked ill.

Then, we told them everything else that had happened to us.

∞

"AMAZING." Standing beside me on the rooftop, Shim had been gazing out at the city, but now he glanced back at me, one side of his mouth quirking up.

I raised an eyebrow in question.

"You." He reached out a hand and pulled down a strand of my green hair the wind was playing with. "We wouldn't have gotten anywhere without you pushing."

"I'm not sure that's a good thing," I remarked self-consciously.

"We are here now, knowing what we know, because of you. Our parents are downstairs, mine most likely still screaming at each other, because you managed to do what they couldn't— negotiate for their release when Agent Bailey contacted us."

"They aren't going to be happy when they learn that I gave away the diary and the journals so they could exchange detention camp for protective custody."

"True, but you were incredible. You had Agent Bailey drooling at the chance to read the diary."

My lip quirked up at the memory, then I frowned. "I didn't think she would keep her word. I thought for sure the agents would crash in here and just take the books from us."

"Yeah, you were smart to have us photograph all the pages first. But if they had just grabbed them, they wouldn't have gotten all our intel on the Helios Headquarters, along with my photos. And they brought our parents here. That has to mean they are going to keep their word, or they are going to detain us all. Like I said, you are amazing."

I rolled my eyes. I was torn between my old way of doubting myself or, maybe, this time believing in myself. Here, in the middle of all this chaos, I had found a new family and friends, and Shim. The things we had learned about ourselves changed everything. Maybe, it was okay if I changed too.

I brushed my shoulder against his, playfully bumping him again as I turned to look out at the strip. I took a deep breath and tried to enjoy just being with Shim. I tried so hard, but it was nagging at me, and I finally just had to ask, "So are we friends? More than friends? Cousins?" He made a choking sound, and flustered, I rushed to add, "Because, it feels like we are more than friends, but I really don't want to be related to you—and maybe finding out our parents have lied to us our whole lives and we're really a-aliens"—I stumbled over the word—"isn't the best time to start a relationship."

Shim's scrubbed his hands over his face and sighed, then looked up, up at the stars. I allowed my eyes to follow the vulnerable line of his throat, the smooth honey-gold skin, the mess of multi-colored chocolate hair falling into his face. Thinking about the Shim I knew from long conversations through the stones and on the boat, I realized I didn't care about being safe this time. "But—" I trailed off as I realized he was shaking. Concerned, I reached out to touch his arm.

Shim's amber gaze studied my face, his eyes full of mirth. He was laughing, laughing at me. His mouth quirked again, and he took over my thought.

"But, you see, Grace, we are inevitable. There are a lot of complications. There are some things I need to take care of. And, maybe you don't want to pin a label on it, maybe you don't want to change your status, but you and I, we are meant to be."

"This sounds like fate, fairytales, and white knight crap." I scrunched up my face as I teased him.

He laughed. "You'd make a better green knight. You are a challenge to me," he declared with a determined look.

"Have you actually read that story?" I said with a grimace. Shim laughed and shook his head. A shiver of excitement raced through me that someone, that Shim, thought of me as complex. Interesting.

His hands slid up and cupped each of my checks in warmth. Holding my face, he stared into my eyes.

My stomach flipped.

"Are we the kissing type of 'more than friends'?" Shim asked, leaning in and placing his forehead against mine.

I nodded, and his lips touched mine. It was a healing kiss, a connecting one—a kiss with intent and promise. After we broke apart, we both sighed.

I looked out at the blanket of city lights twinkling as twilight turned to darkness and the city woke up. "What happens now?" I whispered.

"I don't know. Maybe we should go hang out with our family."

Family. I liked that. After a life of voluntary and involuntary isolation, I finally had people like me. We were the same, we were different, we were...family. I struggled with the word. I didn't feel it the way my mom had. I was still coming to terms with all the members of her foster family. But Shim, Jaxon, Breeze, and Skylar, they had become everything to me. Closer than even my father. Never before had I felt like I had a home. *Home.* That's what they felt like.

With them, I was home.

The End

THANK you for choosing to read The Keystone! Keep reading for a peek at book two in the Elements Series, **The Activator**, where Grace and Shim's adventure continues when they go off-world. Available February 2023

THANK YOU!

Your comments and feedback are so important to me and they help other readers select a book they will enjoy. **If you enjoyed this book, please spread the word! Leave a review** on the platform where you bought it or on **Goodreads** or **Bookbub**. And thank you for telling your friends and posting on social!

To keep up to date on book releases and news, please sign up for my free newsletter serengoode.com. My (mostly) monthly emails will have bonus scenes, free books, news, and other great stuff...and no spam. SerenGoode.com/nltt. And consider joining the Seren Goode ARC TEAM. You can sign-up at https://bit.ly/SerenGoodeARCTEAM.

I sincerely appreciate your support and would love to hear from you at SerenGoodWrites on:

Goodreads - http://bit.ly/Goodreads_SerenGoode
Bookbub - http://bit.ly/BookBub_SerenGoode
Instagram - instagram.com/serengoodewrites
TikTok - tiktok.com/@serengoodewrites
Facebook - facebook.com/SerenGoode
Pinterest - pinterest.com/SerenGoodeWrites

THE ACTIVATOR
BOOK 2 IN THE ELEMENTS SERIES

WHEN THE WALL of water raced towards me, time stopped. My head cleared. My heartbeat slowed to a steady pulse. Paddling faster, my longboard found the glassy blue-green section of the wave, and I popped up. Wind sprayed me with briny water, and the crisp, salty air filled my lungs and poured over into my soul. Exhilarated, I rode the face up to the lip, kicking out the tail of my board, the fins released, and I found my balance.

Finally.

Nothing in my life made sense, except the wave I was riding so I took on its rhythm, letting it move through me, shape me, bring me closer to the *Source*. In the ocean, life made sense. I felt human again, which was ironic because I wasn't—fully human, that is.

The bottom of the yellow sun melted into the horizon as the sky turned a soft red. We had been at Natural Bridges Beach for over an hour and twilight was coming.

The Federal Agents who kept us imprisoned in protective custody hadn't let us communicate with our friends for months. We didn't even know if we would get to spend Christmas with them in two weeks. We were only allowed to leave our apartment once a day. Anyone else would have done real-life things like grocery shop or laundry—we hit the beach and tried to pretend we weren't being watched.

While I headed for the water like it had a tether on my heart. My dad went straight to the tidal pools. In no time, he had a group of kids surrounding him on his marine biology expedition.

My dad, Noah, was human, one hundred percent. My mom, Amé, wasn't from around here—not Santa Cruz, not California, not even Earth. I didn't know this when she was with us. Afterwards, I found her diary where she had confessed everything including how she felt responsible for trapping the others on Earth.

Cause she was an alien.

I was still coming to terms with the idea. Of course, my dad had known. My parents had lied to me my whole life.

It was hard to remember a time when I could trust them.

It took a while to find a wave I liked, and I tipped my nose down, diving under the first couple until the right one came along.

Here it was; this was what I had been dreaming of. I paddled hard. The water glowed copper, and dark shadows moved beneath the surface, but I kept my eye on the building swell. I gave a couple of extra strokes, then braced my hands on the rails and popped onto my feet. Shifting my weight, I extended a leg, turning into the shape of the wave, carving back and forth, rail to rail, the gentle pumping helping me pick up speed.

Someone shouted. I risked a glance at the shore. My father was sprinting away from the tidal pools and he was being chased.

The Helios had found us!

Three people dressed in navy blue suits had disembarked from a boat and were following my dad.

I pointed my board to the shore. Even as fast as I was moving, I was too far away. I watched Noah slip. I gasped and got a mouthful of saltwater. My muscles tensed up, and the board rocked. I willed myself to relax. Wiping out now would only slow me down.

My dad recovered, but the shadowy figures chasing him had made up a lot of the distance.

I reached back and pulled the pin on my leash. As the tip of my board slid up on the beach, I jumped off and hit the ground at a run, splashing through the shallows. In seconds, I was beside my dad.

A gunshot sounded behind us. The sound was deafening, and an involuntary flinch almost folded my body in half.

"Grace!" Noah stumbled again. I grabbed for his arm. There was a scramble as we grasped at each other. I was moving too fast, my surf booties sinking into the sand, but he caught himself and stayed on his feet. There was a pedestrian path that led to the parking area. If we could make it up the hill—

Lights flared. An engine roared.

A large, black SUV barreled down the access road towards us. More shots fired, this time directed at the vehicle. Unfortunately, we were between it and the Helios. The vehicle barely slowed as it left the pavement and ate its way through the dunes. We kept running. The SUV shot past us and did a fancy U-turn that sent a spray of sand on our pursuers. Barely slowing, it changed directions. A side door flew open, and we dived inside.

Our Federal watchdogs were in the front seat returning fire. For once, I was relieved to see them.

"It's the Helios—go!" My dad slammed his hand against the seat back and before he had completed the sentence, we were in motion again.

I was crushed into the leather seats, breathing in a foul combo of stale coffee and body odor. Time did this funny thing when mixed with adrenaline, seconds felt like a lifetime. I could tell by the squeals and the rhythm of the tires that we were back on pavement and had made several sharp turns. We were probably out of the park. And the shooting had stopped.

I sat up. I was only sixteen, but I'd already been in enough of these situations that I'd learned to rebound quickly.

The agent in the front passenger seat who had been doing most of the shooting turned briefly away from the window and looked back at us, accessing. Her gun was still out and her finger was on the earbud in her right ear.

"We expected something like this. It has been happening in the other locations all week. We are withdrawing to a safe house." The agent told us as she turned back to scanning the street for threats.

I yanked my neoprene hood back. I extracted my arms out like peeling a banana. Better. After a whiff of the Feds leather seats, I was unconcerned that I was shedding water and sand all over them. I reached up and pushed my hair back. Much better.

Shivering in my wet swimsuit I had the feeling I had wiped out in an impact zone and I wasn't out of danger yet.

Grace and Shim's adventure continues when they go off world in *The Activator.* Available July 31, 2023

ACKNOWLEDGMENTS

It takes a lot of support to be an author and I want to thank all my family and friends that have helped me along the way. I especially want to thank Randy for always having my back, the LaBo Crew for grounding and pep talks, and my personal cheerleader and fabulous beta reader Lori H.

Seren Goode was born in the Midwest with itchy feet and a dream of far-off places. She has a love of all things alien and a fascination with ritual landscape. Her debut science fiction novel, The Keystone, redefines what makes a family and explores what it means to be human.

A jane-of-all-trades, Seren has studied communications, English, design, marketing, metalsmith, pottery, juggling, and more, and eventually ended up abroad earning a graduate degree in archeology. She started writing fiction while in middle school and thoroughly blames her family for encouraging this habit. A big fan of making her characters do their own work, Seren loves to sit back and watch them unravel a mystery or dig for the truth. When she isn't on the road, she is at home on the Central Coast of California plotting her next book, and her next trip, with her songwriter husband and puppies Clairey and Izzy.

You can follow her at serengoode.com or on:
facebook.com/SerenGoode
instagram.com/serengoodewrites
pinterest.com/SerenGoodeWrites
tiktok.com/@serengoodewrites

www.ingramcontent.com/pod-product-compliance
Lightning Source LLC
Chambersburg PA
CBHW021244190726
48289CB00005B/1479